Cheryl—
Happy reading!
Blessings,
Penny Zeller
Psalm 19:14

Love in DISGUISE

PENNY ZELLER

Maplebrook

Love in Disguise

Published by Maplebrook Publishing

Christian historical romance

Editing and copyediting by Mountain Peak Edits and Design https://mountainpeakedits.com
Proofreading by Angela Watts https://angelarwatts.com
Cover design by Emilie Haney www.eahcreative.com
Interior formatting by Jon Stewart https://stewartdesign.studio/

All scripture quotations are taken from the King James Version of the Bible.

ISBN: 978-0-9760836-3-4 (print)
ISBN: 978-0-9760836-4-1 (ebook)

BOOKS BY PENNY ZELLER

Standalone Novels (Maplebrook Publishing)
Love in Disguise

Love in Chokecherry Heights Series (Maplebrook Publishing)
Love Under Construction
Henry and Evaline (novella)

Montana Skies Series (Whitaker House)
McKenzie
Kaydie
Hailee

Love Letters from Ellis Creek Series (Maplebrook Publishing)
Love from Afar

Novella Collections (Barbour)
Love from Afar (The Secret Admirer Romance Collection)
Freedom's Flight (The Underground Railroad Brides Collection)

Nonfiction
77 Ways Your Family Can Make a Difference (Beacon Hill Press)

Children's Fiction
Hollyhocks

To all of the women who have lost a child through miscarriage or stillbirth. May you find hope, healing, and rest in the arms of our Savior.

Come unto me, all ye that labour and are heavy laden, and I will give you rest.

Matthew 11:28

CHAPTER ONE

Hollow Creek, Montana, 1911

"Those cows are going to drive me plumb out of my mind," Emilie Crawford Wheeler muttered. She stood on her porch, hands on her hips, glaring at the herd of Black Angus cows taking a tour of her front yard.

Heart pounding, she reached for the porch pillar for support. Just because she had inherited the ranch from her late husband didn't mean she particularly cared for the abhorrent creatures.

Their boisterous mooing echoed throughout the otherwise quiet Montana afternoon. Emilie watched as they trampled through her yard, destroying or eating every piece of vegetation in their path.

Her beautiful oak tree sapling, which had withstood storms and hail, became the most recent casualty, its tender limbs snapping beneath a particularly large cow's hoof.

One cow swaggered up the porch steps, as if such a feat were an ordinary, everyday spectacle. "Shoo!" she yelled while removing her hat and flapping it about. The cow paid her no mind, but continued to occupy the far end of the porch.

While concentrating on the cow on the porch, Emilie didn't realize until too late that a Black Angus had leaned its head over the railing and commenced chewing on her hat, slowly and methodically, as if it were part of its normal diet. "Well, I never!" she exclaimed.

She best act quickly if she was to halt the destruction of her newly-planted gardens.

Emilie turned on her heel and ran into the house, ignoring the startled looks from her staff. Instead, she reached into the closet and retrieved Newt's shotgun.

"Almira, dear, please do remember proper etiquette and that you must always conduct yourself as a lady." Mother's admonishment using Emilie's given name threatened to stop her from her course of action.

But she must forge ahead on her mission to finally rectify the problem with the neighbor's cows. And why was it the man was never home when she wished to discuss the situation? Did Mr. Evanson even exist? Or did the ranch running parallel to hers operate itself?

Whoever coined the phrase that desperate times called for desperate measures must have dealt with rogue cattle and their propensity to destroy everything in their path.

"Almira, ladies do not fire weapons. Please do reconsider." What Mother might say were she in Hollow Creek thrummed through Emilie's mind.

"Mother, this is an emergency," she said aloud, nearly stomping through the house.

There was no time for proper etiquette. Today Annie Oakley would be her hero. Miss Oakley was a lady, after all, and Emilie thought of just how accurately she might mimic the woman's skill with a gun.

"Is everything all right, Mrs. Wheeler?" Hattie asked, concern lining the maid's youthful features.

"Quite all right, Hattie, thank you for asking."

"Is it the cows again?"

"Yes, it is, and I have every mind to..."

"Will Cook be preparing steak for supper, Emilie?" Vera, her housekeeper, asked as she entered the room, a smirk on her sweet wrinkled face.

Emilie smiled, thankful for the humorous reprieve from the current situation.

Vera placed a hand on Emilie's arm. "Let us help you," she offered. "Morris has gone to town, but surely you, Hattie, and I can do something to deter the cattle until the hands come to rectify the situation. We might be able to save some of your yard."

"Well, someone has to do something about Mr. Evanson's cows." That someone would be her. While it was never admirable to be prone to temper, and Emilie did not consider herself a temperamental woman, she had all she could take with that ninnyhammer Mr. Evanson and his assemblage of bovine.

This was not the first time they demolished her yard, but it would be the last.

"*Almira, do contain yourself*," Mother would say.

But there was no containing in this matter. Emilie flung open the door and stalked out onto her porch. A few chickens had escaped from the coop and joined the circus in her front yard, squawking and doing their best to avoid being trampled. Emilie checked to be sure no one was in danger of her Annie Oakley ways, then, walking from beneath the porch roof, raised the shotgun to the air and fired a shot.

Several of the cows turned and ran from the yard, but a few stayed staring at her. "Shoo! I said shoo!" Emilie shouted to the remaining cattle.

The cows kicked up dust and continued encroaching upon her property, causing a most appalling commotion.

Jep, one of her hired hands, rounded the corner then, his scrawny torso barely keeping up with his long legs. "We have this all taken care of, Mrs. Wheeler. No need to worry yourself none."

It looked far from taken care of, but Emilie didn't mention such. Two of her other ranch hands appeared on horseback and attempted to herd the cattle back to Mr. Evanson's pasture.

Emilie set the shotgun against the house and patted her skirts, releasing puffs of dust. She was going to faint dead away if she did not get a reprieve from those dastardly cows and their even more dastardly owner.

Vera joined her on the porch. "A trip to Missoula is just the thing you need. Besides, you could deliver those gifts to the orphanage on your way there and see the children."

"What a splendid idea. I shall leave tomorrow morning. However, I think I may just retrieve more presents for the children while in Missoula, and stop there on the way back."

"Excellent plan! Children can never have too many presents. Do you wish for Morris and me to accompany you?"

Emilie thought for a moment, gazing at the seemingly futile effort of Jep and her other hired hands to contain the raucous cattle. "While I do so enjoy the company of you and Morris, I believe I shall make this journey to Missoula on my own."

"Some time away will be of benefit."

Some time away was just what Emilie needed. Being proper-like with a dash of rebellion wasn't for the faint of heart.

Early the following morning, Emilie packed her bags for her trip to Missoula. She needed to retrieve the brand-new hat she'd ordered from Miss Julia Mathilda's Fine Dresses. And not a moment too soon since she was now one hat less due to that cow's insidious appetite. Besides, a break would do her good and shopping did seem to fix many a problem.

Jep carried several wrapped gifts to her Model T to donate to the orphanage. If there was a charity close to her heart, the orphanage would garner that distinction. Each month, she donated a generous check to the institution, as well as a variety of items she purchased in Missoula on her many outings to the city.

Because of the weather and the urgency to return home, she had been unable to stop at the orphanage during her most recent trip. It would be good to stop by, see the children, and gift them with the special books, clothes, and toys she previously purchased for them.

Yes, perhaps a trip to Missoula and the orphanage would improve her mood after having her entire front yard destroyed. At least the west side gardens were unscathed. Huge miracle that was.

Morris started the Model T, opened the door for Emilie to board, and within five minutes, she tasted the freedom of the open road.

Nearly two hours later, she came to a stop at the carriage house behind Missoula's Bellerose Hotel and Restaurant. A fine supper, followed by a restful night's sleep in the feather bed in room twenty-three, the room where she always stayed during her visits, would refresh her mind.

And tomorrow?

Tomorrow the promise of shopping awaited her.

For surely shopping would rid her mind completely of despicable cows and contemptible neighbors.

All would be well.

OH, WHY, oh why, had she not chosen to employ the delivery service? No wonder the clerk at Miss Julia Mathilda's Fine Dresses looked askance when she had declined.

Nevertheless, she straightened her posture and attempted to toss aside the twinge of regret. Determination forced her toward her destination and precluded her from turning around and retracing her wobbly steps to Miss Mathilda's.

Emilie stumbled down the boardwalk toward the Bellerose Hotel and Restaurant as she peeked from one side of the tall tower of parcels to the other. They teetered precariously, and with much effort, Emilie righted them. Several folks sauntered past her, most of whom were careful to watch for the woman wearing the oversized wide-brimmed hat with the six boxes and three bags situated in and on her arms.

Where was the Bellerose Hotel and Restaurant? Shouldn't she have reached it by now?

Emilie's right arm had fallen asleep, and her left ached from its awkward position toting the heavy load. Such stubbornness on her part, this endeavor to carry her own parcels.

But was not such an endeavor a necessary part of her newfound freedom? A freedom Emilie had never before experienced? A freedom she planned to embrace?

Pride might be an appropriate term, not that Emilie would admit it.

Mother's choice word for the situation would be *impudent.* She would be shaking her head and her perfectly-coifed curls with dismay at her daughter's choice. Her voice would take on a disapproving tone. *"Almira Emilie Crawford Wheeler,"* she would say, her hands on hips.

Emilie teetered from one foot to the other, desperately trying to balance on the high heels of her fashionable button-up leather boots. The stack of parcels leaned to the left, then to the right. The three bags situated on her arms slid down to her wrists, causing an off-balanced jolt into the stacked parcels.

She was on the verge of recovering from her precarious situation when the most devastating event occurred.

Someone bumped into her right shoulder. It wasn't that it was a hard bump, or even a rowdy bump, but it did totter her nearly plumb off her feet and toward the left.

And her parcel with the new hat? It plummeted to the ground and tumbled into the street. Flinging the rest of her purchases haphazardly to the side, Emilie darted toward the parcel as it rolled into the path of an oncoming wagon. Desperate to save her hat, Emilie absentmindedly stumbled into the path of traffic.

Just as she reached for the prized possession, a strong hand clasped her upper arm and pulled her back onto the boardwalk. Emilie batted at the firm grip, her focus remaining on the parcel.

Her breath squeezed from her lungs, as she watched a horse trample the hatbox and its precious contents.

No. No. No!

Stunned, Emilie wrenched herself free from the grasp and staggered in shock to retrieve the crushed box. *Surely the hat will be fine. The box is made of only the finest materials.*

She stumbled back to the boardwalk. Holding her breath, she lifted the mangled lid and gaped in horror.

Her precarious situation momentarily forgotten, she winced at the condition of her once-lavish hat. The tattered and formerly ornate ostrich feather floated wistfully to the ground, a sure sign her poor hat had not survived the cruel fate it was handed. Never again would the crushed accessory be wearable.

It had been a splendid hat of 1911 fashion that had boasted a marvelous ostrich feather. Ordered from one of the most renowned millineries in Boston, it emanated elegance and high-class fashion. Now it was ruined.

What was left of it, anyway.

Whatever was she to do? Emilie had intended the new hat to replace the one she wore at present, as the former was becoming far too 1910. While she didn't have too terribly many material weaknesses, she did appreciate the latest fashions.

As if losing a hat to a cow yesterday wasn't bad enough, now she must lose one to a horse.

Could things get any worse? As Emilie lamented her situation, a most ghastly incident occurred. Her toe caught the edge of one of the parcels she had tossed aside, and she lost her footing and tumbled to the ground. She landed in an unladylike heap on the boardwalk.

She closed her eyes for a moment, willing that no one saw her unfortunate lack of respectability. *So much for propriety and decorum.*

Then she remembered all of her parcels, especially the once-elegant hat, strewn all about her. Trying not to appear as inept as she felt, Emilie contemplated how best to retrieve those parcels.

And restore her dignity.

A disturbing thought entered her mind: how would she lift the parcels off the ground and re-stack them in her arms?

An even more disturbing thought then clouded her mind.

Would she ever regain her composure?

"Ma'am?"

Emilie gazed up into the bluest of blue eyes she had ever seen. Her eyes locked with his and she sucked in her breath. Suddenly her parcels and her ill-fated hat were forgotten. She squinted at him. His mouth was moving, but in her discombobulated state, she could neither focus on nor hear a word.

In all of her etiquette lessons, never had there been instructions on how to behave properly when sprawled in a most unrefined manner in the middle of the boardwalk in front of a handsome stranger.

Whatever would Mother say now?

CHAPTER TWO

The stranger leaned down and stooped into her direct line of vision. "Ma'am, you could have been killed by the oncoming traffic."

Oncoming traffic?

"Are you all right, ma'am?"

"I—I..." My, but he was a handsome sort.

"I am sorry I collided with you. It was my fault. Reckon I wasn't watching where I was going. Are you hurt?"

"Am I?"

"I don't know. That's what I'm asking you."

Air caught in her windpipe and she couldn't speak. The handsome man, concern lighting up his face, continued to stare at her.

"Begging your pardon, sir, but what are you asking me?" Her question came out as a breathless gasp.

The man took her elbow and gently assisted her to her feet. "I'm asking if you are unharmed since I ran right into you. Quite by accident, I might add." The corners of his mouth upturned into a cross between a smirk and a full smile. A right fine smile at that. "Did you hit your head?"

From all appearances she must seem quite daft. Could it be that she had hit her head and knocked all sense from it? "Oh. Yes. I am. All right." Emilie dusted the powdery dirt from the dusty boardwalk that had collected on her shirtwaist and skirt. The number of parcels she had managed to gather into a lopsided stack was paltry compared to how many she had purchased.

She reached up and straightened her crooked hat, knowing she must look a fright.

"Please, allow me to retrieve all of your parcels. Do you live far from here?"

Emilie's eyes again connected with the stranger's. "No," she squeaked. Had he asked if she lived far from here or if she was staying far from here? Why could she not concentrate under the perusal of those blue eyes? Eyes that reminded her of the Atlantic Ocean she had visited several times as a child.

"Allow me to assist you with these," he repeated. "It's the least I can do." The man kneeled and, with ease, retrieved every box and placed them in a tall stack against the nearest building. When he came to the open box that held the squished hat in it, he stood staring at it for a moment. "Is this yours as well?"

"Yes." From the blank look on his face, the man seemed to have nary a clue as to what the item had been. Emilie exhaled a deep sigh. "It was a hat. An elegant hat all the way from Boston. I daresay it will never be a hat again."

"That's the truth."

Taken aback, Emilie didn't know whether to be offended or to laugh at the stranger's comment.

"Perhaps we can order you another one—one that I will be paying for since this was my fault." The stranger stacked the hat on top of the other parcels, then scooped them into his arms. His strong arms.

Yes, she had noticed that too.

He was wearing standard working man's clothing, but he was cleaner, as though he hadn't been in the fields or on the ranch that day. He was tall, maybe four inches taller than she was with her heeled boots. Blond hair and a day's worth of stubble on his jaw.

What was the matter with her?

She was staring.

And he had noticed.

This was not like her at all. No one had ever accused her of gawking at a stranger. What a complete embarrassment.

And ever so scandalous. What would Mother say?

"Ma'am?"

"Yes?"

"Would you like to tell me which direction we should go and I'll take these to your destination?"

"It's the hotel."

"You live in the hotel?"

"Yes, I mean, no."

Confusion crossed the man's face.

"I mean to say that I'm going to eat at the hotel's restaurant. I don't live there."

"Which hotel?" he asked.

"The Bellerose."

The man stood back on the boardwalk and gazed to the left and then to the right. "I reckon it's just down the street on the left?"

"Yes."

"After you."

Emilie led him toward the Bellerose Hotel and Restaurant, thankful no one knew her in Missoula like they did in her hometown of Hollow Creek. There could be no gossip this way. She could already see the news in the inferior *Hollow Creek Weekly*:

Emilie Wheeler allows handsome stranger to carry parcels to the hotel for her after he causes the demise of her new hat.

The tongues would wag for sure at that tidbit of juicy information about one of Hollow Creek's wealthiest citizens.

After a few minutes, she stopped in front of the Bellerose Hotel and Restaurant. "I can manage the parcels from here. Thank you kindly for your assistance."

"Are you sure?" The stranger's gaze appeared doubtful. "May I offer to buy you and your husband a noonday meal to make up for the reckless incident I caused?"

Emilie met his gaze. He was offering to buy her a noonday meal? And her husband? Emilie's thoughts veered briefly to Newt. He'd been gone for just over a year. "I'm a widow."

The words leapt from her mouth before she had a chance to stop them. *Oh, dear, another breach of etiquette. I'm sharing far too much personal information with a stranger.*

This man certainly had an odd effect on her.

"I'm sorry to hear that, ma'am."

"Thank you."

"Still, while it is awkward, I would appreciate you allowing me to purchase you a noonday meal for causing you so much trouble. And I intend to pay for the hat as well."

Emilie inhaled. The aroma of something delicious filled her nostrils. Fresh bread? Cinnamon rolls? She had spent so much time at Miss Julia Mathilda's, and then with the mishap...For all Emilie knew, it could be suppertime by now. She inhaled again and her stomach responded with a most awful unladylike growl.

The man's mouth tipped up at the corners.

"You didn't just hear that," Emilie gasped.

"Hear what?" the man asked with a grin. "Shall we request a table?"

What would be the harm in allowing him to buy her a meal? But to dine with her? That was against nearly every rule in the etiquette books. What would Mother say?

"I raised you better than that, Almira Emilie. You should know better than to dine with a complete stranger," Mother would cluck with an austere expression.

But Mother wasn't here. And nowhere did Emilie see any etiquette books. She peered about just to be sure.

No, no Mother, and no etiquette books.

And it was the 1900s after all.

If only Emilie had invited Vera and Morris to journey from Hollow Creek to Missoula with her this time as they most often did. Then they could have joined Emilie and the handsome stranger and all would be well.

And her exemplary reputation would remain intact.

If only that annoying Mr. Evanson and his reckless cows hadn't caused so much difficulty, then she wouldn't have had to embark on a restorative shopping excursion in the first place.

"All right," she heard herself say. "It will be but a moment while I ask the front desk if they will allow me to keep my parcels here while we partake in the noonday meal."

Emilie walked through the door of the hotel and toward the front desk. She took a hurried peek behind her to see that the stranger was standing near the doorway, oblivious of the matters to which she attended.

Not that Emilie would ever see this man again, surely not. But she couldn't take the chance that this poor ranch hand thought her a wealthy widow. He mustn't know she was staying at the Bellerose Hotel for the next two days.

If he was anything like the men in Hollow Creek, he would, without delay, find a way to court her and her money.

And Emilie would have none of that.

Speaking in as quiet of a voice as she could muster, so as to avoid the stranger hearing the conversation, she asked the clerk to place her parcels near the desk for the doorman to take to her room. She would keep the dilapidated hat in case the man requested it for ease of ordering a new one.

Emilie then perused the adjoining restaurant, almost expecting to see her parents at a table in the corner of the room. Mother would be wagging a pointed finger, chastising Emilie in her sternest voice for agreeing to a noonday meal with an unfamiliar man. "*Almira, you, as a widowed woman, ought not to attend an event with a man without a chaperone.*"

Father would be narrowing his brown eyes at her and shaking his balding head. Emilie had disappointed him once again.

Thankfully, Mother and Father lived about as far from Montana as one could get.

"I reckon I should introduce myself," the man said as they crossed from the hotel area to the adjacent restaurant. "I'm Thad Alexander."

"And I am Emilie Crawford," she answered, leaving off her last name, just in case the man had heard of her husband, the well-known and affluent rancher, Newton Wheeler.

Mr. Alexander removed his hat and nodded. "Nice to meet you."

"You as well." The man had manners. Must have been raised right. That would be something that at least Mother would approve of in all her concerns for Emilie's welfare.

Father, on the other hand, would lose years off his life worrying about Emilie's association with a destitute ranch hand.

A destitute ranch hand...

"Really, Mr. Alexander, you needn't feel obligated to pay for my noonday meal. I quite understand our collision was an accident."

"Think nothing of it, Mrs. Crawford. It's the least I can do. And again, I do aim to purchase you a new hat like the one that met with its demise."

An impoverished ranch hand with such exemplary speaking skills. Perhaps his bosses had allowed him to borrow their books from the family library to upgrade his vocabulary. Still, was it becoming of her to expect the penniless man to pay for her meal? What if doing so would preclude him from buying the more important necessities of life like a new pair of boots? And the new hat—could he afford such an expenditure on his meager salary? The concern nagged at her conscience.

"If you're sure..."

"I'm sure, ma'am. If it's all right with you, of course."

He grinned at her, a right handsome smile at that.

Yes, against her better judgment, it was quite all right that they dine for a noonday meal.

Besides, dining with the dapper Mr. Alexander somehow made the incident with the parcels and the flattened hat escape from Emilie's mind.

CHAPTER THREE

Thad could have viewed the incident of colliding with Mrs. Crawford as unfortunate. Except it wasn't unfortunate.

Not all of it anyway.

Sure, he would have to humble himself and pay a visit to Miss Julia Mathilda's Fine Dresses and purchase a women's hat. Fortunately, he would not have to explain to anyone but the clerk at the dress shop why he, Thad Alexander Evanson, should find himself stepping into a store no man had likely ever set foot in before this day.

Worth it, it was, to share a meal with Mrs. Crawford. Dining with a lovely stranger hadn't been on the list of his many things to do today.

No, some things about this whole incident were just the opposite of unfortunate.

Especially since no woman had affected his thinking and common sense the way this woman had in less than ten minutes.

Could it be her eyes, the color of shimmering amber? Or her sweet delicate smile with its air of mystery?

This lack of sleep and all the travel back from the cattle sale has really taken its toll on you, Evanson.

A wave of guilt splashed over him. He had told her that his name was Thad Alexander. Why had he omitted his last name?

Can't have her knowing you own Evanson Cattle Company. Women find out that tidbit of information and they find a way to suddenly grow fond of you and your hard-earned money.

Thad couldn't have that happening, not like it constantly happened in his home in Hollow Creek. He chuckled to himself. At least there was one woman in Hollow Creek who would not be growing fond of him and his hard-earned money. His persnickety neighbor, Mrs. Wheeler, whom he had the fortune of having never met, held as much fondness for him as she held for his cattle.

Providence played a part in Thad's ability to avoid ever crossing her path.

No, he might never see the beautiful Emilie Crawford again, but at least she wouldn't be the wiser as to his income status. Even if Mrs. Crawford seemed more elegant and well-off than some of the women Thad knew, judging by her choice of dress and the numerous parcels she had attempted to carry.

The parcels he'd accidentally knocked out of her hands due to eyeballing a stunning automobile motoring down the busy streets of Mateer Avenue.

Because of his harebrained decision to watch said automobile, Mrs. Crawford could have been killed by the oncoming traffic, as she reached for the hat that he knocked from her arms.

Had the woman even wanted to attend the noonday meal with him at the restaurant inside the hotel? When had her husband passed? What was the proper etiquette in matters such as these?

Thad's knowledge of proper etiquette could hardly be considered robust.

If only Grandma were still alive to offer wisdom in such matters.

The waitress led Thad and Mrs. Crawford to a table in the corner of the dining establishment. In all his times visiting Missoula, which were numerous, Thad had yet to eat at the Bellerose Restaurant. He usually chose to eat at a café or the small home he had purchased on the other side of the city.

Thad pulled out Mrs. Crawford's chair, then took a seat across from her. "It's a nice day today."

"Yes, it is. I love Montana summers." Mrs. Crawford placed the ruined hat beneath her chair, the only item not stacked by the hotel front desk.

"Do you live in Missoula?"

She hesitated for a moment before answering. "A short distance from Missoula. And you?"

"When I'm not out on the ranch or traveling to buy or sell cattle."

"You must be of great value to your employer."

Employer? "Yes, ma'am, ranching is hard work."

Mrs. Crawford nodded as if she understood. Thad didn't mention that he *was* the employer.

The waitress stopped by their table and offered her recommendations for the daily special. They ordered, then sat in silence.

Thad reckoned it was a comfortable silence. He did his best not to stare at her. Of course, some women as lovely as Mrs. Crawford were selfish and rude. Was Mrs. Crawford like that?

Why he cared so much befuddled him.

"I really am sorry about causing you to drop your parcels. And about your hat."

"It was an accident, Mr. Alexander. A quite forgivable one at that."

"Thank you, Mrs. Crawford. I promise I'll purchase you another hat just like the one that was flattened. Maybe I can have it delivered to your home when it arrives." Secretly, and for reasons Thad couldn't explain, he hoped that Mrs. Crawford would agree to meet him for another meal, then he could give the replacement hat to her.

Mrs. Crawford appeared hesitant. Perhaps she didn't want him to know where she lived due to embarrassment. "Or, we could meet here at the restaurant and I could give it to you." Was such a suggestion acceptable? Thad knew as much about etiquette as he did about fancy hats.

Which was nil.

"It took two weeks for my first hat to arrive at Miss Julia Mathilda's. It would likely take that long again. If it's agreeable, we can meet here, and I would bring along my dear friends."

Thad nodded. He understood how important it was to protect a woman's reputation. He would like to meet her friends anyway. Why, he didn't know. "That sounds like a good plan. So, two weeks it is. In two Fridays."

The meal arrived and the waitress set it before them. "Please let me know if you need anything else," she said before efficiently attending to the other patrons in the busy restaurant.

Thad and Mrs. Crawford chorused their thank-yous before Thad folded his hands. "May I lead us in prayer?"

Mrs. Crawford nodded with some reluctance before folding her own hands. Dainty hands with long fingers. Not that Thad made it a habit of noticing women's hands. He closed his eyes and began to pray.

When Thad opened his eyes to see her staring at him, questions seemed to line her beautiful features. What was she thinking? Mrs. Crawford angled her head to one side.

He waited, as Grandma had instructed, for her to take the first bite.

Finally, she gazed down at her food, placed the napkin in her lap and lifted her fork. Was Mrs. Crawford a woman of prayer? Thad found himself hoping so.

"Do you attend church here in Missoula?" he asked, in between bites of meatloaf.

"Not in some time."

He waited for an explanation. When none came, he nodded, wanting to prod, but thinking better of it. While he felt comfortable with Mrs. Crawford, despite meeting less than an hour ago, he had no desire to present himself as off-putting.

Thad decided to change the subject. "You are probably wondering why it was that I lost my eyesight and ran into you on the boardwalk."

A sparkle lit her amber eyes. "I am most curious."

"There was this automobile, the newest built, I reckon, driving by on Mateer Avenue just then. I turned my head to scrutinize it, and that's when we collided."

"I did wonder how someone could avoid seeing me with all of my parcels."

They shared a laugh, and Thad appreciated their easy camaraderie. "That's how. All because of a new-fangled automobile."

"Do you own one, Mr. Alexander?"

Indecision rose within him. If Thad mentioned he owned a motorcar, Mrs. Crawford might see him as wealthy. On the other hand, he didn't want to lie. Hadn't Grandpa said truthfulness was always best?

But you weren't truthful about your name.

Thad brushed the admonishment aside. Maybe he could evade the question. "Ever since I saw the first automobiles in photographs, and then in person, I knew I wanted to someday own one."

Mrs. Crawford nodded with a suspicious smirk. "I am fond of automobiles too, Mr. Alexander, so I quite understand."

"A woman fond of automobiles?"

"They are much faster and more efficient than a horse, truth be told. They offer so much freedom."

"You seem to speak from experience."

Mrs. Crawford said nothing, only blessed him with another of her smiles. Thad selfishly wished the meal could last for several hours so he could spend time with this mysterious woman he had just met.

The waitress returned to offer them dessert. "Oh, I shan't," said Mrs. Crawford.

"I'll take some apple pie and ice cream," said Thad. His belly could scarcely handle another bite, but he wouldn't turn down the decadent dessert he had seen on the menu.

"Ice cream?" Mrs. Crawford asked.

"It's delicious with apple pie."

"Oh, yes, pie à la mode. I declare that I have changed my mind and am going to have a slice of apple pie with ice cream as well."

The waitress took their orders and promised to return quickly with their desserts.

"I recall having pie à la mode years ago. It would be a delight to savor it once again."

"Am I correct in presuming, Mrs. Crawford, that you were not raised in Missoula?"

"You're quite correct, Mr. Alexander. In fact, I grew up in New York City. And you, where did you spend your time as a youngster?"

"In Illinois farming the land with my grandparents."

"Really? What brought you to Montana?"

"The dream of ranching."

"And then, you stumbled upon a kindly rancher, entered into his employ, and your dream came true." Mrs. Crawford tilted her head toward him, as if sharing in his dream. Even if part of it wasn't accurate.

"I like ranching. I can't say it's in my blood, since I'm the first generation in my family to ranch. But I can say there's nothing I'd rather be doing."

"Doing what you love. That's important." A wistful look crossed Mrs. Crawford's face. Would she offer explanations for her statements?

"Yes, I reckon it is."

"Tell me, and I mean no offense when I make mention of this...if you grew up on a farm, how is it that you speak as someone well-educated?"

"No offense taken. My grandma, who, with my grandpa, raised me after my parents passed on, attended a fancy finishing school back East. She had taught my mother all she knew, and when she and Grandpa raised me, she took it upon herself to teach me as well. She immersed me in books, spoke with well-educated vocabulary herself, and encouraged me to never stop learning. To this day, I enjoy reading in the evenings."

"I delight in reading as well, Mr. Alexander. So many adventures to be had within the pages of a book."

"I agree."

"Do tell, who is your favorite author?"

Thad didn't even have to ponder Mrs. Crawford's question. "Robert Louis Stevenson."

"Really?"

"Yes. You've heard of him?"

"Absolutely. He's my favorite author as well."

Thad was taken aback. First the apple pie with ice cream and now they shared the same favorite author? "You don't say. Which book of his is your favorite?"

"That's easy. *Treasure Island.*"

"Mine too."

"I do declare, Mr. Alexander, that we have the same reading tastes."

"That we do, Mrs. Crawford. And why is it, that you like *Treasure Island* best?

"Such adventure and excitement."

Thad nodded. "My thoughts exactly."

The waitress arrived with their desserts. When they finished eating and Thad had paid, they stood just outside the entrance. "Mrs. Crawford, thank you for the pleasure of dining with you this afternoon."

"Thank you, Mr. Alexander, for the delicious meal."

"Do you need any further help with the parcels?"

Mrs. Crawford gave him a look of confusion for a moment before answering, "No, I believe it's all handled."

"Do you have the hat? I will need it in order to replace it."

Mrs. Crawford handed him a box with an item that no longer resembled a hat. But had it resembled a hat in the first place with all of its frou frou finery? Thad pinched the edge of the striped hatbox between his thumb and forefinger, and prepared to salvage his pride. Must he carry such an item?

"I will see you in two Fridays, then. I'll bring the new hat with me."

"I will be here. I daresay you will like my friends, Vera and Morris."

"I look forward to it. Until then, Mrs. Crawford."

"Until then, Mr. Alexander."

Two weeks couldn't arrive soon enough.

CHAPTER FOUR

Thad gripped the striped hatbox and perused the boardwalk near Miss Julia Mathilda's Fine Dresses. He felt as though he had just been hired as a Pinkerton detective on surveillance. First a glimpse to the left, then to the right, then to the left one more time. No one appeared to be paying him much mind.

That was a blessing, for what man stepped foot inside a woman's store? Not even men with their wives would dare such a feat. Thad tipped his hat low over his eyes to aid as a disguise just in case. Thankfully, this was the city of Missoula and not Hollow Creek. Thad's expedition into Miss Julia Mathilda's Fine Dresses would make the *Hollow Creek Weekly* for certain. The owner of the paper, Mr. Coleman, searched, sometimes with underhanded snoopiness, to uncover what he deemed worthwhile stories for his measly two-page paper.

Certain no one cared about Thad's unfortunate duty, he opened the door and entered. *Phew. No other customers.* Relief flooded through him.

Clothes and hats lined the walls. Why would so much space be dedicated to such impractical adornments? Thad wanted to shield his eyes. No man belonged in such a place.

Why had he promised to purchase Mrs. Crawford a new hat again? *Because you were a dolt and bumped into her while staring at that fancy new motorcar driving down the street.*

And...

Because while you would never admit it, you've taken a fancy to Mrs. Crawford.

Thad chastised himself. He had only just met the woman, but he had to admit, there was something about her. Something that made him want to know more about the young widow.

"Hello…sir?"

The clerk did little to hide her consternation at seeing Thad in her establishment, but she was no more dismayed than Thad was to be there. She peeked around him. To see if he had a wife entering the store with him, perhaps?

"Uh, hello, ma'am."

"Are you lost, sir?"

"Uh, no. I'm where I should be."

Not where I should be, but… Thad removed his hat and took a peek behind him outside the large windows containing an assortment of women's clothing. Could folks see him from outside the store?

He plopped the hatbox on the counter.

If he didn't die from embarrassment, then Thad would know for sure miracles still occurred.

"You are in Miss Julia Mathilda's Fine Dresses boutique."

"Yes, yes, ma'am. I am aware of that."

The woman narrowed her eyes. "You're not planning to rob the boutique, are you?"

As if as a robber he would be honest and upfront about his motives. "No, ma'am, nothing of a sort." *Would I be carrying a battered hatbox if I was going to steal?*

"Are you sure? Because if you are, rest assured you'll not succeed." The woman flashed her dark eyes at him in warning. Thad choked back a strangled laugh. What would the clerk do to stop him? Bat at him with one of those outlandish hats?

"I'm not planning to rob the…store. I shouldn't be here."

"That's quite right, sir. You shouldn't. The livery stable or blacksmith shop are more your type of establishment."

Thad nodded. "True, ma'am."

"So, pray tell, sir, just why are you in Miss Julia Mathilda's Fine Dresses if you are not lost, nor planning to rob us? Have you lost your mental faculties? Are you hiding from someone?"

Several someones, as in the entire city of Missoula. "No, ma'am, I am here to buy a hat." The woman placed a hand to her neck. If Thad wasn't careful, he might cause her to have a heart condition.

"Sir, your type of hats are best found at the general store or at the Stetson hat shop over on Fifth Street."

Thad knew his face had to be the color of a ripened strawberry. Thankfully, he hadn't shaved in a couple of days and his whiskers hid the lot of his embarrassment. "Ma'am, please, if you'll just give me a chance to explain..."

"Henrietta, is everything all right?" a voice called, presumably from a back room.

"Miss Mathilda, I think you should come out here post haste." Panic made the clerk's voice wobble.

A thin and stylish woman rushed through a door Thad hadn't even noticed. "Whatever is the problem, Henrietta?"

"This man, he is here to purchase a hat," the woman called Henrietta gasped. She lowered her voice, likely in an attempt to be discreet, although Thad still heard her just fine. "Dear me. I feel as though I may faint dead away at such a thought. This poor man is so utterly confused, Miss Mathilda. Could you please deal with him?"

Miss Mathilda appeared both concerned and exasperated.

"Ma'am...Miss Mathilda, I can explain."

"Yes, sir, you will be offering an explanation, of that I am certain. Henrietta, go retrieve yourself a glass of tea from the back room and recline momentarily while I handle this confused..." Miss Mathilda looked Thad over, clearly at a loss of what to call him. "This gentleman."

"Yes. Yes, Miss Mathilda." Henrietta rushed through the door to the back room.

"Now, sir, do explain yourself."

Thad took a peek out the window where passerby ambled along the boardwalk at a casual pace. He yearned at that uncomfortable moment to be merely a passerby himself. At the very least, Thad wished Miss Mathilda or one of her employees had done a better job filling the window with more dresses so no one could see in.

At that moment, a woman and her husband, a man in a black fedora, decided to pause before the window. The woman pointed at a dress and appeared to be beseeching her husband for its purchase. The man scrutinized the dress and nodded with nonchalance.

Thad held his breath. Would the man see him? Thad placed his cowboy hat atop his head and pulled the brim down on the left side. He could at least shield part of his face from the curious onlookers. An idea came to Thad, and he stooped down, knowing his height made him more obvious.

"Sir! Please do stand up straight and stop cowering behind the counter."

Cowering? Thad reluctantly unfolded himself and stood again to his full height.

"Sir, I must insist you tell me what you are doing," demanded Miss Mathilda, whose bulbous, overly round eyes stared right through him.

"I, uh…" Thad cautiously turned his head to see if the man with the fedora still stood just outside of the store. It was at that moment that the man made eye contact with him, his expression a mix of concern and curiosity. The man then tapped on the shoulder of his wife, who followed the direction of his pointing finger and gawked.

As if Thad were some animal in the Ringling Brothers Circus.

How had he ever found himself in such a circumstance?

"Sir!" Miss Mathilda bristled and drummed her fingers on the counter as though a teacher disciplining a wayward pupil.

Lord, I reckon this is an odd request, but might I become invisible? Knowing that wasn't likely to happen, Thad attempted to appear nonchalant, but the harm was already done. He might as well make the best of the situation. He turned and waved at the man and his wife, much to the woman's obvious distress. The man snickered and led his wife away.

Miss Mathilda couldn't have appeared more vexed as she glowered at him from behind the counter. "I sincerely hope for your benefit, sir, that you did not just cause me to lose a potential customer by your brash actions."

Brash actions? "No ma'am." Thad hoped not, although there were more important matters on his mind. Surely her irritation would subside once he explained his predicament. He cleared his throat. "I am here to buy a hat."

"You do know this is a women's boutique, do you not?"

"Yes, ma'am, I do."

"And you do know that men's hats are not available here?"

"I realize that, ma'am."

Was the room getting hotter? Thad reached up with his free hand and loosened his collar. "Ma'am, I am here to buy a woman's hat. I accidentally ruined her hat, and I'm here to replace it."

"I see." Miss Mathilda raised an eyebrow at him. Did she think him a cad who would intentionally ruin a woman's hat?

"I collided with her and her hat became...ruined." Thad gestured to the hatbox on the counter. "Here it is. I'd like to purchase one just like it, if I could."

The only good thing to occur after going through such embarrassment would be that he would get to see Mrs. Crawford again to give her the new hat.

That would be worth all of the humiliation Thad had suffered.

Right?

Thad reached into the hatbox and pinched the side of the dilapidated hat. He held the hat a short distance from his face and observed it. Squished edges marred the brim. The top of the hat was crimped in several places, and a piece of what might have been a feather stuck to the side.

Who would even wear such a thing?

Doing his best to hide the repulsion he felt, he placed the hat on the counter, then took a step back.

"Oh, dear me. What a dreadful demise to such a fine adornment." Miss Mathilda dabbed at the corners of her eyes with a frilly handkerchief. "Whatever happened to the artificial flowers? The plumage? The ribbons?" She choked the words out, as though she were barely able to speak them.

"Ma'am, I promise, it was an accident. I reckon I'll just order a new hat and be on my way."

"It's quite an expensive hat and takes weeks to arrive from Boston."

"I figured it would take some time to be delivered."

Miss Mathilda placed her hands on the hat and did her best to plump out the smashed parts to no avail. "It's not just any hat, sir. It's the finest of finest. Or shall I say, *was* the finest of finest. Such an unfortunate fate."

Thad wanted to remind Miss Mathilda that it was only a hat and that no funeral eulogy was in order, but he thought better of it. Women baffled him. It wasn't as if someone had passed on, for goodness' sake.

Miss Mathilda gave him a smug look, then took her place behind the counter. She flipped through the pages of a catalogue in an exaggerated motion while shaking her head. Still likely mourning the "dreadful demise," as she had called it of the hat. "There are several hats from which to choose." She narrowed her eyes. "Do you even know the appearance of the hat before you *ruined* it?"

Thad took a deep breath. Miss Mathilda was an exaggerated woman for sure. Sweat trickled down the back of his neck. Could he identify which hat to order? What if he ordered the wrong one? Mrs. Crawford would be disappointed for sure. He cleared his throat and said with more confidence than he felt, "I reckon I could recognize it. The woman who ordered the hat also ordered a bunch of other items and retrieved them earlier today."

"Ah, yes. I do believe I know of whom you speak. One of my best customers. Poor dear that you should ruin her fine hat. Tsk. Tsk." Miss Mathilda turned the catalogue toward him and pointed to some women's hats. "I believe this is the section of the catalogue from which she selected. The artist has rendered several options. Unfortunately, here at Miss Julia Mathilda's Fine Dresses, we do a significant amount of business, and I, therefore, cannot determine, based on mere memory, the particular hat she selected."

The pictures overwhelmed him. Everything from small hats to oversized obnoxious hats filled the pages of the black-and-white catalogue. "Uh..." Whatever happened to the days when women wore simple bonnets?

Miss Mathilda tossed him a priggish glance. "So, you aren't sure of the appearance of the hat you destroyed?"

Destroyed?

How did women even survive day-to-day life if they took their hats so seriously? Thad perused the catalogue, placing his finger on any hat that seemed to be the one. Perhaps he should have focused better on the dilapidated hat. But then, his mind had been more centered on a lovely woman with amber eyes. He flipped to the next page, praying a prayer of gratitude that there were only four pages of hats total. "I...I believe it is this one."

"That style is most popular. Fortunately for you, sir, I have two hats en route from Boston that I have previously ordered. Perhaps I can set one aside for you, but you will have to pay in advance."

"I can do that, ma'am."

"Lucky for you. Now please be advised this is an opulent hat made of the most luxurious materials. Materials one won't find on the dusty streets of Montana." She paused, as if ensuring her words had an effect on him. "And may I remind you that the cost increases significantly due to the necessity of having it shipped all the way from back East."

"I understand."

"Very well." Miss Julia Mathilda told him the amount and after asking her to repeat it twice, Thad plunked the money on the counter, vowing to never again ruin a woman's hat.

"I'll need your name, if you please." Miss Mathilda reached for a piece of stationery and a pen.

Thad pondered her request. Best if he just told her the name he had told Mrs. Crawford, even if it wasn't the entire truth. "Thad Alexander."

Miss Mathilda wrote his name on the sheet of paper. "My suggestion to you is to stop back in two weeks to allow for any delays in transit."

Thad tipped his hat. "Much obliged, ma'am." As he turned to leave, several women entered the store. They pointed and spoke in hushed tones as he slithered past them.

If Thad ever thought his life humdrum, today's events changed his opinion.

CHAPTER FIVE

Monday afternoon after visiting the orphanage and delivering the gifts to the children, Emilie motored the six miles toward her home, thoughts of the orphanage and its occupants never far from her mind. The three-story building, complete with a turret and a spacious porch, was a welcome site.

And a place of hope.

A year before Newt's passing, Mrs. Hagen, the director, arrived at the Hollow Creek Founder's Day Celebration seeking support for the orphanage. Since that time, Emilie had been fascinated by the organization that sought to find a home for all of its orphan children.

Newt hadn't agreed. He had discouraged Emilie from visiting there. "What good would it do you to visit it, Almira? It's a dismal place with children no one wants."

"Those children have lost their parents and have no one. Think of all the good we could do." Hosting benefit teas, volunteering her time, and donating funds had all filled Emilie's mind from the moment Mrs. Hagen sparked her interest at the celebration that day.

Finally, a way for Emilie to make a difference.

After Newt's death, Emilie devoted herself to the orphanage and visited twice a month to read to the children. She also donated a sizable sum to the institution.

The visit to the orphanage had been most welcome, and the children adored their gifts. Her mind wandered for a moment to how her own life would have been if she had been afforded the chance to be a mother. Emilie wiped a tear that slid down her face. The twists and turns of life were not fair at times.

EMILIE THOUGHT of nothing but her noonday meal with Mr. Alexander three days ago. While the events leading to their meal had been quite embarrassing, Emilie discovered a respectable gentleman in the ranch hand. Would they truly meet again in two Fridays? Would he remember their appointment?

Several times, Emilie found herself pondering whether the chance meeting with Mr. Alexander had truly happened or if it was merely a dream.

And why was she so drawn to a man she just met?

Emilie stood, then glanced out the parlor window and did a double-take. Leaning closer to the window, she stared, eyes widening as her mouth dropped open and rounded into the shape of an "o."

The neighbor's cattle had somehow escaped from the neighbor's field and thundered across her property.

Again.

Only this time, they were headed straight for her garden.

The audacity!

Emilie placed her hands on her hips and pursed her lips in a tight thin line. She'd about had it with the antics of Mr. Evanson and his disregard for her and her land. Such disrespect had gone on for too long.

Far too long.

Lifting her pink walking skirt, she marched across the floor toward the front door—and none too softly either—causing the polished floor boards to creek. *If those cattle ruin my garden, so help me…* So help her, she would borrow Morris's rifle and turn those impudent bovines into beef!

It was 1911. Surely Mr. Evanson could become current with the times and manage to enclose his *entire* ranch with barbed wire fencing, rather than ignoring the one remaining section of wooden fence on the border between the Wheeler and Evanson residences. An area far too close to Emilie's house and gardens.

Why should that particular section be treated any differently than the rest of his expansive ranch?

Emilie shook her head and let out a frustrated sigh.

"Mrs. Wheeler, is everything all right, ma'am?"

Emilie stopped at the sound of her maid's voice. She turned and tried her best to keep her voice calm. "Yes, Hattie, I'm fine. Would you please ask Jep if he'll see to stopping the neighbor's cattle from destroying what's left of my garden?"

Hattie covered her mouth with her hand and, with the dramatic effect the young girl had mastered, gasped, "Oh, Mrs. Wheeler, that's positively awful! Whatever shall be done? Yes, I'll let Jep know right away." Hattie turned on her heel and headed out the door to alert the ranch hand of the situation.

As Emilie watched Hattie, she allowed herself to smile in the midst of her frustration. Hattie's drama kept things entertaining. The young girl worked hard and needed her salary to help support her family. Fond of the maid and knowing of her situation, Emilie often stuck a few extra dollars into Hattie's pay as a bonus.

And Hattie had a liking for the young ranch hand, Jep. Emilie was sure of it. Not that Emilie was an expert when it came to knowing what it felt like to be in love.

Glancing down at her wedding ring with its sizable diamonds, her mind recessed for a moment from the infuriating cattle situation to a time of the recent past. Her thoughts reverted to her husband, Newton, and she sighed. Of all the men to have married, couldn't she have married one who loved her?

Enough of such thoughts. Reflecting on things I have no control over will most certainly not bring me peace of mind.

Now standing on the front porch of her stately home, Emilie could see the commotion caused by those ornery cattle. Dust everywhere, deep holes from their trampling hooves ruining her manicured yard. She shook her head.

Enough was enough.

Perhaps it was time for her to pay Mr. Evanson a visit. She'd never met the man, for he seemed to always be gone, whether in the fields or on out-of-town business. But meet him this time, she would, for there was a time for just about everything that needed to be handled, even dealing with contemptible men like her neighbor.

Yes, she would visit him today, just as soon as Emilie was reassured that her prize tomato plants would survive the earthquake they'd been subjected to. She'd climb into her Model T and drive herself right over to Mr. Evanson's home. Then she'd demand he replace her garden, build a more secure fence to keep his cattle on his own property, and pay her the expenses for her headache.

And if Mr. Evanson didn't comply?

Well, Emilie would just beckon the sheriff and resolve this matter once and for all.

JEP AND two of Emilie's other hired hands had managed to herd the cows back to Mr. Evanson's property.

"If you'd like, we'll go right on over there, Mrs. Wheeler, and give him a talking-to about his cattle," said Jep.

Emilie smiled at her favorite ranch hand, despite the anger that riveted through her concerning the damage from the cattle. A hard worker, Jep was also as reliable as they came. She could see why Hattie held a fondness for the kind and considerate young man.

Jep's scrawny thin build disguised his strength and aptitude for the sometimes-difficult labor that working on a ranch brought. Freckles dotted his face and his strawberry blonde hair stuck out at odd places beneath his hat. Sparkly green eyes, in the shape of round saucers, even when he wasn't surprised, had a gentleness about them. A gentleness Emilie figured was due to the fact that Jep had helped raise his six younger siblings after his father died.

"Thank you, Jep. I would appreciate that, as I am not of the mind right now to speak to Mr. Evanson. I'm not sure why the cattle have rushed through the yard yet again. I thought Newton had resolved this matter last year in his dealings with our neighbor."

"Not sure either, ma'am. It appears the fence was knocked over in some manner or another. Reckon I can go over and talk to Mr. Evanson about the whole ordeal since..."

Since you no longer have a husband to do the speaking for you.

Jep's unspoken words caused a lurch in Emilie's heart. While Newt could hardly be considered as one who excelled at taking difficult matters into his own hands, he had spoken with Mr. Evanson about the cattle last year when it had happened.

A mere month before Newt had succumbed to a fatal case of pneumonia.

And right before Emilie had become a widow less than three years after her wedding vows.

Now Emilie had to handle most things on her own, not that that had changed dramatically since Newt's death. He rarely came through on topics of grave concern to her, God rest his soul. Such things, Newt had noted, were merely an inconvenience, nothing for him to give a second thought to when he had so many other things on his mind.

Last year Newt spoke with Mr. Evanson about the cattle, not because Emilie's beloved petunias were at stake, but rather because Newt never liked the neighbor in the first place. As a matter of fact, he'd previously had at least three run-ins with the owner of the Evanson Cattle Company.

Newt had even mentioned something about suspecting Mr. Evanson and his hired hands of rustling cattle. A topic Emilie overheard Newt speaking about with their ranch foreman. "Never trust Mr. Evanson or his hired hands," Emilie had heard him say.

Surely if there was any indication of cattle rustling, the sheriff in Hollow Creek would have taken notice by now.

"Mrs. Wheeler? Didn't mean to upset you none about Mr. Wheeler's passing."

Emilie swallowed and forced a slow smile toward her ranch hand. "Oh, Jep, I know that, and I appreciate your concern. Yes, please do go speak with Mr. Evanson."

Emilie had never met the deplorable man, even though he lived less than a mile away.

Newt insisted it wasn't necessary.

CHAPTER SIX

Thad rode his horse toward the former O'Reilly property. Mr. O'Reilly, the previous owner, had fallen on hard times and was unable to pay the mortgage. Mr. Salonen at Hollow Creek Bank and Trust had done what he could to work with him, but in the end, it wasn't enough. Mr. O'Reilly returned to Ohio, and his property was sold.

Thad recalled the moment he strode into the bank and discussed purchasing the O'Reilly land. Mr. Salonen, eager to be relieved of the acreage, sold it to Thad just minutes before Newton Wheeler arrived to express his own interest in the property.

While it added nearly 1,000 acres to Thad's current land holdings, it also created further friction and animosity between him and his neighbor.

Thad dismounted and gazed upon the surrounding scenery. Evanson cattle roamed the former O'Reilly property. In one direction, the breathtaking Bitterroot Mountains rose high above the ranchland, their snow-covered tips seeming to reach the blue sky. To his right stood the Wheeler home, barns, corrals, a family cemetery, and numerous large trees. If he squinted, he could barely make out one of the Wheeler ranch hands in the distance. Beyond that to the right lay the rest of the Evanson property, which included his own house, barns, the bunkhouse, chicken coop, corrals, and acreage, reminding him of all God blessed him with.

The point of contention was how the Wheeler property separated his land from the O'Reilly property. Hence the desire on Newton's part to purchase the O'Reilly land. While unconventional to have his property split into two pieces, Thad knew there had to be a way to compromise.

But Newton Wheeler hadn't seen compromise as an option.

He recalled one of his confrontations with his argumentative neighbor.

"Can I pay you for usage of a strip of your property to access both pieces of my land?" he'd asked Newton one day in town.

Newton Wheeler, a tall thin man with rust-colored hair and what Thad termed a permanent scowl, pushed Thad's suggestion aside as Thad attempted to elaborate.

"I'll pay you, Wheeler, and I'll keep it fenced off and properly maintained."

Newton stepped closer to Thad, his skinny frame half of Thad's, but his ego twice the size. "If you were so concerned about your cattle getting from one side of your property to the other, you should have avoided purchasing the O'Reilly property altogether and instead looked for another spread."

"Just like you, I aim to expand my holdings, and I didn't figure it would be an issue."

Newton's intense stare through dark beady eyes confirmed his hatred toward Thad. He jabbed a finger toward him. "Listen here, Evanson. You'll not use one piece of my property for your nefarious schemes, whether you compensate me for it or not."

"Nefarious schemes?"

"I'm wise to your less-than-lawful cattle operation. Word is you and your men have rustled a few cattle in the area to build your herd. If I were you, I'd stay far away from any Wheeler property unless you care to explain to the sheriff about how your herds have increased so quickly and extensively."

Was Newton threatening him? Thad fisted his hands at his sides. To be accused of cattle rustling was not something he, nor the law, took lightly. "Wheeler, I know we haven't gotten along since the day we became neighbors, but to accuse me of something illegal, that you know full well I would never have a part in, is unwarranted and won't be tolerated. I've built my herds through hard work, perseverance, and much prayer."

Newton's expression indicated he doubted Thad's assertion.

Thankfully, the law had seen the truth. Thad would no more rustle cattle than be a frequent shopper at Miss Julia Mathilda's Fine Dresses.

Thad mounted his horse again and rode toward the edge of the O'Reilly property. Should he ask Mrs. Wheeler if he could make an arrangement to access his property via hers? Would she be more open to his proposition than her late husband had been? Might be an uphill battle considering the very real possibility her husband had sullied Thad's reputation.

THAD OPENED the door to his home and placed his hat on the table. Yanking his boots off with one hand as he walked, he finally crashed on the bed. But as exhausted as he was, sleep eluded him.

He contemplated his plans for the coming days and weeks. Soon he would board the train in Missoula to visit his friend and mentor in Texas. When he returned, he would meet with the bank to discuss securing a spread of land between Hollow Creek and Missoula.

Thankfully, most of his employees tried their hardest to help make the Evanson Ranch run smoothly, even in his absence.

Thad shoved aside thoughts of trips, bank appointments, and ranch chores and settled on something—or someone—more pleasant.

Over and over again, Thad gave thought to the woman he had just met in Missoula. An interesting woman, that Mrs. Crawford.

Beautiful.

Intelligent.

Two weeks seemed like an awful long time to wait to see her again.

But why was Thad so taken with her?

Was it the easy camaraderie? That he felt like he had known her for years instead of minutes?

That they shared much in common: from their interest in automobiles, to their preferred author, to their choice in favorite desserts?

Mrs. Crawford had crowded his mind the rest of the day after meeting her, during his drive home to Hollow Creek, and all the minutes in between.

Thad chuckled to himself at the reminder of his visit to Miss Julia Mathilda's Fine Dresses. Never would he tell a soul of his misfortune of entering that store and causing a commotion for the proprietress, as well as her flighty clerk.

Thad clasped his hands behind his head and stared at the ceiling in darkness. The silence in the house always bothered him. Had he married Catherine, he would have come home to her greeting. She would ask how his trip went and if things had gone as he had hoped. Thad would inhale the aroma of supper she had saved for him and she would tell him about the shenanigans their children engaged in while he was away.

But Thad hadn't married Catherine and he wouldn't be coming home to a wife and children anytime soon.

Maybe even never.

The thought unnerved him. He didn't want to be alone forever, and at thirty, he wasn't getting any younger.

It was just as well.

Because when he finally married, if God ever had that on His list of plans for Thad's life, it would be a marriage between two people joined together by love. Like Grandma and Grandpa's marriage had been.

Marrying Catherine would not have achieved that ideal.

Thad knew he wouldn't just settle for any woman as his wife, even though there was no shortage of interest from the fine women in town. But did they like him for him or did they like him because of the wealth he had amassed?

Thad never knew for sure.

But he wasn't willing to take the chance. Even if he was eighty-four when he finally settled into matrimony.

The sound of the ticking clock reminded Thad there weren't many hours before he would have to awaken and start a new day. Nonstop chores would beckon him on his growing ranch. He rolled over on his left side and stretched his long legs over the side of the bed, trying to get comfortable. He liked his work as a cattle rancher, even if the hours were long.

It had always been his dream.

Thad employed numerous ranch hands and he did what he could to treat them in a Christian way as Grandpa had taught him. He paid them a fair wage and gave the men time off when they requested it.

Thad had friends at Hollow Creek Church and at the church he attended often in Missoula. Basically, his life was complete. To make it sound as though he was missing out on love would never be something he would readily admit, even if he was lonely.

And he was.

Thad mentally listed the things in his mind he had to do to prepare for his trip in a few days. Then, swinging his legs over the side of the bed, he sauntered toward the pitcher for a glass of water.

Peering out the window, he noticed in the distance a light shining in the Wheeler home. *Apparently, I'm not the only one having trouble sleeping.* The Wheelers had enough wealth for electricity, something Thad hadn't upgraded to as of yet.

Why make his home comfortable with all the modern conveniences if he was rarely here? And moreover, if he had no one to share it with? So instead, Thad remained in the humble home the previous owner had built on the land, even though he could afford much better.

Thad stared for a while at the Wheeler place. He didn't know much about his nearest neighbor, only that he had never much cared for the husband, who died about a year ago. Thad had never met the widow, but judging from her husband, she would be in her late thirties or early forties and bearing a cantankerous attitude just like her departed husband possessed.

He attempted to recall if he had ever seen Mrs. Wheeler at church in Hollow Creek. Not that Thad was able to attend one of the two churches in town too often as of late. Instead, he visited Pastor Shay's church in Missoula most recently, as Missoula was where Thad was on most weekends for business.

Thad's thoughts returned to the Widow Wheeler. In trying to be a good neighbor, he thought many times about offering his condolences over her loss, but had never gotten around to it. He had been so busy these past few years with getting Evanson Cattle Company started and spending so much time away from home, whether on the range of his extensive ranch or on business.

"Just as well," he muttered. There had been no kindness between him and Mr. Wheeler.

Thad had attempted to make amends.

But Newton Wheeler had resisted and not in the kindest of ways.

More like threats from the mealy-mouthed man who thought he could get anything he wanted because of his affluence.

It hadn't helped that just recently Thad's cattle had broken down the fence and trampled through the Wheeler property twice while Thad was gone. That certainly didn't improve pleasantries between neighbors. He would have to make good and sure his ranch hand, Floyd, fixed the fence properly so there was no chance of Thad's herd trespassing onto his neighbor's property yet again.

Turning around and heading back to bed, he attempted to let all of his thoughts seep out of his mind. But the image of a woman he'd met in Missoula contributed to the sleepless night.

CHAPTER SEVEN

Emilie marveled at the tender buds beginning to sprout. Buds that would soon become flowers. Fortunately, those contemptible cows hadn't trampled her flower garden in the back of the house. She gritted her teeth. It was bad enough the animals had rendered some of her other plants useless. The growing season in Montana was painfully short, to say the least. Thankfully, some of her flowers were perennials. However, her vegetables were not.

She adjusted her hat on her head, then reached for her Haws watering can. Rather pleased with herself for investing in such a fine purchase, Emilie tilted the can and watered her young blooms.

Newt would arch one of his already-pointy eyebrows at Emilie when he saw her doing "servant's work". However, Emilie delighted in caring for her many gardens. It gave her purpose. Newt would tell her she was absurd to do anything that could dirty her hands or cause any amount of sun to rest upon her fair skin.

Emilie rolled her eyes at the thought. Planting and watering were hardly servant's work in her mind. Why, if it wasn't so utterly unconventional, Emilie would toss her wide-brimmed hat to the side and roll up the sleeves of her blouse to soak up the sun's rays. She could hear Newt's voice now: *"You're not a working-class servant."*

Or Mother's voice, *"Be ever so sure to slather on your almond oil and heavy powder. There will be no freckling among the women in our family."*

Indeed not.

Emilie rolled her eyes again, but remained fully protected from the sun's rays. She was a woman of opulence, after all.

The spring day was crisp and clear and full of wonderful noises, like birds chirping and the faint sound of a calf calling for its mother. And the sound of Hattie sweeping the front porch and humming what sounded like a hymn.

Moments later, Emilie poked small holes into the ground and planted some more seeds. Could a woman ever have too many flowers?

She rose from her kneeled position and placed a hand on her lower back. Gardening did take its toll on her, but it was nothing a hot bath couldn't remedy when she turned in for the evening. Emilie closed her eyes and tilted her head toward the sun, but only for the tiniest of moments.

When Emilie opened her eyes, she saw something, or someone, in the distance. Squinting and straining to ascertain who it was, she watched Jep's familiar gait come into view. He didn't see her, but continued toward the western side of the house, clutching something in his hands.

Father sometimes accused Emilie of being quite nosy. Emilie preferred the word "inquisitive." She strolled along the side of the house, following the strains of Hattie's harmonious voice. When Emilie reached the edge of the house, she stopped when she heard Jep sauntering up the stairs to the porch.

Emilie removed her hat and clutched it in her gloved hand. Eavesdropping on her hired help? Mother would call her meddlesome. Emilie trusted her employees to the fullest extent, but she often suspected Jep's fondness toward Hattie. And vice versa.

Snug against the house, Emilie dared herself not to breathe while she listened as intently as she could.

"Uh, hello, Hattie."

"Oh, Jep, I didn't see you there."

Emilie smiled to herself. That could explain why Hattie had continued to sing, even while Jep wandered up the porch steps.

"Reckon I'm sorry to interrupt you."

"Oh, that is no problem. No problem at all."

Oh, to be young again. Emilie peered around the corner of the house with caution. From her vantage point, she could see the back of Hattie and the side of Jep's face. Fortunately for Emilie, the young man would never win an award for being attentive and aware.

Jep removed his hat with one hand, displaying his unruly strawberry blond hair that sprouted in spikey disarray from its many cowlicks. "I...uh..." One hand remained behind his back. What could he have for Hattie?

The excitement was nearly too much for Emilie to bear. For she had never experienced a blossoming love like what was shared between Hattie and Jep.

"Yes?" Hattie's voice squeaked.

"Um...I..."

Emilie watched Hattie's head bob up and down, encouraging Jep to continue with his sentence.

"You see, I...well, it's like this, Hattie. I picked these for you." Jep brought his left hand from behind his back and thrust a handful of wildflowers at Hattie.

"Oh, Jep, they're lovely. How did you know I like flowers?"

Even from her incognito position, Emilie could see a flush on Jep's freckly face. "Reckon I just knew. That's all."

"Thank you, Jep."

Jep nodded, slapped his cowboy hat on his head, and rambled down the porch steps toward the field. Was it Emilie's imagination or was he standing just a bit taller than he had when he had first approached Hattie?

Emilie hastily slid her head back behind the corner of the house, lest either of them see her. *"Snooping about is just so unbecoming."* Mother's voice rang in her ears. Emilie brushed it aside, and instead giggled to herself at what she just witnessed.

Jep's secret infatuation for Hattie was no longer a secret.

That evening, Emilie settled into her comfortable chair in the parlor after taking a long and relaxing bath. She opened the pages of her latest book by Robert Louis Stevenson, longing to escape into a world of adventure.

She wondered if Mr. Alexander was partaking in a Robert Louis Stevenson book this evening as well, after a hard day of work on his boss's ranch.

A knock at the door interrupted her. "Mrs. Wheeler?"

Hattie stood in the doorway, her face unsure. "Yes, Hattie, what is it?"

"May I speak to you, ma'am?"

"Is everything quite all right, Hattie?"

"Quite all right."

"Come in, then." Servants in Emilie's parents' house were treated far differently than Emilie treated her help. They had never been so freely allowed to approach her family. But things were different for Emilie. She considered some of her employees as friends. Hattie was one of them. Or rather, she considered Hattie the younger sister she never had.

"Mrs. Wheeler, I'm sorry to bother you, but I have a concern."

"Please, have a seat, Hattie."

"May I shut the door, ma'am? You see, this is a sensitive matter."

"By all means." *A sensitive matter?* "Hattie, is your family all right?"

"Yes, ma'am."

Emilie breathed a sigh of relief. Hattie's father had succumbed to an illness that made it difficult for him to work. Thankfully, in recent months, he had improved significantly. "What ails you, Hattie?"

"Mrs. Wheeler..." Hattie paused and twisted her fingers together.

"Yes?"

"You are the nicest employer I've ever had. Not that I've had any other employers, mind you, but you've always treated me so kindly, what with paying me well and caring about my family and all."

"Hattie, you're not thinking of leaving my employ, are you?"

"No, ma'am, nothing like that."

"Oh, good. You see, Hattie, I am quite fond of you as well."

Hattie nodded, her large hazel eyes darting around the room. "I have but a question, and since you're always so kind to me, I thought I would ask."

"Please, go ahead."

"When you were in love, what was it like? I know this is a sensitive question and probably improper to ask, but I was hoping you could help me."

"When I was in love?"

"Yes, you know, when you were in love with Mr. Wheeler. Not after you were married..." Hattie cleared her throat. "I mean, when you were courting, or about to start your courtship."

"Oh." Emilie thought back to those early days of courtship with Newt. A very brief courtship.

"If this causes you sadness, seeing as how Mr. Wheeler has passed and all, you can tell me to mind my own business."

"You are fine in asking, Hattie. While I do miss Mr. Wheeler, it is appropriate for me to discuss him."

Hattie leaned forward then in expectation. "If you're quite all right speaking of such matters with me, what was it like to be in love? How did you meet?"

Emilie was honored Hattie felt comfortable enough to ask such questions. Emilie hadn't even asked such things of her own mother.

But then, she and Mother were not close in the least.

"Newt—Mr. Wheeler—was a business associate of a friend of my father's. At a charity ball, it was suggested by my father that I meet Mr. Wheeler."

"And when you saw him, did your heart flutter? I mean, hoping you don't mind my forwardness in asking."

Emilie sighed. Her heart had never fluttered around Newt. How could she discuss such delicate matters with Hattie?

"That's too private. I'm so sorry." Hattie pressed the wrinkles from her uniform. "How did you know Mr. Wheeler fancied you?"

"We danced several dances at the charity ball. Mr. Wheeler was an accomplished dancer, and we entered into courtship not long after." Emilie recalled that her dance card had been primarily filled with Newt's requests. At the petition of her father, perhaps?

"Oh, yes, I recall him being a lot older than you." As soon as she had said it, Hattie bit her lip. "Begging your pardon, ma'am."

"That's quite all right, Hattie. I'm honored you have sought me to discuss this. I know you don't get to visit with your mother as often as you would like. And yes, you are correct, Mr. Wheeler was twelve years my senior. His business in New York was well-established when we met. We courted for several months, then married in a lavish ceremony. Mother was thrilled. Father was ecstatic."

"And you? Did you *just know* you had found the one God chose for you?" Hattie looked as though she could barely remain sitting at such a thought.

I'm not sure God had a thing to do with it. Rather than voice her thoughts, Emilie instead said, "We had a whirlwind courtship, a splendid outdoor wedding that Mother was almost nearly unable to pull together in such a short amount of time, and then Mr. Wheeler moved us to this ranch he inherited after his uncle passed."

"I've heard weddings for rich folk take a long time to plan. Oops! Begging your pardon again, Mrs. Wheeler."

Emilie laughed. "Weddings do take a long time to plan. Most need a year or so to succeed in properly arranging a wedding. But Mother didn't complain. She was just thrilled for me to be married."

And not continuing life as a spinster.

"I'm eighteen, and I'm not thinking about marriage yet. But I do think Jep might fancy me."

"Really?"

"Yes. Oh, Mrs. Wheeler..." Hattie placed a hand to her neck and plopped back in the sofa in a most unrefined manner. "Today he surprised me on the front porch. You know how I love to sing hymns while going about my work?" Hattie seemed to have forgotten all about her nervousness at approaching Emilie, as she sat upright again and nearly bounced off the sofa.

"Yes?"

"Well, I had no idea at all he was standing there on the porch with me. And then, lo and behold, there he was. And there I was. Standing face to face. I mean, I have seen and spoken to him many times here at the ranch and thought him quite dashing, but there he was standing so close to me. I thought my heart would beat plumb out of my body. And that's not all." Hattie paused for the briefest of seconds to catch her breath. "He handed me this beautiful bouquet of wildflowers that he picked. I do hope it is all right that he picked the flowers from your property."

"It's perfectly fine, Hattie."

"Oh, thank goodness. So he handed me the flowers, and it was all I could do to...what is it they say in those cultured books...retain my composure."

"What a thoughtful gesture. You should place them in a vase and display them."

Hattie bobbed her head. "Oh, I will, Mrs. Wheeler." She paused and appeared thoughtful. "So, you see, I think Jep may fancy me."

"I think it sounds very likely."

"Do you really think so? I mean, I think he might have been staring at me that one time when I was serving the ranch hands pancakes and eggs last week. But I didn't dare look. Mama always said it's impolite to stare, even if someone is staring at you." Hattie held a hand to her heart. "I still can't stop thinking about him. But don't worry, my daydreams won't get in the way of my work."

"I'm not worried, Hattie."

"Thank you, Mrs. Wheeler, for allowing me speak with you about this."

"Anytime."

"I best be going now. I have a few more things to finish before turning in." Hattie rose, curtsied, and dashed out the door.

Emilie pondered the young woman's excitement and fought not to envy it.

For Emilie had never known what it was like to be in love.

BRIGHT AND early before Emilie barely stepped a foot outside, she saw Jep running toward her. "Good morning, Mrs. Wheeler," he said, clearly out of breath.

"Good morning, Jep." Emilie stepped onto the porch and reached for her watering can.

"I'd be much obliged if I could speak to you in private for a pint-sized minute."

"Of course, Jep. Walk with me as I see to my gardens."

"Yes, ma'am." He fell into step beside her, slowing his long lanky stride to match her short narrow one.

"Is everything all right, Jep?"

Jep removed his hat and scratched the back of his head. "I believe so. I just needed to ask what a fella can do to let a woman know he fancies her."

Emilie stopped and stared at Jep. "Begging your pardon?"

"Sorry, ma'am, if that's not all right to ask. I was just thinkin' since you are a married woman...well, were a married woman that is, that you might know a thing or two."

"I will help you if I can."

"Appreciate that, Mrs. Wheeler. See, there's this beautiful young lady that I fancy. You even know her. She's the prettiest girl I've ever set eyes on." Jep stared off into the distance, as if imagining the object of his affection. "I really want to see if she likes me too. I can't know for sure, but I do know that I can do things to show my interest, right?"

"Jep, did you happen to speak to Morris or one of the ranch hands about this?"

Surely one of the men would be better for Jep to discuss such delicate issues. Although Emilie was flattered both Jep and Hattie looked to her as a mentor of sorts.

"I did speak to Baxter about it, but he wasn't too knowin' about things."

"Well, what have you done so far?"

"I have given her flowers. Aww, maybe I should have asked first. See, these were wildflowers picked from your fields, Mrs. Wheeler." Jep hung his head. "Sorry 'bout that. I shouda asked first."

"I think the wildflowers were a grand idea, Jep. I don't mind one bit if you pick them from the fields. As you know, I love flowers of all types."

"Yes, ma'am, I do know that and thank you."

"I would keep doing thoughtful gestures such as the flowers and maybe say 'hello' to her every now and again."

"Oh, I do plan to do that, Mrs. Wheeler. Sometimes I stare at her, but it's only because she's so pretty and all." Jep cleared his throat. "And, well, there's this barn dance comin' up next week at the Rettig place. Reckon I'd like to see if Hat...uh, this girl I fancy, would like to go with me to the dance."

"That sounds like a splendid idea, Jep."

"Yeah, I thought so too. Do you think we could both have next Saturday afternoon off? I reckon you give us lots of weekends off with you travelin' to Missoula and all, and I don't know if it's all right to ask if you're not goin' to be gone, but...I mean, I'd like the time so that um...this girl I fancy, could get ready for it and we would have time to ride into town and be there for the potluck that's before the dance."

"I think that would be fine."

"Thank you, Mrs. Wheeler. Meaning no offense, but I sure like you a whole lot better than Mr. Wheeler, God rest his soul, as my mama would say."

"Well, thank you, Jep. Please see to it you've done all Baxter needs you to do before you leave on Saturday."

"Oh, I will. You know I'm a hard worker, ma'am."

"That I do."

"I keep prayin' God will guide me in all this. I don't want to court Hat...I mean...the girl I fancy, that is, unless it's God's will and all."

Emilie knew absolutely nothing of God's will. Only that He ignored her when she had desperately pleaded with Him about the thing closest to her heart and, prior to that, when she had asked that He heal Newt.

CHAPTER EIGHT

"Hello, Mrs. Wheeler. I have your tea for you," Hattie said, interrupting Emilie's thoughts on a bright and cheery Wednesday afternoon.

"Thank you, Hattie."

"Yes, ma'am."

It had been a few days since the barn dance, and Hattie hadn't yet spoken of it to Emilie. Her curiosity was getting the best of her, so she decided to bring up the subject.

"Hattie?"

"Did you need something, Mrs. Wheeler?"

"I was wondering how the barn dance went with Jep? If you don't mind me asking?"

"I don't mind you asking at all, ma'am." Hattie glanced at the sofa. "May I sit for a moment?"

"Please do. I'm eager to hear all about the barn dance." Emilie had never been to a barn dance. Mother would say how uncivilized such an outing was if Emilie were ever to attend one.

"Oh, Mrs. Wheeler," Hattie's head bobbed up and down so fast that Emilie worried she might cause herself a headache. "It was splendid. Jep was so dapper and so gentlemanly. The whole evening was as though a dream." Hattie paused, her eyes glazed in a dreamy state, as she stared absentmindedly at a spot on the far wall of the parlor.

Emilie giggled at Hattie's apparent woolgathering. "Please do go on, Hattie. I am most anxious to hear."

"Yes, where was I? Oh! I thought I might faint dead away when he took me in his strong arms and spun me around." Hattie sighed. "It was as though a dream had overtaken me. I couldn't concentrate yesterday nor today. Oh, dear me! Not that I'm not doing my work as expected, it's just that...I am in love with Jep, Mrs. Wheeler. As Pa used to say, it's as plain as the beak on a chicken." Hattie hesitated, a look of concern crossing her face. "Although I am not sure if he feels the same."

"It's quite possible he does."

"I have a confession to make. I once read...just a few words, mind you, of the story *Cinderella* in *Perrault's Fairy Tales* that was on the table. Begging your pardon, but I loved the part about the handsome prince. Jep really is my handsome prince, although I thank the Good Lord daily that I don't have an evil stepmother or evil stepsisters." Hattie wrinkled her nose. "Please forgive me, Mrs. Wheeler, but I hope you don't mind that I read a few pages of your book. It was after the day had ended and all my work was finished."

"I don't mind if you read my books, Hattie. All I ask is that next time you do ask permission first."

"Oh, yes, ma'am. I shan't forget to do that."

"I'm thrilled to hear the barn dance went well."

"We rode home in his wagon, but we didn't speak much. He hasn't spoken to me today, but I only did see him from far away, after all. You do think he still fancies me, don't you, Mrs. Wheeler?"

"I'm quite sure he does, Hattie."

"Do you recall when you couldn't stop thinking about Mr. Wheeler?"

Emilie wasn't sure how to answer the question. There had never been a time when she couldn't remove Newt from her mind, other than when she did her best to pray he would recover from his illness.

Although, in retrospect, Emilie had no idea the proper way to pray or even if God heard her.

Obviously He either hadn't heard her or had chosen to ignore her, as Newt had succumbed to his illness.

"It's as though Jep fills my every thought. A kinder, gentler man I've never met."

No, Emilie couldn't recall a time when Newt had filled her mind because she fancied him. But there was another who had consumed her thoughts deep into the night.

Mr. Alexander.

LONG AFTER Hattie returned to her duties, Emilie remained sipping her tea in the parlor wishing for the first time that the days would go faster than ever so she could see Mr. Alexander again.

Oddly enough, already she and Mr. Alexander had more in common than Emilie and Newt had ever had. They both shared the same favorite book and author and had a love for automobiles. Then, there was the pie à la mode. Perhaps they could partake in such a dessert during their next meal at the restaurant.

Emilie appreciated Mr. Alexander's offer to purchase her a hat to replace the one he ruined.

Had he thought of her at all since their time at the restaurant? Perhaps he was already courting another. But goodness! What was she even doing thinking of courtship with a man she had just met? And only a year after Newt's untimely death?

Yet, a man of Mr. Alexander's character and attractiveness likely had many women from which to choose, especially in a city the size of Missoula.

For sure, Emilie could not divulge to Mr. Alexander about her wealth. She must remain "Mrs. Crawford" and use her chosen first name with her maiden last name. Once, and indeed if, she discovered he cared for her, and not the wealth she had accumulated, then Emilie would disclose her true identity.

Could it be Emilie was merely lonely and that was why Mr. Alexander so filled her thoughts?

While it could never be said that Emilie and Newt were in love, it had been pleasant to have a husband, a partner of sorts.

Even though Newt had never seen Emilie in that capacity. She figured he saw her as more of a nuisance than anything else. Being twelve years his junior, Newt had commented more than once that Emilie's ways seemed childish.

Would Mr. Alexander think the same? He appeared to be nearly the same age as Emilie, so hopefully not.

She would just have to do her best not to be immature or reckless, as Father had once called her, simply for having opinions of her own. Especially when such opinions were looked down upon in today's polite society.

What would Father think of Emilie's involvement with women's suffrage?

Someone like Father could never understand, as he had likely been mature and sophisticated at a young age.

Emilie replaced her teacup on its saucer. Father and Mother had always expected her to act a certain way so as not to embarrass the family name. It was nice to be able to be herself for once and experience the unabated freedom she had here in Montana.

Even if some folks in Hollow Creek thought her eccentric.

Emilie strolled to the fireplace. She took the wedding photograph from above the mantle and stared at it as she often did. Newton appeared regal in his fine clothing—almost like royalty. His rust-colored hair combed to one side and his serious facial expression reflected his austere personality. Thin, wire-rimmed spectacles did little to disguise his intense gaze. Even his right hand, which was placed on her shoulder appeared rigid. He cocked his head to one side—in the opposite direction of hers. Had Newton had second thoughts about their marriage?

He died so soon, before she'd ever grown to love him.

But would she have ever loved him the way a wife ought to love a husband? Not fanciful feelings, but true, abiding love like that which she saw in Vera and Morris, her hired help, who had been married for decades?

Memories crowded her mind of the day Mother and Father broached the subject of marrying Newton. It came unexpected and unannounced, in the usual spontaneous nature of her selfish parents. A trait she, as a deliberate and meticulous planner over all details, did not inherit.

Emilie rubbed her thumb along the outside edge of the gold-plated frame and took a step back in time…

"But, Mother, I've only known Newton for a couple of months. And…I don't love him."

Father cleared his throat and slipped from the room, leaving Emilie and Mother to their conversation. Quite like him to avoid any type of discussion about anything of importance to Emilie. She could count the number of meaningful conversations they had ever shared on one hand.

Mother's small round eyes penetrated through Emilie's very soul. "Love isn't all there is, Almira."

Emilie had resisted the urge to argue. She detested when Mother called her by her given name of Almira. She much preferred her middle name of Emilie and let Mother know on many occasions. Mother resisted right back and insisted Emilie appreciate her name.

"Do you love Father?"

"Pish posh, Almira. What a private question to ask and unladylike at that. Of course, I love your father in a conventional sort of way. You will someday grow to love Newton in such a way as well."

"A conventional sort of way?"

"You know that our families encouraged us to marry to preserve the family fortunes."

"It would be nice if I could choose whom I might marry." The words tumbled from her mouth before she could restrain them.

Emilie took great pains to plan most of her life and couldn't quite suppress the words she spoke, especially when they were words she ought not speak.

Mother's eyes had grown large at Emilie's statement. "Almira, you might want to consider the fact that you, at the age of nearly twenty-five, are considered a spinster. Shall your father and I long for grandchildren but never have the joy of them in our lifetime? Shall all those years of instruction you received regarding how to be a well-bred woman in a high society home be for naught? Wasted? Just withered away? Shall you deny your father and me the knowledge of knowing that you are secure in your financial future by marrying a man of greater means than even we possess? And what of the Crawford family line? You are our only child. Shall the line just perish when you someday pass on? Come now, Almira. Think rationally."

Of course, it was always about the Crawford family line and about Mother's and Father's desires. Never about her. It never had been. How many times had she been left behind with a nanny while Mother and Father gallivanted all over the United States and Europe? More times than Emilie could count.

"Don't make an error here, Almira. You are nearly beyond the age of marriage and aren't getting any younger. Don't be foolish and wait until you have some fluttery feelings in your heart for a man. Such things never happen. Be orthodox in your decisions and realize that Newton is graciously offering his hand in marriage to a woman most men would pass by because of her age."

But hadn't Emilie experienced fluttery feelings for Mr. Alexander, even though she had just met him?

Emilie had gritted her teeth at Mother's comment. So she was more like charity? Was she really that hard on the eyes that no man would ever consider her? Was she really such an elderly spinster that her days of finding true love were over? Was there really no such thing as falling in love that she must marry to secure her financial future—and please her parents—and marry only for those reasons?

Mother placed her well-manicured hands on her hips. "You're giving me that look, Almira, the one that you inherited from your grandmother. She was always a bothersome woman."

Fantastic. Now she was like Grandmother Crawford once again. Did Mother have no respect for Emilie's feelings at all?

Mother softened her face for a brief moment and uncharacteristically placed a hand on Emilie's arm. "Almira, dear, just say you'll marry Newton so my heart will be at peace, won't you? You don't want your mother to have heart trouble now do you?"

"No, Mother."

"Good. And your father, he gets himself in such an upheaval when things don't go his way. You don't want him to have an upheaval, do you? You know he can't concentrate or even sleep when he has those moments."

Always the guilt. "No, Mother."

"Good. Then say you'll marry Newton. He's a nice man and somewhat handsome. Plus, he is financially stable. What is there not to like?"

Emilie hadn't cared about those things. She'd only wanted to marry someone for love. Why had that been so hard for Mother to understand?

CHAPTER NINE

Morris drove Emilie and Vera to Missoula, seemingly taking his time. If Emilie had her druthers, she would have been the one to drive, for Morris drove much too slowly. His unhurried acceleration reminded Emilie of riding in a wagon with a broken wheel.

Not that she'd ever ridden in such a mode of transportation. But still...

The miles seemed endless. Emilie struggled with patience at the slow pace and resisted the urge not to aimlessly drum her fingers. Instead, she clasped her hands tightly. Had she ever been more jittery in her life? The thought of meeting Mr. Alexander again threw her into quite a state. Would he remember about their agreed-upon convergence?

Emilie stared at Morris's profile. The darling elderly man with his thick goggles stared intently at the long dusty road ahead of them. His right ear was bent from the strap of his goggles, and his wispy gray hair fluttered in the breeze. "Right fine day for a ride," Morris commented, without taking his eyes off the road.

"That it is."

Vera leaned forward from the backseat. "Morris, are you quite all right?"

"Yes, dear, I am quite all right."

A few moments later, Morris yawned, and that gave Emilie the opening she sought. "Morris, why don't you nap in the backseat while I take a turn at motoring?"

"Sure thing, Mrs. Wheeler." Morris guided the car to the side of the road and slowed to a stop. They needn't worry about much traffic on the road to Missoula. Although with Morris's unhurried pace, if there was a horse or wagon, they could easily catch up and pass.

Morris climbed out and assisted Emilie from the automobile. Mother would have Emilie's hide at such a brazen thing as motoring the butler and his wife.

Yet, this way, she would make it to Missoula in time to check in at the hotel before her meal with Thad.

Vera plopped her ample self into the passenger seat. "Poor Morris. He's been so drowsy of late. I do hope he's not coming down with something."

"It's probably the sunny weather. It's perfect for a nap," Emilie said, trying to reassure her housekeeper and friend.

"I suppose you're right."

"There's nothing wrong with me, dear," Morris chimed in from the backseat.

"He wasn't supposed to hear that," Vera whispered.

Emilie giggled. She did adore Vera and Morris. Such a delightful married couple and such an inspiration to her. While they had their moments of disagreement, she knew the two loved each other more than life itself. Vera once mentioned that there was only One she loved more than Morris, and that was the Lord Jesus. Emilie had marveled at that comment. What would it be like to love the Lord so much?

But Emilie quickly dismissed the thought of a distant and faraway God who didn't listen to her prayers and the thought of loving such a God.

She remained so disappointed in the choices the Lord had made for her.

Brushing the thoughts aside, Emilie focused on the road. It was time to make up for Morris's tarrying.

On the straight, open road, Emilie reveled in her freedom. A cursory glance at Vera indicated the older woman shared her delight of motoring at a decent speed.

The thrill of independence rippled through Emilie. She needed this excursion to Missoula. Staying confined to her spacious and extravagant home often got terribly lonely and tiresome.

Especially lonely.

"Do tell me about this fine young man," quipped Vera, her goggles pressing into her chubby face and causing her round cheeks to protrude. "And not to worry, Morris is fast asleep."

Poor Morris, although she was grateful he slept. It gave Emilie time to share some details with Vera since the only thing she had mentioned previously was that the three of them were meeting a dapper ranch hand for lunch in Missoula. Mother would cringe if she knew all of the juicy morsels of information Emilie was about to share with her hired help and the boundaries of propriety such a friendship violated. "His name is Mr. Alexander and he seems kind and forthright. He hails from Illinois and now works somewhere near Missoula on a ranch."

"How did you meet, if you don't mind me asking."

"Quite by accident."

"By accident? Oooh, do tell."

Emilie tittered. "Goodness, Vera, if you don't sound a bit like Hattie in her dramatic presentations."

"Oh, yes, our dear Hattie presents a talent for the melodramatic."

It was difficult to hear each other above the motor and the wind whooshing by their heads, forcing Emilie and Vera to shout to hear each other.

Fortunate for Emilie that Morris was hard-of-hearing, as well as asleep. Some topics of conversation were for womenfolk only.

"We ran into each other, quite literally, on Mateer Avenue. That's when the parcels flew out of my hands. My new hat was squished in the street by a horse. It all happened so fast."

"Oh, your poor hat." Vera placed a chubby hand on her face in dismay. Emilie wasn't the only one who loved fine hats. Much to Vera's delight, Emilie had purchased her a wide-brimmed hat with a variety of brilliant decorations adorning it during her first trip of the year to Missoula.

"Let me guess," said Vera, "the handsome ranch hand then assisted you to your feet?"

Handsome indeed.

Emilie didn't have to take a peek at Vera's expectant face to know the woman's eyes had grown large beneath her thick goggles. "He did. I do declare, Vera, he is a dashing one, that Mr. Alexander."

"I remember when I first met Morris. He was standing across the room at a barn dance. Oh, Emilie, you should have seen him. All dressed in his best trousers and those gleaming green eyes..." Vera placed a hand to her chest as she swooned. "Seems awful strange, but I think he's even more dashing now than all those many years ago."

"Such a darling thing to say, Vera."

"It's the truth. And I just knew there was something about Morris from that first time he asked me to dance. Oh, sure, I had seen him around town at the mercantile and such. Apparently, according to my friend, Mary, Morris had been asking around about me. He was new to town, you see. Just hired on at the livery. The Lord brought Morris to our small town. I'd like to say it was just for my sake, but Morris blessed so many folks in our old town and now here in Hollow Creek."

Emilie realized she had never heard how Vera and Morris met until now. "So you knew right away there was something different about Morris?"

"Oh, yes. Most of the young men I knew only cared about fishing and hunting. Morris liked to partake in those things too, but he also cared about helping others. That's what endeared him to me from the start. In the coming days after that first dance, I noticed Morris's heart for blessing others. Any way he could make life easier for someone else, he sought to do so. I would sometimes miss a need, but not Morris. What with his keen observation skills and all, he noticed many a time those he could assist. So yes, those green eyes, that dark unruly hair, and those broad shoulders were dashing, but it was Morris's heart for others, and most importantly for the Lord, that drew me to him."

Emilie pondered what Vera had just told her. Morris no longer possessed broad shoulders, but more of a sloping variety. He no longer had dark unruly hair, but sparse gray hair. His eyes were still green, but they didn't see as well as they once had. Yet, Vera loved him all the more.

Could Emilie ever possess a love like that? Sadly, she'd certainly not experienced such a love for Newt.

"Tell me, dear," Vera continued. "Does this Mr. Alexander love the Lord?"

Emilie took a deep breath. Both Vera and Morris attempted many times to speak with Emilie about the love of the Lord. But Emilie had either changed the subject or pretended not to hear. Vera had gotten the hint a time or two, but that hadn't stopped the grandmotherly woman from inviting Emilie to read her Bible and attend Grace Church, one of the two churches in Hollow Creek, and the one Vera and Morris regularly attended.

And it certainly didn't stop Vera from constantly giving credit to God for everything.

"Well?" Vera asked.

Precious but persistent woman. "I'm not sure."

"Oh."

"You see, we didn't much discuss God. But Mr. Alexander did bless the meal, a most eloquent prayer, I might add. I think he might have asked me something about the Lord too, but I don't rightly recall."

"I know you don't like me to discuss the Lord, Emilie, but it is the most important thing. Be sure Mr. Alexander loves the Lord with all his being."

From Emilie's peripheral, she could see Vera bobbing her head up and down, her tight bun shaking slightly. "Yes, Vera."

Vera patted Emilie on the arm. "Now, then. Mr. Alexander is meeting you at the hotel restaurant for the noonday meal..."

"And to bring me a new hat."

"Oh, what a gentleman."

"Indeed."

"Does he know you live in Hollow Creek?"

Emilie shook her head. "No, I told him I live a short distance from Missoula. I know, Vera, that since you are a religious woman, you would never condone an outright lie. However, I don't feel at this time I should be forthright with Mr. Alexander about my true identity."

"Might I ask your reasoning?"

"As you may have noticed, the men in Hollow Creek are none too shy about attempting to separate me from my wealth. I am hoping to disguise that I am a wealthy widow, at least for the time being. I have told him my name is Emilie Crawford."

"I see."

But did Vera see?

"Please, Vera, if you wouldn't mind, I would appreciate that we kept my true identity a secret for now."

"I will keep your identity a secret, as you wish, Emilie. However, I won't lie."

"I understand. Thank you."

Vera promised to speak with Morris about Emilie's predicament with Mr. Alexander, much to Emilie's gratitude.

They continued in pleasant conversation over the putter of the engine for many miles, taking pleasure in the freedom of motorcar travel. Emilie pushed on the gas pedal, lurching the automobile to a faster speed. The two women laughed. "I do love this mode of transportation," Vera declared.

"As do I." Emilie pressed on the gas pedal again, and the scenery whizzed past.

"Uh, Vera? Mrs. Wheeler?"

"Yes, Morris?"

"I've been trying to get yours and Vera's attention for some time now. Reckon something just flew out the back of the automobile what with this nifty speed we're going and all."

"Begging your pardon?"

"Something flew out the back of the automobile."

Emilie slowed the motorcar and safely stopped. "Whatever was it, Morris?"

"Not absolutely sure, but it looked like your prized feather pillow."

CHAPTER TEN

Thad wondered if perhaps the Lord was teaching him something about pride. Why else would these turn of events cause him to have to visit Miss Julia Mathilda's Fine Dresses not once, but twice in the span of less than a month?

He must humble himself. That remained the obvious answer to his dilemma.

Lord, I'm wagering this is an odd request, but could the hat please have arrived at the shop and not have had some delay between Boston and Missoula? Thad winced at the thought he might have to visit the women's store a third time if the hat hadn't arrived in the time frame Miss Mathilda mentioned.

It might not matter how beautiful and interesting Mrs. Crawford was. Thad would have to nix the idea of another trip to the establishment that caused him an awkwardness he had not ever known before.

With a sigh, Thad strolled down Mateer Avenue, attempting to take his mind off the disturbing task at hand and focus on Mrs. Crawford instead. In less than an hour, he would be dining with her at the hotel restaurant. He longed to know more about the mysterious woman who had captured his attention.

Reckon I ought to thank that obnoxious hat or else I might never have met her. Thad preferred to thank the Lord instead. The hat was nothing but a nuisance. How could women even wear such cumbersome items? His own cowboy hat didn't protrude a huge diameter like the hat fashions becoming so popular in Missoula. He had even spied a woman wearing one in Hollow Creek.

Thank You, Lord, that I am a man and don't have to wear such things.

He should also express gratitude for having to step foot inside that Mathilda store to purchase the hat that would allow him to meet with Mrs. Crawford once again.

Thad wouldn't humble himself quite that much.

People lined the busy boardwalk, and as Thad neared the store, he tried his best to be incognito. He glanced in front of him, then behind. No one appeared to be paying him any notice.

He stopped at the front door and conjured up a Bible verse. "*Have not I commanded thee? Be strong and of a good courage; be not afraid, neither be thou dismayed: for the LORD thy God is with thee whithersoever thou goest.*" When the Lord authored the Bible, He for sure hadn't had a women's hat and dress establishment in mind. Rather, He spoke of how Joshua was about to enter the Promised Land.

Still, the Lord's words gave Thad hope. Even if sauntering into Miss Julia Mathilda's Fine Dresses had absolutely nothing in common with the Promised Land.

Thad turned the doorknob and stepped into the unchartered enclave no man in his right mind would enter. *You did it once before, Thad. You can do it again.*

Unfortunately, he lamented, the store was full of women.

Much worse than his first journey into the unknown realm of women's fashions. Last time it had only been that exaggerated clerk named Henrietta and Miss Mathilda.

He held his breath and braced himself for what was to come.

As if on some sort of cue, several heads oscillated toward him at once. Eyes widened, whispers started, and Thad took a giant step backward.

It wasn't too late to run away.

But then, how would he ever retrieve the hat? Mrs. Crawford was depending on him, and if he ever expected to win her heart...

Whoa! Win her heart? When did you become so sappy?

Thad tossed his inner voice aside and straightened his posture. This visit to the shop could not be any worse than his last visit.

Or could it?

The clerk named Henrietta hemmed in on him immediately and gasped. Apparently, she still hadn't recovered from his prior social call.

"What is *that* man doing here?" whispered a robust woman with the largest hat Thad had ever seen. It made the hat he was retrieving for Mrs. Crawford look like a miniature bonnet.

"No man in his right mind would ever step foot in a boutique. Do you suppose confusion has overcome him?" This from a thin woman with an enormous beak-like nose and a high-pitched voice.

"Good morning...sir," Henrietta wheezed.

"Hello, ma'am. Is Miss Mathilda here?"

The beak-nosed woman's eyes went from large to extra-large. "Do you suppose he is Miss Mathilda's beau?"

"Not likely," snapped an older woman, wrinkling her nose as if she inhaled a foul odor. "I've heard that Miss Mathilda's beau is a dandy. This man is far from a dandy. He is more of a ranch hand."

Thad narrowed his eyes. For one, there was nothing wrong with being a ranch hand, and for two, his trousers and shirt were his Sunday's finest. No, he would never be a dandy, and that was all right with him.

"I'll get Miss Mathilda right away," said Henrietta, rushing toward the back of the store.

Within moments, Miss Mathilda entered the room. "Sir. You are back for the hat?"

Good. No explanation necessary. "Yes, ma'am. Much obliged you remembered me."

"You're rather difficult to forget, as your type is not our typical clientele," said Miss Mathilda. "Please wait a moment, and I'll fetch the hat for you."

"Thank you, ma'am."

Miss Mathilda retreated again to the back room, leaving Thad with...he counted six pairs of eyes on him.

"Why are you buying a woman's hat, sir?" a young girl asked.

"For a woman who..."

"Ooohhh..." Swooned a woman with a mound of red hair that nearly overtook her pinched face. "What a gentleman."

At that, all the rest of the ladies nodded, even the beaked-nose lady, the robust lady, and the grumpy older lady. Suddenly, their countenances changed from disgust to appreciation. "Are you purchasing it for your wife?" the young girl asked.

"I..."

"Oh, isn't that quaint? He's decidedly doing his best to remain humble and purchase a gift for his beloved. What a whimsical thought."

The crowd of five high-society women and one young girl all nodded in agreement. "Whimsical indeed," agreed the crotchety elderly woman. "It's not every day a man embarrasses himself so just to purchase a gift for the love of his life."

Thad knew his face rivaled the color of those bright red flowers in that bothersome Mrs. Wheeler's flower gardens. But this type of attention was far better than the women thinking him a dolt.

Maybe.

"When he met his wife, he never knew that one day, he would be paying a visit to Miss Julia Mathilda's Fine Dresses to acquire the gift his wife has been eyeballing in the window since last month."

"It's their anniversary today."

"Oh, yes, and what an exquisite gift this gentleman is procuring! If it wasn't their tenth anniversary, he might have purchased his wife something modest, like a simple hairpin. But seeing as how this is a monumental anniversary, Mr...what did you say your name was?"

Whimsical?

Their tenth anniversary?

He shuffled his feet and returned his attention to the woman's question. "Uh, Mr. Alexander."

"Oh, yes, Mr. Alexander here decided to procure a hat all the way from back East for his wife for this significant occasion. The topmost of accolades to you."

Thad looked from woman to woman and soon lost track of who was speaking and about what. The commotion of the busybody high-societies overwhelmed him. Why was Miss Mathilda taking so long to fetch the hat? Had she gotten lost in her own shop?

Was it normal for a man like him to feel lightheaded?

"I so appreciate a man who takes the time to arrange for a clandestine retrieval of an item so desperately important to his beloved. There just aren't enough men like you in the world anymore, Mr. Alexander."

"Indeed. Are you also planning a memorable dinner, just the two of you at Reynold's Restaurant?"

Reynolds Restaurant? Was that the frilly restaurant over on Sixth Street where the aristocracy of Missoula dined? Thad would hardly want to visit such a place.

"It's critical in this day and age that a woman has time alone with her husband, without the children in tow. Highest of praises to you."

Wife?

Children?

"It's exhausting to say the least for a woman to consume herself daily with the tasks of organizing charity events and tending to volunteer duties. So consuming of her time. And here you are, Mr. Alexander, ensuring that your lovely wife has time away from such duties for your anniversary. God bless you, fine sir!"

If Miss Mathilda didn't return soon, Thad might just test his new boots out and see how far and how fast he could run. Out the door. And all the way back to Hollow Creek.

Finally, she returned. "Please pardon the delay. I wanted to be sure the hat was just the one you wanted." She opened the box and removed an unsightly display of feathers, flowers, and ribbons.

That's a hat?

"Oooohhhh, such an attractive accessory," one of the women squealed.

Looks like a bunch of frou frou to me.

"Why, if my husband thought to purchase me that hat, I would faint dead away from appreciativeness," squawked another.

"It's the one," said Thad, praying that the meddlesome women didn't return to their creative stories.

"Fabulous." Miss Mathilda placed it back in the box. "Henrietta, do wrap it in brown paper for Mr. Alexander, please, and add a colorful ribbon for the occasion."

Henrietta, who had been mostly silent up until now, bobbed her head up and down. "Yes, Miss Mathilda. Anything for this kindly gentleman."

Kindly gentleman? Thad quirked a brow. When had Henrietta decided he was anything but a cad?

"Mr. Alexander, while you are here, might I interest you in purchasing a brooch for your wife to go with her exquisite hat?"

"My wife?"

"Yes. I overheard the women discussing your plans to surprise your wife with the new hat. I fear I may have misjudged you." She leaned forward toward Thad and whispered. "I'll not let them know you ruined the first hat."

Thad gulped. Had the high-society ladies heard Miss Mathilda's comment? But one glance in their direction told him they were far too busy gossiping about him to have heard the Miss Mathilda's latest words.

"Well, Mr. Alexander? May I present to you a couple of marvelous adornments?"

Without awaiting Thad's answer, Miss Mathilda retrieved four brooches from a glass display box. "Here are four different choices. Suffice it to say they are all magnificent, but this one is by far my personal favorite."

And likely the most expensive, he thought.

Miss Mathilda pushed the brooch toward him. "What makes this one so well-deserving of your attention is that it accompanies a set of matching earrings. What woman..." Miss Mathilda leaned toward him again and lowered her voice, "especially a treasured wife of ten years..." She pulled away "doesn't deserve only the best Miss Julia Mathilda's Fine Dresses has to offer? For that matter, are you aware, Mr. Alexander, that my boutique rivals those found in prominent cities? You'll find no finer jewelry, except perhaps in expensive stores in New York City, Chicago, or Boston."

Thad suddenly remembered he needed to meet Mrs. Crawford at the hotel restaurant at noon. How long had he been in Miss Mathilda's? Hours?

He retrieved his pocket watch, flicked it open and stared at the time. He had exactly fifteen minutes before he was to meet with Mrs. Crawford, and he wanted to be on time. "I'm not sure, I uh...need to go soon..."

"Then I would make a decision post haste. We here at Miss Julia Mathilda's Fine Dresses do not want you arrive late to greet your wife. Ladies, shall we have a vote?"

The busybodies crowded around Thad to more closely view the four choices. "Are these enough options or shall I retrieve more? I have at least fifteen selections."

Thad nearly choked. If they had to look at all fifteen selections, he would make it to the restaurant just in time for Christmas.

"I vote for the brooch with the earrings. Your wife will adore such a choice."

"I second that."

"I concur."

"There really is no other reasonable option."

"Don't you just love how the gold cameo glitters in the light?"

"It will complement the hat in the most remarkable way and make a treasured ensemble for you to present to your beloved."

Thad deliberated the scene before him. Why would he purchase the cameo set? Wasn't that presumptuous? He had only just met Mrs. Crawford. He certainly did not want to marry her. "I'm sorry, ma'am, but I won't be taking the brooch and earrings set."

"But it is such an impeccable choice." The woman with red hair placed a hand to her forehead. "I may just have a dreadful attack of the vapors if you don't choose it."

Vapors or not, Thad would not be yielding to their influence. Maybe when he and Mrs. Crawford were courting...Not that he was planning on courtship anytime soon.

"But Mr. Alexander, I daresay I could have Henrietta wrap it in a padded jewelry box with gold-embossed wrap. After all, you wouldn't want anything less on your special day." Henrietta scooted to the side at Miss Mathilda's words.

Thad didn't even have a special day. How had he ever gotten himself into this predicament? If he purchased the set, that would be yet another horse purchase that wouldn't happen. Nope. He'd not be plunking down any money for the jewelry. Not today. Maybe not ever.

All this talk of his "wife" and "children" and his "ten-year anniversary" had spiraled Thad into an uncomfortable imaginary world. Thad thought he himself might have a vapor if it continued. *What are you thinking, Evanson? You're a man. Men don't have the vapors. You've been in the company of these daft women for far too long.*

It was too soon to even imagine Mrs. Crawford liking him, let alone being more than just an acquaintance. Too distant into the future to even contemplate. He took a deep breath. "Ladies, I am not interested in the jewelry," Thad heard himself say in a voice he didn't trust to be his own. But it must be, for it was the only masculine voice in the establishment.

The older lady started toward him, her thin lips in a straight line. "Sir, this is reprehensible."

"Hear, hear," one of the other women said, raising her voice.

"I've never been so vexed in all my life," hissed another.

Thad glanced out the window. He was sure everyone on Mateer Avenue heard this absurd exchange. He wanted to disappear, but he was trapped by a group of women with crusty expressions.

Clearly, he had fallen from grace in their eyes.

Taking slow and methodical steps, Thad inched backward toward the door with the enormous hatbox in his hand. He would have to break into a trot on the boardwalk just to make it to the restaurant on time if he didn't leave now.

The women inched toward him. And then, with one gigantic step and an abrupt turn, Thad dodged out the door. He did not dare look back.

Having survived the past half-hour, Thad knew he could now survive anything life tossed his way.

CHAPTER ELEVEN

Emilie, Vera, and Morris waited inside the restaurant at the front counter for Thad. Emilie inhaled the delectable aroma of mashed potatoes, meatloaf, and apple pie, and her stomach grumbled in response. The grandfather clock against the wall of the restaurant chimed noon.

Five minutes later, she and her hired help remained standing by the front counter. Customers entered and exited in a span of a few minutes. The waitress asked once again if they wished to be seated. "We're waiting for someone," Emilie reiterated, hoping her voice sounded polite, rather than annoyed. The waitress tossed her a sympathetic look and nodded.

Would Thad bother to show for their meeting? Emilie's heart dropped at the thought. Yet, the man did not owe her anything, except for the new hat he promised to purchase for her and deliver to the restaurant.

Disappointment began to settle in.

She resisted the urge to tap her toe on the floor in impatience.

"Now, now, Emilie, all will be fine." Vera placed an affectionate hand on Emilie's arm.

Emilie's voice was barely above a whisper so as to avoid any of the patrons over-hearing the conversation. "What if he doesn't arrive?"

"He will be here."

"But what if he forgot?"

Vera, her eyes tender and kind, leaned toward Emilie. "Do not worry, dear. If he said he would arrive, then he will."

"It's just that..."

"'Be careful for nothing; but in every thing by prayer and supplication with thanksgiving let your requests be made known unto God.'"

Emilie brushed Vera's quote aside. Was there an answer to every dilemma within the pages of the Bible?

"He wants you to be anxious for naught, dear one."

"Thank you, Vera." Emilie offered a weak smile at the woman who had become so much more than mere hired help. She had become like the grandmother Emilie never had the privilege of having.

Morris tipped his head and offered a reassuring smile. He, too, had become precious in Emilie's life.

Five more minutes passed, but it seemed like an eternity to Emilie. She flattened any wrinkles in her skirt, something she had done no less than twelve times prior.

She patted her hair, hoping all the pins were in place. Vera's words popped into her head about God's Word. Did He really want His children to pray about things even as simplistic as whether or not a man kept his word?

Just as she was about to ponder the thought further, Thad strolled through the door with an oversized hatbox in his hand. "Beg your pardon, Mrs. Crawford, for my tardiness. I was detained at the dress shop."

Emilie begged her breathing to normalize. "That's quite all right, Mr. Alexander. I appreciate the time you took in retrieving my hat." Her eyes darted to the box. She couldn't wait to hold the fine accessory in her hands. Instead, she forced her thoughts to other matters. "Mr. Alexander, may I present to you my beloved friends, Vera and Morris Weeks."

Mr. Alexander set the box on the floor and removed his hat. "It's a pleasure, Mr. and Mrs. Weeks." He nodded at Vera and shook Morris's hand.

"The pleasure is ours," Vera said, and Emilie hoped the woman and her husband remembered not to mention anything personal in nature. That they lived in Hollow Creek and not Missoula, that Emilie was wealthy, her real last name, and that Vera and Morris were her servants.

"Reckon it's nice to finally meet you," said Morris. "We've heard kindly things about you."

Heat rose up Emilie's neck and splashed onto her face. What she wouldn't do for a fan at a moment like this. Mr. Alexander graciously avoided her eye and instead focused on Vera and Morris. A good thing, too, for it would not do for Emilie to faint dead away from embarrassment.

Saving them all from an awkward silence, the waitress approached them. "Is this the other person in your party for whom you've been waiting?"

"Yes, ma'am," answered Emilie.

"Right this way. I regret I do not have a table for a party of four. Rather, I do have two tables nearby with two chairs each. Will that suffice?"

"That will suit us," said Mr. Alexander, taking Emilie's elbow in his hand.

A tingle traveled up Emilie's arm at his touch. She caught a whiff of a scent of fresh soap and eyed him from the corner of her eye. It appeared Mr. Alexander had recently shaved. She sucked in her breath. My, but if the man didn't look dapper.

"This table is for the two of you," said the waitress to Emilie and Mr. Alexander. "And for you fine folks, this table crosswise." She pointed to another table for Vera and Morris.

Mr. Alexander set the hat box beside the table and pulled out Emilie's chair. "Thank you," she squeaked.

"Mrs. Crawford, again, I do apologize for my tardiness." He took the seat directly across from Emilie.

"I thought perhaps you might have forgotten." Had she really just admitted those insecure thoughts? Why was it that words departed from her mouth without her wherewithal to stop them?

"Oh, I hadn't forgotten." Mr. Alexander's voice was low and his eyes held her gaze. Had she noticed before just how brilliantly blue his eyes were?

Of course, you did, silly. You noticed that upon your first glance of him.

"I do thank you kindly for purchasing a new hat for me, Mr. Alexander. I am most anxious to see it, if you don't mind."

"Not at all." Mr. Alexander retrieved the box and handed it to her. "It's rather cumbersome. Who knew a woman's hat could be awkward?"

Emilie giggled. She opened the box and her eyes lit upon the extravagant hat. "Oh, it's even more magnificent than I remember." She fingered the lavish brim. If it wasn't so improperly improper, she would place the hat upon her head this very instant.

"I reckon a woman gets excited about a hat just like a man does about a new horse."

"Likely so. I have to admit I would never become overly enthusiastic over a new horse, much the same as I imagine you wouldn't over a new hat."

"You imagine correctly, Mrs. Crawford."

Emilie sighed and situated the hat in the box. She would delight in it later. For now, she wanted to take pleasure in her time with Mr. Alexander. The moment she had anticipated for the better part of the past week; the moment she thought would never arrive.

After the waitress arrived and took their orders, Mr. Alexander leaned toward her. "How was your week, Mrs. Crawford?"

Never once had Newt asked how her day or her week had gone. "It went well. I am fond of gardening and anything pertaining to flowers, but also vegetables. As such, I managed to plant a few more flowers and tend to the ones already planted." The thought of those obnoxious cows of Mr. Evanson's fluttered through her mind, and she pushed the thought aside. Why think of someone as dismal as that neglectful Mr. Evanson and his ornery cows on an otherwise charming day? "How was your week?"

"Busy. The ranching business takes a lot of time, not that I'm complaining, but I find that I am quite perfectionistic when it comes to making sure my job is well done."

"I am certain your boss appreciates his ranch hand being so conscientious."

Mr. Alexander's peculiar expression took her aback. Had she misspoken? Before Emilie could contemplate further, he continued. "Grandpa always taught me the importance of hard work. He was fond of quoting the verse, *'And whatsoever ye do, do it heartily, as to the Lord, and not unto men' from Colossians 3:23.'"*

Emilie nodded, but she wasn't familiar with the verse, nor that book of the Bible. Perhaps she should brush up on her knowledge, or lack thereof, of God's Word to impress Thad. That contemplation shocked her. Hadn't she placed the Lord out of her life after the tragedy? "You seem well-versed with Scripture, Mr. Alexander."

"Knowing the Lord is the most important thing." His blue-eyed gaze once again held hers. Did Mr. Alexander wonder if she felt the same about the Lord? Emilie recalled Vera inquiring about Mr. Alexander and his knowledge of the Lord. The older woman would for certain be pleased at his proclamation. But as for Emilie's knowledge of the Lord...

Well...

Emilie bit her lip and rejected the urge to fidget. "Would you agree, Mrs. Crawford?" he asked, as if he had read her mind.

"Regrettably, Mr. Alexander, I am not as accomplished in the Lord's Word." Would he judge her for her admission?

Instead, an affable smile lit Mr. Alexander's face. "Our gracious Lord gives us yet another day to hide His Word deep in our hearts. Our relationship with Him is priceless, and He wants us to yearn to know Him more."

Emilie swallowed. But how could she yearn to know Him after what had happened? She had never known Him anyway, not really. "Yes," she squeaked.

"So, you love flowers and vegetable gardens?"

Thankful for the change in conversation, Emilie bobbed her head. "I do. It's my favorite pastime, although I can't say there is one flower I favor over another. They are all beautiful, from the dandelion growing all on its own in the meadow to the purposely-planted rose bush."

"My grandma loved her gardens. Whenever she wasn't teaching me or tending to chores, she could be found in her gardens."

"Did your grandparents pass recently?"

"It's been about five years. When Grandma passed first, it was less than a month and Grandpa passed too. They had been married for so long that I don't think Grandpa could continue through this life without her. He missed her something awful. Grandpa said he knew she awaited him in Heaven and he longed to see her again." A wistful look crossed his face.

Mr. Alexander, just like Emilie, knew the pain that came with loss.

"I'm sorry, Mr. Alexander, for your loss."

"Thank you. And I'm sorry for the loss of your husband, Mrs. Crawford. It must be difficult."

"Thank you." While the loss of Newt had been difficult, it hadn't been as painful as the loss of her baby who had never had a chance to be born. But Emilie didn't make mention of that to Mr. Alexander. Instead, she glanced over at Vera and Morris, hoping they were savoring their meal in the fancy restaurant.

Emilie expected Vera and Morris to be engaged in conversation. Instead, however, Vera was squinting in Mr. Alexander's direction. Was she staring? Emilie attempted to catch Vera's eye to no avail. Vera continued with a watchful eye toward Mr. Alexander, while Morris happily ate mashed potatoes. Emilie made a mental note to ask Vera about it later.

"Are you ready for dessert?" the waitress asked a short time later.

Emilie looked up from her plate and her eyes connected with Mr. Alexander's. He raised an eyebrow. "Apple pie and ice cream?"

"Pie à la mode?" Emilie asked.

They laughed together then, and Emilie revered in their shared camaraderie.

"Two pie à la modes," said the waitress. "I'll return shortly."

"Would you and Mr. and Mrs. Weeks care to join me for a stroll after our noonday meal?"

"That sounds delightful. I am sure Vera and Morris would take pleasure in a stroll." While the two had joined Emilie often on her escapades to Missoula, they hadn't had much opportunity to simply peruse the city.

"Have you been friends with the Weeks's for many years?"

"About three years. My late husband introduced us." While that was the truth, it had actually been Emilie who had chosen the couple out of four other applicants to work at the Wheeler Ranch. Vera and Morris were the perfect fit from the start, both as employees and as friends. For what would Emilie do without them, especially since she had been widowed?

No one else knew the secrets she held in her heart, as Vera did.

If Emilie made it a practice of expressing gratitude to the Lord, she would have thanked Him for Vera.

After finishing their desserts, they met outside the restaurant for their stroll, Vera and Morris seeming to be almost as eager as Emilie to venture through the city. The sun shone brightly and the fresh breeze promised the weather wouldn't climb to an uncomfortable temperature. Emilie donned her new hat.

Could the day be any more perfect?

"Reckon it sure is a nice day," said Morris, reaching for Vera's hand.

Emilie tossed aside a feeling of envy at the kind of marriage Vera and Morris shared.

"It sure is," declared Vera. She turned and squinted again at Mr. Alexander. Then, as if realizing she was staring, Vera averted her eyes to the boardwalk before her. "We haven't explored the city much. This should be a real treat."

Mr. Alexander offered his elbow, and Emilie slipped her hand through the crook of his arm and rested it on his forearm. Her pulse fluttered. She minded each step she took, careful not to stumble in her nervousness. Mr. Alexander certainly had an effect on her.

"So you don't spend much time in the city?" Mr. Alexander asked.

Emilie sucked in a breath. Vera's comment made it sound as though they were unfamiliar with Missoula. Would Mr. Alexander realize Emilie had lied about living in Missoula? Her mind searched to her exact answer when he had asked where she lived during their meal time two weeks ago. *A short distance from Missoula. Yes, that was what I said. That again will be my standard answer. No sense in letting Mr. Alexander know I am a wealthy widow from Hollow Creek.*

But it's not all right to lie.

No, but it can be necessary.

It's never necessary.

Emilie chided the argument she had with herself and realized she hadn't yet answered Mr. Alexander's question.

Vera pressed her lips together and nodded her head in Emilie's direction as if to hint that Emilie should answer the inquiry.

"We live a short distance from Missoula. My, but there is Miss Julia Mathilda's Fine Dresses. Speaking of the boutique, thank you, again, Mr. Alexander, for replacing my hat. It is quite comfortable and remarkably stylish."

Mr. Alexander peered at her, seemingly perplexed by her change of topic. "Yes, you are welcome, Mrs. Crawford." His eyes traveled to the dress shop and he cleared his throat.

At just that moment, a tall woman in elegant clothing with a nose the shape of a bird's beak stepped from Miss Julia Mathilda's Fine Dresses. She glared at Mr. Alexander, an obtrusive look that made her already long and narrow nose seem all the more pointed. "I'm most disturbed to see you again, Mr. Alexander," she huffed. "You are a rather obtuse man."

Mr. Alexander tipped the brim of his hat, but said nothing.

Emilie glanced behind her as the woman stood gawking. "What a peculiar woman."

"That she is."

When Mr. Alexander offered no further explanation, Emilie returned her focus to the lively city around her. A fraction of the size of New York, and so much more populated than Hollow Creek. What had made Newt decide to ranch in Hollow Creek, rather than Missoula? She reveled in visiting the city and could have easily been happy living there.

The four of them ambled in pleasant silence until they came to a brown-brick church with a tall steeple where they stopped. "I attend this church when..." Mr. Alexander cleared his throat. "Would the three of you care to join me tomorrow for services?"

"Oh, we would be most delighted!" squealed Vera.

Emilie shifted from one foot to the other. Of course Vera would be ecstatic about church.

Mr. Alexander continued. "The services begin at eight o'clock. I can retrieve you, or we can meet here."

"We will meet here," Emilie answered, a little too quickly.

"Yes, we can meet you here," confirmed Morris. "How's the preaching?"

"Solid and convicting," said Mr. Alexander. "Where do you attend church?"

Morris opened his mouth, then shut it. Emilie cringed. Would he say they attended Grace Church in Hollow Creek? "We haven't attended for a while," she blurted. *More appropriately, I should say hardly ever.* Would Mr. Alexander think her unreligious?

"Pastor Shay is a gifted man of God. I always walk away from services with a desire to know more about this awesome Lord we serve."

Emilie released the breath she had been holding. Mr. Alexander hadn't condemned her, rather he had made a comment about the services. "Is it a large service?"

"Around 250 folks or so."

"I recall as a child in New York City the church we attended hosted several hundred people." Emilie didn't make mention that she had rarely attended the church. She caught sight of Vera, who offered a gleaming smile.

"Oh, Mr. Alexander, you sound as though you are a man of God. What a wonderful thing," exclaimed Vera.

Mr. Alexander chuckled at Vera's outburst. "The Lord has been patient with me all these years, and I hope to be more like Christ with each passing day."

Vera placed a hand to her bosom and blinked. "Oh, my, but I declare that is the truth for us all. I remember when I first met Morris. Such a handsome man he was."

A sheen of red traveled up Morris's weathered face, and Vera continued. "The best thing about Morris was his love for the Lord. In all our difficulties, and I daresay we have had many, Morris has remained steadfast in his devotion to our Savior. Me, on the other hand, I have struggled a time or two."

Morris planted a gentle kiss on his wife's face. "The Lord brought us together, you and me."

"That he did, my dear Morris."

The two gazed at each other with a look so tender that Emilie wasn't sure if she could continue to watch them without feeling as though she were intruding on their special moment. Envy crept into her heart. Followed by guilt. *I shan't be covetous of my dear friends.*

"Let's plan on meeting here at forty-five minutes past seven," said Mr. Alexander. "The pews fill quickly, and we'll want to have a good seat."

Emilie did her best to hide her reservations about tomorrow's plan. She hadn't given God much thought in recent days. Would she be welcome in His house?

CHAPTER TWELVE

Thad settled into the bed at the humble house he purchased for when he stayed in Missoula. The day had gone well, and he found he took a liking to spending more time with Mrs. Crawford. Her expressive eyes drew him in, he appreciated her pleasing personality, and admired her intelligence. It would be helpful to know for sure her standing with the Lord so he would know if he could possibly pursue their growing friendship.

He closed his eyes, eagerly anticipating time spent with Mrs. Crawford tomorrow at church.

In all his visits to Missoula, and there had been many, Thad had attended Pastor Shay's services each time. The man possessed a gift for speaking the Truth.

And conviction was always important in Thad's constant hope of growing more like Jesus each day. He often fell short, especially in a couple of areas he constantly prayed about.

Five minutes after Thad arrived at church the next morning, Mrs. Crawford and Mr. and Mrs. Weeks arrived. "Good morning," he said, noticing Mrs. Crawford looked especially pretty today.

"Good morning, Mr. Alexander," Mrs. Crawford responded.

"Vera here is champing at the bit to hear the service," said Mr. Weeks. "We rarely miss a church service, unless we're ill."

Thad noticed Mrs. Weeks jab an elbow at Mr. Weeks, as the man continued. "I mean, uh, we do miss church sometimes."

From what was insinuated by the trio yesterday, they didn't attend church often. Thad pondered the varied responses. "Should we go inside and find a place to sit?" he asked.

Mr. and Mrs. Weeks held hands and started toward the entrance. Mrs. Weeks whispered something in Mr. Weeks's ear and he whispered back, a little too loudly, "Sorry about that, dear."

That left Mrs. Crawford standing alone. Should he take her elbow and guide her in? "Shall we, Mrs. Crawford?" he asked. He never recalled feeling so nervous around a woman. Mrs. Crawford surely had some sort of effect on him.

"Yes, we shall." She smiled up at him and he almost forgot how to breathe. All this would be for naught, however, if Mrs. Crawford wasn't the religious woman he hoped her to be.

They meandered up the four steps and into the foyer where Pastor Shay stood welcoming the congregants. "Good morning, Thad," the pastor greeted him.

"Pastor Shay, I would like to introduce you to my friend, Mrs. Crawford."

"Mrs. Crawford, it is a pleasure to meet you."

"Likewise, Pastor Shay."

Mr. and Mrs. Weeks claimed seats in the front pew. He hoped no one else had already staked a claim to it. He heard Mrs. Crawford gasp. "Goodness, but they chose the front pew?"

"All the better to hear the sermon, I reckon."

"Yes, but still, that is awfully close."

What concerned Mrs. Crawford so? The more time Thad had spent with her, the more he wanted to know about her. This was no exception.

They took their places next to Mr. and Mrs. Weeks. "This is a sizeable church," exclaimed Mrs. Weeks. "So much bigger than our church in...ummm, our church where we go."

"Where do you attend, Mrs. Weeks?" Thad asked.

"We...well, let's see. We listen to a thought-provoking sermon and partake in fellowship with a potluck."

"Yes. We have that here as well. Is it a church in Missoula?"

"No. Rather, it's outside of Missoula."

The kindly older woman could certainly be evasive. The organ began to play then, much to Mrs. Weeks's delight. "Oh, Morris," she squealed, "do you hear the music?"

"That I do, Vera. Kinda hard not to hear the music."

Thad grinned. He could see why Mrs. Crawford adored this couple.

After the announcements, the congregation stood for the first hymn. When Thad was a youngster, Grandma once told him it didn't matter what his voice sounded like, so long as he used it to worship the Lord. To this day, Thad was grateful for that advice because no one would be seeking him for a place in the choir anytime soon.

Mrs. Crawford, on the other hand, had a captivating voice. He leaned closer to hear the words she sang. He caught a whiff of her perfume and inhaled. Grandpa was right. There was nothing more beautiful than a woman worshipping the Lord. Thad attempted to keep his attention on the hymn he knew by heart, but found himself watching Mrs. Crawford read the words of the hymn while singing them in her enchanting voice.

Chiding himself for allowing himself to watch her instead of focus on worship, Thad struggled to return his attention to the front of the church. The voices of the choir rang loud and clear, and Thad did his best not to sound like the croaking frog he often heard in his own ears.

After the singing of several hymns, Pastor Shay took his place at the podium. "Welcome, everyone. Please turn to Exodus. Today we are going to talk about idolatry."

Thad opened his Bible. He noticed Mrs. Weeks shared her Bible with Mrs. Crawford.

Had Mrs. Crawford forgotten hers?

"The Lord says in Exodus 20:3 '*You shall have no other gods before me*' as one of the Ten Commandments. Idols are addressed elsewhere in the Bible, which we will look at in a moment." Pastor Shay paused. "We tend to think of idols as the idols mentioned in the Old Testament. However, even in today's world, we are guilty of worshipping idols. Perhaps not the small carved images mentioned in the Bible, but other idols. People, money..."

Thad listened as Pastor Shay spoke of idols. Conviction permeated his heart. Thad recalled that in the not-too-distant-past, and still at times, his ranch had been his idol in the midst of his ambition to be successful. Put far above God, Thad had sought to become efficacious at his dream, even to the detriment of spending little time with his Lord and Savior. Placing an emphasis on running his ranch and ensuring its profitability caused Thad to miss many a Sunday church service.

Days had passed when Thad had not spent the time to utter even the most meager of prayers.

He still struggled at times with not allowing the ranch to be the most important thing in his life and instead placing God in His proper place—the number one position—in his life. Repentance and help from the Holy Spirit had guided Thad in his pursuit of loving the Lord with all of his being, rather than loving his ranch more than anything.

Thad still did struggle with toiling far beyond the hours he ought. His wise and godly ranch foreman, Pete, often reminded him that was why Thad hired employees.

Reverting his mind back to the sermon, Thad listened intently to Pastor Shay's words. Moments later, his guests again drew his attention. Mrs. Crawford leaned her head slightly toward Mrs. Weeks while sharing the elder woman's Bible. Mrs. Weeks proclaimed several softly-spoken "amens" in agreement to Pastor Shay's words. Mr. Weeks focused on the pastor, seemingly absorbing every word.

Did any of the other congregants ever struggle with an idol, as Thad had?

When the service commenced, Thad and his guests followed the other folks exiting the church. "That was an outstanding sermon," declared Mrs. Weeks. "Wouldn't you say so, Morris?"

"Indeed. Always appreciated sermons like that. Straight out of the Bible and making a fellow think. I see why you come to this church, Mr. Alexander."

"What did you think, Mrs. Crawford?" Thad asked. He observed that Mrs. Weeks appeared to be awaiting Mrs. Crawford's answer as well.

"Pastor Shay does deliver a good sermon," she said. "I appreciated his insight."

Thad wanted to ask Mrs. Crawford more questions about her thoughts of the sermon, but thought better of it. He would instead prefer to ask her over a meal just between the two of them.

Another meal? Would she even care to partake in another meal with him? Thad didn't have any reason to ask her to meet him again at the restaurant next Saturday. He didn't need to present her with another hat.

No, there was only one real reason he wanted to invite her to the restaurant again. That was to spend more time with her. Get to know more about her, especially her thoughts about the Lord.

Thad noticed that Mr. and Mrs. Weeks had commenced in a serious conversation between the two of them. "Mrs. Crawford, may I speak with you?"

"Yes?"

They stepped aside from Mr. and Mrs. Weeks and the lingering church folk. "Would you care to join me next Saturday for a noonday meal at the Bellerose?"

A smile shone on her face. "Why, Mr. Alexander. I do believe you are growing accustomed to our tradition of meeting at the restaurant."

Thad hoped Mrs. Crawford couldn't detect the red heat rushing up his neck. "Well, Mrs. Crawford, I do believe you are accurate in your assumption."

"Could it be the pie à la mode? I must admit the Bellerose does present a fine dessert."

Thad chuckled. "Perhaps it is the company," he teased.

She rewarded him with a giggle of her own, soft and sweet, a sound he wished he could hear more often.

If only she lived in Hollow Creek.

"Shall we set a time, then?"

"Noon?" he asked.

"I shall see you Saturday then, Mr. Alexander."

"Until then."

"Until then."

What was it about this woman Thad had met only three weeks ago?

"Much obliged for the invitation to church," said Mr. Weeks, interrupting Thad's thoughts.

"Glad you and your wife could make it, Mr. Weeks."

"You can call us Vera and Morris," piped in Mrs. Weeks. "Seems we will be seeing more of you from the sounds of your conversation with Emilie. Not that we were listening, mind you."

"We weren't?" asked Mr. Weeks.

Mrs. Weeks shot her husband a warning look. "We might have been listening, or we might not have," corrected Mr. Weeks.

"Nonetheless, please do call us by our first names."

"Very well, Vera and Morris. And I'm Thad."

Thad caught Mrs. Crawford's eye. Did she wish for them to call each other by their first names as well? "Mrs. Crawford..."

"Please, do call me Emilie," she said, as if to read his mind.

"Reckon you can call me Thad." Why was he teasing her so?

"Thad it is. Until next week..."

"Until next week." But for Thad, Saturday couldn't come soon enough. Something about Emilie Crawford was quickly reeling him in.

CHAPTER THIRTEEN

Emilie adjusted her hat, then tipped her watering can to sprinkle the oxeye daisies in her flower garden. The pink and white colors on the blooms were breathtaking, and she made a note to herself to plant even more of the delicate flowers next year. Next, she moved on to her petunias. Leaning down, she patted the dirt around the flowers, which had been ruffled by the recent windstorm. A storm that had blown over one of the outbuildings and had damaged a fence near the house.

What a difference today's weather was from last night.

The early-July sun was hot, but not too hot, and Emilie marveled about the perfectness of the day.

That was, until she heard the first rustle and *moo*.

Glancing up, she saw a cow stepping through the fence and into her garden. But not just any cow. It was another of Mr. Evanson's detestable animals. How had it gotten in?

Then Emilie spied the culprit. The windstorm must have knocked down the gate.

"Shoo!" she shouted and ran toward the Black Angus, which had been followed by two other cows. Emilie's eyes darted about, searching for a stick. Finally, she located one not far from her hollyhocks. Retrieving it, she stood and waved the stick. "I said, shoo!"

The cows eyed her briefly, then chose to ignore her. Instead, they continued sauntering through her prized flower garden and toward her black–eyed Susans. "Oh, no you don't!"

Wishing she hadn't worn her fancy shoes out to garden, Emilie nearly tripped while running toward the animals. But she was too late.

The first cow had taken a huge bite of Emilie's thriving black-eyed Susans. "NO!" she shrieked.

"Mrs. Wheeler, are you all right?"

"Digby, have you seen Jep?"

"Don't rightly know, ma'am. Could be that he's out in the field."

"Never mind. Please do come quickly. The Evanson cows are eating my flowers."

"Don't you worry none, ma'am. I'll set right to gettin' them outta here." Digby ran toward the cows and herded them back toward the Evanson property.

But not before they had trampled a sizeable portion of the flower garden and had eaten most of her black-eyed Susans.

"That does it. I am going over right now to speak with that despicable Mr. Evanson."

"Mrs. Wheeler, don't know if it's my place to say so, but I reckon maybe myself or Jep or Baxter oughta go over there 'stead of you."

"Not this time, Digby, although I appreciate the thought. No, this time, I am going to give that man a piece of my mind. First, I had to worry about my tomatoes. Now the flowers. Next, it'll be the saplings I planted near the house. No, Digby, I'll handle this once and for all. That irritating man will regret the day his bothersome cows ever chose to step over onto my property."

Digby picked up the downed fence and temporarily set it to rights. "But ma'am, with all due respect, the cows are only tryin' to get to the other side."

Emilie stopped and turned toward her most-recently-hired ranch hand. "I beg your pardon, Digby?"

"I wasn't meanin' nothin' bad by it, but them cattle, they just wanna get to the other side with them other cattle." Digby nodded toward the field on the other side of the flower garden where numerous cows grazed.

Narrowing her eyes, Emilie allowed her gaze to travel to the other field.

More of the Evanson property.

Goodness gravy! Who in their right mind would purchase land that wasn't connected to their original holdings and had to be accessed through another ranch?

For certain someone completely daft.

"Digby, the cows do not get to decide where they will congregate. Furthermore, it is not my problem Mr. Evanson has a piece of property on either side of my acreage."

"I know it ain't your fault, ma'am, and I don't mean nothin' by it, but, well, it's just that the cows don't understand where they are supposed to go and where they ain't."

"Where they aren't, Digby. Where they aren't."

"Beggin' your pardon, ma'am?"

"Nothing. I am going to drive over to the Evanson place in the automobile. I will be back before long." Emilie could walk to the Evanson Ranch, as it wasn't that far. But why walk plumb through a perfectly good pair of shoes stomping all the way to the home of her adversary?

"You sure you don't want someone to go with you?"

"Quite sure." Who gave a thought to propriety in a time of emergency such as this?

And an emergency it was.

Emilie lifted the edge of her skirt and stomped from the garden, feeling every rock and pebble beneath her high-heeled boots. She would give that reprehensible Mr. Evanson a piece of her mind if it was the last thing she did.

Why, if Mr. Evanson had a kind ranch hand like Mr. Alexander, none of this would have happened. Too bad Mr. Alexander wasn't her neighbor instead of Mr. Evanson.

Not stopping to right her hat, nor to retrieve a drink of lemonade, Emilie bumbled directly toward her automobile. She cranked the engine, then slid inside behind the wheel. She started down the road none too slowly.

Less than five minutes later, she pulled into the entrance to the Evanson ranch. The house came into view first, a white home in desperate need of a good whitewashing. Why didn't Mr. Evanson take the time to care for his property? *Of course, it stands to reason that a man who doesn't take care of his own property isn't going to care about someone else's.*

Emilie parked the car, then opened the door and rushed to the front door, where she pounded without restraint. "Mr. Evanson!"

When there was no answer, she turned and began stomping toward the barn. In dark contrast to the home, the barn was in excellent condition. Figured someone of Mr. Evanson's character would have misguided priorities.

"Mr. Evanson!"

"Ma'am?"

Emilie turned to see a short boxy man standing behind her. "Mr. Evanson, may I have a word with you?" *Oh, my. What would Mother say about my seething tone? And approaching a complete stranger, a man no less, in such a manner? Thank goodness Mother is a million or so miles away.*

"Uh, ma'am..."

Emilie held up a hand to prevent Mr. Evanson from speaking another word. She was going to say her piece.

No. Matter. What.

"Mr. Evanson, I have come to tell you that I have absolutely, positively, had it with your lack of decency."

"Ma'am, I..."

"Hush, Mr. Evanson, please." Emilie took a deep breath, and for the first time, took in the man's appearance. He had large brown eyes protruding from years of wrinkles, making him seem almost froglike. Dark brown hair, dusted with gray, fringed around a bald spot on his head. Stout, but fit, likely from years in the ranching business, Mr. Evanson was bow-legged and about two inches shorter than her own five-foot, seven-inch height.

Yes, Mr. Evanson looked exactly as she had anticipated.

Before the man could speak, Emilie proceeded. "As I was saying, Mr. Evanson, I am ashamed to have you as a neighbor. You have no regard for me or my property. When are you going to get that fence of yours mended once and for all?"

"What fence, ma'am?"

"The fence between your land and my land." Emilie held her breath, attempting not to inhale the noxious smell of sweat and liquor permeating from Mr. Evanson's person.

"The one that's right up there next to one of them so-called gardens of yours?"

Emilie gritted her teeth. Mr. Evanson was even more despicable than she could ever have imagined. From what she had heard, he didn't go to town much. And for good reason! Not many would likely welcome such a reprehensible man.

"My so-called garden is an actual garden."

"Ma'am, I ain't..."

And his language was horrendous. Did he have any proper education at all? "Mr. Evanson, I refuse to listen to any more of your excuses. After finishing here with you, I am going straight into Hollow Creek and speaking with the sheriff. If you don't think you need to fix the fence to preclude your irritating animals from trespassing onto my property, then maybe a night or two in jail will do the trick for you."

"Ain't meanin' no respect, ma'am, but I don't have a clue what you're talkin' about with all them fancy words. I did catch the word 'jail' though, and the word 'sheriff.' He's a nice man to be sure. Done a real fine job keepin' the law here in Hollow Creek. Why just yesterday, I heard he done caught a horse thief that's been up to no good."

"Mr. Evanson, I am thankful the sheriff caught the criminal, but we are talking about you and your cows."

"Like I been tryin' to tell ya, those cows ain't..."

"They *are* getting into my gardens, Mr. Evanson. First, my vegetable garden and now my flower garden. I'll have you know that today they tried to eat all of my black-eyed Susans and quite nearly succeeded."

"A shame for sure. Wonder how they got over there. Sometimes cows don't have a brain in their feebleminded heads."

"It was likely the windstorm that blew through here last night, knocking down the fence that you should have properly fixed. But no matter. They are your cows and they are trespassing onto my property and damaging my prize flowers. This is absolute nonsense."

"Tres...what did you say, ma'am? Like I done said, I don't know all them fancy words."

"Oh, never mind. Just keep your cows on your own property. Please."

"I'll go fix that there fence once I get done with my other chores. Don't you worry yer pretty head none, Mrs. Wheeler."

"Please make it a priority. It is just not neighborly to continue to allow your cows to roam onto my land. My late husband spoke to you about that and now here I am speaking to you a year later about the same thing. Something must be done."

"Yep, fer sure."

"See that you fix the fence, Mr. Evanson. See that you fix it *properly* so that no more of your herd slips through and ruins my gardens." Emilie hoped her heavy emphasis on the word "properly" was understood by the daft little man.

With that, she stormed from the yard and to her automobile. Cranking the crank a little harder than she ought, she fired up her Model T, then drove toward town. The audacity of that peculiar man. Promising to mend the fence after he finished his other chores.

Where were his priorities?

How incredibly vexing.

Emilie was festered up more than ever now. What was it Mother had said a time or two? That Emilie had an Irish temper, even though she possessed not one ounce of Irish in her blood?

She'd be sure the sheriff got an earful.

CHAPTER FOURTEEN

Thad parked the wagon next to the barn and began unloading the feed. It was only three o'clock in the afternoon and already he was behind schedule thanks to a wagon wheel that needed to be fixed in town.

"Mr. Evanson, you ain't never gonna believe what happened just a bitty while ago."

"Give me a hand here with the feed, will you, Floyd?"

"Sure thang. Boss, you ain't never seen such a thang ever in your life before. This woman had a real hornet in her bonnet, only she wasn't wearin' a bonnet, but one of them newfangled hats fancy women like to wear."

Thad threw the feed over his shoulder. "What woman, Floyd?"

"Why that feisty Mrs. Wheeler, of course."

"When did you see Mrs. Wheeler?" Thad had never seen Mrs. Wheeler. Well, not up close anyway. He'd seen who he believed to be her from across the fields in her gardens. Thad wouldn't recognize her even if he did see her in town or at church.

"She was here just a bitty while ago. Boy, was she festerin' like nothin' you ain't never ever seen. A real tornado of a woman."

"She was angry?"

"Yep. Shore was. But the funny thing was..." Floyd flung the bag of seed on the ground, then slapped his knee. "The whole time she done thought I was you! She kept sayin'

Mr. Evanson this and Mr. Evanson that. I tried to tell the ornery woman that I wasn't you, but she wouldn't listen. Just kept on badgerin' on."

"She thought you were me?"

"Yep. Ain't that a funny thought?"

Frightening was more like it. Floyd was the opposite of Thad in just about every way. "Well, that stands to reason since Mrs. Wheeler and I have never met. I've met her husband, but I've never met her."

"And you don't want to neither. It's not somethin' any man should have to go through. Surprised I am still alive after that tongue-lashin' she gave me."

"Why was she mad?" Thad reached for another sack and nodded at Floyd to do the same.

"Somethin' about them cows of yours gettin' into her so-called garden again. I don't know why she was so angry. I told her I would fix the fence after I got my other chores done."

Thad sucked in a deep breath. Even he knew such a statement wouldn't go over well with Mrs. Wheeler, or any woman who wanted an immediate solution to her "serious" problem. "And what did she say?"

"After she went on about some woman with black eyes named Susan and how she was gonna go to the sheriff and get me thrown in jail, she left. I wasn't sorry none to see her go."

"Let's go now and fix that fence, Floyd."

"But what about the feed, Boss?"

"The feed can wait. I have no idea why those cows keep getting out, but we need to fix this problem once and for all."

"Why, Boss, you scared about goin' to jail?"

"No, Floyd, it's not that."

"I reckon Mrs. Wheeler is a handsome woman and all."

Of course. To Floyd, Almira Wheeler, who was closer to Floyd's age, would be a handsome woman. Thad, on the other hand, would never think such a thing about the quarrelsome neighbor lady.

"Let's go, Floyd. God would want us to be neighborly. And after we fix the fence, I'll have you take her some of our best Evanson Cattle Company Angus steaks as a truce of sorts."

"No offense, Boss, but it's gonna take a lot more than the best Evanson Angus steaks to convince that woman to forgive you."

Thad didn't doubt that. Not for a moment.

THAD WAS not thrilled to see that Floyd had not fixed the fence properly in the past. It was as if his ranch hand had done the job as hastily as possible and had given no thought to doing the job well. Thad thought many times about firing the inept ranch hand, whom he suspected also imbibed while on the job.

This, apparently, hadn't been the first time Floyd had been careless and failed to adequately repair the fence. No wonder Mrs. Wheeler was fit to be tied. Thad couldn't blame her.

And a couple of Evanson Cattle Company Angus steaks was hardly a sufficient apology.

But it was a start.

After Thad and Floyd repaired the fence, Thad sent his employee to finish the rest of his daily chores. Standing alone in the hot summer sun, Thad peered through across the fence and saw the meticulous gardens Mrs. Wheeler had painstakingly planted. With being gone so often and with the property being so far from the barn and other places on his acreage where Thad spent most of his time, he had never paid much attention to the gardens. However, from the looks of it, she did indeed spend an inordinate amount of time perfecting them. His gaze found the trampled flowers not far from the fence and he cringed.

Grandma would be upset for sure if cattle had trampled her flowers.

He somehow needed to ask for Mrs. Wheeler's forgiveness and make restitution. The woman had every right to be angry with him.

Thou shalt love thy neighbor as thyself. The Lord's second greatest command entered Thad's mind.

He shook his head. He hadn't been doing a commendable job of executing that command. Even if Mrs. Wheeler and her late husband had been difficult neighbors, Thad, as a man trying his best to imitate Christ, needed to make sure he was a good neighbor himself.

And Thad needed to speak with his foreman and mentor, Pete, about what to do about Floyd's lackadaisical work ethic and whisky problem.

He took one more glance at Mrs. Wheeler's gardens. His mind immediately went to Mrs. Crawford. Did she have gardens such as these? Did she carefully tend to them in the way Mrs. Wheeler so obviously did? How would she feel if her neighbor allowed his cattle to trample all of her hard work?

Something needed to be done about the situation. There was no doubt about that. He needed to do all he could to ensure there would be no more issues with his cattle in the future.

Thad found Pete in the barn a short time later. He always appreciated his mentor's wisdom and maturity. He hadn't had a chance to speak with his ranch foreman for more than a few minutes since returning from his most recent trip to Missoula.

"Hello, Pete. Do you have a minute?"

"Sure, Thad." Pete set his work aside. "I was needing to talk to you about a few items as well. But first, how was your trip to Missoula?"

"It went well."

"Were you able to see the woman and give her the new hat?" A twinkle lit Pete's eyes.

"I did. We had a pleasant time at the restaurant, then we went to church the following day. Pastor Shay's church."

Pete chuckled. "That man knows how to preach a sermon." He paused. "So, am I to understand correctly that you fancy this woman?"

"I do. Mrs. Crawford is smart, funny, and pretty. We have a lot in common. We made plans to meet again next week, this time on Saturday, for another noonday meal. Before long, the waitress will know exactly what we plan to order without us even having to mention it."

"At some point, I imagine you will ask her to court you."

"Well, there are three problems."

"Oh?"

Thad sighed. "She is a rather evasive woman. I always meet her at the hotel restaurant. I'm not sure, but I think she may be embarrassed by where she lives, although that confuses me. She had the funds to buy that hat and a tall stack of parcels, so she doesn't seem destitute."

"That does seem odd."

"Yes, and then there's the fact that she lost her husband only a year ago. I am not sure if there's room in her heart for another man this soon. And lastly, and most importantly, I am not at all sure if she is a religious woman."

"It may be too soon to worry about her husband, as you two haven't spent much time together, but the possibility of being unequally yoked..."

"Each time I have brought up the Lord, Mrs. Crawford presents a vagueness I can't quite explain." He paused. "I'm ashamed to admit I'm tempted to fancy her whether or not she knows the Lord."

"Something for us to lift up in prayer," suggested Pete.

Thad nodded. "I have been and I would appreciate yours and Anne's prayers as well."

"We are happy to pray for your situation, Thad."

"Thank you. I appreciate that. There is one other matter I need to discuss. It involves Floyd."

"Ah, yes, Floyd."

"Reckon he's the reason the fence between us and the Wheeler Ranch isn't being properly fixed. Apparently Mrs. Wheeler's flowers were trampled again. With being gone so much, I haven't taken the proper notice and responsibility of getting it fixed. Until today. That was when I noticed Floyd hasn't been fixing the fence."

"My apologies, Thad, for not keeping a better eye on Floyd. What with my broken leg finally healing and all, I haven't been as attentive as I should be."

"Neither of us has been, Pete. Between ranch work, my trips to Missoula on the land deal and to see Emilie, and the trips to Texas, I haven't taken full responsibility either."

"You mentioned that Floyd hadn't properly fixed the fence. That could explain why the sheriff rode out here to see you today."

"Floyd did say that Mrs. Wheeler was going to talk to Sheriff Keats about the situation."

"Yes, and he arrived while you were in town. That's what I was needing to speak to you about."

"I'll go into town tomorrow to see the sheriff. I also need to figure out a way to make amends with Mrs. Wheeler. Apparently, according to Floyd, Mrs. Wheeler thinks Floyd is me."

"You don't say?"

"Downright amusing seeing as how we aren't much alike."

"There's a lot of truth to that statement," chuckled Pete.

"Any suggestions on how to deal with Floyd's lack of integrity as far as ranch chores are concerned?"

"Floyd needs a talking-to, that's for certain. He has a lazy streak, although I do know he struggles with staying away from the saloon."

"I was afraid of that." Thad knew that Floyd grappled with the temptation of whiskey. "Is he still attending church?"

"He is. I know what it's like to struggle, Thad. You know that. I myself had an issue with the bottle for years. I wasn't the husband nor father I should have been in those days. But when I gave my life to the Lord, Jesus changed my heart and I became the man the Lord wanted me to be. The Lord helped me, although it wasn't immediate and took some time and a lot of effort on my part, but as you know, I haven't touched whiskey in over seven years. I pray we will be able to assist Floyd. I know he wants to overcome this, but I have smelled liquor on his breath in recent days. That was the other thing I needed to discuss with you."

"I smelled it as well. Let's pray for the right way to handle this, Pete. He needs to know he caused Mrs. Wheeler undue hardship with his actions and that he'll have to help her repair her gardens. He also needs to know we will stand by him and assist him with overcoming his drunkenness."

If there was one thing Thad hoped to accomplish in Floyd's life, it was to encourage him to be the man Thad knew he could be. He figured that keeping Floyd employed would be the best way to influence and encourage him.

THAD RODE into town the following day to speak with Sheriff Keats and set things to right. He found the lawman in his office rifling through wanted posters that had just arrived. "Sheriff Keats?"

"Thad, I was just out at your place yesterday. Come in and have a seat." Sheriff Keats motioned for Thad to take a seat in front of the sheriff's worn mahogany desk.

Thad plopped down in the wooden chair. He and the sheriff had been friends since Thad had moved to Hollow Creek.

"I heard you stopped by. I presume this has to do with the Wheeler Ranch and my cattle?"

"Your trespassing cattle, to be precise. Reckon you've allowed them through the fence and onto Mrs. Wheeler's land. They've trampled her flowers and vegetables to smithereens."

"I discovered Floyd wasn't fixing the fence as well as he ought. I aim to set things right with Mrs. Wheeler."

"I would highly recommend you do that," said Sheriff Keats. He tapped his pencil on the desk. "Perhaps you or one of your hired hands could assist her in replanting more flowers."

"Reckon that's a good idea, Sheriff. I never intended for the cattle to ruin her gardens. I'm out of town a lot and haven't paid the attention I ought to the ongoings of the ranch, specifically the fence that wasn't properly mended. I take full responsibility."

"I told Mrs. Wheeler you would make the appropriate amends. I don't think she would have minded half as much about your cattle on her property if it wasn't for all the hard work she pours into those gardens. Hester says the flower garden alone is prize-worthy and that she has suggested more than once that Mrs. Wheeler start a garden club in Hollow Creek."

Thad nodded. "I perused the gardens briefly when I checked out the fence. The ones that hadn't been ruined by my cattle were impressive. I agree with Hester."

"Hester also said Mrs. Wheeler declined the suggestion, but made mention that she enters some of her best flowers and vegetables in the county fair in Missoula."

"I feel badly about what has transpired."

"I figured you would. I told Mrs. Wheeler that you wouldn't intend to damage her gardens on purpose. Unfortunately, she gave me the impression she doubted my statement."

"I have never met the woman, Sheriff, but I have met her husband. He came over on a couple of occasions, one being to discuss the cattle roaming on his property. I thought, after having Floyd tend to the fence, that it was fixed once and for all. I was wrong." Thad thought back to the day when Newton Wheeler had approached him about the fence. He also recalled when Mr. Wheeler accused him and his hired hands of rustling cattle. There was no truth to the serious charge, and it was later discovered that some cattle rustlers from Wyoming had come through town and done the deed. But it hadn't changed the way Newton Wheeler felt about Thad.

"Ah, yes, I remember Newton Wheeler, God rest his soul. Mrs. Wheeler doesn't visit town much. As a matter of fact, counting yesterday, I think I've seen her two times in town since she moved here a few years back. I noticed she doesn't attend church, and Hester says Mrs. Wheeler has only been in the mercantile a total of four times. And you know that Hester knows all of the ongoings here in Hollow Creek." At the mention again of Hester's name, Sheriff Keats's eyes lit up.

Thad chuckled at the sheriff's comment. Sheriff Keats and Hester had been courting now for nearly a year. Things worked well for the couple: Hester reported the gossip and Sheriff Keats upheld the law. Many times, Hester, in her gossip, had given Sheriff Keats tips that assisted in solving a crime. The two had been drawn together by their love of curiosity. It worked well that Hester worked for her parents, who owned the mercantile, and therefore was able to be a busybody in her "spare" time.

"While Mrs. Wheeler doesn't come to town often," Sheriff Keats continued, "Hester did make mention that the widow does spend a fair amount of time volunteering at the orphanage. I'm surprised you haven't crossed paths with her there, Thad."

"I am, too. I wasn't aware she volunteered there. Unfortunately, I haven't been as gracious of a neighbor as I should be. I should have paid a visit to Mrs. Wheeler upon her husband's passing. With her being the only close neighbor within a couple of miles, it would make sense for us to get along. I aim to change all of that when I make amends over the cattle incident."

"Mrs. Wheeler is a nice woman. Quite handsome one at that, although not as handsome as my Hester."

Thad pondered Sheriff Keats's comment. The sheriff was about two or three years younger than Thad to his way of estimating. And Mrs. Wheeler was in her late thirties or early forties. It surprised Thad that Sheriff Keats found the much-older woman attractive. "I haven't seen the woman to know."

"She's classy, and from what I hear, kind and generous too. Hester said Mrs. Wheeler is extra cautious when it comes to the menfolk in Hollow Creek. Something about them wanting to part her and her money, of which she has quite a bit of, according to Hester."

"That makes sense." Thad knew exactly what Mrs. Wheeler experienced as one of the wealthier folks of Hollow Creek. How many women had pursued Thad only because of his wealth?

"So instead, she spends considerable time in Missoula, from what Hester says."

Thad nodded. That made two of them. Business quite often kept him in Missoula where transportation was readily available to travel elsewhere should he need it.

"And did you know she drives an automobile? Hester hinted around that we might should purchase an automobile after we're married. I told her horses and wagons suited me just fine. Besides, when the lawbreakers take off into the mountains, I won't be chasing them in some motorcar. A horse can travel over rugged terrain much easier."

"I have seen her automobile parked at her house," said Thad. "It's a Model T."

"I told her I would speak with you about the cattle. I would appreciate it if you could clear this up."

"Will do, Sheriff."

Thad left the sheriff's office with just the idea on how to make amends with Mrs. Wheeler.

EMILIE WAS reading in the parlor when she heard the rap at the door. She glanced out the window. Mr. Evanson? What was he doing here? And at such an hour?

Glad she had spoken to Sheriff Keats about the cow situation, Emilie realized that perhaps the sheriff had gone to speak with Mr. Evanson.

Not wishing to have to meet with the man, Emilie instead walked quietly to the side of the parlor and listened as Vera answered the door.

"Hello?" Vera's straightened posture gave her the appearance of utmost authority.

"Yes, ma'am. I'm here to give two of our mostest prized Evanson Cattle Company Angus steaks to Mrs. Wheeler, a truce of sorts. These here are the best steaks this far West."

No rival for the infamous Wheeler Angus steaks to be sure, thought Emilie.

"Mrs. Wheeler is unavailable at this time," said Vera. Emilie smiled. Vera was a gem. The woman always knew when Emilie didn't wish to be disturbed.

"That's right fine, ma'am. I'm just here to give her a steak or two, that's all. Oh, and to tell her I'd be plenty sorry about the cattle gettin' into her so-called garden. Hope this can make up for it."

Her so-called garden? Why did that despicable man always use that term? There was nothing "so-called" about it.

"I'll give Mrs. Wheeler your gift, Mr. Evanson, but I'm not sure this will make up for the many flowers and vegetables your cattle destroyed. This is the third time just this spring they have managed to wreak havoc on Mrs. Wheeler's property."

"Yes, ma'am, except that I'm not..."

Vera didn't give Mr. Evanson a chance to argue. Good for her. "Sir, I hope you have taken it upon yourself to mend that fence once and for all. It's downright unchristian what you've allowed your cattle to do time and time again."

"Yes, ma'am, and yes, I have mended the fence all proper-like. There shouldn't be any more cattle gettin' into that there so-called garden of Mrs. Wheeler's. No, ma'am. No more cattle at all."

Emilie could imagine Vera's stern look directed at Mr. Evanson. "Well, I certainly hope that is the truth, Mr. Evanson. I will let Mrs. Wheeler know you stopped by."

"One other thing, ma'am..."

"Yes?"

"I aim to help out Mrs. Wheeler with the fixin' of her plants and make it much better than it ever was. Will you let her know that?"

Emilie cringed at the suggestion.

"I will, Mr. Evanson. Thank you."

With that, Vera shut the door calmly and found Emilie in the parlor. "Mr. Evanson brought you a couple of his ranch's fine steaks to make up for the mishaps in the garden. He also said he would assist you with fixing your plants."

"Thank you, Vera, for handling that for me. Would you please place the steaks in the icebox?"

"Certainly, Emilie. And my, but what an odd little man," declared Vera.

An odd little man indeed. But then, one couldn't choose her neighbors.

It was something Emilie had completely forgotten to ask Vera about in the busyness of returning to Hollow Creek and the fiasco with the cows. "Vera, when we were in Missoula, I noticed something peculiar."

"Yes?"

"I noticed that while at the Bellerose Hotel and Restaurant, you appeared to be giving Mr. Alexander a curious, yet bizarre glance."

"I did?"

"Yes. I can't quite explain it, and perhaps you were only in a daydream, but I wanted to ask you about it."

Vera rolled her eyes upward as if to give deep thought to Emilie's inquiry. "Oh, yes. I remember now. It would seem that I have seen Mr. Alexander somewhere before."

"Perhaps in Missoula during one of our visits there?"

"Perhaps. I can't say for sure."

Emilie thought about what Vera said, then shrugged. For certain, Vera would be seeing more of the mysterious man from Missoula who was swiftly stealing Emilie's heart.

CHAPTER FIFTEEN

Emilie stood back to admire her latest blooms. It would be some time before they recovered fully from the havoc the cows wreaked on them, but some were slowly making a comeback. She sighed. Protecting them from bovine-wrought calamity was a full-time job.

Emilie focused her gaze toward the road, where a man on horseback approached her home.

Who would be calling this late in the afternoon?

She squinted, attempting to recognize the visitor. But the tall man with a rotund belly and bushy dark curly hair and filthy attire was no one she knew.

The man strutted up the porch stairs, a bouquet of flowers in his hand. Emilie shook her head. "Not another one," she muttered.

Suitors desiring her hand in marriage, and an expeditious way to become a wealthy man, embarked on her doorstep frequently since Newt's passing. And even though Emilie rarely went to town, they still found a way to find her and express their fraudulent intentions.

Emilie sidled alongside the house, determined to eavesdrop, but avoid being seen at all costs.

Peering around the corner, she caught a better glimpse. The man flopped the wilted flowers back and forth and cleared his throat before pounding on the door. He turned his gaze and Emilie sucked in a deep breath and whipped her head back around the corner, praying he hadn't seen her.

Best just to listen and stay hidden.

"Hello?" asked Vera, as she opened the door.

"Well, well, Mrs. Wheeler. Ain't you a sight for sore eyes? You're even purdier than they say you is."

Emilie covered her mouth to stifle her amusement. She could imagine Vera's expression at the man's mistaking her identity for Emilie's.

"Sir..." Vera began.

"I brung these flowers just for you. I picked 'em all by myself. Do you like flowers, Mrs. Wheeler? I ain't realized your house would be so ginormous. It's prit near got more rooms I'll bet than all the houses in town put together."

"Sir, what is the purpose for your visit?"

Good for Vera. She'd not expose the truth that she was not Mrs. Wheeler. While her dear employee would never lie; Vera *would* protect Emilie from vagabonds such as the one presenting himself on the front porch. For that, Emilie would forever be grateful.

"The purpose for my visit? Why, it's to court you."

Emilie shivered, although not from the weather.

"Sir..."

"No need to say nothin', Mrs. Wheeler. You're a handsome woman to be sure, and I'd make you a fine husband. I could run this here ranch for you. You see, I been a bit down on my luck in recent days. But I think that would all change if you and me started to court and got ourselves married."

"Mr...."

"No need to make your mind up right this minute. I can come in fer supper and sit awhile and we could discuss our plans then."

"There will be no plans. I do not wish to court you now or ever. Now, please see to it that you climb back on your horse and ride to Hollow Creek post haste."

"But, ma'am..."

"No ma'am-ing me. Be off with you and don't come back. And take that odious handful of weeds with you."

Emilie longed to see the exchange between Vera and the man, but did not dare reveal herself. "You won't be givin' me a chance?" the man asked.

"No, now off you with this instant."

Emilie imagined Vera's plump hand waving the intruder away.

The man stomped off the porch and left a puff of dust in his wake as he rode away.

Emilie waited what seemed like an eternity while the man disappeared from sight. She found Vera on the front porch, rug beater in hand.

"The nerve! The audacity! That scoundrel. How dare he!" she said, whacking the innocent rug with the rug beater.

"Vera?"

"How dare he make his presence known and attempt to swindle you." Another hard whack initiated a dust cloud. "He thought it a wise idea to have supper and discuss his courtship plans, did he? I'll show that ruffian to never step foot on the Wheeler property again." Three more whacks, the rug nearly folding in half. There would be no dust left in the rug once Vera was finished with it.

Emilie stifled another giggle. Vera's gray hair had partially emerged from its tightly-wound bun. Her flushed cheeks, rounded eyes, and pursed lips gave testament to the fact that, while Vera was a godly woman who would nary hurt a fly, she was prone to temper when defending those for whom she cared.

The thought warmed Emilie's heart. She had made an exceptional choice in hiring and befriending Vera.

Morris arrived in the wagon. "Vera, are you all right?" he asked, his short legs attempting to skip one of the stairs as he ascended the porch.

"Enough of this absurd nonsense," said Vera with yet another whack to the rug.

"What nonsense? Emilie, is Vera all right?" Morris's thick gray eyebrows knitted together in one long bushy strand.

"I'm quite all right, Morris. Just defending our Emilie from another preposterous charlatan set on swindling her."

That evening while sleep eluded her, Emilie again replayed the earlier events in her mind. The entire ordeal was far from humorous due to the fact that yet another man wanted to separate Emilie from her wealth. However, it was amusing to witness Vera being mistaken for her. And Vera's frustration taken out on an innocent rug.

"EMILIE, ARE you ready to go?" Vera's voice interrupted her thoughts and she turned to find Vera standing in the doorway.

Emilie set a photo of her and Newt in its rightful place on the mantle. "Yes, just allow me to retrieve my carpetbag."

"Morris and I will be waiting for you in the automobile."

Emilie reached for her carpetbag from the ornate table in the parlor. She opened it to quickly examine its contents. Satisfied she had everything she needed for the overnight trip, she closed it again. "Hattie?"

The maid appeared in the doorway. "Yes, ma'am?"

"We'll be back in a couple of days. Enjoy your time off with your family."

Hattie's round face glowed in the sunlight that beamed through the window. "I will, ma'am. Oh, and Mrs. Wheeler?"

"Yes, Hattie?"

"I've got some exciting news if you have a moment."

"I always have a moment for you, Hattie. What is it?"

Hattie's face turned redder than Emilie's petunias in her flower garden. "Jep asked me to court him."

"Oh, Hattie, how thrilling." Emilie gave her maid a hurried hug.

"I just had to tell you, Mrs. Wheeler."

"I'm glad you did. I best be going so we reach Missoula in a reasonable amount of time." Emilie patted her arm and left the house.

Morris assisted Emilie into the back seat, then took his place in the front with Vera. Emilie couldn't decide who was more excited to head to Missoula, her or the long-married couple in the front seat. The two of them always delighted in getting away for the weekend to the city. And now that it seemed that Mr. Alexander—Thad—would be making their luncheons a weekly tradition, Vera and Morris might just be seeing more of Missoula than they had ever imagined.

No matter who was more excited, the entire plan worked well. Emilie would have a chaperone and perhaps another chance to meet with Thad, and Vera and Morris would have time in the city.

Later, Emilie checked the time on the elegant grandfather clock in the corner of her hotel room. Ten minutes until she was due to meet Thad for their noonday meal. She checked her image in the mirror. Thinking she had perhaps been too well-dressed during their other noonday meetings, Emilie had brought one of her less-extravagant dresses so as not to arouse suspicion that she might be well-off. After all, she wanted Thad to be interested in her for her, not for the tidy sum she kept safely in two separate banks.

Although it was likely too late for Thad to think about her wealth, or lack thereof. Twice he had seen her in extravagant dresses from Miss Julia Mathilda's Fine Dresses, and he knew the cost of the pricey hat he replaced.

Still, to allow him to know the extent of her wealth would never do. If one was to ever love her for her, as Emilie dearly dreamed of in a suitor, he mustn't know the balance of her bank account and her real estate holdings.

Emilie patted her swooped-up hairdo. She beamed at her ability to mimic the latest Gibson Girl fashions with her hair in a perfect coiffure resembling the ones she'd seen in advertisements. She tugged one strand of shorter hair from its pinned place and allowed it to hang fashionably over her forehead as she'd seen in the latest issue of *Ladies Home Journal*. She may be a woman living in a small ranching community in a rural area in the uncivilized West, but that didn't preclude her from being stylish.

She hoped Thad didn't arrive early for this social event, as Emilie needed time to present herself downstairs without him knowing she stayed at the hotel. She hated the thought of lying, but it was better than the alternative. For what would the man think if he knew Emilie often stayed at the finest hotel in the city? That would never do.

Vera and Morris took a seat in the corner of the restaurant, while Emilie seated herself at a table not far from a window. She watched as passersby walked up and down the street. Couples, arms linked, strolled happily along while a mother pushed a pram. On the street, a variety of motorcars, buggies, and wagons transported passengers to their destinations.

What would Thad do if he ever found out her true identity? That she only visited Missoula and didn't live here? That she was a rich rancher's widow and not a common woman?

Emilie, lying is never right. Nanny's words from years ago rang through her mind.

Lying is wrong, but I can't have Thad believing I'm wealthy. Not until I know if he likes me just for being me. That is, if he does someday grow fond of me.

After ten minutes, Thad hadn't yet arrived and Emilie began to worry. Did the man not understand promptness? She worried her bottom lip and fussed with the handle on her reticule. Had she misread that Thad enjoyed her company the last two times they had met? She reminded herself he was late last time. Perhaps punctuality was not on the man's list of admirable attributes.

"Emilie?"

Emilie looked up to see Thad standing by the table. She attempted to open her mouth, but at first words would not come.

"Are you all right?"

Still no words, so she nodded.

"May I join you?"

Again, she nodded. What must he think of this continuously bobble-headed woman who couldn't speak? Blush crept up her cheeks. He was more dapper than she remembered with his thick dark blond hair and those intriguing blue eyes. He wore fine clothes and sported a pocket watch, although she could tell by his strong hands that he was not a stranger to working hard.

"Sorry I'm a few minutes late. I own a horse with a mind of its own." He flashed her a handsome smile.

And Emilie thought she might lose consciousness all at once right there at the table.

When she didn't respond, Thad continued. "It's nice to see you."

"Yes, and you as well." Finally, she could speak after all.

"How was your week?"

Suddenly, she couldn't remember last week.

"We sure were busy this past week on the ranch." Thad retrieved the napkin from the table and placed it in his lap. "It seems we'll be adding more cattle to the herd."

Emilie leaned forward, catching his every word. While she didn't know a whole lot about cows, she did know a thing or two about the business because of her own cattle operation.

The waitress appeared by their table. "Can I get the two of you something to drink?"

Glad for the diversion, Emilie focused her attention on the waitress. "Yes, I'd like a glass of tea, please."

"I'll take a cup of coffee."

"Very well. I'll get those for you and be right back to take your order." The waitress handed each of them a menu. "Our special today is cream of potato soup and broiled steak with parsley butter and pecan pie for dessert."

They placed their orders, and the waitress left with a promise to bring their food soon. "I apologize for being late. I honestly don't make it a habit of not being punctual."

"Truth be told, I did wonder that."

Thad laughed, an easy laugh that Emilie was becoming fond of. "I promise next week I will be on time. Early, in fact."

Emilie's pulse quickened. Next week? Thad truly was making their luncheons into a tradition, not that Emilie was complaining. She would have to be sure to leave her hotel room even earlier so he wouldn't catch her coming down the stairs and into the restaurant. Although could a ranch hand afford to feed them each week with his shortage of hard-earned funds? Should she request a less-expensive place in which to dine?

"Are Vera and Morris here?"

"They are over in the corner. They are becoming quite accustomed to this restaurant. Those two are such a delight. An inspiration to me of sorts."

"An inspiration?"

"Yes, they truly do love each other."

"I don't remember much of my parents, but my grandparents were that way."

"My parents do bicker some, but I know they do love each other."

"I was going to ask if perhaps you, Vera, and Morris would care to join me again for Sunday services."

Emilie hesitated. Last time at the church she felt uncomfortable as though she really didn't belong. Her thoughts returned to her baby and how the Lord had taken him from her.

"Emilie, may I ask you a question?"

"Yes?"

"Are you a religious woman?"

"I—the Lord and I aren't as close as we should be at the moment."

"Reckon I figured something of a sort."

Emilie folded her hands in her lap. Perhaps someday she could share with Thad the sadness in her heart. But after only knowing him such a short time, such things were neither permissible nor proper. Perhaps they might never be.

The meal arrived and the subject was forgotten. But Emilie couldn't help but wonder if Thad thought less of her because of the distance between her and the Lord.

The thought bothered her, for in this short amount of time, she had come to care for the man who sat directly across from her.

CHAPTER SIXTEEN

No matter what business Thad attended to these days, Emilie remained on his mind much of the time. He regretted being late once again to their noonday meal. She must think him obtuse for his lack of punctuality.

And he cared what she thought of him.

A lot.

From Missoula, Thad often boarded the train to travel for business. Many times he traveled to Texas to visit his friend Milt, who had been instrumental in assisting Thad with his dream of ranch ownership. Today Thad was traveling to Illinois regarding the order and subsequent shipment of some cattle.

Thad walked into the Johnson Brothers Nursery. Replicating the nurseries that were becoming ever more popular in New York and other prominent cities, the Johnson Brothers Nursery offered everything from seeds to flowers; from strawberry plants to saplings.

"May I help you, sir?" a man with round spectacles inquired, looking up from arranging some containers of plants.

"Yes. I need to purchase some saplings, strawberry plants, and flower seeds."

The man nodded and retrieved a crate in which to place the smaller items.

"I'm commuting by rail back to Missoula tomorrow, so if you could please pack them suitable for travel, I would appreciate it."

"Absolutely, sir." The man busied himself retrieving the items Thad had requested. "Do you have any particular flowers in mind?"

"I'm not familiar with flower types. What are the ones that come back year after year?"

"Perennials?"

"Yes. I'll take several of those, although you could throw in two or three of the yearly types as well."

"And for the seeds, sir?"

Thad thought a moment. "A mixture of types, about six or seven packets, please."

"I have some black-eyed Susans here. They make fine flowers."

"Reckon that sounds good," said Thad, perusing the sketches on the outside packets of the envelopes. Perhaps Emilie would appreciate those flowers along with the other seed packets he purchased for her. Thad took a closer look at the variety of seeds. "Some daisies as well."

"How about some dahlia roots?" the clerk asked.

"Sure." Thad had no idea what dahlia roots were, but if they went toward making peace with Mrs. Wheeler, they were worth it.

The clerk did a thorough job packing the plants into crates. "These are prize-winning dahlias. As a matter of fact, Mrs. H.L. Stewart has won many a blue ribbon at fairs in Chicago for these dahlias. We order the roots directly from her."

When the clerk finished, Thad paid for and loaded the plants into the wagon he rented from the livery stable for the day. Wouldn't Mrs. Wheeler be thrilled to receive an abundance of saplings, strawberry plants, flower plants, and dahlia roots to add to her gardens? Perhaps she would be able to forgive Thad for being a lousy neighbor once she perused the fine selection he had chosen for her.

And Emilie. Thad would surprise her with the numerous seed packets during their next noonday meal visit. He knew she loved flowers. Perhaps someday he would learn where she lived and he could see the flowers she had already planted.

As Thad drove the wagon through the crowded streets of the Illinois city, he thought of Emilie and their most recent noonday meal and subsequent visit to Pastor Shay's church. Emilie had seemed mighty uncomfortable that first time she visited church with him, Vera, and Morris. But this time, she seemed more relaxed.

What was it that had come between her and her faith?

Thad aimed to find out.

EMILIE CLIMBED the stairs to her room, weariness lining every muscle. She eyed, as she always did, the door next to hers. A door that always remained closed, except when Vera entered the room to dust it on rare occasions.

Vera would dust it more often if only Emilie would give her permission to do so.

Emilie stopped in front of the door and placed her hand on the doorknob. Dare she enter?

Taking a deep breath, Emilie turned the doorknob with one hand and opened the door. The musty odor filled her nostrils, and shadows from the candle in her hand flittered on the walls. Emilie took a step inside. It was just as she had left it.

Emilie brushed her hand along the edge of the walnut baby crib. The tiny mattress inside reminded her of the baby who had never had the chance to rest his precious head upon it. A blue and yellow crocheted baby blanket hung over the side of the crib, made with love by Vera.

Vera. The only other person besides Emilie and the doctor who had known about the baby.

Emilie had kept her condition a secret, although she knew Hattie and Morris suspected. A secret because from early in

Emilie's pregnancy, a peculiar concern had preoccupied her mind for her beloved little one.

Neither Hattie nor Morris nor any other of Emilie's hired help had ever entered the room that had once been meant for happiness.

A room that now only radiated sadness.

Not even Newt had known he was to be a father. He died before Emilie's stomach had become swollen with evidence. Would Newt have been elated as Emilie had been? Apprehensive? Concerned? Disappointed?

Emilie would never know.

Two months after Newt died, Emilie lost her baby at just over five months of pregnancy. Morris had fetched the doctor after Vera told him Emilie wasn't feeling well. When the doctor arrived, it was already too late.

Emilie never got to hold her little son, so perfectly created.

The tears slid down Emilie's cheeks. Why had the Lord allowed such a thing? Wasn't Newt's passing enough?

While Emilie had never known much about the Lord, nor had she often attended church in the past, the loss of her baby had sealed one thing in her mind. The Lord hadn't cared enough about her to allow her baby to live.

And no amount of attending Pastor Shay's church would ever change her mind to the contrary.

THAD SAUNTERED up the stairs to Mrs. Wheeler's house with the crates of plants and saplings in his arms. A young woman answered the door.

"May I help you, sir?"

"Yes, I'm looking for Mrs. Wheeler."

"I'm sorry, sir, she is not here right now. May I pass on a message to her?"

"Please give her the message that this is a delivery from Mr. Evanson, her neighbor. Here are some saplings, strawberry plants, and flowers to replace the ones that were trampled by the cattle. Where should I set them?"

The young woman's eyes rounded. "Oh, my. Mrs. Wheeler will be ecstatic at these gifts. Please tell Mr. Evanson 'Thank you'."

"Ma'am, I..."

"You can set them right inside the door, sir. I might have to take a quick peek at them myself once my chores are done, mind you. Thank you and have a good day."

Obviously, the maid was so enthusiastic about taking a gander at the plants that she forgot about Thad. He hadn't even had a chance to tell her that *he* was Mr. Evanson. Instead, the maid had told him to have a good day, waved him away, and promptly closed the door.

Thad stood there for a moment staring at the closed door. Should he make a proper introduction? For all he knew, Mrs. Wheeler still thought Floyd was Mr. Evanson. He shrugged. More pressing matters demanded his attention at the ranch.

He would introduce himself another time.

Thad shoved his hands in his pockets and descended down the porch stairs. *Reckon that was a mighty fine idea, Evanson. You might just make amends yet.*

EMILIE RETURNED from the orphanage and was greeted by Hattie the second she entered the door.

"Mrs. Wheeler, you will never believe what was delivered for you."

Emilie wanted to inquire, but Hattie's exuberance precluded her from getting in even one word.

"Mr. Evanson, you know, the next-door neighbor?"

Yes, Emilie knew good and well who that obnoxious Mr. Evanson was. "Did he bring by more steaks?" Surely, the odd little man would realize at some point that steaks were not the answer to making amends.

"Oh, no, Mrs. Wheeler. Not steaks. Not this time." Hattie flailed her right hand toward two crates on the floor. "I hope you don't mind that I asked his hired hand to place the crates inside on the floor."

"Not at all."

Hattie chewed on her lip. "His hired hand was a nice man, although he didn't have much to say."

Emilie kneeled by the crates. Flowers, roots, and what looked like strawberry plants and saplings filled the wooden boxes. She gasped. Had she ever before seen such an assortment of magnificent plants all begging to be planted?

"I knew you would be thrilled, Mrs. Wheeler, knowing how you like plants and all. I think Mr. Evanson figured you would not be so angry with his cows after all once you saw these two crates."

"When did his hired hand stop by?"

"When you were at the orphanage, about three hours ago, to be exact."

Emilie was surprised Mr. Evanson hadn't delivered the plants himself. But no matter. If he sent his hired hand to deliver the plants, that was fine by her. Emilie had no desire whatsoever to converse again with that idiosyncratic man who referred to her prized flower beds as "so-called gardens". She inhaled the rich aroma of the flowers and closed her eyes. Was there ever a scent more heavenly than flower blooms? "I'm going upstairs to change into my gardening attire, Hattie. I can't wait another moment to plant these glorious plants." *Even if that obtuse Mr. Evanson shouldn't have been so negligent in allowing his cattle to trample my gardens. But... perhaps this will make partial restitution.*

CHAPTER SEVENTEEN

Emilie's favorite time arrived once again. Each month on the third Wednesday, she met with her newly-made friends, all of whom were rancher's wives who lived in the towns between Hollow Creek and Missoula. Each of the women had excellent social standing and had graciously accepted her into their social circle. They all knew about Newt's death, but none knew of Emilie's other devastating loss in life.

This month was Emilie's turn to host the women. One by one, they arrived at her house, a plate of goodies in their hands. There was Joy, a woman close to Emilie's age, with two young children. Joy lived up to her name and was a kind and gracious woman with a contagious smile. A friend who was forever trying to convince Emilie to rely on the Lord *and* to attend church even if it meant attending at one of the two Hollow Creek churches.

Someday perhaps Emilie would heed Joy's advice.

And wouldn't Joy be ecstatic if she knew that Emilie had attended Pastor Shay's church in Missoula not once, but twice? Emilie decided to keep that information to herself for now. She could only imagine the mini-sermon it would encourage.

Then there was Rhoda. In her fifties, Rhoda was a no-nonsense type of woman, and one who freely shared her opinion about all things, especially women's suffrage and the importance of seeing the movement come to fruition.

Carlotta had lived in Montana the longest. Her husband was not only a rancher, but also a politician. If one didn't know Carlotta well, they'd think her stuffy. However, her kind heart and polished, elegant demeanor demonstrated otherwise. At age forty, Carlotta barely looked a day over thirty with her perfectly coifed brunette hair and blemish and wrinkle-free complexion.

Emilie greeted her friends at the entrance to the parlor with a hug. "It's so good to see you all. I daresay once a month is hardly enough to see some of my favorite and most dear friends."

"Indeed, Emilie, indeed." Rhoda set a plate of scrumptious desserts on the round table in front of one of the sofas. "Cook outdid herself this morning with her choice of pastries."

"They look delightful, Rhoda. Thank you for coming." Emilie showed Rhoda to a seat on the mahogany sofa.

"Joy, what a delight to have you here." Emilie beamed at her favorite of the group.

"It's a delight to be here. The children are with me. I hope you don't mind." Joy carried her youngest in her arms, while her young son grasped her hand. "Nanny was ill today, so I brought them with me."

"Not a bother at all. To the contrary, I love to see little Foster and Nanette." Emilie planted a kiss on baby Nanette's chubby cheek. "I'm sure Hattie wouldn't mind at all keeping the children entertained while we tend to our gathering."

Carlotta stepped in last, her fashionable appearance lending proof to her well-bred background. "Hello, darling Emilie." She took both of Emilie's hands in hers. "How have you been since we last spoke?"

Emilie showed Joy and Carlotta to the paisley sofa across from the mahogany sofa where she and Rhoda sat. "Things have been good. With the exception of one not-so-minor detail."

"Do tell," Carlotta said.

Vera arrived to pour tea in the charming pink-flowered teacups Emilie and Newt had received for their wedding gift from a friend of Emilie's parents. "Well, that pesky neighbor of mine, Mr. Evanson, has once again allowed his nuisance cattle into my garden area. A couple of days ago, they trampled many of my prize flowers and ate a good number of my black-eyed Susans."

"Oh, dear." Rhoda held a gloved hand to her chest. "Not a good thing at all. What is it with that ornery man? This isn't the first time this has happened."

"No, it has happened several times." Emilie sighed. "That awful windstorm we had blew over the fence, and sure enough, the cattle found their way into my garden again."

"Did you go speak with the man?" Carlotta asked. "I know Newton had done so prior."

Rhoda took a sip of tea. "I believe I recall something about Newton not holding Mr. Evanson in high regard. Something about Mr. Evanson's hired hands rustling your cattle?"

"You are correct. Newt never did care for Mr. Evanson. The cattle rustling was later proven unfounded, although Newt, bless his soul, never relented on his suspicion. But it for certain didn't help to have Mr. Evanson's cattle running rampant through our yard, knocking over the fence. As such, I didn't take too kindly to having to deal with the man." Emilie reached for a piece of lemon gingerbread cake and placed it on a saucer.

"I'm quite disheartened to hear about the cattle incident," said Joy. "From all accounts I have seen at church, Mr. Evanson is a polite and kind man with a heart for assisting others. He makes it a priority to assist widows and orphans and seems bent on living out the Gospel."

"It's quite possible we speak of two different people, Joy," said Rhoda. "Are you sure there aren't two Mr. Evansons?"

Joy shook her head. "Not to my knowledge, Rhoda. Although, I have only spoken to him a handful of times, my husband has spoken with him more often. From what my husband says, Mr. Evanson has no other kin in the area."

"Well, I have attempted to speak with him to no avail. And do forgive me, Joy, but Mr. Evanson was anything but a polite and kind man with a heart for assisting others. There is nothing neighborly about cattle being allowed to trample someone's yard."

"I do wonder why anyone would put a ranch in the location where your house sits. Did you ever ask Newton about why his uncle chose to build this fine home in its current location?"

"I wonder that as well, Carlotta. And no, Newt never mentioned why we have Mr. Evanson's property on either side. Most of our acreage, as you know, is to the rear of the house, with the exception of our small front yard and my garden area."

"We are all so sorry to hear about your destroyed flowers, Emilie. Is there anything we can do to help? Perhaps I could have my husband speak with Mr. Evanson next time we see him at church," suggested Joy.

"Thank you, I appreciate you all. The good news is that Mr. Evanson did have his hired hand deliver two crates full of saplings and flowers just yesterday. Needless to say, I have already planted them."

The women laughed. "Oh, dear Emilie, you do love your flowers," said Rhoda.

"That sounds like the Mr. Evanson I have met at church. Perhaps he is attempting to make amends," said Joy.

"Indeed," remarked Carlotta, taking a sip of her tea. "Pray tell, is he now in your good graces?"

"Not yet in my good graces. However, it does bode well for his cause. I do so hope his cattle remain on his property. For what good will it do to have to continually replace my plants, especially in light of this short growing season? But enough about my concerns. How have you all been?" Emilie glanced from friend to friend. What a blessing they were to help quell her loneliness after moving to Montana. She pondered whether to tell them about the kind and dapper gentleman she had met in Missoula a few weeks ago. Perhaps if things escalated to courtship, she would share the information with her friends. Until then, Emilie figured it best to keep it to herself. For what might her friends think? Would they think it was too soon for her to be expressing interest in someone else since Newt had only been gone a year?

Emilie's heart thumped wildly at the thought of seeing Thad again, and with much effort, she returned her thoughts to the task at hand and the entertainment of her dear friends.

The women discussed various events in their lives while partaking in tea and treats. The subject then turned toward what charitable cause they wished to undertake for the month of July. "In August, we planned to do something for the orphanage, and we always do the coat and mitten fundraiser in November," said Carlotta, the proclaimed spokesperson. "In September, we decided to all travel to Helena to raise money for the suffrage movement. We'll do the drive for school supplies for the Hollow Creek and surrounding area schools in October. Does anyone have any ideas for this month?"

"There are a number of worthwhile causes out there, to be sure," said Rhoda. "Emilie, how are you handling the constant requests for donations now that Newt is gone?"

"Mostly, I avoid town. It's difficult to know who really needs help and who is just taking advantage," replied Emilie.

"That is the truth, for sure." Carlotta nodded, "So while we all want to be generous, it's most unpleasant to hear from those seeking funds each time we go to town. Discernment is the key."

"I agree," said Joy. "The Lord calls us to care for the poor, the widows, the orphans, and the grieving in our society. He implores us to be generous with what He has blessed us with, for after all, it is all His. However, it does take a great amount of discernment. Have you prayed about the matter, Emilie?"

Emilie swallowed. Pray? She hadn't prayed since the day she prayed that the Lord would save...best not to think about that now. Tears would be inappropriate at such a joyous gathering with her friends. Besides, Emilie hadn't even known her new friends at the time of her pregnancy. "That is a good idea, Joy."

"Joy, do you have any ideas for this month's charity?" Carlotta asked.

"Actually, I do. There is a new foreign missionary organization in the area that I suggest we all consider joining at our earliest convenience. It seeks to send missionaries to China and also to raise funds to purchase Bibles for our local area, as well as other foreign missions."

"What a delightful idea, Joy. Yes, I make a motion we join this movement," exclaimed Carlotta, clapping her hands together.

Rhoda nodded. "I second the notion. Where do we sign up?"

"I agree as well," said Emilie. "Can you sign us all up, Joy? Perhaps we should devote at least a month to this benefactor."

"Yes, I would be elated to sign all of our names to the roster." Joy beamed. "Such a worthwhile cause, and one that is close to my heart since my grandparents were missionaries."

The remainder of the time was spent partaking in fellowship and enjoying one another's company. If Emilie made a habit of praying to the Lord, she would have thanked Him for the blessing of friendship.

And a day without loneliness.

CHAPTER EIGHTEEN

Emilie kneeled beside the miniature grave marker in the private Wheeler Cemetery. Her hands shook as she placed a bouquet of flowers from her gardens on the headstone. No one except Vera knew about the baby and no one visited the cemetery except Emilie.

A tear rolled from her cheek and fell to the ground below. "Lord, I know You and I don't talk much, but why did he have to die before he even had a chance to live?"

No answer came. Instead, birds chirped overhead and a soft whistling breeze whispered through the surrounding trees. In the distance, a horse neighed. Life went about its normal routine.

But not for Emilie.

A stab in her heart brought about the sobs. Would the pain of losing him ever lessen? Would she ever find peace in the midst of her sorrow?

The doctor had told her that her baby had been a boy.

A boy who would never run and play in the meadows, play jacks with his friends when he was older, or open presents on Christmas. A sweet child whom Emilie would never snuggle in her arms or plant a kiss on his soft chubby cheek.

"Did you need more babies in Heaven, Lord?"

She didn't—couldn't—understand why her son hadn't lived.

Thankfully, the cemetery was isolated enough that no one could hear the anguish in her sobs or her grief-stricken cries for answers.

Emilie gazed up at the sky. A lone bird flew, wings spread wide, as it coasted along on the breeze.

Would her son have looked like her? Like Newt? Would he have had a serious personality? Fun-loving? Adventurous like Emilie? Solemn like Newt?

She would never know.

The tears came in rapid succession then; Emilie unable to stop them. She asked the Lord over and over for an explanation, as she always did when she visited the tiny grave, which was often.

If only He had saved her baby. If only God's plan had been for her son to live. If only...

Finally, after some time, Emilie rose and visited Newt's grave. Moments later, she opened the gate to step out into the meadow beyond the cemetery.

Her wounded heart would never know the answers to some questions.

And her heart would never heal from some of the tragedies life had bestowed upon her.

THAD STOPPED at the bank window before entering to make a deposit and perused the sign in the window:

Electrifying and astounding!

Esteemed birdman, Eugene Ely, will take to the skies in his aeroplane in a show you won't want to miss.

Date: June 28

Place: Fort Missoula

Come one, come all.

Tickets available at: Smith Family Shoe Shop, Tom's Mercantile, Miss Julia Mathilda's Fine Dresses, The Bellerose Hotel and Restaurant, Reynold's Restaurant, Missoula Banking Company, and from men selling tickets in the streets throughout the city.

Streetcar transport to and from the field, along with admittance, is seventy cents. Must have a ticket to attend.

The written words alone enticed him, not to mention the thought of seeing a real aeroplane take to the skies as a bird. What must it be like to fly in such a vehicle? There was no doubt in Thad's mind that he would attend the show. Should he ask Emilie to accompany him? Surely, with her interest in automobiles, she would also take delight in seeing one of the newest inventions.

Thad walked into the Missoula Banking Company and purchased four tickets. If Emilie, Vera, and Morris wouldn't or couldn't attend with him, Thad was certain he would be able to find someone who could use the tickets. The event was next week, so he'd hasten asking her during their noonday meal tomorrow.

The following day, Thad met Emilie, Vera, and Morris at the Bellerose Hotel and Restaurant. As had become the tradition, Emilie dined with Thad at one table, while Vera and Morris dined together at a table nearby. Each time Thad met with Emilie, he determined that he enjoyed their meetings more and more.

"I have a surprise for you," he said, after the waitress took their order.

"Oh?"

Her eyes lit up at his suggestion. Thad doubted he could ever tire of looking into them. "I just so happen to have four tickets to the Eugene Ely aeroplane event next week." He placed the tickets in front of her.

"Eugene Ely, as in the aviator?"

"One and the same."

Emilie clasped her hands together in delight. "Oh, Thad, I have read the papers about him. Isn't he the one who took a flight from aboard a Navy ship last year?"

"He is."

"I just know Vera and Morris will be delighted to join us." She paused. "Thank you, Thad."

"I have one other surprise for you," said Thad, reaching for the bag he'd placed beneath the table when he arrived.

"Another surprise? As in two surprises in one day?"

The way her eyes gleamed made Thad wish he had brought her a surprise every time they met. "Yes, two in one day. Close your eyes."

Emilie closed her eyes, and Thad placed the contents from the bag into her hands. "You can open your eyes now."

Her eyes fluttered open and she gasped. "Seeds? How did you know?"

"Someone mentioned she loves flowers and flower gardens. I figured it only appropriate to present to you some seed packets, although you may have to wait for next year to plant them."

"Thad, I love the seeds. Thank you so much."

He watched as Emilie perused each seed packet, her eyes lighting anew as she took in the sketches of each type of flower.

"Wherever did you find these? Do they sell them in Missoula?"

"I had to travel to Illinois..." Thad paused. It wouldn't do for Emilie to think him wealthy enough to purchase train tickets at his every whim. "I had to travel there for my boss."

As soon as the lie left his lips, Thad felt the choking sensation in his chest. His boss? *I am the boss.*

"Do you travel often?"

"On occasion. Another place I travel to is Texas. My...boss has a friend and mentor there who has been assisting him in the development of his ranch."

Again, the stab of conviction in his heart. Thad shoved it aside.

Sometimes lying was necessary, right?

Wrong.

Although you did travel to Illinois, and you do travel to Texas to meet with Milt, so not all is a lie.

Thad bit back the extreme urge to be honest and truthful. He would, he promised himself, when the proper time came.

When he no longer had to worry about Emilie's motives.

They dined, then decided to join tomorrow for church. Thad was thrilled Emilie agreed once more to join him at Pastor Shay's church. This would be her fourth time. If she loved the Lord as he hoped she did, Thad would soon be asking Emilie to court him.

EMILIE LISTENED intently to Pastor Shay's sermon. Each week she attended, she grew more comfortable. She had even remembered to bring her Bible this week.

Emilie found herself longing to visit the church, which surprised her. Wasn't it just recently that she cried out to Him yet again in anguish over her son? Wasn't she still blaming the Lord for not allowing her baby to live?

Why then was she suddenly more open to the idea of attending church with Thad, Vera, and Morris than she had been before? And why then was she suddenly eager to listen to the sermons Pastor Shay preached?

The other times she attended church, Emilie had squirmed uneasily in her seat. Restlessness overtook her. Such was not the case today. She almost felt at ease being in the house of the Lord.

"Please turn in your Bibles to Matthew 11:28," said Pastor Shay, after the hymns, announcements, and offering.

Emilie observed the speed at which Thad and Vera found the passage. From what she could tell, it obviously wasn't toward the front of the Bible, nor toward the back. She flipped through the pages, so crisp and new in a book she rarely opened. After what seemed like minutes, Emilie finally found the passage. Taking a deep breath, she yielded her attention to the pastor as he preached.

"*Come unto me, all ye that labour and are heavy laden, and I will give you rest*," Pastor Shay quoted from the Bible.

Emilie pondered the verse and listened as Pastor Shay spoke of Jesus wanting those who were overwhelmed, worried, afflicted, saddened, discouraged, or anxious, to give their concerns to Him.

Did that mean He wanted Emilie to give Him the heartbreak she felt over the loss of her son too? But why when He could have prevented it?

As if Pastor Shay read her mind, he continued. "There is and always will be heartbreak in this world. We wonder how God could allow bad things to happen. Illness, death, wars."

Emilie sat up straighter in the pew. Yes, why did God allow bad things to happen? Why had her baby died? Why had Newt, a normally healthy young man, contracted fatal pneumonia?

"We don't know the answer as to why some things happen the way they do. It seems that God, whom we know to be loving, wouldn't allow diseases, atrocities, and the like. But we also know we live in a fallen world, and we will not escape the hardships of life this side of heaven. But there is good news. We have hope because we have Jesus."

After Pastor Shay finished his sermon and the closing hymn had been sung, the elderly reverend with kind gray eyes spoke once again. "If you have not placed your faith and trust in Jesus, would you come forward now? As Second Corinthians 5:17 says, '*Therefore if any man be in Christ, he is a new creature: old things are passed away; behold, all things are become new*'. He promises us that when we repent and believe, we can have new life in Him. I would be honored to pray with you about making the decision that will change your life for eternity."

Emilie squirmed in her seat. She had never placed her faith and trust in Jesus. How could she when she barely knew Him?

She absolutely could not.

Two people walked to the front of the church toward Pastor Shay. Emilie watched as the pastor prayed with them. One of the people, a woman, was crying as she prayed.

An odd pressing of conviction filled her heart. What would it be like to trust in Jesus? To put her faith in Him? To have new life in Him, as Pastor Shay mentioned?

She wasn't sure what all of that meant, but she did know she wanted to have the hope that could be found in Jesus.

Before she could halt their movement, her legs propelled her to her feet. Her feet ushered her to the front of the church.

A pull so strong and so real tugged on Emilie's broken heart.

So broken that only One could heal it.

On that day, Almira Emilie Crawford Wheeler's life changed for eternity.

"A CELEBRATION is going on in Heaven right now," whispered Vera, as she hugged Emilie in a firm embrace.

Emilie had no idea of what Vera spoke. Why would there be a celebration in Heaven?

But Emilie couldn't ponder that thought at the moment. For it seemed as though something life-changing had just happened to her. Within her.

Something she didn't fully understand.

Only that Pastor Shay told her that now she was the Lord's.

"Vera and I, why, we've been waiting for this moment for forever it seems," said Morris, as they stood outside the church moments later. Could that be a tear slipping down the weathered cheeks of the elderly man Emilie had come to adore?

Emilie noticed Thad standing a few feet away, watching her. He walked toward her and took her hands in his.

At his touch, a jolt traveled up her arms. He said no words, but leaned toward her so close that she could smell the fresh scent of soap on his skin. So close that if he wanted to kiss her, he could.

Not that Emilie would mind.

With a light touch of his thumb, he stroked her tear-laden cheek ever so tenderly.

Never would Emilie forget that day in the summer of 1911.

CHAPTER NINETEEN

True to his word, Thad stopped at the hotel to retrieve Emilie, Vera, and Morris promptly at two o'clock.

I wonder if he thinks our agreed-upon meeting place is unusual, Emilie mused. She watched as Thad parked on automobile next to the boardwalk.

"Ooh, we'll be going in style to see the aeroplanist," quipped Vera.

"I didn't know Thad had a motorcar," added Morris, "and a right fancy one at that."

Emilie hadn't known that Thad owned an automobile either. It didn't seem fitting for a poor ranch hand to own such a mode of transportation.

Perhaps he wasn't as destitute as she thought.

After all, he had purchased her meal all of those times at the restaurant and now the tickets for the Eugene Ely show.

Or maybe Thad used his money wisely and saved every penny, hence having some funds for activities such as luncheons.

Not that whether Thad was wealthy or not made much difference to Emilie.

She was falling in love with him no matter his financial status.

The important thing remained that Emilie not allow Thad to know of *her* considerable wealth.

Thad grinned as he approached them. Just the sight of him took Emilie's breath away. She pushed aside the realization she had never had those feelings for Newt.

"What a nice automobile," commented Morris.

"Yes, it is. I'm borrowing it from a friend. Wouldn't mind owning it, however. It's a brand new 1911 Cadillac." He tossed a look of admiration toward the motorcar, then continued. "Should we go so we aren't late?"

Thad opened the passenger-side door and Vera and Morris climbed into the backseat. "I'm so glad you suggested this outing," said Vera. "I've never seen an aeroplanist."

"Nor have I," agreed Emilie. Thad gently cusped her elbow and assisted her into the front seat. His touch sent flutters to her stomach.

When they arrived, Thad handed the tickets to the ticket taker, and they entered the festivities.

Already people were crowding the area, anxious to see this new remarkable machine. The delicious aroma of funnel cakes waffled on the air, and a popcorn wagon wheeled by the crowd. Sounds of trumpets, clarinets, and flutes indicated the beginning of the band concert.

"Would anyone care for a funnel cake?" Thad asked.

Emilie's stomach grumbled in response, and she willed the unseemly noise to quiet. Thad eyed Emilie suspiciously, likely hearing the undignified cacophony of her stomach's desire for food. "I can retrieve four funnel cakes and be back post haste," he said, a teasing glint in his bluer-than-the-bluest sky eyes.

"I'll go with you, Thad," suggested Morris, and he and Thad started toward the funnel cake merchant. Each time Thad purchased their noonday meals, and now today when he paid their admission expenses, Emilie felt a twinge of guilt. She didn't want a man who struggled financially to continually pay her way. What if he was unable to purchase food for himself because of his generosity toward her and her friends? The thought of causing such an imposition, especially to provide unnecessaries for her, disturbed Emilie.

Should she say something?

"Such a thoughtful man," said Vera.

"He is. I just worry about him not being able afford such extravagances."

"I think he's fond of you, Emilie."

"Really?" She hoped she didn't sound too eager at Vera's suggestion.

The men returned and handed the funnel cakes to Emilie and Vera. Covered with a light dusting of sugar, Emilie couldn't wait to indulge in the special treat.

"I'm sorry, but they didn't have pie à la mode," teased Thad.

Emilie giggled. "We'll have to wait to have that again at the Bellerose."

Thad nodded. "I look forward to it." He held Emilie's gaze for a moment.

Could it be true as Vera mentioned? That he really was growing fond of her? But they had known each other for such a short time.

They finished eating their funnel cakes as more and more people gathered in the field. Emilie could barely contain the excitement that rippled through her. If driving the motorcar hadn't been a rush to her system, surely flying would. "Have you ever thought about flying in an aeroplane?" she asked Thad.

"Indeed I have. I've always marveled about how God made the birds of the air to float so peacefully on the breeze. What would that be like?"

"Mr. Ely seems to have discovered that very thing."

"Yes, and people say that someday, even common folk will fly in aeroplanes." He turned and smiled at her a smile that made Emilie's heart beat at least one hundred times faster than it currently thrummed.

Just then, a brisk breeze blew and Emilie's wide-brimmed hat—the one Thad had replaced for her—went flying off her head. Emilie reached up in surprise. "Oh, dear. My hat!"

Thad left her side and chased the wayward hat as the wind caught it and carried it to the east. Emilie covered her mouth, attempting to stifle her laugh, as Thad, with his long legs and broad shoulders chased after the hat.

It finally settled at the foot of a spectator some distance away.

"Thad is such a gentleman," commented Vera, "retrieving your hat for you."

"I would chase your hat too, Vera," said Morris with a glint in his spectacled eyes. "Even if it meant crossing rivers or climbing mountains to do so."

Vera reached up to ensure her hat was firmly attached to her head. "Oh, my sweet Morris. I do know that. Such a gem you are." She placed a kiss on her husband's weathered cheek.

Emilie contemplated the conversation between the dear older couple. They had been married for longer than she had been alive and loved each other more and more with each passing year it seemed. She blushed as the thought of Thad entered her mind.

He returned a few moments later carrying Emilie's hat. She reached up, attempting to smooth her windblown hair. "I must look a fright."

"Not at all," Thad said.

Emilie knew she was blushing more than a person ought.

Thad stopped in front of her and with both hands placed the hat on her head with a gentleness Emilie had come to admire. "You might want to secure your hat. It seems we may have quite the brisk winds this afternoon." His twinkling eyes and his lopsided grin did something to Emilie's insides she couldn't quite explain.

Whenever she was around him, Emilie's heart palpitated and her mind raced. Such a foreign feeling, but she recognized it as only one thing.

She was falling in love with Thad Alexander.

This must be what Hattie meant when she spoke of her affection for Jep. Emilie now finally understood.

"I don't know what it is about that hat, but it sure has caused its own adventure."

"That it has," she agreed.

Thad chuckled. "I'm just thankful I don't have to replace it again."

"As am I. I know it was a pricey expenditure."

Thad shrugged. "If by chance, Mrs. Crawford, your hat takes flight again, I'll gladly chase it for you again."

"I'm much obliged for your assistance, Mr. Alexander."

He held her gaze for a minute longer, then took his place beside her. Emilie treasured these times of their coquetry and pondered them long after their time spent together.

If only Thad resided in Hollow Creek and they would be able to see each other more often.

Of course, if he resided in Hollow Creek, he would come to know the truth about who she really was.

"How many folks do you reckon are here?" Morris asked, interrupting Emilie's thoughts. She looked over at her butler and noticed he and Vera remained holding hands. A warmth filled her chest.

She discreetly studied Thad's profile. What would it be like for her and Thad to experience what Vera and Morris shared?

Much, much too soon to even contemplate such a conjecture, she chided herself.

Thad studied the crowd. "Looks to me like a couple thousand at least."

Obvious anticipation rippled through the audience as they eagerly waited for Mr. Ely to fly his aeroplane. "I heard Mr. Ely's plane was delivered here by railroad," said Thad.

"In a boxcar?"

"Yes, and that's the way he plans to deliver it to his next destination."

"Amazing how modern it all is, especially for Montana," marveled Emilie. Such things were the custom in New York, but even with its uncultured status, Montana was becoming more modernized. Missoula, anyway. Hollow Creek still had some distance to travel before it was the least bit contemporary.

"Makes me wish I could have been the one to invent such a contraption."

Emilie gazed at Thad's profile again. Strong. Capable. Handsome.

Oh, so handsome.

He intertwined his fingers with hers, causing a jolt to radiate up Emilie's arm.

A loud rumble filled the air, and the aeroplane roared to life. Mr. Ely drove the plane a short distance before taking flight. Slowly, he increased his altitude.

The crowd oohed and aahed. Within moments, the spectators observed astonishing tricks as the plane dipped and swooped in the air. The cacophony of the crowd's applause thundered in her ears.

Emilie had never seen anything like it in all her years.

Mr. Ely landed, then took flight two more times. Once again by himself, and a second time taking another man with him. The man could have flown all day and into the next and the crowd would have given him their continued undivided attention.

Late into the evening, the show concluded. Emilie's ears rang from the day's noises as Thad drove her, Vera, and Morris to the hotel.

Thankfully, Thad didn't ask to drive her "home." Instead, he opened the doors to the Cadillac and assisted his passengers from the automobile.

Later that night in her hotel room, a thought occurred to her. She recalled the day weeks ago when Hattie had asked what it was like to be in love. Emilie hadn't known then.

But she knew now.

And in the words of Hattie, Emilie's heart did flutter. More than once when around a certain ranch hand from Missoula.

CHAPTER TWENTY

Thad parked the 1911 Cadillac in front of the humble house at 2807 16th Street. He had use of his friend, Jonathan's, automobile for one more day. A right fine automobile at that.

Perhaps when the money came in from his latest cattle shipment, a new Cadillac purchase would be in order.

While he appreciated Missoula and all the city had to offer, Hollow Creek remained his home. He would have it no other way.

If he and Emilie were to someday marry, would she desire to continue residing in Missoula, rather than on the Evanson Ranch in Hollow Creek?

If only Emilie lived in Hollow Creek. Not only would he see her more often, but the problem of where they would live would be of no concern.

Whoa. Back up the wagon, Evanson. Since when did you start thinking of marriage? Thad swallowed hard. Such a thought had entered his mind on more than one occasion in recent days.

Odd since he had known Emilie for such a short amount of time.

But there was something about the woman who had captured Thad's attention from the second he returned her scattered parcels and set to right the deflated and annihilated hat.

At Pastor Shay's church, Thad's prayers had been answered when Emilie had gone forward and surrendered her life to

Christ. He hoped for both of them to grow in the knowledge of the Lord together.

Today at the airshow, Thad had wanted to kiss Emilie when he delivered her, Vera, and Morris to the hotel. Her gaze as she had looked into his eyes told Thad's mind something his heart already knew.

That he was in love with her.

Emilie was lovely, to be sure, but there was so much more than that to her. Grandpa repeatedly mentioned how outer beauty faded over time while inner beauty lasted a lifetime. He encouraged Thad to choose someone who was beautiful inside.

The woman of Thad's affections possessed that inner beauty.

Thad removed his boots and took a seat at the table. A photo of Grandma and Grandpa taken at the Chicago fair sat nearby on the shelf—one of the few possessions Thad had brought from the ranch to the Missoula house. The photo, taken about a year before they passed on, showed the true essence of their characters.

Not many folks smiled for photographs. After all, it was a serious affair to have your photo taken, and an expensive one at that. But Grandpa had grinned a crooked smile Grandma said Thad inherited.

Even though both Grandma and Grandpa were advanced in age when the photograph was taken, their youthful spirits had shown through their abundance of years.

"What, pray tell, were you so happy about?" Grandma asked upon first seeing the photograph.

Grandpa placed a kiss on Grandma's cheek, to which she blushed in response. "I was thinkin' about my lovely bride," Grandpa answered with a twinkle in his blue eyes.

"Oh, my!" Grandma had blushed again, then wrapped her arm through Grandpa's, apparently enjoying every second of Grandpa's obvious affection for his bride of so many years.

A love that had transcended through time.

And a love that existed because two people loved each other with a deep abiding love based not only on outer appearance.

Grandpa had gone from a tall and strong young man to a hunched over elderly gent with a bad back. His thick brown hair had been replaced by a shiny bald spot with a slight fringe touching the nape of his neck. Grandma had gathered some girth around her once-trim waist. Her brown hair had been replaced with a bun of gray.

Once Grandma had asked Grandpa if he still found her to be comely, to which Grandpa answered, "Sure as rain, I do." Grandma giggled and whispered to Thad that Grandpa needed new spectacles.

Thad wanted a love like his grandparents had shared. Not perfect by any stretch, but enduring and with God at the center.

Emilie was the first woman Thad envisioned having that type of marriage with. No other woman, Catherine included, had affected him the way she did. He couldn't wait to see her again tomorrow for a Sunday drive in the Cadillac after church.

Seeing her only on the weekends wasn't enough.

Reckon you've gone sappy, Evanson.

Sappy indeed. And sweet on one lovely woman from Missoula.

AFTER CHURCH, Thad delivered Vera and Morris to the restaurant at their request, and he and Emilie went for a drive. "You and your friends are fond of the restaurant," Thad mused aloud, finding it odd that he didn't ever retrieve or return Emilie to her home. Should he inquire? He didn't want to embarrass her.

"Yes. The Bellerose is a fine restaurant." Emilie offered nothing more. Was she ashamed of her home? Had she lost her home when her husband passed? Was she temporarily residing at the hotel?

He had so many questions he wanted to ask. Thad began to open his mouth to ask those very things, but when he noticed the sight of her, he found he could utter no words at all.

Emilie wore no hat today, and the breeze blew a few strands of hair around her face.

The site of her took his breath away.

Thad had never seen anyone so captivating.

A honk sounded, garnering Thad's attention. Nearly side-swiping another vehicle, he returned his gaze to the road and righted the motorcar.

It would never do to crash Jonathan's Cadillac.

And all because Thad's attention had been centered, not on the road ahead of him, but on a certain woman beside him.

Emilie seemed not to notice the near-collision, but instead gazed out her side of the Cadillac. Her soft scent of lavender perfume rode on the breeze and tickled Thad's nose. "It's a right fine day," he said, his voice sounding awkward in his ears.

"That it is. Fine day, fine company, and a fine automobile." She turned and blessed him with one of her smiles.

"Reckon I'm growing quite fond of Jonathan's motorcar." *And quite fond of you, Emilie.*

Emilie said nothing for a moment, then nearly bounced in her seat as she fully faced him. "May I drive it?"

May she drive it? Thad's first thought was one he didn't utter aloud, so instead, his mouth uttered another equally featherbrained question. "The automobile?"

Emilie giggled. "Yes, Thad, the automobile. Did you think I was speaking of a horse?"

"Uh, yes, of course, the automobile. Well, let's see here..." A woman driving a 1911 Cadillac? Oh, sure, it could be done. It was 1911 after all, and Thad had seen several women driving a motorcar in his travels. But with no practice?

Whatever his reservations, it would be nearly impossible to say no to Emilie.

"I promise I won't cause a debacle and that I will handle the automobile with the utmost of care," she continued, with an upward and self-assured tilt of her chin. "I promise I'll keep my eyes on the road."

"Have you driven a motorcar before?"

Emilie hesitated for a moment before responding. "Not a Cadillac, but I have motored before, yes."

"You are full of surprises, Emilie."

She leaned toward him, her expression expectant. "May I, Thad? Just for a short distance?"

Thad weighed the decision in his mind and finally relented. When they were outside of town and away from so many other automobiles and wagons, Thad pulled to the side of the road. Jonathan would kill him for sure.

He offered a prayer that Emilie's driving wouldn't put their lives at risk or ruin Jonathan's Cadillac.

But Thad would do just about anything for Emilie, even something as crazy as allowing her to drive the borrowed automobile. *Besides, she said she's driven a motorcar before.*

He emerged from the vehicle, walked to Emilie's side, and opened her door. He reached for her hand and assisted her from the automobile, allowing his fingers to clasp hers for a bit longer than necessary.

The warmth of her hand in his messed with his senses. At this rate, Emilie might just talk him into motoring the automobile from Missoula to New York City.

Emilie gazed up into his eyes. He looked into hers. Should he kiss her?

He sure wanted to.

Before Thad could argue with himself, he leaned down and found her lips with his. Her kiss was just as he imagined. Soft and passionate. He placed his left hand on her lower back and held her in his arms, pulling her closer. They broke apart just briefly before Thad's lips found Emilie's once again. This time, he kissed her with the passion existing in his heart from the moment he knew he was falling in love with her.

"Emilie..." he muttered, as they drew apart once more.

Her eyes were wide as she regarded him. Had Emilie enjoyed the kiss? Should Thad have resisted the impulse to kiss her as they weren't yet courting?

Thad cleared his throat. He had a remedy for that. "Emilie, will you do me the honor of courting me?"

Her hand flew to her neck and her eyes widened all the more. Would she say yes?

"Yes, Thad, I will court you."

For the first time in his life, a thought entered Thad's mind.

This could be the woman the Lord had planned for Thad all along. Emilie could be *the one*. The one that the Lord had sent to be his wife. Someone who would love him for him, not for his wealth. A love like his grandparents had shared.

"Reckon we should continue our drive, Mrs. Crawford." *Before I decide to plant yet another kiss on your pretty face.*

"I reckon so, Mr. Alexander."

Thad escorted Emilie to the driver's side of the automobile, opened the door for her, and helped her behind the steering wheel. Then, with a multitude of prayers, Thad climbed into the passenger side of the Cadillac, resisting the urge to hold tightly onto the door.

With an impressive start, Emilie pulled the Cadillac from the side of the road and onto the street. If he'd thought her a sight to behold while she was his passenger, Emilie was even more so now. The wind whispered through her hair, tugging a few more strands loose.

"What a fine automobile," Emilie said after some time.

"It is. I'm thinking about owning one myself someday. Say, Emilie, where did you learn to drive a motorcar?"

Seconds ticked by before she answered. "I've had the experience of driving a time or two. I really am quite fond of it. Perhaps I might consider owning a Cadillac myself."

Thad finally relaxed and leaned back against the seat. Could the day get any more perfect?

A few miles later, they arrived at the turn-off for the Mount Sentinel trail. "Wait until you see the view, Em," Thad said, still thinking of the kisses they had shared and her agreement to court him.

They took the trail slowly, mostly because Emilie didn't have proper shoes for the hike, and partly because Thad wanted to revel in every moment spent with her.

"There's an 'M' up here somewhere," he said. "Made with some rocks from some University of Montana students a couple of years back."

"This is an incredible view from here," Emilie said, stopping and gazing upon the valley below.

"Not as incredible as the woman before me," Thad said. She was a view he could admire all day and never tire of it.

EMILIE COULD quite possibly never tire of spending time with Thad. He took her by surprise with that first kiss by the side of the road as they switched places in the Cadillac.

Probably not nearly as surprised as he was that she hadn't crashed the borrowed motorcar.

As they stood with the view of Missoula below them, Emilie reveled in the fact that Thad asked her to court him. More than once, Emilie pondered whether she had heard him correctly. Then she wondered if it had been long enough since Newt's death. And if she should yet tell Thad her true identity and where she really lived and that she was really a wealthy woman.

She would have to be forthright with him soon. No courtship should begin on an untruth. Would he be angry when she told him the truth?

Emilie had never before felt the butterflies taking up residency in her stomach when Newt had kissed her, which wasn't often.

Her feelings for Thad continued to grow.

So many emotions rippled through her.

Especially the emotion of happiness.

Emilie hadn't wanted the day to end. When they returned to the Cadillac, she relayed her upcoming plans. If only she hadn't committed to a meeting several months ago. "I won't be able to meet you at the restaurant next weekend," she said. "Vera, Morris, and I are going to Helena to a women's suffrage meeting."

Thad quirked an eyebrow. What did he think of women's suffrage? So many men were against it, including Newt and Emilie's own father.

"I'll miss you next week, Emilie. Perhaps in the following week we can meet again?"

"I would very much like that." She would surely miss him next week as well.

"And before too long, I'd love to take you to the Missoula Garden Park, seeing as you love flowers and such."

"I would delight in visiting the botanical gardens." Emilie clasped her hands together. The only thing more exciting than visiting the gardens was visiting them with Thad.

"I figured we could ride the streetcar to the gardens."

"A streetcar? I haven't yet ridden on the Missoula streetcar."

Thad grinned. "Make that a first time for both of us."

A few moments passed, then the question that had been in Emilie's heart spilled from her mouth. "Thad?"

"Yes?"

"How do you feel about women's suffrage?"

"Reckon I'm not concerned if a woman decides to fight for the right to vote."

A huge sigh escaped Emilie's lips and she caught Thad's amused glance at her release of breath.

"Does that surprise you, Em?"

Em. She liked his nickname for her.

"It does. You see, some men..." *Unfortunately, including Newt...* "Have the idea that women are empty-headed and are not equipped with enough brains to make a wise political decision in casting a vote."

"I believe women, just like men, come with all types of intelligence. Some are smart, some are not."

"I agree. Some people have started anti-suffrage movements and have even published pamphlets regarding their opinion."

Thad nodded. "I've heard of those movements. Those folks are entitled to their opinions, of course, but I am of the belief women should have a share in determining who becomes their next president as well as other elected officials."

Emilie's admiration of Thad grew another thousand notches. How thankful she was that he shared her views on something so important to her. "Some men are stating that the right of women to vote will actually have a negative impact on our society."

"My grandma was all for women's suffrage. She was far ahead of her time in her thinking and looked forward to the day when women could vote. She stayed up-to-date on all the current events. My grandpa supported her views, although at first he expressed concern."

"I'm thankful Vera and Morris feel this way as well. They've attended many meetings with me throughout Montana. As Morris would say, my mother would squawk like a festered chicken if she knew." Emilie giggled at the phrase Morris had said on more than one occasion about more than one individual.

"'Squawk like a festered chicken'...I'll have to remember that."

And so it went, all the way back to the restaurant, a pleasant camaraderie between Emilie and Thad.

With the bonus of one last kiss until two weeks from now when they would again meet.

THE FOLLOWING evening, Emilie climbed the stairs to her room. Standing near the bureau, she knew the choice she was about to make was the correct one.

With care, she removed the gold wedding ring from her left finger and placed it on the bureau. With the acceptance of Thad's courtship proposal, wearing Newt's ring would hardly do.

Besides, Emilie couldn't wait to begin a new chapter in her life.

CHAPTER TWENTY-ONE

Thad drove to Hollow Creek and parked his wagon in front of Hollow Creek Church, one of the two churches in his hometown. It had been some time since he had frequented there, since he'd most often been in Missoula on Sundays. Thad missed the humble church and its congregants.

Most of them, anyhow.

Climbing from the wagon, Thad looked both ways. One glance toward the town of Hollow Creek, the other to the church and slightly beyond. Just to be sure none of those pesky women who had sights on courting him were around. Seeing none of the usual "suspects," Thad sauntered toward the church doors, nodding at several of his friends as he did so.

Praising God for the warm sunny day, he almost didn't see her.

But when she bumped into him, Thad surely knew she was there.

"Mr. Evanson, for what do I owe this pleasure?"

Her high-pitched voice, recognizable and shrill, grated on his nerves. He tipped his hat. "Good morning, Miss Chisolm."

Dora Chisolm smiled what was likely her biggest and best smile that showcased far too many teeth for one mouth. "Good morning to you, too." Miss Chisolm batted her eyelashes at Thad, failing to hide the fact she had her sights on him and had for some time. "I made this just for you." She thrust a loaf of bread at Thad. "I'm sure you don't often have fresh bread, with not having a wife and all."

Thad remained courteous while Grandma's words flitted through his mind. *A man is always a gentleman. Always.*

"Thank you, Miss Chisolm. I appreciate your generosity."

"We can't have you going hungry." Dora Chisolm cackled a piercing laugh and batted her eyelashes again. She twirled a stray tendril of hair between her finger and thumb.

"Well, I best be on my way. I don't want to miss the start of services. Thank you, again, Miss Chisolm."

"Oh, my pleasure. Truly it is."

Thad took a deep breath, and with his Bible in one hand and the loaf of bread in the other, he continued toward church.

"Mr. Evanson, is that you?"

No mistaking that voice. The Southern accent, all the way from Alabama, called out to him before he had even taken three steps. "Yes, ma'am, it is." He turned to see Cleo Flickinger standing behind him.

Other churchgoers gawked. Some of the men smirked and some of the women tittered, as if the day Thad Evanson became a married man was closer than ever.

Only it wasn't. Not if a woman wanted him for only his money, like Dora and Cleo did. No, if all of the women in Hollow Creek and anywhere else in Montana, or even in the world, only had their sights on Thad because of his wealth, they would be better served looking elsewhere.

"I made this apple pie for y'all." Miss Flickinger blushed, the red creeping up her cheeks matching her fiery red hair.

"Thank you."

"You are most certainly, and I mean most certainly, welcome."

Thad noticed a piece missing from one of the outer edges of the apple pie.

"Oh, that. Sorry 'bout that, Mr. Evanson. I got a mite hungry this morning after preparing it and sampled it. It's right good if I do say so myself, and I think you'll find it delicious."

"I'm sure I will. Much obliged, Miss Flickinger."

The woman lingered for a moment, her eyes wide as she stared. "I just happened to hear there's a barn dance coming up the weekend after next. I know someone who would welcome the opportunity to attend the dance with y'all."

Thad did all he could to hide his smirk. While he wasn't a betting man, Thad bet he knew who wanted to attend the dance with him. "I'm sorry, but I will be out of town this next weekend."

Out of town hopefully meeting with Emilie.

"Really? Oh, that is not good news, Mr. Evanson. I will let myself, I mean the woman who was inquiring, know that you'll not be available for the barn dance. I'm quite sure she'll be grief-stricken."

Grief-stricken? Over that? While Cleo Flickinger was a somewhat fragile woman, Thad doubted one barn dance would do the woman in. "I best get into the church, ma'am. Services will be starting soon. Thank you for the apple pie."

"You are most welcome. And if there is a change of plans the weekend after this, y'all be sure to let me know so I can pass it on to my…my friend."

"I'll be sure to do that."

Thad juggled the bread, the apple pie, and his Bible and entered the church. He strolled up the center aisle to the church pew where his foreman, Pete, and his wife, Anne, sat.

"It looks as though the women of Hollow Creek are taking mighty fine care of you," Pete teased.

Thad took a seat. "That they are. Glad to see you back."

Pete clamped a strong hand on Thad's shoulder. "It's good to be back."

Thad had noticed Pete's five-day absence. The ranch just didn't operate as smoothly without Thad's right-hand man at the reins. And Floyd having to take things over in the interim…

The Lord sure tested Thad's patience when it came to Floyd. He definitely didn't possess the patience Pete had for the lazy employee. But nor did Thad possess the courage to remove Floyd from his employ at the Evanson Cattle Company.

"How is your family, Anne?" Thad asked.

"They're doing all right. It's been difficult since Grandfather passed, but we were able to settle Grandmother in with my mother. Thankfully, they both have a strong faith. God will see them through this."

Thad nodded. "I'll continue to pray for them."

"Thank you, Thad."

Thad placed the bread and apple pie on the pew beside him. The music began to play and he reached for a hymnal, but not before noticing Shauna Hillard's eyes boring into the side of his head from across the aisle. He tipped his head in polite greeting.

The coquettish look in Miss Hillard's eyes did not go unnoticed. Thad knew she had set her cap for him.

A thought that didn't interest him in the least. Not after the day he overheard a certain conversation. Prior to that, Miss Hillard had sparked an ever-so-slight, somewhat dull interest in Thad last year. She seemed nice and wasn't painful to look at, however...

When he'd overheard Shauna Hillard speaking with some friends at Dell's Mercantile, he'd almost been unable to breathe. The brash and cheeky comment confirmed his suspicions about most of the eligible women in both Hollow Creek and Missoula. *"Once I persuade Thad Evanson to marry me, I'll never have to work again at that ridiculous millinery. I'll have him build me a grand house, not like that pile of rubble he lives in now. I'll host tea parties and you all will be invited. I'll own every elegant dress ever seamed together, and nary a week will pass without the purchase of a new hat. I'll be the envy of every woman in Hollow Creek and Thad won't be the wiser of my intentions. Further, he'll not give another thought to Cleo or Dora."*

Thad wouldn't marry a woman who wanted only his money and the success he'd built with hard work, sweat, long hours, and much prayer.

That was why Thad avoided telling Emilie he was the successful owner of the Evanson Cattle Company. She would never know by the way he dressed or the way he presented himself that he was anything more than a common ranch hand.

Unless, and until, God led Thad to speak the truth.

But what about asking for her hand in courtship? Shouldn't you have told her the truth then? Thad brushed aside the quarrelsome thoughts.

Reverting his attention to the hymnal, Thad raised his voice and began to sing with the rest of the congregation one of his favorite hymns.

When I survey the wondrous cross
On which the Prince of glory died,
My richest gain I count but loss,
And pour contempt on all my pride.

Not only had God given Thad eternal life through the death of Jesus on the Cross, but God had also been there in the smaller, much more mundane events of his life.

Like not allowing Thad to marry someone like Miss Hillard or Catherine.

SUPPER AT Pete and Anne's home was always a treat. While a meager home in contrast to Thad's, and especially the neighboring Wheeler home, Anne managed to create a welcoming atmosphere that reminded Thad of his grandparents' home in Illinois.

Anne teased him that while women constantly gave him home-baked goods, he couldn't very well live on bread and apple pie. And Thad never turned down a homemade meal.

"How have the trips to Missoula been?" Pete asked after supper was served.

"Good."

"And Mrs. Crawford?"

Thad looked from Pete to Anne, knowing that, upon Thad's permission, Pete had told Anne about Thad meeting the lovely and mysterious Emilie.

"Reckon I have some news to share, but it must remain between the three of us for now."

Pete and Anne gave their word, and Thad continued. "I have asked Emilie Crawford for her hand in courtship."

Anne beamed. "That's wonderful. Congratulations."

"Yes, congratulations. So...when do we get to meet her?"

"Soon, I hope. Perhaps when things slow down here with my traveling and the cattle sales, we can all go to Missoula so you can meet her. She's a fine woman."

"We shall look forward to it," smiled Anne.

Emilie would like Anne. Pete too.

Thad couldn't wait to see the woman of his affections again.

"CARE TO join me in the barn?" Pete asked after supper. "Got some whittling I'd like to show you."

Thad followed Pete and took a seat in one of the two chairs opposite Pete's humble workbench. "I've taken to carving some toys for Little Petey for Christmas."

"Will you and Anne be traveling to Billings to see family for the holidays this year?"

"We aim to. Still several months away, but I figure it's never too early to start on Christmas gifts."

Thad chuckled. "A wiser man there never was."

"Now if only finding something for Anne could be this easy. I've been thinking of carving a duck for her. You know how she loves ducks."

"She'd like that."

Pete nodded and showed Thad the toy train set he was whittling for his grandson. "Think he'll like it?"

"He will. You've got some talent, Pete."

"Thanks. Say, I'd like to speak with you about something on my mind."

Thad leaned back in the chair and clasped his hands behind his head. Pete had become so much more than a hired hand over the years. He'd become a close friend, a confidant, and a mentor. "What's on your mind, Pete?"

"First of all, congratulations on courting Emilie, but have you told her who you really are and where you live?"

Thad shifted in his seat. "You know my reasons for keeping those things to myself. Especially with what happened with Catherine and Miss Hillard..."

Pete stroked his graying beard. "I'm hearing what you're saying, and I respect you. But Emilie ought to know the truth, especially since you two are courting."

"You're right, Pete, and I know it's prideful and displeasing to the Lord to lie. I just...I reckon I'm hesitant about how to go about it. She obviously has some money since she dresses well, but then so does Shauna Hillard."

"Displeasing as all get out to the Lord when we aren't truthful. Even when we think we have acceptable reasons for dishonesty."

"It's not that I've been completely dishonest. She knows I work on a ranch, and I do have a home in Missoula, and she knows all but my surname."

Pete's kind, but serious gaze caused Thad discomfort. "Seems like a trough-full of excuses. I respect you as an employer, as a friend, and most importantly as a brother in Christ. Consider my words, and I'll be praying for you for wisdom."

"Thank you, Pete. I've always appreciated your straightforward approach to matters of concern."

The conversation changed to the upcoming branding and the cattle sale in Missoula in the fall.

But Pete's admonition was never far from Thad's mind.

CHAPTER TWENTY-TWO

Watching the sunrise from her back porch, Emilie took in the view of the mountains. Never had she seen anything so magnificent. Such a contrast from the crowded city streets of New York. Her ranch edged its way toward the Bitterroot Mountains with gently sloping grasslands giving way to timber-covered valleys, which stretched toward spectacular mountain peaks. She closed her eyes and inhaled, allowing her lungs to draw a deep breath. Newt's uncle, who purchased and owned the ranch before his passing, had been a wise soul to invest in such a location.

What a peculiar circumstance that she should now own a ranch consisting of thousands of acres—a ranching empire of such magnitude, she at times could not believe it herself. Not that money had ever been a shortage for her, for she had always known wealth. But in the open country, symbolizing the freedom for which she'd always longed, the value of her estate meant all the more.

Before the recent weeks of coming to know the Lord more fully, Emilie might have considered such a benefit the mere circumstance of her husband's untimely death. But recognition of the Lord's favor struck her now as the only reason she should be blessed enough to own such a place.

The temperate breeze enhanced, rather than detracted, from her tranquil surroundings, and Emilie ensured her wide-brimmed hat remained firmly on her head, lest she prone herself to the freckles Mother so adamantly warned her about. She took in another deep breath, exhaled, and whispered a prayer of gratitude to the One she had come to know better in recent days. His Word now invited her each evening to delight in the love, truth, and wisdom found within its pages. He beckoned her to learn more about Him and the eternal life He promised through His Son. Emilie still had so much to learn, and someday she would accept Vera's offer to attend Grace Church in Hollow Creek with her and Morris.

Were it not for her foe, a careless neighbor with overbearing cattle roaming at their whim, Emilie's life would, in recent days, mirror perfection. At least the fence now appeared to be properly fixed.

"Emilie?"

She startled and flung her eyes open to see Vera standing a few feet from her. "Oh, hello, Vera."

"Sorry to interrupt you. May we speak for a moment?"

"Certainly."

Vera shuffled from side to side, her hands clasped behind her back.

"Vera, is everything quite all right?"

Her friend's eyes blinked rapidly beneath her spectacles. "Emilie..." She placed a hand on Emilie's arm.

"Yes?"

"The Lord has placed something on my heart I feel I really must speak with you about."

"Please continue."

Concern settled in Vera's eyes. "Emilie, you must tell Thad who you are. You two are now courting and lying is no way to begin a relationship, especially with the man you may someday marry. You must be honest and forthright with him."

Emilie bit her lip. A flurry of thoughts shuffled through her mind. What would Mother say about Emilie's housekeeper being allowed to speak so freely to her employer? Especially about such an intimate matter? What must *Vera* think of Emilie for telling untruths to Thad? What should Emilie do?

"Thank you, Vera, for your concern."

Vera's brows knitted together. "I wouldn't broach such a topic if I didn't believe it wasn't of the utmost of importance."

"I appreciate that, but you must understand why I haven't been able to discuss the truth with Thad."

"You are concerned he would only be after your wealth."

Emilie nodded. "I want someone to love me for me, not what he can gain from marrying me." The words pained her to say, and she recalled how an alliance for furthering the wealth of two prominent families was the reason for her marriage to Newt. She swallowed hard, knowing the man she dedicated her life to for a few short years never loved her. "I care about Thad and hope we have a future together, but…I will tell him when the time is right."

"I don't want you to be making a mistake." Vera paused. "The Lord makes it clear in His Word that lying is unacceptable. Besides, there have been many a time Morris and I have nearly disclosed more than we ought while visiting with Thad in Missoula. You know we won't lie, but in loyalty to you, we won't divulge your secrets."

"Of which I appreciate."

"Besides, Thad must not be destitute since he is able to purchase noonday meals for all four of us each time we eat at the Bellerose."

Emilie could not be irritated with her dear friend's concern, for she knew Vera cared about her in a way no other friend ever had. However, she could not take Vera's advice forthwith.

Over the next three weeks, Emilie and Thad saw each other each weekend without fail. They spent all day on Saturdays together and most of the Sundays as well. They ate at the restaurant, strolled around the city, attended church on Sunday, and delighted in the affection blossoming between them.

On this particular Sunday, as with each Sunday evening, Emilie didn't want her time with Thad to end. When had she cherished a man's company so much?

Suddenly, she felt guilty. Shouldn't she have fancied being in Newt's company?

Shouldn't Newt have taken pleasure in spending time with her?

But their marriage had only been one of convenience. The tying together of two wealthy families to secure a future generation. A generation who never had the chance to live.

Emilie dismissed the thoughts that rolled through her mind. Why ruin such a delightful day with dismal thoughts?

"We spoke of the botanical gardens some time ago. Would you care to join me for a visit to the Missoula Garden Park next Saturday? I hear the flowers are a sight to behold."

Emilie's heart skittered at Thad's invitation. She would never tire of spending time with him. If only he resided in Hollow Creek...

"I have always wanted to visit there, but haven't yet. I would love to."

Would Thad find it peculiar that she had never before seen the botanical garden even though she supposedly resided in Missoula?

"How does one o'clock sound? We could meet here for our noonday meal, then take the streetcar to the gardens."

"Delightful."

Thad offered her a lopsided smile and her heart nearly stopped.

And then her heart did stop when he planted a kiss on her waiting lips.

CHAPTER TWENTY-THREE

The week passed slowly and Thad found himself wishing time away, something he determined never to do, for life was precious. While he took great pride in usually having everything in his life under control, the days leading up to spending more time with Emilie wreaked havoc on his ability to focus on his work.

Did she feel the same way he did?

She had, after all, accepted his offer of courtship.

Guilt niggled at him then, for the hundredth time. Courtship most oftentimes led to marriage. Before he asked her to marry him, Thad would need to share with her his real last name, his real occupation, and who he really was.

Would Emilie forgive him for the untruths and understand his rationale?

What was the Lord's plan in all this?

Certainly not to be deceptive.

Pete's words echoed through his mind. *"Displeasing as all get out to the Lord when we aren't truthful. Even when we think we have acceptable reasons for dishonesty."*

Thad did his best to shove aside convictions of the ills of lying. He'd had a perfectly good reason to do so. He only prayed both the Lord and Emilie would understand.

Finally, Friday afternoon arrived. Ensuring that Pete, Floyd, and the rest of his ranch hands had everything under control, Thad walked to the barn that housed his Model T.

As he rounded the corner into the barn, Thad drew a deep breath at the site of his most prized mode of transportation. Oh, for Grandpa to have seen such a thing of splendor!

He would have been dazzled by the newest invention of transportation almost as much as Thad was.

Thad had taken some time to order an automobile, not sure he really needed it when he had a good horse. But enough time spent in Missoula told him that automobiles were the future. Even if most of the folks in Hollow Creek and the surrounding areas still drove wagons.

He stood beside his 1910 Model T touring car as he always did before an outing, admiring the paint finish and leaning in to run his hand across the diamond-tufted leather seat. Brand new off the factory line, Thad had paid the handsome sum of $950 for the fully-equipped beauty, not including the cost of delivery to Missoula. Not one to usually be so unconventional with his money, he almost hadn't purchased it.

However, now more than ever, Thad knew the investment in the Model T was a wise one. In the past, his trips to Missoula were more sporadic. But now that he was courting Emilie, Thad determined he would be spending every weekend in the foreseeable future in Missoula until winter came and the roads became impassable.

Thad would miss her something awful when that time came. He might have to just purchase a sleigh and continue to meet her for their noonday meals.

Donning his motoring duster coat, driving hat, and goggles, Thad cranked the starter, then climbed into the Model T.

His arms tingled with excitement as he started down the road. How fast could it safely go?

It was a question he asked himself each time he embarked on the open road.

Several miles and a few automobiles, buggies, and wagons later, Thad came up behind a slower-moving motorcar. Upon closer examination, it appeared very similar to the automobile he'd seen parked at that bothersome Mrs. Wheeler's house.

If it was, in fact, the Wheeler automobile, Thad figured one thing. He and Mrs. Wheeler must both be fond of motorcars, but that was where the similarities with the uppity woman ended. He couldn't tell who the three people were in the touring car, only that whoever was driving caused the motorcar to creep along at a painfully slow pace. If the occupants ever expected to reach their destination, they'd never reach it at that speed.

As he passed, Thad glanced over. *Well, I'll be.* Was that a child driving the automobile? There was no way he could tell with her thick goggles and hat. And what of the poor sleeping individual in the backseat, his hat-covered head lolling to one side?

The motorcar lurched forward at an increasing speed. *Ah, the thrill of a well-built machine!* The touring car accelerated with no problem and zoomed past the other motoring car, leaving it quite literally, in the dust.

It was not ten minutes later, as Thad tested the limits of his newfangled possession, that his Model T ran off the road and took a bumpy detour into a field.

Pride goeth before a fall... Hushing the words of truth that crowded his mind, Thad, with heart racing, maneuvered his way onto the road once again, but not before the automobile he'd recently passed at a great speed slowly crested the hill.

"Hopefully that wasn't the brash Mrs. Wheeler after all. She'd have one more thing to add to her list of not taking kindly to me," Thad muttered.

Thanking the Lord his own brashness hadn't caused him to wreck his new motorcar, Thad continued toward the city, his mind on a woman he was falling in love with named Emilie Crawford.

"WELL, GOODNESS gravy! Did you ever see such a cad?" Emilie asked as the other Model T passed them.

"Never in all my days," declared Vera, as she adjusted herself on the pillow Emilie had provided so she could see above the dashboard. Her petite stature had nearly made it impossible to drive, were it not for the plump patchwork pillow. "I'm quite content to just mosey along at a peaceful speed. Are you sure you'd like for me to continue motoring, Emilie? I wouldn't want to be the cause of ruin to your fancy automobile."

"Don't worry yourself, Vera. You take all the time you need to get us to the city. This is to be an adventure, remember? And besides, you've never driven a motoring car before. Enjoy yourself."

"Oh, that I am, Emilie, that I am."

"Well, the man who sold it to me said it was one of the best and most modern available today." Emilie recalled the day last year when she'd purchased the automobile. What would Mother say if she knew Emilie had made such an impulsive decision?

Emilie returned her attention once again to Vera. "I imagine you can't wait to tell your friends in the quilting circle of your adventure."

"They'll say I have the best boss in the entire world for certain."

Emilie laughed at Vera's comment. While Vera and her husband Morris were on her payroll, she thought of them as friends more than employees. Mother had mentioned when she and Father came to visit briefly after Newt's death that Emilie presented herself as far too comfortable and familiar with the hired staff. She had brushed Mother's comments aside. Why did hired help have to be treated as less than important, the way that Mother and Father had always treated their staff?

Yes, Emilie expected her help to work hard, but she rewarded them well. Those who exhibited laziness were quickly removed from her employ.

Morris, who was sitting in the backseat, shifted. "Everything going all right up there?" he asked, stifling a yawn.

Emilie laughed. "Poor Morris. Plop him in a motoring car and it lulls the man to sleep."

"We're fine, dear love," chuckled Vera.

"All right then," Morris answered, brushing his mustache with his gloved hands before nodding off again.

A wind gust propelled the automobile to the left-hand side, and Vera righted it. "Although, Morris, you did just miss seeing a boor of a man traveling at speeds far too fast for these roads." Vera paused. "Wait a moment, is that the very man of whom we speak?"

Emilie surveyed the road a short distance ahead, straining to see through her driving goggles. Sure enough, the other Model T was traveling slowly and bumpily over a field. "Where is he going?"

"I think perhaps he left the road in his haste to be a braggart."

The automobile continued over the bumpy terrain before making an abrupt re-entry onto the dirt road. "Well, goodness," said Emilie. "It's best we stay far away from him. Seems he's a danger to society. I'm shocked he is allowed to maneuver such a fine motorcar with his carelessness."

"Your mother would squawk like a festered chicken if she knew how close we were to such a cad," remarked Morris.

Emilie nodded. "Indeed she would."

"The Lord was watching out for us. For what would have happened if he had crashed into us? I suppose it's for the best

I'm not an expeditious driver." Vera gripped the steering wheel with more force until her wrinkled knuckles turned white.

Emilie nodded. While she didn't mind Vera's slow progress toward the city, she did mind the way time appeared to crawl at a pace slower than a turtle. To spend time again with Thad Alexander couldn't come quickly enough. And to attend the Missoula Garden Park with the man of whom she was growing ever more fond of?

A perfect dream about to become a reality.

CHAPTER TWENTY-FOUR

Thad and Emilie stood with Vera and Morris at the corner of Bobbin Street, eager to catch a ride on the streetcar to the Missoula Garden Park. When Emilie caught a glimpse of Thad walking down the boardwalk toward her, her heart forgot to beat for a moment.

What was it about this man?

His kindness, generosity, and upstanding character drew her to him. So had his love for the Lord, something Emilie was increasingly beginning to realize the importance of in her own life with each passing day.

Attempting to gather her wits about her, Emilie smiled as Thad reached for and kissed her hand, causing her heart to beat faster than it ought. "Hello, Emilie."

"Hello, Thad."

"I understand you're taking our Emilie to the Missoula Garden Park today. What a delight since she loves flowers and trees," chattered Vera.

Emilie blushed when Thad's eyes connected with hers. "Yes, well, I'm looking forward to this as well. I've never yet been."

"Neither have we," commented Morris. "It'll be a treat for us all, especially Emilie. But I must warn you that she may not wish to leave once we set foot on the grounds if it is as impressive as we've heard it to be."

Thad chuckled and Emilie relished the sound of his laugh. She'd only heard Newt laugh once and that was when Father had quipped a nonsensical joke about living in the Wild West.

Surely even then, Newt's laugh was more of a courtesy than anything else. No, Emilie had never been able to make the man she had married express more than a thin-lipped smile.

If only she could bottle Thad's laughter and listen to it over and over again once she returned home to Hollow Creek.

"We'll have to coerce her with some pie à la mode, I reckon," said Thad. "Perhaps then she'll be willing to leave the blooms behind."

"Never. Not even for all the pie à la mode in the world," Emilie teased back.

"Here comes the streetcar now." Morris gathered his and Vera's things and took a step back.

Emilie hoped Thad didn't wonder why a woman who "resided" in Missoula hadn't yet taken the opportunity to ride the streetcar. Did he suspect her dishonesty?

Guilt pricked her conscience. The more Emilie grew to care about Thad, the more the chicanery pressed on her heart and her mind.

If their courtship progressed to an engagement, she would have to present the truth.

How would Thad take to that truth?

More importantly, the more Emilie grew to know the Lord, the more she desired to please Him. Surely lying was displeasing to a holy God.

Vera's recent words wove through Emilie's mind: "*The Lord makes it clear in His Word that lying is not acceptable...*"

Emilie shoved the disturbing thought aside. She'd not ruin such a pleasant day deliberating the predicament in which she found herself.

Thad gently took her elbow and assisted her into the streetcar. "Would you like to sit by the window?"

"Most definitely!"

EMILIE'S ENTHUSIASM for riding the streetcar and attending the botanical gardens was contagious. Just as it had been when she drove Jonathan's automobile. Thad thought of the time driving in the Cadillac. Someday, he would have to take Emilie for a ride in his Model T.

Someday when Thad told her he owned an automobile.

He slid into the narrow wooden seat beside Emilie and across from Vera and Morris. He pretended to watch out the window, but his eyes never quite made it past Emilie's profile. Even with her silly hat, he had the perfect glimpse of her perfect face.

A face that lingered in his thoughts long after they met each weekend. At some point, after more prayer, he would ask her to marry him.

After he told her the truth about himself, of course.

But not today. Today, Thad would savor the time he spent with Emilie without any thought of the consequences his dishonesty might bring.

And to watch the pleasure on her face as she looked upon the expertly manicured hedges, trees, and flower gardens would be a sight to see. Thad heard there was nothing like the botanical gardens in all of the West.

Intently, yet discreetly, viewing Emilie's beauty, Thad didn't react quick enough when Emilie swiftly turned her head to point something out to him.

"Oh! Thad, are you all right?"

"Reckon that feather on your hat is a might bit dangerous."

"Thad, I am so sorry. I had no idea. I could have poked out your eye." She rested a delicate hand on his arm.

"I'm fine, Em. Just wasn't expecting it."

"I should say not. I truly am sorry." She leaned closer. "I see a scratch under your eyebrow. Shall we have it checked out by a doctor?"

"Mrs. Crawford, I assure you I am just fine. I'll not waste a moment of time at the doctor's office for a pint-sized scratch. You should see some of my scars from the ranch. This is nothing."

"Quite the truth, Mr. Alexander. I suppose it would be embarrassing for a grown man to show up on the steps of the doctor's office only to pronounce he'd been attacked by an ostrich plume."

Thad chuckled and drank in her smile. What would it be like to kiss her each and every day? In the morning, in the afternoon, and in the evening? To hold her in his arms? To plan a future with her?

He envisioned them sitting together on the porch of his Hollow Creek home, discussing their day.

Reckon you're getting far ahead of yourself, Evanson.

Emilie removed a handkerchief from her reticule and held it toward his eye, gently patting at the place where the ostrich plume had taken its vengeance. "Perhaps a dab at it...it's bleeding slightly."

Thad's heart stalled at her tender touch. "Thank you, Em."

"You're welcome. Are you sure you're all right?"

The concern in her eyes captivated him. Was she the one the Lord had chosen for him? He could only pray it was so.

THANK GOODNESS Mother wasn't here. What would she think of Emilie spending time with a man outside of her social standing? Not a banker, attorney, or businessman, but a ranch hand?

Mother would squawk like a festered chicken, as Morris would say.

And Father would have a fit within a minute.

For that reason, and that reason alone, Emilie had chosen to stay in Hollow Creek after Newt's death, rather than return to New York.

To be able to make her own choices from meager matters to more important affairs like courtship gave Emilie a sense of value. And it coincided well with her independent spirit.

Pathways extended everywhere from the entrance of the park. "This is breathtaking," she declared. In her many travels, she'd seen a wider variety of enchanting gardens, but never so green, plush, and unassuming as the oasis before her.

"I've never seen anything like it," Vera said. "Morris, shall we go over and see the pond with the ducks?"

Taking Vera's hint without so much as a second thought, Morris nodded. "Be obliged to take my lovely bride to see the pond."

Vera giggled like a young girl instead of a woman of all of sixty-five, and placed her arm through her husband's. "Shall we meet somewhere in an hour or so?"

"How about that gazebo?" Emilie pointed to an octagon-shaped enclosure a short distance ahead.

"Superb idea," said Vera giving Emilie a knowing glance, "but on second thought, why don't we make it instead for a couple hours from now?"

Vera and Morris started off in the direction of the pond, while Emilie and Thad wandered in the opposite direction. Emilie slipped her hand through the crook of his arm. "What a testament to God's creation. Thank you for bringing me here, Thad."

"From what I've have heard," said Thad, "this is just the beginning. It extends several acres and has a host of trees, flowers, and shrubs. It'll likely take us all day to complete our tour."

Pausing to grab a pamphlet from a man at a narrow stand not far from the gate, Emilie and Thad then continued on their way.

"The aspens are some of my favorite trees. We have several of those at..." Emilie stopped short. She'd almost mentioned the Wheeler Ranch. Such an admission would never do. Not when Thad suspected she lived in Missoula, in perhaps a dainty house. "At places I've seen," she corrected herself.

They stopped to thoroughly take in the view before them. Thad faced her then, the tender gaze in his eyes causing Emily to plumb forget all about nature. He brushed her lips gently with his and time stood still.

A moment later, they resumed moseying down the path. Chirping birds in a variety of sizes and colors nestled in the birch, aspen, and cottonwood trees. "The robins are one of my favorites. They stay around, it seems, all winter," Emilie said.

"They do seem a hardy sort. Did you have many gardens in New York City?"

To tell Thad of the lavish gardens surrounding the Crawford Estate would surely reveal the wealth of her parents. "Yes, I have seen some gardens in New York, but there is something about the West. Something that keeps me here."

"I know what you mean. I plan to make this my home forever." He paused and took her hands in his. "And Em, do you plan to live here for the remainder of your days?"

His question caught her off guard. Did he mean for her to answer his inquiry with regards to residing in Missoula, as that was where he believed she lived? "I...I..."

"In Missoula," he said, as if reading her mind.

How could Emilie answer that when she really resided in Hollow Creek? "Yes," she finally answered, hoping that would suffice.

His eyes held an expression she couldn't ascertain. "I like Missoula," he said.

So did Emilie. A little less than she liked Hollow Creek, but she could be happy living in either place, couldn't she? Could she leave the Wheeler Ranch behind and move to be with Thad in Missoula if he asked her to marry him?

Didn't courtship most often result in marriage?

In Thad's case, she hoped so, as he had stolen her heart.

But would he understand when Emilie told him the truth that she didn't already live in Missoula? That she had lied?

Emilie bit her lip. What if when she revealed her true identity, Thad decided to discontinue their courtship? For who would desire to marry a liar? It was no way to start a friendship, a courtship, and most definitely a marriage.

Lord, I'm new to praying, but I ask for you wisdom...

"Em?"

His voice interrupted her thoughts. "How about a walk to the stream?"

Emilie nodded, thankful for the reprieve of the thoughts that badgered her. She again placed her arm through his elbow, realizing how comfortable and natural it felt. What if they spent time together every day?

She was quickly realizing that there was nothing she would rather do than spend time with Thad.

In the distance, children's voices echoed throughout the air. "You look mighty lovely today, Emilie."

"Thank you." Had Newt ever told her she was lovely? Not that she could recall, although she had once overheard him speaking to a friend about it. What if she had met Thad before meeting Newt? Her life would have been so different. She would have been spared much loss. The loss of Newt and especially the loss of...

Why, Lord? I don't understand. While she had grown to know more about God, she was far from understanding His ways.

"Emilie, are you all right?"

"Yes, I'm fine." She would do her best not to allow such sad thoughts ruin an otherwise perfect day.

"Shall we continue?"

And so they did, arm in arm down the pathways, admiring God's handiwork.

CHAPTER TWENTY-FIVE

A young boy's words interrupted the otherwise quiet solitude, as Thad and Emilie later wandered through a flower garden. "I beg your pardon, young man?"

"I said, mister, can I interest you and the missus in a picture of yourselfs?"

"A picture? As in a photograph?"

"No, sir. This is more like one of them caricature drawings."

"A caricature?" The puny boy wore high-water britches and his hair was in need of a good cutting.

"Yeah. If you'll just take a seat on that there bench, I'll get to work straightaway and it'll only cost you a nickel."

Thad glanced at Emilie. "Shall we allow the young man to draw a picture of us?"

The boy's brown eyes darted from Thad to Emilie and he shifted from side to side. "I promise it'll be worth the money. I only do my best work."

"Are you from around here, lad?"

"Yes, sir. I work for the garden. You see, they hire me to draw folks."

Thad suspected the boy was lying from his shifty gestures. "So we will be hiring a professional artist, then?

"Yep, sure thing, mister. Po-fessional and all. Now, do we have a deal? I'll draw a picture of you and the missus, and you'll pay me a nickel."

Thad could have told him that Emilie wasn't his wife, but the innocent mistake was a compliment. What would it be like to marry someone like Emilie? Would such a refined woman ever consider him for a husband?

"Well, what's it gonna be, mister?"

"What do you think, Emilie?"

"I think it would be delightful. Then we'll have a way to remember this day."

"Yep, you sure will, ma'am. You'll remember it all right. Now you and the mister just look as ord-nary as you can." After they sat on the bench, the boy pulled out a tattered notebook and began drawing.

"I'll allow you to do this under one condition," said Thad.

"Sure, mister, whatever you say."

"Will you do two caricatures?"

"Two?"

From the joyful appearance on the boy's face, Thad thought he had suggested the lad eat nothing but ice cream every day for the next year. "Yes, two."

"Yep, I can do that. I can."

"And will they look the same?" Emilie asked.

"As same as I can make 'em."

The boy began drawing then, pausing every once in a while to view his work.

"What's your name, lad?"

"Please, mister, don't interrupt the artist when he's drawin.' Sides, my name is Stanley."

Stanley continued to draw. When he finished, he tore the paper from the notebook, causing a ragged edge. "Here's one of them, mister. That'll be a nickel and then I'll draw the other one."

Thad dug into his pocket and pulled out a nickel. Stanley glanced from side to side and behind him and did so once more before pocketing the nickel. The likeness between the real Emilie and Thad in the caricature was impressive.

"Sir, if you'll just put that aside for a minute, I'll draw the other one."

Thad set the picture on the seat beside him.

"Shall we smile for this one, Stanley?" Emilie asked.

"Whatever you'd like ma'am. Reckon your usual faces is fine."

A few minutes later, Stanley finished the second picture. "Here you go. That'll be another nickel."

Thad again dug into his pocket, only this time, he pulled out a dollar. "Here, Stanley, for doing such an outstanding job."

Emilie concurred. "Where did you learn to draw like this?"

"Reckon when God was givin' talents out, he gave me this one." Stanley shrugged. He looked again from side to side and all around the perimeter of the garden before pocketing the dollar. "Thanks for the extra money, mister. I best be goin' now. Unless you're wantin' for me to draw some birds or flowers or somethin.'"

A loud voice erupted from behind them. "Stanley Miller, you little ruffian!"

"Oops, gotta go. Have yourselfs a good day." With that, the scrawny boy with threadbare clothing escaped down the pathway.

And into the firm grasp of a tall man with a scowl.

The young Stanley did his best to escape from the clutches of the man. "There'll be no running away now, lad," the man told him. Stanley's short legs ran in stationery circles.

"Is there a problem here, sir?" Thad asked, as he and Emilie approached the man.

"There is. This young man has been doing his best to scam the visitors to our fine park for some time now. I have told him before and I will tell him again that this behavior is not tolerated."

"Stanley, if the man lets go of you, will you promise not to run?"

Stanley turned and looked from his captor to Thad and back again. "I reckon so."

"Good. Now, Stanley, why don't you go visit with Emilie a moment while I have a visit with this man. Emilie, would that be all right?"

"Certainly. Come along, Stanley. Let's have a look at the ducks on the lake."

Thad focused his attention on the man. "I'm Thad Ev... Alexander." Thad stole a quick glance toward Emilie, who had already walked a short distance away with Stanley.

"Chester Wilmers. I am the manager of this park."

"It's a pleasure to meet you, sir. I wanted to assure you that Stanley was not causing any problems. Actually, he is quite the artist." Thad produced the caricature Stanley had drawn. "He sketched this picture of Mrs. Crawford and me."

Mr. Wilmers narrowed his eyes. "I see. Might I ask why you are coming to the defense of the young Stanley?"

"I think he has a talent, Mr. Wilmers. He kindly drew our picture and didn't appear to be committing any crime. His clothes indicate he doesn't have much money."

"No, he doesn't have much of that, I am afraid. One of the women in my employ told me the lad lost his father two years ago and that Stanley's mother has been doing all she can to raise Stanley and his two younger siblings."

"Might we be able to help him out, Mr. Wilmers?"

"How do you mean?"

Thad thought for a moment. "Perhaps Stanley could set up a small easel and draw caricatures of interested folks as a memory of their time at the Missoula Garden Park. I know for Mrs. Crawford and me, this is a souvenir we'll be able to keep forever."

THAD IMPRESSED Emilie with his kindness toward Stanley. He had convinced Mr. Wilmers to allow Stanley to set up an easel and draw pictures of guests at the park at their request. She admired how he promised to purchase the items for Stanley to start his own little business. Under one condition, of course. That when school started up again, Stanley would focus on his studies and work at the park on Saturdays only.

Thad was a thoughtful and considerate man and was becoming more endearing to her the more time she spent with him. At times, their courtship seemed almost too good to be true.

With the exception of a few minor deceptions.

They wandered through the gardens for some time in comfortable silence until they took a seat on one of the benches to eat some candied apples from a nearby stand. "I'm enjoying my time with you, Emilie."

Emilie returned his smile. "I am too, Thad. Thank you for helping Stanley."

"Seems a shame his father died with Stanley being so young and all. I recall quite well what it's like to lose a father."

"I'm sorry about your parents, Thad."

"Not a day goes by when I'm not thankful for loving grandparents who took me in and raised me after my parents' death. I'm glad Stanley still has his mother."

Emilie nodded. "I don't understand why the Lord takes people from us—people we love." Never before had Emilie cared to spend time in God's Word as she had in recent weeks after that day at Pastor Shay's church. When winter arrived and she could no longer travel to Missoula, she would contemplate attending Grace Church in Hollow Creek. Wouldn't Vera and Morris be ecstatic over that decision?

Still, while she had grown in her faith, there were, nevertheless, many things Emilie didn't understand. Her baby son's death was one of those things.

"I don't know either. Some things aren't easy to understand." Thad paused for a moment, then continued. "Emilie, I'm sorry about your husband's passing."

"Thank you, Thad."

Newt.

Should she reveal to him her late husband's name? Or should she continue to refer to him as "my husband?" The closer she and Thad grew, the more likely it was that someday he would come to know Emilie's husband's name. Should that day be today?

But if Emilie did reveal Newt's name, Thad would know for certain of Emilie's abundant wealth. Was it too soon to trust his feelings for her? That those feelings would change if he knew she was wealthy?

She weighed the decision in her mind. On the one hand, if she and Thad were courting, oughtn't they be honest with each other? And if she were honest about Newt, then it would make it easier to be honest about where she lived and her name. The stress of hiding so many things and keeping up with the lies had taken a toll on her. Vera and Morris as well. For when would one of them accidentally slip? To acknowledge Newt's name could take the prior dishonesty in a new direction—a good direction.

On the other hand, how would Thad take the news? Newt had not been a popular man. He had a reputation, God rest his soul, for not treating his employees fairly and not offering fair prices for cattle. And for gouging the prices on his own cattle, depending on the buyer. He also rarely donated to charities, whether by volunteering or monetarily.

Would Thad still hold an affection for her based on Newt's business practices?

Emilie thought of how hard she had worked to improve the reputation and image of the Wheeler Ranch. She paid her employees well, purchased gifts for her hardworking staff on occasion, and had given them days off when requested. As far as the cattle buyers and sellers were concerned, Emilie had been sure Jep, Digby, Baxter and the rest of her ranch hands treated them with utmost respect and honest prices.

What should she do?

"Em?"

"Sorry, Thad. Please excuse my absent-mindedness."

Thad cleared his throat and took her hand in his. "Emilie, I realize you miss your husband. Was I wrong in asking to court you? Has it been too soon after your husband's death?"

It had been just over a year since Newt's passing. Emilie wasn't sure what the etiquette books might say about the mourning period, as she had never before been in such a situation. Did the etiquette change if your husband hadn't truly loved you? If you hadn't truly loved your husband?

Guilt assaulted her at the thought.

Whether she missed Newt or not, it was horrible he had passed on at a young age.

One thing was certain, Emilie didn't want to miss out on a future with Thad. She stared into his blue eyes, the eyes that reminded her of the ocean. "I think it is acceptable for us to court, Thad."

He blew out a deep breath. Glancing both ways, presumably to see if they were alone, Thad then placed a quick kiss on her waiting lips.

Ah, to have those kisses all the time.

They sat in comfortable silence for a few minutes. She wrestled with the thoughts and emotions filling her mind. Should she tell Thad about her baby? As if in answer to her dilemma, he reached for her hand and held it. His warm touch gave her comfort and courage.

"Thad, I also grieved the loss of a baby."

"I am so sorry. I had no idea."

Tears threatened. "I don't understand why the Lord took him from me. He was so tiny and so precious when he died.

Not nearly big enough to survive in the world yet. I never even got to hold him, not even once."

Thad's hand tightened over hers and he faced her. "Emilie, I don't know what to say."

"My husband didn't even know I was going to have a baby. He wasn't around much." She didn't add that he never paid much attention to her when he was around. "The only ones who knew were the doctor and Vera. I didn't tell my parents either. And, while I never really knew much about God before my son died, I did know one thing afterwards—that He wasn't anyone I wanted to worship."

"I'm sorry about your son, Emilie. I can't imagine losing a child."

Forceful sobs shook her body then. Guilt followed as Emilie wondered if she should have shared something so intimate with Thad. Guilt at expressing her true pain.

Guilt at forsaking the Lord.

Thad reached for her, and she leaned into his waiting arms. His chin rested softly on her head, and she reveled in the tenderness of his embrace.

He allowed her to cry as long as she needed, his hand gently stroking her back.

"I don't understand God's ways either sometimes, Em," he murmured.

While confiding in Thad would not bring back the baby she lost, sharing with him had made her burden lighter.

THAD HELD Emilie in his arms. Emotion choked him at what she had disclosed. To lose a child and a husband? No wonder she had distanced herself from the Lord. Thad had heard in a sermon once that in tough times, folks either draw closer to Him or distance themselves from Him. Emilie had chosen the latter.

He had lost his parents and his grandparents. Both losses had been tough. Thad knew firsthand about grief.

Emilie's choking sobs tugged at his heart and compassion filled him. He pulled her closer and held her. He cared for this woman and was beginning to love her. Thad would hold her for the next several hours if that was what she needed from him. He wanted to be there for her. Wanted to share her pain, sadness, and grief. And on better days, Thad desired to share her happiness, excitement, and joy.

As Thad sat there holding the woman he was growing to love, a thought occurred to him.

Emilie Crawford was indeed the one with whom he wanted to spend the rest of his life.

CHAPTER TWENTY-SIX

Thad loaded the first bags of feed into the back of the wagon. He could have sent Pete, Floyd, or any one of his other ranch hands, but had decided instead to make the trip to town himself. Last time he sent Floyd to retrieve feed, he arrived back at the ranch with half of it spilling out of the bags.

He'd had to get harsh with Floyd in recent days. Thad tried to be patient and assist him in his recovery from his addiction to the bottle, but his patience was wearing thin. Besides the poorly-fixed fence between the Evanson and Wheeler properties, Floyd had also forgotten to do other simple chores. Even so, Thad had done all he could to give his employee another chance and show to him the same grace the Lord was forever showing Thad.

But he had given Floyd an ultimatum.

One month to improve his work ethic, including no whiskey while on the job, or he would need to search for other employment.

Thad hopped down from the back of the wagon where he had arranged the feed bags just so. As he headed back to the livery stable, he noticed someone familiar walking in the opposite direction.

Could it be? "Vera?"

"Thad?" The woman scrutinized him, probably to be sure it was really him. After a moment of assessing him, she squealed, "How delightful to see you." She balanced a crate in her arms.

"You as well, Vera. Can I assist you with that crate?"

"That would be most appreciated. Thank you. Our wagon is just up ahead."

Thad took the crate from Vera and followed her. He placed the items carefully in the back of the wagon.

"Are you visiting Hollow Creek, Thad? Emilie will be so disappointed she missed you. While she did contemplate coming to town with me today, she decided against it at the last minute. You know how she is with her flowers." Vera's speech accelerated, as she shook her head and rolled her eyes. "Seems the growing season in Montana just isn't long enough. And what with the fall weather settling in, Emilie wanted to cut some blooms for the vases before the flowers all died away from the first freeze." She paused and blinked rapidly. "Listen to me, babbling on so."

"Emilie? Emilie Crawford, the woman you and Morris accompany when we meet for noonday meals at the Bellerose Restaurant in Missoula?"

Vera arched a brow. "Thad, you know good and well of which Emilie I speak," she teased. "The Emilie of whom you have grown quite fond." She gently ribbed him in the side.

Thad knew his face must be redder than the overly-ripe tomatoes Pete's wife, Anne, had delivered to his house yesterday. Yes, he had grown quite fond of Emilie Crawford. Figured he might just love her in fact. "Yes. I know which Emilie," he murmured.

Vera's eyes darted beyond him. "So tell me, Thad, do you visit Hollow Creek often?"

"Uh..." how could he explain that he didn't *visit* Hollow Creek, but that he *lived* there? Thad shifted. The lies he had so carefully told to protect who he really was were coming unraveled. Lies he never should have told. He wanted to kick himself for his foolishness. What would Vera, and more importantly, Emilie, think when they learned the truth?

"Well, I best be going. The better part of the day is getting away from me. I still must visit the millinery. Pleasure to see you, Thad," her words remained rushed and her countenance skittish. He'd never seen Vera be anything but calm and unruffled.

"You too, Vera." Thad resisted the urge to wipe the perspiration from his brow.

Perspiration not so much from the heat of the day, but more from the untruths he'd hidden so well these past months. Vera rushed away, peering over her shoulder twice at him before disappearing into the millinery.

A tall, skinny young man with wayward orange hair threw a sack of flour in the back of the same wagon Thad placed Vera's crate. He squinted at Thad and took a big step forward on lanky legs. "Say, sir, you look familiar. Do I know you?"

"Name's Thad."

The man extended his hand. "Nice to meet you." He paused and scratched his head. "I'm Jep. You sure do look familiar. Have I seen you somewhere before?"

"Maybe here and there." Thad's mind was still on Vera and the fact she was in Hollow Creek. Did Emilie travel from Missoula to visit the town?

Jep chuckled. "That's a good one. Reckon I'll have to remember that. I'm from here and there too, 'cept mostly from here."

Another man approached them. "Say, have you seen Vera? I forgot to tell her Mrs. Wheeler will be wantin' us to pick up some coffee beans."

"She done went yonder to the millinery," said Jep. "When she's done lookin' at the fineries there, I can tell her."

"Thanks, Jep." The man faced Thad. "Say, I'm Digby."

"Thad."

They shook hands and the man turned his attention to Jep. "I need to stop over at the barber shop before we head back."

"Take your time. Reckon Vera'll likely be at the millinery for the better part of the hour."

Digby chuckled and retreated to the barber shop at the other end of the boardwalk.

Thad pondered the coincidence, only he didn't believe in coincidences. What were the odds that Vera would be in Hollow Creek discussing the retrieval of items for Mrs. Wheeler? And why would she be here with Jep and the other man? Where was Morris? Why was Vera here purchasing items in Hollow Creek rather than Missoula where she lived? And what was her connection to Mrs. Wheeler?

"Jep, your friend there mentioned a woman named Mrs. Wheeler. How is that you and Vera know her?"

Jep stroked a non-existent beard. "We work at the Wheeler Ranch." A proud smile lit his face. "I'm one of her ranch hands."

"Vera works at the Wheeler Ranch too?"

"Sure thing. Vera, Digby, and myself."

"Do you know Vera's husband, Morris?"

The young man nodded. "Sure as rain, I do. Morris is Vera's husband."

"And does he work at the Wheeler Ranch?"

"Sure does."

The entire conversation perplexed Thad. Vera and Morris must travel to Missoula often from their employ with Mrs. Wheeler to visit Emilie. A considerable distance for ranch employees. Confusing, but not unheard of. "You all work for Mrs. Wheeler, as in Newt Wheeler's wife?"

"One and the same. But Mr. Wheeler, God rest his soul, passed on 'bout a year ago. Do you know Mrs. Wheeler?"

"Can't say as I've ever met her." If there was a connection between Vera, Morris, and Mrs. Wheeler, could there be a connection between Emilie and Mrs. Wheeler as well? Surely she knew the woman her friends worked for. "Do you know a woman named Emilie?"

"Yes, I know an Emilie Wheeler. She's the owner of the Wheeler Ranch."

There was an Emilie Crawford and an Emilie Wheeler and they both knew Vera and Morris?

Could it be they were one and the same?

No. Couldn't be.

A crazier idea there'd never been. Thad attempted to remove the notion from his mind, but the confusion wouldn't relent.

His neighbor, Mrs. Wheeler, was an older woman, with a cantankerous disposition like her late husband's. Right? Emilie Crawford was a wonderful woman who had captured his heart. The thought of the woman Thad fancied for the past few months sent a jolt through him. He missed her and couldn't wait to see her again. He returned his thoughts to the conversation at hand. "I thought Mrs. Wheeler's first name was Almira."

"Oh, that's her given name, or at least that's what Hattie told me. She goes by Emilie. Hattie says the name 'Almira' is too stuffy or somethin' or other like that."

"There's no way it's the same woman," he muttered more to himself than to Jep.

Thad found himself nearly speechless, but full of questions. Did Emilie ever visit Hollow Creek? If so, they could easily meet here instead of Missoula. Were she and Mrs. Wheeler good friends? Did Emilie have relatives here?

"Say, I'm thinkin' I know why you are familiar. Don't you work for Mr. Evanson?"

"I am Mr. Evanson." He blurted the words he'd attempted to conceal before he could give it a second thought.

"You are Mr. Evanson?" Jep's eyes grew round. "Well, don't that beat all? You're Mrs. Wheeler's neighbor. She almost came to town today, but traveling to Missoula always tuckers her out."

Jep's words further befuddled Thad. "Does she travel to Missoula often?"

"She does."

"Does she visit Emilie Crawford?"

Jep scratched his head. "Don't rightly know who Emilie Crawford is." He paused. "Mrs. Wheeler takes Vera and Morris with her most times to Missoula. She told us about a place she visited with all kinds of flowers and such. Mrs. Wheeler loves flowers."

An uncomfortable fuzziness clouded Thad's mind. The Emilie of whom Jep spoke sounded very much like the same Emilie he had grown fond of in recent months.

He had to find out for sure.

For there was no way *his* Emilie—Emilie Crawford—could be one and the same as Almira Wheeler.

CHAPTER TWENTY-SEVEN

Emilie fluttered about her gardens, taking in the remnants of the last days of warm sunshine. The extended summer had certainly been nice, but it wouldn't be long before the first frost. Oh, how she wished the peaceful and perfect summers in Montana lasted longer. The winters were frigid, harsh, and confining. She didn't look forward to them.

The blooms of her flowers lent their faces toward her. Best she cut some of her favorites now to enjoy before the frost got to them. Leaning down, she snipped some of the stems and blossoms of the treasured black-eyed Susans that had survived the Evanson Ranch cow stampede. She placed the flowers into her bag and moved on to the daisies.

That's when she saw someone standing near the fence between her ranch and the Evanson Ranch property line. At second glance, Emilie recognized the contemptible Mr. Evanson.

"Hello, Mr. Evanson," she said between gritted teeth. Leave it to that loathsome man to ruin the day.

Mr. Evanson smirked and placed a hand on the fence post beside him. "Hello, Mrs. Wheeler," he said in almost a sneer.

"What do you need, Mr. Evanson?" *Lord, please forgive me for my lack of patience. I also ask for forgiveness in advance for any rudeness that comes from my mouth in this conversation with this difficult man.*

She thought of Pastor Shay's words about how one was not perfect the second they gave their life to Christ. Such things took time, and even then, no one was perfect this side of heaven.

Emilie returned her thoughts to Mr. Evanson, awaiting his answer.

"Just checkin' to see if the new fence we put in is workin' to keep the cattle from your...flowers."

Mr. Evanson appeared to be mocking her, which irritated Emilie to no end. "It is working so far, thank you."

"Good."

Emilie inhaled at the wrong time. She wrinkled her nose. When had Mr. Evanson last had a bath? The mingled odors of sweat, cigar smoke, and liquor permeated the air. Wetness covered the front of his shirt in the shape of a "u." For a man so well thought of in the community, he certainly possessed neither good manners nor good hygiene.

"Was that all you needed, Mr. Evanson?"

"With all yer complainin' I figured I better make sure you ain't gonna go runnin' to the sheriff again and tattle because of your little plants."

Her little plants? Did the man have no concern for anyone but himself?

And to think she might have personally thanked Mr. Evanson for the flower delivery. "As long as you be neighborly and keep your fence fixed, we shall have no problems, Mr. Evanson."

He shook his head. "Oh, and one more thing ya's ought to know..."

"Yes?" Goodness but the man had poor grammar!

"I ain't Mr. Evanson, though I wish I was."

"Begging your pardon?"

"Like I said, I ain't Mr. Evanson."

"What do you mean?"

"Reckon you think I am Mr. Evanson, right?"

"Yes. That is what you have led me to believe."

"Ain't no such thing, Mrs. Wheeler. I ain't never told you nothin' of a sort. You just went along and planted the idea in that head of yours." He stuffed his fingers beneath the straps of his suspenders. "Get it, *planted*? Since this is all about plants?" He laughed an obnoxious laugh that made his already-large nostrils flare above an ungroomed mustache.

"I imagine that I presumed."

Was he lying to her?

"Yep, you did."

"Then if you aren't Mr. Evanson, who are you?"

"Name's Floyd. Floyd Marsh."

"Do you work for Mr. Evanson?"

"Yep. I'm his best ranch hand."

If Floyd Marsh was Mr. Evanson's best ranch hand, Mr. Evanson might ought to hire better employees. "Well, thank you for clearing that up, Mr. Marsh." Emilie did her best to rein in her sarcasm.

"So you can go on and blame someone else next time you have trouble with cattle. Ain't my fault at all. Even though I reckon I got an earful about it."

"I take it Mr. Evanson knows about the situation?" What if she had jumped to a conclusion and had told the sheriff before even ensuring the real Mr. Evanson knew about the broken fence?

"That he does. He thinks you're puttin' up a fuss for nothin'."

"Oh, he does, does he? I best go now, Mr. Marsh. Good day."

All this time, she believed Floyd Marsh was Mr. Evanson. Who was the *real* Mr. Evanson?

THAD PUZZLED about meeting Vera and Jep all the way home. He should have been more persistent in asking Emilie where she lived. Of course, if he had, she likely wouldn't have been upfront with her answer. She had been so reticent about her home.

He was all but engaged to her, yet didn't know where she lived.

Just why was it Emilie had insisted that he deliver she, Vera, and Morris to the Bellerose Hotel and Restaurant time after time?

What had she been hiding?

Emilie doesn't know where you live either.

He pushed aside the nagging thoughts.

Minutes later as he rounded the corner to the road leading to his ranch, Thad spied someone in the field at the Wheeler house.

Not just someone, but a familiar figure.

She stood bent slightly over some flowers. While her face was hidden by a sizeable hat and her back was to him, Thad knew it had to be her and none other.

Emilie.

Thad's heart galloped faster than his horse had in a horse race he won years ago.

Emilie.

The woman he loved. The woman he wanted for his wife.

He suddenly forgot all his other obligations for the day. Reluctantly, Thad pulled on the reigns, urging the horses to stop.

Emilie continued to tend to her flowers. The sight of her both took his breath away and placed consternation in his heart. Questions bombarded him, even as the apparent truth rose to the surface.

But why was she at the Wheeler Ranch?

Was she friends with Mrs. Wheeler?

Or...Simultaneously, the muscles in his neck tightened and his pulse increased several notches.

Hadn't Vera mentioned that Emilie chose to stay behind and not come to Hollow Creek? Had Emilie changed her mind at the last minute? How long was she in town before heading back to Missoula?

A troubling thought again emerged in his mind. If Emilie Crawford and Almira Wheeler were one and the same, why had she lied?

Why had he not noticed before that his neighbor was the woman he cared about?

He watched as Emilie moved from flower to flower. She appeared to linger periodically, perhaps to inhale the scent of the blooms, and he recalled the joy she received from partaking in their visit to the botanical gardens last week.

She exhibited elegance and gracefulness, as she tended to the gardening, and Thad could see strands of her blonde hair escaping from her enormous hat and resting on her shoulders.

She was so close he would need only to walk a short distance to be in her presence.

But his feet refused to carry him farther than the confines of his location on the buckboard.

Warring notions assailed him.

Thad blew out a breath. Should he continue on his way? Stop and ask her the million questions assaulting his mind? Pretend he never met Vera and Jep in Hollow Creek today?

Emilie looked in his direction. She placed a hand above her eyes, as if to shield the sun.

With a lethargic movement, he raised a hand to wave.

Awaited her response.

With some hesitance, she returned his wave. Had she recognized him? He slowly climbed from his place in the wagon. "Lord, reckon I could use some help." Even his beseeching of the Almighty's assistance came in ragged and muttered breaths.

More questions crowded his mind, as his feet defied him and began to walk toward her. Thoughts warred within him. Embrace her, as he so often did, or demand to know the truth? Perhaps there was a reasonable explanation for her untruths.

Lie not to one another, seeing that ye have put off the old man with his deeds...

Thad attempted to brush aside the verse from Colossians.

Wherefore putting away lying, speak every man truth with his neighbor...

Thad sighed. "I know lying is wrong. I have been dishonest as well."

He paused to scan the blue sky above and offer a pleading prayer. "Lord, I'm not sure what's happening here. Please don't let her be Mrs. Wheeler."

CHAPTER TWENTY-EIGHT

Did her eyes deceive her? The man who stopped in front of her property looked so much like Thad.

The broad shoulders, long legs, and confident demeanor gave proof that it was, indeed, him.

Emilie's heart stopped.

He waved and she stared, then was finally able to force her astonished self to raise a hand and return the wave. It was clear he recognized her.

What was Thad doing in Hollow Creek?

What would he think about Emilie when he discovered she lived here? As a godly man, Thad no doubt expected others to be forthright.

I live not far from Missoula.

Hollow Creek would stretch that statement by a comfortable bit and then some.

Could Emilie lie again and tell him she was visiting Mrs. Wheeler?

Thou shalt not lie.

Emilie brushed the admonition she'd read in the Bible aside. *Surely, Lord, You understand my predicament. I can't just tell Thad who I really am, not yet.*

But why the hesitation? From what she knew of Thad, he wasn't the kind of man who would superficially only love her for her wealth.

Yet, at some point, Emilie would have to admit the truth. After a lengthy courtship, it was only proper for a man to ask for a woman's hand in marriage.

Unless they broke off the courtship.

Emilie shuddered at that thought of losing him. She was falling in love with Thad and entertained the thought of someday spending the rest of her life with him.

But you won't be spending one more day of your life with him if you continue to base it on a lie, she chastised herself.

Lying was wrong. Even Emilie, new in her faith though she was, knew that to be true.

Lord, I beseech thee to assist me in this predicament...

But did the Lord assist those who had broken His commandments?

If only they were in Missoula right now, about to dine at the restaurant, or perhaps attend an event.

Emilie's stomach roiled and nausea overcame her.

For her lie was about to be revealed.

THAD CONTINUED toward her on heavy legs. What would he say when he came face to face with her? Should he ask if she was staying with Mrs. Wheeler? If she was only visiting Hollow Creek for the day? If she *was* Mrs. Wheeler?

He longed to take her into his arms and plant a kiss on those full lips of hers.

And yet...

There was no smile from her, only a somber expression that likely mirrored his own.

"Hello, Thad."

"Hello, Emilie."

Never in their time of knowing each other had they been at a loss for words. He struggled for the questions he desired to ask of her, but the words hid, stuck in his throat.

"I just saw Vera in town. She mentioned you gave thought to visiting Hollow Creek, but that you were sidetracked by flowers. That sounds like the Emilie I know."

"Thad, what are you doing in Hollow Creek?" Her voice, as well as her demeanor, appeared troubled.

Thad cleared his throat. "I, uh..."

"Are you here for a visit?"

"Emilie, I need to tell you something."

Where did he begin?

JUST WHY was Thad in Hollow Creek? And what had Vera mentioned to him in town? Would Vera have betrayed her confidence and told Thad that Emilie, in fact, resided here and not in Missoula? And that she was Emilie Crawford Wheeler, rather than merely Emilie Crawford?

"What is it, Thad?"

"First, I'd like to know how long you're in Hollow Creek visiting."

Emilie swallowed hard and sought the Lord's assistance. But did He assist with such a grievous error? "I...Thad..."

"Yes?"

"I live here."

"Here at this house or here in Hollow Creek?"

His usually brilliant blue eyes took on a stormy gaze. Why would her living in this house be so dreadful to him?

"Thad, please understand..."

"Understand what, Emilie?"

Emilie tossed a glance at her surroundings. The day had been so perfect when she awoke this morning. And then Mr. Evanson, or rather, Mr. Marsh, decided to pay her a visit. And now Thad was here demanding to know the truth.

A promising day turned unfavorable in a matter of hours.

If Thad loved her—truly loved her, he would understand the reasons behind her deceit.

Right?

"Emilie?"

"Thad, you need to know something."

"Yes?"

Thad appeared impatient, something she had never seen him express before, unless she counted the time he awaited Eugene Ely's flight.

That type of impatience was far from the agitated persona Thad now exhibited.

"I live here. In Hollow Creek."

"But you said you lived in Missoula."

"If I recall correctly, I mentioned I live *not far* from Missoula."

"Hollow Creek could hardly be considered adjacent to Missoula, Em."

Not so many days ago, Emilie had loved it when Thad used the nickname only he used for her. Now, with a sharper edge to his voice, the nickname lacked its charm.

"Are you visiting Mrs. Wheeler?" Thad asked.

"Thad..."

"Is she a friend of yours?" He narrowed his eyes. Did he have something against Mrs. Wheeler?

"Thad, I *am* Mrs. Wheeler."

"You are Mrs. Wheeler? Mrs. Almira Wheeler? The wife of Newton Wheeler?"

"Yes, one and the same."

There was a tightness in his eyes and, if Emilie was not mistaken, the vein in his forehead appeared more prominent. He did have a right to be upset, she supposed, but yet, she had never seen him like this. "I suspected as much from my conversation with your ranch hand, Jep, in town," he said.

An awkward silence between them filled the air. There was much she wanted to say—needed to say—but the words wouldn't come.

CHAPTER TWENTY-NINE

Thad surmised Emilie was Almira Wheeler, but hearing it from her own lips shook him. Why had she said her name was Emilie Crawford? And how had she convinced her hired help to lie for her as well? He turned his attention to his home in the distance. The houses really weren't far from each other. How had he not ever known who his neighbor was? *Because you spent so much time in Missoula that's how. And because you never took the time to introduce yourself or to even pay your respects when her husband passed.*

He had been selfish.

Emilie. *His* Emilie was married to Newton Wheeler.

Newton Wheeler who had accused him of cattle rustling.

Imagine that.

He gritted his teeth. Why had she lied to him?

"I was led to believe you lived in Missoula, Emilie. But here I find out you not only live in Hollow Creek, but that you are my neighbor." His heart raced and his temper flared. Had he ever been this angry? This disappointed? This hurt? Normally he wasn't prone to temper, was actually a calm man, in fact, but something about this entire situation frustrated Thad like nothing ever had.

"I'm your neighbor?"

"Yes. I live right over there." He jabbed a finger in the direction of his house.

Emilie placed her hands on her hips. "You told me you lived in Missoula," she accused.

"I do have a house in Missoula as well."

"But you failed to inform me that you also have a home here, and I discover you are my neighbor. A difficult neighbor at that." She narrowed her eyes and held her chin high.

"Come now, Emilie, you haven't been the easiest neighbor either."

She ignored his unkind remark, and he chastised himself for it.

Moments passed in silence, but it felt like hours. Emilie spoke again. "All this time, I believed you to be a ranch hand living in Missoula, not my neighbor. You made mention your name was Thad Alexander."

"Alexander is my middle name. And what of you, Emilie Crawford? What happened to Almira Wheeler?"

"Alexander is your middle name? Why not include your last name?"

"At least Thad Alexander *is* part of my name."

"Emilie Crawford is part of my name as well. My full name is Almira Emilie Crawford Wheeler." She paused. "My parents named me Almira after a relative. I've never been fond of the name, so instead, I go by Emilie."

Thad softened his posture for a minute. Maybe this was all a misunderstanding that could be resolved.

But he shoved those thoughts aside. "Why did..."

"How come..."

Their voices chorused in accusation. Thad gestured at her to go first, then folded his arms across his chest.

"How come you told me you lived in Missoula and declined to give me your full name?"

"And why did you tell me the same, Emilie?"

Thad heard footsteps as Jep approached them. "Hi there, Mr. Evanson. Reckon I heard some commotion just now. Mrs. Wheeler, are you all right?"

"I am, Jep. Thank you for inquiring."

Jep nodded, seemingly grateful he wouldn't have to intervene in the heated argument. "All right, then, Mrs. Wheeler. I'll just go about my own business then. Please holler if you need anything."

"I will, thank you, Jep."

The ranch hand nodded and retreated back the way he came.

Thad watched him go and wished again that he'd never met Vera and Jep in town.

"So you are telling me that you are Thad Evanson, my neighbor, and the owner of the Evanson Cattle Company?"

"One and the same."

Her pained expression tugged at him. "Just an hour or so ago, as I am cutting blooms in my garden, I discover one of your ranch hands on my property. One whom I thought was you all this time. Floyd Marsh—I believe is his name? Or is that a lie as well?" Her voice took on an edge, and she didn't give him time to interrupt. "After Mr. Marsh tells me that he is not you, which I had presumed him to be you since the very beginning, he proceeds to tell me who he is. And then he tells me that you think I'm—I believe his exact words were you think I'm 'puttin' up a fuss about my flowers for nothin'." Her amber eyes flashed with hurt and anger.

Thad shifted from one foot to another. He recalled when he had said those words. Long before this day, and long before he knew her true identity. "And, Emilie, what did you do? You threatened to turn me into the sheriff all because of a broken fence. Not to mention the difficulties I had with your husband."

"Leave Newt out of this. He has no bearing on any of this mess. Because you refused to properly fix the broken fence, I lost many of my best flowers and vegetables. You would think a kindly neighbor— a gentleman—would repair the fence on the first request."

"I will leave Newton out of this, except to say one thing. Your husband accused my men and me of cattle rustling. That was a charge I don't take lightly. I have an exemplary reputation, one that your late husband nearly destroyed. It took some time to clear our names. When it was discovered who truly rustled the cattle, there was never an apology or another word spoken from your husband. I'll say no more about Newton now that I've made my point."

Emilie made a huffing sound. "You haven't exactly been a good neighbor."

Thad saw someone peek through the window of Emilie's house. Vera perhaps? Emilie was fortunate to have so many care about her. "Tell me, Em, why did you lie?"

"Because of men like you who try to take advantage of wealthy widows."

"Men like me? I am wealthy in my own right. I don't need to take advantage of wealthy widows to secure more funds. God has richly blessed me. I just secured a sizeable spread that spans nearly all the way to Missoula. The Evanson Cattle Company is one of the largest ranches in Montana."

"Why did you lie about who you were?"

Thad tilted his head back and let out a sorrowful chuckle. "Ironically, for much the same reason you did. Because of women who try to marry a man for his money."

"And you believe I was trying to do that?" She glared at him.

"How could I know the *real* you, Emilie? Apparently, the woman I thought I knew wasn't who you really are."

"Thad, I am so disappointed. I thought we cared for each other, that we..."

"I thought we cared for each other as well. I actually loved you."

At his stern declaration, he saw tears in her eyes. Why were they fighting like this? Hadn't he truly loved her? Hadn't they loved each other? Hadn't he wanted to someday make her his wife after a reasonable amount of time for courtship?

Warring thoughts packed his mind, each vying for the win.

"I think we should break off the courtship." The words leapt from his mouth far harsher than he intended and so opposite from what he had wanted to say.

The pain in her eyes at his comment broke Thad's heart. He should take her into his arms and work through their differences. He should put all this behind them. Remember the love between them.

But Thad didn't take her into his arms. Nor did he, at this time, desire to work out these differences.

For something known as pride clouded his vision.

She sniffed, but composed herself. "If that's what you want, Thad."

"That's what I want."

"Goodbye, Thad."

"Goodbye, Emilie," he ground out.

He turned on his heel and stomped away. Climbing into the wagon, he beckoned the horses down the road, traveling far faster than he ought.

But on the way from Emilie's ranch to his, something happened.

Shrouded with guilt and disappointment in himself, Thad felt his heart break.

CHAPTER THIRTY

Emilie wasn't sure how long she stood there after Thad left. Her mind reeled, as she attempted to process all she had discovered.

Thad Alexander, her beau, was really Thad Evanson, her neighbor.

The neighbor she strongly disliked.

The neighbor who strongly disliked her.

How could she love the man, but also dislike him?

Pain so deep it made Emilie feel as though she may lose what she ate for the noonday meal descended upon her. Thad was not the man she thought him to be. Not in name, and not in character. She had never seen him so angry. Yes, she had lied to him, but he had also lied to her.

Contrasting thoughts and emotions filled her mind.

Why hadn't she made some attempt to reconcile with him?

Why hadn't she seen the truth?

Then she recalled his harsh words and his desire to sever their courtship. Had Thad ever really cared about her?

Emilie finally forced herself to put one foot in front of the other, then slowly turned and faced Thad's house. Never in all her years would she have imagined that to be the home of the man she had grown to love.

A façade.

The tears flowed, as though a river overburdened with water after a hasty snow melt in the spring. She fought to catch her breath. Would all of this have happened if she hadn't lied to him?

If Thad had been the only one who had been deceitful?

*Lord, please...*the words of her distress didn't come. Hadn't Vera once said something about an Intercessor? Emilie searched her mind for those words. Yes. It was a verse in Romans: *"Likewise the Spirit also helpeth our infirmities: for we know not what we should pray for as we ought: but the Spirit itself maketh intercession for us with groanings which cannot be uttered"*. Emilie squeezed her eyes shut. *Please intercede for me. I know not the words to pray.*

She stumbled into the house and into Vera's waiting arms. Through sobs, Emilie told Vera of the error she had made, bracing herself for her friend's rebuke about how wrong dishonesty was. After all, Vera had previously warned Emilie about the ills of lying.

But Vera said nothing, only held Emilie in her arms as a mother would hold a distraught child.

And on that day, Emilie lost a part of her heart she feared would never again be recovered.

THAD COULDN'T sleep that night. He looked out the window over and over again across the field to Emilie's house. A window on the second floor remained lit, even deep into the night.

Was sleep evading her as well?

Thad berated himself over and over. He never should have been so cruel and so hypocritical. Had he not done the same thing for which he condemned Emilie?

He was usually mild-mannered and calm. Why then had he been so quick to place blame and even quicker to destroy the delicate love between he and Emilie?

Because something upset your perfect world. The words came as a harsh reproach, one that bore much truth.

Thad climbed from his bed and kneeled. *Lord, please forgive me. I have been so wrong. If there's any way...any way at all, please bring Emilie and me back together.*

Weariness overtook him and competed for the guilt weighing on his shoulders. He never should have spoken so sternly to Emilie, never should have been so rude and prideful. *Charity is kind;... Doth not behave itself unseemly, seeketh not her own, is not easily provoked...*The words of First Corinthians flooded his mind.

He'd been anything but charitable to Emilie.

Would she ever forgive him?

Would he ever forgive himself?

One thing Thad knew. He would never love another the way he had loved Emilie Crawford.

EMILIE MOPED in her bedroom for four days. She rarely left the confines of the second-floor room and had little appetite. The early fall rain fell steadily, adding to her already-somber mood. With each thought of Thad, Emilie struggled not to brood or slip into a melancholy slump. Why had she chosen to lie to him in the first place?

Why had he lied to her?

No wonder Newt didn't like the man.

Emilie reached for the pencil-drawn caricature on the bureau. Stanley's likeness of her and Thad almost brought a smile to her face.

Almost.

If she had not been so distraught at the loss of a relationship that had come to mean more to her than any relationship ever had.

In the sketch, Emilie and Thad were holding hands. Stanley drew amazing detail for such a young fellow. He even captured the love in their eyes for each other.

Or perhaps it just appeared that way.

A tear dropped onto the paper with its jagged edge, and Emilie hastily placed it back on the bureau before more dampness could ruin it.

Enough had been destroyed these past days. The caricature need not be added to the list.

Plopping on her pillow and gazing at the ceiling, a realization came over her. She had loved Thad—still did. Even if there was no hope for them ever to resolve the issues that came between them.

Oh, why hadn't she been more diligent in discovering who Thad really was? What else had he lied about?

Had he ever really cared for her?

Would her broken heart ever mend?

It made it all the worse that Thad was the one who had broken their courtship. He refused to give their relationship another chance whereby ending the tender love blossoming between them.

Or what she thought was blossoming between them. For all Emilie knew, that could have been a lie as well.

She buried her face in her pillow once again, as the tears fell anew. A knock at the door interrupted her persistent heartache.

"Emilie, dear?"

She sat up in her bed. "Yes, Vera?" she croaked.

"May I come in?"

Emilie wished Vera could leave her well enough alone. She wasn't hungry, nor was she desirous of spending any time outside the walls of her bedroom. She chastised herself then, for her friend only wanted to help.

"Yes," she answered.

Vera stepped inside the room and closed the door. "How are you feeling, Emilie?"

"Most dreadful."

"May I have a seat?"

Emilie nodded at the chair beside her bed. She swung her legs over the side of the bed and faced Vera as the woman sat.

"Now, Emilie, you know I care for you as I would if you were my own daughter."

"Yes, Vera, and I thank you for that." It was one sliver of comfort amidst all the recent upheaval.

"Good. Now, I have watched for four days as you have brooded in your bedroom. You haven't uttered more than a word or two, and you've not eaten enough to feed a bird. Now, Emilie, this cannot continue."

Emilie thought of the time Nanny rebuked her as a child for sneaking six snickerdoodle cookies from the kitchen when Cook's back was turned. She made it all the way to her room, devoured half of them on the way there, and the other half while crouched on her bed under the covers. Vera reminded Emilie of that day with her face taut in sternness and her pointed gaze.

"Emilie?"

"Yes, Vera?"

"Have you been listening to a word I've said?"

Emilie folded her arms across her chest and did her best not to look like the pouting child she felt she was at that moment. "Yes, I have, Vera. Thank you for caring for me."

"I care very much for you. You have every right to be distressed over the happenings with Thad. You can continue to cry daily, several times in fact, if necessary. But I must intervene when I see that you are quickly suffering from melancholy and becoming morose. It isn't healthy not to eat, and it certainly isn't healthy to stay confined to this bedroom, no matter how well-decorated it is."

"It's not like I can go anywhere. It's raining outside, after all."

"Now you sound like a petulant child, Emilie, and there will be none of that."

Goodness, but what would Mother say if she heard the hired help speak to Emilie with such reproach? "Yes, Vera."

"Now, I have been praying the Lord would bring you and Thad back together. You made a handsome couple for certain, and if it was truly love between you, this matter won't hinder you from renewing your courtship."

"That's just it. He lied to me. He failed to tell me he's Thad Evanson, the man whom Newt strongly disliked. The man who allowed his cattle to run rampant through my gardens. What if he lied to me about other things as well?" Tears formed again in Emilie's eyes and slid down her face.

Vera leaned forward and placed a hand on her arm. "Oh, Emilie. I know this is hard. Lying is an awful thing. It erodes trust faster than the weather changes here in Montana. There's a reason why the Lord clearly admonishes it. Being dishonest with each other has created this mess."

The charitable woman could have mentioned that Emilie had lied almost as much as Thad had, but instead, she hinted at such in the most gracious of ways.

"After some time, you and Thad must sit down and discuss this matter at length. It's the only way to mend this unfortunate tragedy."

"Please forgive me for saying so, but if this is what it's like to be in love, I'll have none of it."

"Emilie…"

"Every time I think about him, or even glance in the direction of his house, I think about this—this catastrophe all over again. The way we both lied to each other, the fact of who he really is, that he broke our courtship, even the way his cattle ruined my flowers. The heartbreak hurts, Vera."

"I know, dear. You and Thad love each other."

"Loved, as in 'past tense.'"

"Just because the two of you had a squabble doesn't mean it's over for good. Morris and I have had our share of bickering over the years, and here we are still married and more in love than ever."

"That's you and Morris. He didn't lie to you about a half dozen items of importance. Morris didn't break off your courtship, rather than making amends."

"Well, regardless of whether you reunite in the coming weeks, or decide to remain apart, there is something of utmost importance. You must move on with your life, however difficult that may be. Enough of the long face, Emilie. You appear as though you are a bad-tempered child."

"Vera, I am not a child."

Vera ignored her comment. "You'll not pass the days away in sorrowful demise here in your bedroom. Not under my watch. No, Emilie, you need to return to your life. Become involved again with your flowers, spend time at the orphanage, go visit your society friends...as a matter of fact, don't you have a meeting in Helena to raise money for the suffrage movement?"

"I do."

"Exactly. You best be thinking about your wardrobe. Morris says he can feel it in his bones that the weather is going to clear soon. You'll need to be in touch with the ladies and see about the details of transport to Missoula to catch the train. There's much to do in the next couple of days. Moreover, have you arranged to once again read at the orphanage? You haven't been there in over a week. The children will miss you."

"I suppose you're right."

"Yes, of course, I am right. How about you, Morris, and me taking a trip to Missoula? We haven't been there in a couple weeks, and before we know it, the snow will be flying and we'll be stranded here in Hollow Creek."

"I have no desire to visit Missoula."

"Whyever not? You love the city."

"Because Thad isn't there."

"No, but he's your next-door neighbor."

"Need you remind me?"

Vera gave her "the look" again. "Now, we are going to pray and then you will have exactly ten minutes to freshen up before afternoon tea." She folded her hands and proceeded to offer a prayer.

"Vera?"

"Yes, dear?"

"Thank you."

"For being harsh with you? You know I don't aim to be, Emilie, but..."

"No, Vera, for caring about me," said Emilie, embracing the older woman in a hug.

Whatever would she have done if Newt hadn't hired Vera as the housekeeper of the Wheeler Ranch?

CHAPTER THIRTY-ONE

Thad dreaded the advice he knew was about to come. Pete had that expression on his face. The one that looked like a cross between determined and annoyed. "Can we talk for a moment, Thad?"

He nodded and took a seat in the barn on a hay bale across from Pete.

"Now, I reckon you didn't ask me for my advice. You may not want to hear in the least what I have to say. But, Thad, I'm going to say it anyway."

"Pete..."

Pete held up a hand. "I know I'm your foreman, but I'm also your friend, and I'd like to think, also your mentor of sorts. Am I correct?"

"Yes, Pete, you are."

"Good. So I understand you and Emilie had a falling-out of sorts. I gather it stems from the fact that the two of you weren't upright and honest with each other."

Pete didn't wait for Thad to respond. Instead, he continued. "Now, I think being dishonest is one of the worst things a man can be."

"You know I had my reasons."

Hadn't they already had this conversation?

"I know you had your reasons, but the two of you need to discuss this quarrel and come to some type of understanding and soon."

"Why the hurry?"

Pete blew out a mouthful of air and shook his head. "Thad, reckon I'm gonna put this as tactfully as I can. You have been nothing short of challenging lately."

"Challenging?"

"Temperamental, irritable, impatient..."

"I get the message, Pete."

"Good. I know you've needed to be tougher on Floyd, and the one positive thing that comes out of this mess is you being harder on his lack of work ethic and his whiskey habit. But, Thad, the constant cantankerous attitude you've been displayin' toward all of us needs to cease."

"You're not one for mincing words."

"Glad you get my meaning. Now, Anne and I have been praying for you. We've been praying that if it's the Lord's will, you and Emilie would reconcile. If it's not His will, that He would give you the grace to continue on without her."

"I loved her, Pete."

"And you still do."

Thad shook his head. "Not after her lies."

"And *your* lies. I want you to get back into living. Spend time at the orphanage again. Come over for supper. Anne will make you your favorite meal. Go to the upcoming church potluck. Go to Missoula."

"There's no need for me to go to Missoula now."

"And why is that? I know the land deal is finalized, but you do have a house there, and you might as well pay a visit to the city before the snow sets in."

"There's no need to go to Missoula because Emilie is not there."

"True. She's right next door."

Pete stood and gave Thad a pat on the shoulder. "You know I think of you as a younger brother. I wouldn't be giving you this lecture if I didn't care about you."

"I know, and I appreciate that."

"Now, you have five minutes to ready yourself before we round up some cattle that have taken the notion to stray."

If only it took five minutes to rid Thad of the turmoil filling his heart.

That night before turning in, he reached for the piece of paper with the caricature Stanley had drawn of him and Emilie. It didn't take a picture for Thad to remember all the wonderful things about Emilie. Her smile. Her full lips he kissed on several occasions and yearned to kiss again. Her long blonde hair. Her sweet personality and caring heart. Her newfound love for the Lord.

Thad placed the sketch back in its place of honor on the small table by his bedside. If only he could rectify the discord between him and the woman he loved.

VERA HAD been right. Attending the suffrage meeting in Helena with Joy, Rhoda, and Carlotta had done her some good, as had visiting the orphanage and reading to the children. However, Emilie hadn't wanted to attend church, much less the potluck that followed.

Both Grace Church and Hollow Creek Church merged to offer an annual joint potluck with everyone meeting for the sermon at Grace Church and joining the potluck at Hollow Creek Church.

Emilie sighed and followed Vera, Morris, Hattie, and Jep up the stairs. Did the folks in Hollow Creek know of the dreadful trauma her heart endured in the past week? Had tongues waggled at the gossip about her and Thad? Did *The Hollow Creek Weekly* boast front-page news about the demise of Emilie and Thad's courtship?

If any of those things were true, no one gave any indication. Emilie scooted into the pew next to Vera and Morris and prepared herself for the service. Across the room, she spied Thad. Had he not wished to attend Pastor Shay's church today?

As if he felt her eyes bore into the back of his head, Thad turned and gave her a quick glance. Not a lingering gander, but a brief glimpse reserved for a stranger.

Emilie's heart broke all over again.

After the service, the congregants left for nearby Hollow Creek Church. As she exited through the door of the church, Thad arrived at the same time. Their arms brushed.

For a moment, a jolt rushed through her. She wished he would take her hand, as he had so many times during their outings in Missoula. Or perhaps he would tuck her hand through his arm.

But he did neither.

Deciding not to give Thad a second thought, Emilie moved past him and down the stairs, being ever so sure to keep her nose slightly tilted upwards.

Emilie, you are most certainly putting on airs.

Airs or not, Emilie wouldn't give Thad the satisfaction she missed him. It was a matter of survival, really. If she allowed herself a second glance in his direction, she may not be able to rein in her emotions.

Greeting the folks she knew, which were few, Emilie stood in line moments later to retrieve her meal.

"As a special treat," the reverend was saying, "We have some ice cream to top our apple pie."

Emilie's eyes connected with Thad's. *Pie à la mode* she mouthed, without giving a second thought.

He did the same at exactly the same time.

Fighting back tears, Emilie recalled all of the times at the Bellerose Restaurant. If only…

But such whimsical thoughts didn't heal a broken heart.

CHAPTER THIRTY-TWO

The news that Mother and Father were coming for a visit brought about a certain distress in Emilie's heart. Yes, she loved her parents, but their timing couldn't be worse. With her and Thad at odds after discovering each other's identity, the last thing Emilie wanted to do was hear from her parents that she needed to return to New York City.

Forgive me, Lord. My attitude toward my parents should be one of honor and gratitude.

Tomorrow they would arrive by train in Missoula. Emilie would send Morris in the Model T to retrieve them. Until then, she would set her mind on other things.

Like Thad.

Emilie reached for her knitted shawl and stepped out onto the front porch. The sky sparkled with stars, and with the exception of a calf calling to his mother in the distance, all was quiet.

Tiptoeing to the edge of the porch, Emilie leaned against the railing and sipped her tea. She stared across the field to Thad's home. He, too, had a porch on his home. She squinted. Could it be that he stood on his porch as well?

Emilie could make out a dark figure in the moonlight. He appeared to be facing her direction, although she couldn't be certain. She lifted her free hand to wave slightly, then thought better of it.

Thad made his intentions clear.

He wanted nothing to do with her.

Emilie bit her lip and averted her eyes from the figure across the field to a vacant spot beyond the porch. She had told him the very same thing.

The irony of it struck her harder than she'd anticipated. Emilie found what she had deemed might possibly be true love, only to have it expunged from her life under the cloak of deception.

If only things could have remained a secret and she could have continued believing Thad to be someone other than her neighbor.

Emilie raised her head again and strained her eyes through the darkness. The figure remained on the porch across the field. His broad shoulders, tall, muscular physique, and a cowboy hat atop his head.

It could be none other than Thad.

There would be no sleep for her tonight. Not with a broken heart to nurse.

THAD SAW her in the distance standing on her porch. The woman who had captured his heart like none other, then broke it just as fast. He had loved her; of that he'd been certain.

But Thad couldn't live with the fact she had lied. He couldn't forgive her.

But you lied too… The impact of the words slammed into his heart with a force he couldn't ignore.

Yes, but…

Thad was without excuse. He was just as guilty at not being forthright with her as she was with him. Why could they not forgive each other?

He had been so wrong to deceive her. Far too hard on her about her deception and far too easy on himself. Conviction pricked his heart.

Thad stared across the field and saw her slender figure leaning against the railing between the two pillars of her porch.

At the church potluck, Emilie made it clear she wanted nothing to do with him. Their eyes had connected on more than one occasion. He made an effort to be at the doorway at the same time as she was as they left the church.

What had Thad hoped to achieve? A chance to speak with her? To take her hand in his and declare to her that he still loved her? That these last days without her had been nothing short of misery?

Then why hadn't he?

When the reverend spoke of the ice cream and pie, their eyes met. Had she recalled the times at the Bellerose Restaurant eating pie à la mode? Did she relish those memories as he did?

Several times throughout the passing days, Thad caught himself pondering about their next meeting in Missoula.

A sober reminder there would be no more such meetings renewed the sorrow of losing her all over again.

Thad watched as Emilie retreated to the house. Did she miss him? He missed her. If only he could find some way to rid himself of the stubbornness and pride that precluded him from telling her.

THE DOOR opened and Emilie heard the voices from the parlor. She returned her book to the bookcase and rose. *Lord, I beseech Your help. Grant me patience and fortitude.*

Three different voices besides those of Morris's and Vera's greeted her ears. Mother, Father, and an unknown man's voice. Had Mother and Father brought an additional guest? Emilie rounded the corner into the foyer and greeted them. "Please, do come into the parlor."

Mother, Father, and a stranger followed Emilie.

"Almira, darling, it's been far too long." Mother paraded across the floor, arms open wide.

"Hello, Mother."

Mother kissed one of Emilie's cheeks, then the other. She then gently clasped Emilie's arms with her hands. "How have you been?"

"I've been fine, Mother, and you?"

"Oh, just grand. Busy with all of the social affairs, as usual."

Father stepped forward then, along with a stranger, a man in a fedora. Father took her hands in his. "Almira, you remember Donald W. Smith, III, from when you resided in New York? His father owns the famous D.W. Smith Bank."

Father retreated and the man stepped forward and reached for Emilie's hand, as recognition dawned. With his dark beady eyes remaining on her face, he leaned and kissed her hand. "It's a pleasure, Almira. While I haven't seen you in some time, I have heard so much about you. And you may call me Donald, without the 'W', the 'Smith', or the 'III.'"

What a gracious gesture.

Emilie recalled when she first met Donald Smith years ago. He failed to leave a favorable impression on her. Just another in a string of suitors.

Vera brought a tray of tea and set it on the table. "Would anyone care for tea or a slice of almond sugar cake?" Emilie shot Vera a grateful glance. Something about Mr. Smith's demeanor left her a bit unsettled.

Everyone took a seat and Vera served the tea and cake.

"Mother, I wish you would have told me Mr. Smith was joining you and Father for a visit."

Mother nodded toward Father. "To my considerable delight, it was actually your father's idea, Almira."

"Yes, it was my notion." Father puffed out his chest and tossed a self-satisfied look to each person in the room, apparently hoping for accolades.

Mr. Smith aimed an egotistical grin and what could be construed as a wink in Emilie's direction.

Emilie pressed her lips together. She didn't need her parents attempting another matchmaking scheme at her expense. Fortunately, this time they would not succeed, for she was quite adept at finding her own husband, thank you very much.

Calling him Donald was too informal, too friendly. She would drop the 'W' and the 'III', but she would keep it as Mr. Smith.

She certainly would not encourage Donald W. Smith, III, to set his cap for her.

CHAPTER THIRTY-THREE

"Almira, why don't you give Mr. Smith a tour of the ranch?" Mother suggested at breakfast the next morning.

Emilie winced. She could already foresee Mother and Father's intention to arrange a courtship between her and Donald Smith.

A courtship she was not in the least bit interested.

"Yes, Mother," she acquiesced.

Mr. Smith gave her a cocky grin. "I'd love to see the ranch." He wiped the edges of his mouth with the napkin. "I believe I'm ready."

But Emilie wasn't ready. She hadn't even started eating the breakfast Cook prepared. She nodded, then took a bite of the scrambled egg. Not that she had much of an appetite. Between thinking about Thad and the sudden arrival of her parents, and then the surprise of bringing a potential suitor, Emilie hadn't much fortitude these days to partake in any additional activities.

Mr. Smith scooted his chair back, and with precise movements, rose. "Well, shall we, Mrs. Wheeler?"

Mother beamed. "It is a most pleasant day for a stroll, is it not?"

Father grunted with a nod of his balding head.

Mr. Smith sidled to the opposite side of the table where Emilie sat, pulled out her chair for her, and offered his hand. Emilie placed her napkin on the table and stood, reluctantly allowing Mr. Smith to assist her to her feet.

"Allow me to retrieve my shawl. I'll be but a moment." Without waiting for a response from Mr. Smith, Emilie retreated upstairs to her room.

"Is everything all right, ma'am?" Hattie asked.

"Please pray for me, Hattie," Emilie whispered.

"Are you ill, Mrs. Wheeler?"

"No, Hattie, I feel fine, other than I'm lacking patience today."

Hattie bobbed her head in such a hasty manner that it nearly caused the pins in her hair to come loose. "Oh, yes, ma'am, I'll be sure to pray for you."

"Thank you." Emilie wrapped the shawl around her shoulders and took a deep breath.

Something told her she would never be fond Donald Smith.

Especially when comparing him to Thad Alexander Evanson.

Emilie missed his company so much it hurt.

Moments later, Mr. Smith invited Emilie to put her arm through his. She considered declining, not giving a care to any breach of etiquette it might cause.

Then, as if they were the best of chums, the presumptuous Mr. Smith patted her hand. "Ah, Mrs. Wheeler, but you do live a reclusive existence," he said when they left the house.

Emilie gritted her teeth. "To the contrary, Mr. Smith, there's nothing reclusive about it. I have my staff, my friends, my church family, and my neighbors." One neighbor in particular that she wished hadn't left her life and taken a large part of her heart with him. "However, I do see how one might think Hollow Creek remote when having just arrived from New York City."

"Well, someday, perhaps you will have all of the conveniences of the city once again."

"I'm quite content, Mr. Smith." Emilie hoped she didn't sound too brusque. No sense in giving Mr. Smith something to complain about to Mother. "How is the banking business?"

"My, but I do recall that you are not like most women, who know better than to concern themselves with the subject of business."

"I run my late husband's ranch. It's my business to know business."

"Yes, well, a meager cattle ranch differs immensely from a string of banks."

Meager? If only you knew just how expansive the Wheeler Ranch is.

"Not so much, Mr. Smith. We are both ensuring our customers receive a quality product."

Mr. Smith raised a bushy eyebrow. "I don't see the similarities, but to avoid conflict, I'll not broach the matter further." As if he had completely erased part of their conversation—a part he disliked—his countenance changed. "When we met in New York, Father ran the day-to-day operations of the banks. Now that he has advanced in years, the oversight of the banks is my sole responsibility. A responsibility, I might add, that is undoubtedly impressive. If only I had someone with whom to share my life, I daresay my life would be complete."

Mr. Smith paused for a moment and grinned at her; a grin that appeared somewhat insincere. The edges of his curled black mustache twitched and the smile never reached his dark eyes.

I'll not be the one to share your life, Mr. Smith.

They continued their stroll down the lane. Mr. Smith strutted in an exaggerated swagger, Emilie on the crook of one arm, while he held his other hand to the lapel of his expensive suit. He reminded her of an arrogant peacock.

And while Emilie considered birds to be her favorite animal, she'd never been particularly fond of peacocks.

A rider on horseback in the distance, riding on the boundary between the Wheeler and Evanson properties, garnered

Emilie's attention. Only when the horse and its rider drew closer, did she see who it was.

Thad.

Her heart nearly leapt from her chest at the sight of him. Long legs, broad shoulders, and so comfortable on a horse. The edges of his blond hair curled beneath the back of his hat and his strong hands guided the reins.

"So then, shall we make it a priority to become better acquainted?" Mr. Smith's unwelcome interruption disrupted her thoughts of Thad.

Mr. Smith's forwardness was not unexpected, although it was shocking nonetheless. "Begging your pardon?" But she heard nary a word more of what he said for her focus was on the man guiding cattle on horseback.

Thad rode toward them. Oh, how she wished for one more moment with him. To erase the dissension between them. To feel the warmth of his arms around her, even for the briefest of moments.

"Almira, do pay heed to my words," Mr. Smith admonished.

"Again, begging your pardon, Mr. Smith."

But Emilie's attention wasn't in the slightest on Donald Smith, but on Thad.

Their eyes connected. If possible, Emilie's heart galloped through her chest all the more.

"Hello, Thad."

Thad tipped his hat. "Emilie."

His eyes held hers and she longed to reach out to him. Tell him she was sorry. That she loved him. She missed him. That they were meant to be together.

But, of course, she couldn't say all those things. Especially not with Mr. Smith standing at her side. She found it difficult to breathe as their shared gaze continued. He appeared as dapper as ever. Cherished moments they had spent together in Missoula as Emilie Crawford and Thad Alexander permeated her thoughts. She remembered his kiss, his nearness, the way he'd held her...

Did Thad recall all of those special moments as well?

"And I am Donald W. Smith, III," boasted Mr. Smith, breaking the spell between Emilie and Thad.

"Nice to meet you, Mr. Smith. I'm Thad Evanson." Thad didn't reach for a handshake or remove himself from the horse.

"Almira and I are out for a pleasant excursion this splendid morning." Donald gripped the top of Emilie's hand and pressed it firmly into the crook of his arm. "I've arrived all the way from New York City to see her."

Thad looked from Emilie to Mr. Smith, and then back to Emilie again, a wariness in his eyes. "Is that so?"

No, it's not so! She gave her head a slight shake.

"In that case, welcome to Hollow Creek." Thad's gaze held Emilie's once again and she longed to break free from Mr. Smith's grasp. What must Thad think?

"I can't say as I really care much for this remote village, but considering the importance of visiting Almira, I made the arduous journey."

"Enjoy your stay." Thad tipped his hat. "Emilie."

She watched as Thad rode away, taking another piece of her heart with him.

"Who was that idiosyncratic man?" Mr. Smith asked.

"He's my neighbor."

Mr. Smith nodded and cocked one of his bushy eyebrows. "Shall we continue on our stroll?"

Emilie heard no more of what Mr. Smith said as they meandered down the lane, for only one man held her attention.

SURLY AND cantankerous would best describe Thad's mood in recent days. Ever since his disagreement with Emilie, he hadn't been himself.

And his hired help had taken the brunt of it.

Several times, Thad had had to apologize for his ill-tempered behavior. And numerous times, he'd had to seek the Lord's forgiveness.

Surely there was a way to win back the affection of the woman he had grown to love.

Or so Thad thought until that obnoxious Mr. Smith cornered him.

"Well, hello, there. Mr. Evanson is it?"

Thad looked up from his duties to find Emilie's guest standing near the barn.

"I hope I'm not disturbing you. I went for a stroll and found my way to this location."

"What can I do for you, Mr. Smith?"

"Seeing as how you work for Almira's neighbor..."

"I *am* Almira's neighbor. The owner of this ranch."

Thad felt the surge of competition flow through his veins. Just what was Emilie's relationship with Mr. Smith?

"Very well. You are the owner." Mr. Smith perused the ranch, his eyes settling on Thad's house and allowing his disdain to show. He straightened his posture. Hoping to increase his average stature, perhaps?

Thad followed Mr. Smith's gaze and was again reminded how badly the house needed a good whitewashing.

"Do you know why I am visiting Hollow Creek, Mr. Evanson?"

"No."

Mr. Smith flexed his shoulders, causing him to have an overly exaggerated posture. "Almira is my fiancé. We've entered into courtship."

"Is that so?"

"Yes, it is. You see, soon Almira will join me back in New York City for our wedding. She has plans to sell the ranch. Perhaps you would like to purchase it."

Before Thad knew Emilie was the owner, he would have appreciated the chance to own more acreage. Since discovering Emilie's identity, however, Thad had no interest in her land.

He had interest only in her.

But Thad had ruined any chance of a life with her because of his dishonesty, pride, and stubbornness.

"Almira and I have known each other for years. You see, I am an affluent banker in New York City. I own a fashionable home on 67th Street, one that Almira has long desired to make her own. It won't be long until she is my wife. We plan to marry in the next couple of months. She has even expressed interest in a December wedding. Rushing it? Yes. But when two people are in love..."

Thad's stomach lurched in unrest. If Emilie had been fond of Mr. Smith, why had she agreed to court Thad?

"You see, after Newton passed, Almira was hesitant to ever love again. Being the upstanding and esteemed man that I am, I gave her the time she needed. When she invited me to the ranch, I knew it was time to again pursue her. Almira is a handsome woman, don't you think?"

"Yes, she is."

Mr. Smith snorted. "I just thought you should know she is spoken for."

A thought suddenly occurred to Thad. "If you and Emilie are courting, why is it you call her Almira? She told me she prefers to be called 'Emilie.'"

Thad's question didn't faze Mr. Smith. "She has allowed those below her station, such as servants, and the like, to refer to her as her middle name of Emilie. Those of us who know and love her—including myself and her parents—know her as Almira."

"I see."

"I was hoping you would. Well, I best be on my way back to Almira's home. She and I are having a special supper. I plan to present her with her engagement ring in the near future."

Mr. Smith might as well have punched Thad square in the gut.

It would have felt better than the upheaval in his stomach and the aching pain in his heart.

Had his love for Emilie meant nothing?

CHAPTER THIRTY-FOUR

"Would you care to have the noonday meal with me at Olga's Café in town?" Emilie asked her mother the next morning. It had been awhile since Emilie spent time with Mother. As a matter of fact, Emilie couldn't recollect the last time she and Mother shared the company of each other without anyone else around.

"That sounds splendid."

Mr. Smith entered the room. "I should like to come too, Almira."

Irritation rose within her. "This will be just Mother and me." *Take that, Mr. Donald W. Smith, III.*

Mr. Smith's thin lips folded downward to a pout. "If you say so. But what shall I do in this bucolic home while the two of you are away?"

"Father would savor your company, of that I am sure," Emilie said. "Now, I must summon Morris and have him drive us to town."

Moments later, Emilie and Mother sat in the backseat of the Model T touring car. Morris, good-natured as always, drove them to town while telling humorous stories the entire way. He promised to keep secret Emilie's fondness for driving the automobile. Once again, she was thankful for the trusted staff with whom she'd been blessed.

When they reached Olga's Café, Morris exited the automobile and assisted Emilie and Mother. Taking a look to the left and then to the right, Mother perused the dusty town of Hollow Creek.

"What do you think, Mother? I know it's been some time since you've visited. Our town has grown a bit since then."

"I must say, Almira, that this town exudes rustic charm. The boardwalk, even with its uneven boards, is positively winsome, and the church steeples remind me of a backwards town your father and I once visited, quite by accident, when we were lost once."

Emilie felt a sense of pride for Hollow Creek, a pride she'd not felt until she had decided to engage herself more in her community. She had Thad to thank for that.

If only he knew how much he had helped her. Especially in her faith.

And his comfort as she shared about the loss of her baby. Such an intimate topic to share with him. Thad had shown much compassion toward her then. But did he now think her foolish for disclosing such a private matter?

Emilie swallowed the thoughts of Thad and led Mother to Olga's Café. "What a quaint establishment," exclaimed Mother as they entered.

They sat at a round corner table near the back, the only table available in the room of four tables, and placed their orders. "Are you enjoying your stay in Hollow Creek?" Emilie brushed aside the fact that conversations with Mother were, and always had been, strained at best. She witnessed women and their mothers conversing with ease at church and longed for the same type of relationship with her own mother.

"As much as can be expected. I do miss New York and my friends." Mother sipped her tea. "I fail to understand why you would care to stay in such a desolate place. New York has so much more to offer, and what with Newton gone, there really is nothing to keep you here. Sell the house, Almira, and move back to New York, won't you?"

Emilie was afraid the conversation would turn to this topic. "Mother, I'm quite content in Hollow Creek and have no intentions of returning to New York for more than a visit."

"What about Donald Smith? He fancies you."

"Yet, I don't fancy him."

Mother appeared disturbed by Emilie's blunt statement. "May I ask why not? Donald has everything a woman could hope for in a husband. He's wealthy, powerful, and a dandy. That house you once admired on 67th Street? Donald recently purchased it. It could be yours, Almira."

"Those things don't mean anything to me anymore, Mother." Not since the Lord had caused her priorities to slowly begin to shift.

"As I mentioned when you married Newton, you place far too much emphasis on love. You could grow to love Donald in time. You've only to give it a chance. And if you don't grow to love each other, you will always have companionship."

"My heart belongs to another."

"Oh, Almira. I know how you must miss Newton something dreadful. But he's gone now. You must move on and make a new life. You're so young to waste it all alone in that extravagant, but gloomy, house."

"I do miss Newton, but my heart never truly belonged to him. As you are well aware, we were married for convenience only." She glanced around, thankful the café was now empty of other customers.

"I'm bewildered. You say your heart belongs to someone else?"

"Yes, Mother. It does. But it's not Newton."

Mother's austere facial expression reminded Emilie of those days when Emilie had forgotten proper etiquette as a child. "Please explain yourself."

"After Newton passed and..." Emilie stopped short of mentioning about the loss of their baby. Mother had never known she was once to be a grandmother. Emilie deemed it best that way. She took a deep breath and continued. "My days were filled with loneliness. As such, I did meet a fine and upstanding, godly man. He has stolen my heart."

"Then where is this man of whom you speak?" Dramatic as usual, Mother craned her neck and glanced about the entire cafe.

"We had a disagreement."

"Please do not tell me this man is a destitute soul who was only eyeing the Crawford and Wheeler family fortunes."

"Nothing of a sort, Mother. In fact, he's wealthy in his own right."

Mother pursed her lips, making them almost invisible. "What has happened to the daughter your father and I raised? You traveled to Montana and became a free-spirited, fanciful dreamer. Really, Almira. Do come back to New York. Things have been difficult for you here. Forget about this man with whom you've had the disagreement and start over in the city. There's nothing left for you here."

"I do appreciate your advice, Mother. But I love this man, and with the Lord's help, I hope we someday reconcile."

A look of tenderness filled Mother's eyes then, and she reached across the table for Emilie's hands. "I apologize, Almira, that I have, at times, been overbearing. It's just that as my only child, I have only wanted the very best for you. Your father and I do miss you and had hoped someday you would remarry and settle in close proximity to us."

"I understand. I miss you too, but my life is in Hollow Creek."

They sat in silence for some time, eating their meals, although Emilie's appetite had waned. She watched outside the window as the reverend and his wife passed and an idea emerged. "Mother, tomorrow is Sunday. Would you and Father care to join me for church services?"

Mother peered up from her soup and Emilie realized how much she had aged in the past couple of years. While Mother would always be a handsome woman and she appeared younger than her forty-nine years, time had taken its toll on her. Fine lines etched around her hazel eyes and strands of gray hair emerged. No matter that they hadn't seen eye to eye more times than not, the truth was that Emilie loved her mother very much.

"Church?"

"Yes. Hollow Creek has two churches, and I attend Grace Church. The reverend preaches an outstanding sermon and the congregants are quite friendly." Not that Emilie had always thought so. For the longest time, she'd had no use for the churches in her town, or any church for that matter. When Thad finally convinced her to go to the church in Missoula, all of that changed. When she returned home, she'd found a church family she had never known existed.

"Well, we continue to attend church on occasion when time permits or when someone is getting married or has passed. I suppose we could attend your church during our time in Hollow Creek."

"Thank you, Mother. I have learned much about Jesus in these past couple of months." The words popped out before she could rein them in. Dare she share with her mother all she had learned about the Lord? All she had learned because Thad convinced her to attend services? All she now knew because the patient Pastor Shay in Missoula and Reverend Arkley at Grace Church shared with her about Jesus's loving sacrifice?

Emilie pondered the thoughts rippling through her mind. Thad had made such a difference in her life by inviting her to attend church services that day in Missoula. An eternal difference.

"Jesus? Oh, yes, the Baby in the manger. Your father and I have been faithful about attending church during Christmas.

The Valerio family, you remember them? We attend Christmas services then visit at their home afterwards for festivities."

"Yes, the Baby in the manger who grew up and died for us."

Mother appeared perplexed. "I remember someone mentioned that at Easter one year. Did I tell you that your father and I attended during Easter a few years back?"

"He was born to die, Mother, so that we could live forever with Him in Heaven."

"You sound like you've been taking lessons from the reverend."

"Only listening intently." Emilie's heart raced. For so long, her family never knew the truth about who Jesus was and what He had done for them. Suddenly, she couldn't wait to share all of this with her parents. "Mother, my life has changed since I decided to live for the Lord. In ways I never would have imagined."

"Of what are you speaking, Almira? I know about Jesus dying, although I found it to be such a tragedy."

""Not a tragedy, Mother. He did die, but three days later, He rose again. His death on the Cross was the only way we could be forgiven for all of our sins and have eternal life. He took all of our sins upon Himself. I've repented of my sins and have trusted Him as my Lord and Savior. I put my trust in Jesus and am now living my life for Him."

"Please tell me you have not been driving that automobile. That would be dreadfully sinful."

Emilie nearly laughed at Mother's severe expression and her abrupt change in subject. "All the times as a child when we attended church—the times I can count on one hand—those times meant nothing. I decided to continue to live my life without the Lord here in Hollow Creek. Newton had no use for church. He called it 'the house of hypocrites.' I agreed with him. I figured all that the folks in the church wanted was my money. How wrong I was. Tha...this man who introduced me to the Lord shared with me so much about Jesus and that He has a plan for my life."

"So the Lord, whom you now know, has He repaired the animosity between you and the man you love?"

"Not yet. But if it's His will, I know our relationship will be restored." If only Emilie felt as confident as she attempted to sound. But knowing the Lord was so new to her. A verse Reverend Arkley quoted recently flowed through her mind. "*And we know that all things work together for good to them that love God, to them who are the called according to his purpose.*" She couldn't recall from which book of the Bible the verse originated, but surely Emilie could trust the Lord's words even in matters as personal as her love for Thad, couldn't she? He would work it out according to His plan.

"Goodness, but I guess it takes faith to believe God will restore even a broken relationship. It sounds as though you have grown much in your knowledge of the Lord."

Emilie had to admit, her faith wavered at times. "It's a growing process," she said. Thad had told her the very same thing when he'd shared his own struggles.

Mother sighed. "Your father and I will attend church with you tomorrow, Almira."

"Thank you, Mother."

"And we'll bring Donald along as well."

CHAPTER THIRTY-FIVE

Mr. Smith twirled his waxy mustache the next day at the breakfast table, seemingly in deep contemplation. "Almira, perhaps you and I could go on a picnic today. It would indeed be a waste not to take full advantage of this beautiful day."

"Mr. Smith..."

"Donald."

Emilie ignored him, much his disturbance—and Mother's too. "I will have to decline. After church, I intend to give Father a tour of the ranch."

"Church? Yes, your mother mentioned something about us going to services. I attend on occasion and am sure to donate benevolent sums of money to a variety of charities." His mouth quirked upward in smug appreciation of himself. "I find it only fitting you know what kind of man I am."

Oh, I know what kind of man you are, that is for certain. Emilie gazed across the table at the man who desired to court her. Mr. Smith had attempted, without success since the day he arrived in Hollow Creek, to win Emilie's heart. Several times she brushed off his advances or made excuses not to spend time with him, but he relentlessly pursued her all the more. This morning, his yearning for success seemed even more apparent.

Mr. Smith reached up and smoothed his dark hair on either side of a prominent and perfectly-even part atop his head. Emilie stifled a giggle at the thought that he likely used enough Macassar Oil for three men.

"My sweet, are you staring at me?"

His sweet? Nausea rose in the pit of her stomach. "No, Mr. Smith, indeed I am not." Not staring at him with interest, that was for certain. Staring at him with amusement, perhaps. But she'd not confess such a notion.

"It's so becoming when you smile. Your eyes light up in a way that reminds me why I am here. To win your affection."

"Mr. Smith, I..."

"We aren't that different, you and I. We both have a taste for the finer things in life and are both business-minded. However, once you become my wife, you'll spend all of your time arranging charity events, and in general, submitting to my whims. I shall take abundant pleasure in showing you off to my business associates. You would look quite lovely as an ornament of sorts as we attend important events that will further enhance my standing in society." He quirked a bushy eyebrow at her.

An ornament of sorts?

Emilie shivered. Never had she been more unimpressed and repulsed by a man than she was Mr. Smith. "We are both business-minded. You have that much correct. However, I take great pride in running the day-to-day business activities of the ranch. When Newton passed, it was up to me to see that the Wheeler Ranch not only survived, but thrived. While I have a foreman and other employees who assist me in such matters, I take on a fair amount myself."

"Yes, yes. To be expected when one is taken unawares by the death of her husband. Under normal circumstances, a proper woman, especially one of your breeding, wouldn't undertake duties not intended for a mere woman. No matter, however, because when you become my wife, you will transfer all of the duties of the Wheeler Ranch to me. Of course, in all likelihood, the ranch will be sold. Our lives will be in New

York City, and neither of us shall have any need to have ties to this remote part of the world."

Vera walked in then to clear the table. She hummed as she partook in her duties, methodically wiping the table and working more slowly than usual. Emilie appreciated that her housekeeper and dear friend cared to look out for her. She knew Vera's slower movements were due to the kindly older woman knowing she may be needed to come to Emilie's defense.

"Yes, it was unexpected. Therefore, I undertook the ranch duties from a business standpoint," said Emilie. "I have no desire to sell the ranch, and even a lesser desire to return to New York City on a permanent basis. I instead prefer to remain in this remote part of the world. This is my home."

"Commendable, indeed, my sweet, that you have done your best attempt to run this...ranch."

I am not your "sweet," Mr. Smith! Emilie inwardly cringed. Even when she first met the man years ago, she hadn't thought highly of him. There was something sinister about him.

"However," continued Mr. Smith, "It's not so commendable that you insist on maintaining the management of this ranch for the long term. Even less admirable is that you would desire to stay in Montana. Some women these days are becoming too headstrong for their own good. Take the women's suffrage movement, for instance. A woman should know her place. The temporary management of a ranch is one thing, my sweet, but far too many women, and I fear you may be headed in this direction, believe all sorts of asinine notions. One day you are in charge of ranch operations, the next you are expecting to vote."

"I do expect to vote someday. I fully believe women will be given the right to vote in our lifetime."

Mr. Smith's mouth twisted and tightened in a way that made him look as though he had sampled a rotten apple. He rolled his eyes and gave her a harsh squint. "I abhor this nonsense of women thinking they need to have voting rights. What are those suffrage women thinking? You should see all these women in an uproar in New York with their frivolous meetings and their idolizing of Elizabeth Cady Stanton and Susan B. Anthony. Empty-headed fools, I daresay!"

Lord, I beseech thee that I would not loose my tongue in retaliation to Mr. Smith's absurd gibberish.

Mother shifted uncomfortably in her seat, and Father's stern look Emilie's way did nothing to dissuade her.

They'd had this discussion before.

"Further, your ignorance about the subject indicates to me that women are a foolish lot believing they can conduct any sort of business outside what is intended for them to do." Mr. Smith silently dared Emilie to contradict him.

Oh, Emilie wanted to contradict him, all right. And when she did, she aimed to win.

But the look of distress from both Mother and Father persuaded her not to acquiesce to Mr. Smith's bait.

"I think we shall leave the room post haste," remarked Father. He stood and pulled out Mother's chair. "Do try to control your tongue, Almira."

"Indeed," agreed Mother, a warning look in her concerned expression. "We'll see you in a few minutes for church." Together, they left the kitchen.

"Yes, Almira. Do try to control your tongue," Mr. Smith smirked.

Vera stopped clearing the table and stared, clearly stunned. She shook her head and looked from Mr. Smith to Emilie, and then back to Mr. Smith again.

As if to rein in his own irritation, Mr. Smith calmed his tone to an exaggerated drone. "My sweet, you look as though you are about to lose your composure. Your lips, they are pursed and your face so very red, like a red raspberry, to be exact. Are you quite all right?"

Emilie glanced at Vera, who stood completely still. She of all people knew about the wrath that was about to be unleashed on the unsuspecting Donald Smith. And when Emilie did, Mother would remind her to rein in her Irish temper, even though Emilie had not an ounce of Irish coursing through her veins.

Emilie took a deep breath, then another deep breath. Then prayed some more. "Mr. Smith..."

"Ah, my sweet, I told you to call me 'Donald.'"

The audacity! Emilie balled her hands into fists. "Mr. Smith, I will have you know that I *am* one of those empty-headed fools who attends frivolous meetings and who thinks very highly of both Mrs. Stanton and Miss Anthony. Women should have the right to vote. They should be able to run a business if they so choose. They should be allowed to live in remote parts of the world if that is their desire." Emilie failed to temper her voice.

Would Mother and Father have to recline momentarily due to her tirade? She offered a prayer of gratitude that they had left the room.

Mr. Smith's eyes grew dark. "Almira, that is quite enough. You don't mean what you say. Besides, to my extensive knowledge, there are no suffrage movement meetings in Hollow Creek."

"You are right about only one thing, Mr. Smith, and that is that there are no formal suffrage meetings in Hollow Creek. However, they are quite common in Missoula, and I have partaken in several. When and if I do decide to marry again, I aim to be the godly wife spoken of in the Bible first and foremost. I will put the Lord first, my husband and family second, and tend to the raising of my children, should I be blessed with any. In addition, I will continue to manage the Wheeler Ranch, speak out for the right for women to vote, and attend meetings that promote such ideals."

Mr. Smith leaned forward across the table and narrowed his eyes. "Now, now, Almira. Do not lose your composure over this."

"You and I are nothing alike, Mr. Smith. You may have your opinion, and I will have mine. However, be sure to know that I have no intention of courting you, much less entering into marriage with you."

"Good riddance. No wife of mine will be so obstinate and bullheaded. If your parents knew what was right for you, they would demand you return to New York City at once. All of this primitive living in an uncivilized state has made you head-strong and unyielding to any practical advice."

"It is a good riddance, Mr. Smith." Emilie lowered her voice. She stood and pushed in her chair. "Now, if you'll excuse me, I must prepare myself for church services."

"I doubt your reverend takes kindly to your preposterous notions. You should be grateful I agreed to your parents' proposal to seek a courtship with you. Not many men would be interested in a woman such as yourself."

"That is fine, Mr. Smith. If it is the Lord's will for me to remarry, He will orchestrate it in His perfect time." *And oh, how I pray it is the Lord's will that Thad and I resolve our disagreement.*

"You and your religious talk. Another reason your boldness needs to be tempered. I fear it might not work between us after all, Almira."

"You are absolutely right, Mr. Smith," interjected Vera. "Any type of partnership between you and Mrs. Wheeler would never work because she is one of the kindest, most gracious people I have ever met. And you, Mr. Smith. You are quite daft."

Donald Smith's beady eyes grew twice their size and took on a chilly glare. "Of additional and utmost importance, Almira, your staff should never be able to address anyone in the household, much less a cherished guest, in the manner of which she just spoke. Unfathomable! She would be sent packing were she a member of my staff."

"Mr. Smith, Vera is a trusted and hardworking employee, as well as a friend. The last thing I would do is send her on her way. And you, a cherished guest? Hardly." The last sentence flowed from her mouth before she could stop it.

"But goodness. Do the two of you find it so necessary to continue your bickering?" Mother asked, entering the dining area and appearing quite shaken. "Please, Almira, do curb your Irish temper."

"Mr. Smith and I were just parting ways," said Emilie. "I must now go prepare for church services. I will see you momentarily."

"Donald?" asked Father.

Donald cast an ill-mannered glance in Emilie's direction. "With all due respect, Mr. Crawford, I will no longer be seeking your daughter's hand in marriage."

"That is just as well," piped up Mother. "For her heart belongs to another."

CHAPTER THIRTY-SIX

Morris drove Emilie, Father, Mother, and Mr. Smith in the automobile, while Jep, Hattie, and Vera took the buggy to church services. Sworn to secrecy about Emilie having driven the Model T, Morris continued to act every bit the chauffeur.

Emilie would have preferred to drive the automobile herself, but dared not cause a spectacle, especially since the disagreement between she and Mr. Smith had caused Father considerable apprehension and another crease in his already-furrowed brow. Mother, surprisingly, had taken most of it without as much hullabaloo as Emilie expected.

That was an answer to prayer.

Morris pointed out various sites along the way to town, most of which Emilie was certain neither her parents nor Mr. Smith cared for more than a smidgeon. As a matter of fact, Mr. Smith had not spoken at all since they left the house. Not that Emilie was complaining.

When they finally reached the church, Morris assisted Emilie and Mother from the automobile. "I do declare," announced Mother, "I am relieved to be on stationary ground once again. I would have much preferred the buggy to this..." she waved a hand toward the automobile, "this contemptible mode of transport."

"I have made mention many times over that I might purchase an automobile, but your mother has shown her deepest opposition," grunted Father.

"You don't need an automobile," answered Mother, adjusting her wide-brimmed hat on her head.

"Oh, but I do."

"No, Ernest, you do not."

Father crossed his arms over his thin chest and clenched his jaw. "Our daughter has an automobile but I do not. Do tell how this is fair."

Emilie almost laughed at her father's apparent tantrum. Usually, Father got whatever he desired. Bullheaded, stubborn, and proud, Father almost always got his own way. On those rare occasions when he did not, there was always an outburst of his usually-calm demeanor.

"Almira has an automobile because our dearest Newton, God rest his soul, purchased it for his transport." Mother looked down her pointed nose at her husband. "You, my husband, do not need one. Our chauffeur takes us wherever we need to go in the finest of buggies."

Shuddering inwardly at the thought of Mother discovering Emilie herself had purchased the automobile *after* Newt's passing, Emilie focused her attention on other families arriving at church. There would be more than one of her parents exhibiting an outburst if the truth was known.

Father groaned. "I may someday come home with a fine new Ford and be the envy of all the neighbors."

"Let's do go inside before you cause a spectacle, Ernest."

"Would you like it if I denied you a new hat?" Father sent his wife an ominous look.

Mother's eyes grew large. "You wouldn't dare."

"I would."

"Mother, Father, please. We need to get inside. Can we postpone this conversation for another time?"

Father was the first to acquiesce. "For you, Almira, we will adjourn this debate."

Emilie sighed. Spoken like the attorney Father was.

The strains of the organ flowed through the door, as Emilie and her guests entered the humble white church with the tall steeple.

"Reverend Arkley, I present to you my mother, Cecelia Crawford; my father, Ernest Crawford, Esq.; and their family friend, Donald W. Smith, III."

Reverend Arkley, in his usual amicable way, graciously greeted the three, then asked a few questions before greeting those next in line.

"Oh, how quaint," remarked Mother. "Do you have your own pew, Almira?"

Emilie didn't explain the irony that if a pew was only for family members, as Mother intended it to be, that Emilie would not need her own pew. "Let us sit here," she offered instead.

Hattie and Jep joined their respective families, and Morris and Vera gave Emilie a questioning glance. Usually, they sat with Emilie at church. She nodded. They were her friends, as well as her staff. The elderly couple clamored into the pew first, followed by Emilie, Mother, Father, and on the end, Mr. Smith.

"Does your staff always sit with you?" whispered Mother.

"Yes, Mother, they do."

"Oh, Almira. So many pertinent things you have forgotten since the days of your upbringing."

Father, who must not have heard the previous conversation, leaned over and said, none to discreetly, "Does Almira's staff always sit with her?"

"Yes, Ernest."

"Etiquette must be different in Montana."

"Lacking, more like," answered Mother, none too quietly.

Emilie resisted the urge to shake her head and roll her eyes and instead focused on the reverend, who had taken his place at the front of the church.

After announcements, they opened their hymnals and began to sing. Emilie had never known the words to some of the most beloved hymns until Thad took her to Pastor Shay's church. Now the words that exuded worship for the Lord warmed her heart each time she uttered them. She had made it a point to commit to memory each and every word.

"Please now turn to page 106," announced Reverend Arkley.

"This is one of my favorites," Emilie told Mother, as she raised her voice to the chords of *Holy, Holy, Holy*.

"I'm not familiar with it, but it does sound lovely," said Mother, still flipping through the worn hymnal. "They could use some new hymnals. Perhaps your father and I could make a donation toward such."

Emilie paused from singing for a moment to answer her mother. "That would be most generous. Thank you, Mother."

Within five minutes, her gaze found him. Emilie knew Thad attended Hollow Creek Church rather than Grace Church. Yet, for reasons unknown to her, there he was in Reverend Arkley's congregation.

Thad stood on the opposite side of the church, looking dashing in his finest Sunday clothes. She could see his mouth move to the words, and it was clear he focused on only one thing during the hymns—worshipping God.

She almost stopped breathing for a moment, taking in Thad's devotion to his Savior. Thad taught her so much in so little time about the Lord. If nothing ever became of their relationship—if it was never repaired—Thad Alexander Evanson would always hold a place in her heart like no one else.

For he was the one who had introduced her to Jesus Christ.

When the singing concluded, everyone took their seats and passed around the donation plate. Emilie fixed her eyes briefly again on Thad. At that moment, he turned and caught her eye. Seconds, which felt like minutes, passed as their eyes connected. Emilie wished she could read the expression behind the handsome blue eyes that returned her stare.

How I miss you, Thad.

Would God see fit to restore the love that had begun to bloom between them? Emilie, more often than not lately, began to have doubts. Could she really trust the Lord to bring her and Thad together? God had so many more important matters to tend to...sick and dying people, poverty, orphans, illness and disease.

Emilie saw from her peripheral that Mother followed Emilie's glance. But Emilie didn't want to break the moment between her and Thad, so she ignored Mother's silent rebuke.

Mother had other ideas. "Almira Emilie Crawford Wheeler, it's unbecoming to stare at a gentleman in such a way," she hissed.

At least this time, Mother kept her voice down.

Thad chose that moment to return his gaze to the front of the church and Emilie did the same. But she remained staring at his back and those strong shoulders. She recalled the times they shared an embrace. If only...

"Thank you all for coming today," said Reverend Arkley. "I see we have some guests. Welcome to Grace Church. We are delighted to have you." He nodded his graying head toward Mother, Father, and Mr. Smith. Emilie caught Mr. Smith's smirk and offered a prayer heavenward for the pompous man.

After all, Emilie had learned just last week that one was to pray for one's enemies.

THAD HADN'T intended to visit Grace Church instead of his own church. It just happened.

Happened when he saw Emilie's Model T motoring toward the church.

Happened when he gave his hundredth thought to the fact Emilie was promised to another.

Happened the instant he realized he wanted to see her again.

Even from afar.

And there she was. Sitting with Vera and Morris, an older couple he presumed to be her parents, and Mr. Smith. He yearned to take her into his arms again and apologize for all he'd done to cause her pain. For his role in their failed courtship.

But he couldn't

And he wouldn't.

For her heart now belonged to Mr. Smith.

CHAPTER THIRTY-SEVEN

When they returned home, Emilie gave Father a tour of the ranch. They strolled through her gardens and meandered past the closest fields. Try as she might, Emilie couldn't take her mind off searching for a sight of Thad. What was he doing at this very moment? Did he miss her like she missed him?

Father was silent most of the time during the tour. He had always been a man of few words, except in the court room where he presented a debate like none other. Perhaps that was why he so often won the cases he took on as his own.

That evening, Mother joined Emilie on the front porch. "What did you think of the church services today, Mother?"

"It was a pleasant time. Reverend Arkley does have a unique way about him that makes one want to sit up and take notice of the topic at hand."

"I agree. For the longest time, I didn't attend church in Hollow Creek. I'm so glad I changed my mind."

Mother looked thoughtful, but said nothing. Emilie would remember to pray for her and Father often. Hadn't Pastor Shay once preached on the importance of praying for the unsaved?

"I must ask, Almira, about the young man you exchanged glances with during the service."

"Yes?"

"He appeared quite interested in you."

He did? That's comforting, for I couldn't read from Thad's expression what his thoughts were toward me today.

"He's a nice man. Godly, kind, thoughtful, and generous."

"A hireling, I suppose."

"He does work on a ranch, yes."

"Almira, do I need to remind you such a man is far beneath your station?"

Emilie sighed. How much should she tell Mother about Thad?

Mother continued. "I know you are not fond of Mr. Smith. Truth be told, I have grown less fond of him during this visit. He was most brash in his conversation with you this morning and I had every mind to put him in his place. The only thing keeping me from doing so was decorum. Nonetheless, your father thinks of Mr. Smith as a son, so it is natural your father would want you to court and eventually marry Mr. Smith. You have expressed your concerns to me."

"My decision remains, Mother. I will neither court nor marry him."

"Yes, we have discussed this. You mentioned your heart belongs to another."

"It does."

Mother sighed. "Might I ask if the young man at church is the one to whom your heart belongs?"

"He is the one."

"I assumed as much."

Silence lingered between them until Mother again voiced her concerns. "Almira, some men will only be interested in your money, of which you have a tidy sum. Not only do you have your own funds and the funds from Newton's estate, but you also will someday inherit all your father and I own. I daresay you will never be lacking."

"Yes, Mother, I know. I'm well aware there are men only looking to take the money of a lonely young widow. However, Thad—that's his name—isn't like that."

"How can you be sure?"

Emilie turned to face Mother. How many times had she dreamed of being able to carry on a worthwhile—even intimate—conversation with her mother? From the time she was born, Emilie was raised by nannies, then sent to boarding schools. She'd never had the type of relationship with either of her parents that "normal," less affluent girls had. She never had the kind of relationship where she could speak to Mother about anything and know that Mother loved her regardless. Yet, here they were, sitting on the porch, discussing Emilie's future.

"Mother, I know you and Father care for me. I appreciate that. However, Thad is wealthy in his own right. When we met, neither of us knew the other was well-heeled."

"What a relief to know of his financial state." Mother, in her normal dramatic fashion, rested a hand to her forehead. "If you're sure we cannot persuade you to return to New York?"

"No, Mother, I'm sorry."

"And we cannot persuade you to marry a man of your father's choosing? The son of one of his lawyer friends or business associates, perhaps?"

Emilie shook her head. "I desire to marry for love this time, Mother."

Mother took Emilie's hands in hers and gave a firm nod. "Then Almira, you must follow your heart toward the one to whom your heart belongs."

THE NEXT morning, Mother journeyed to town with Vera in the buggy. Father, and presumably Mr. Smith as well, joined Morris to go fishing, something Father endeavored to do while visiting the primitive land of his daughter.

Emilie walked out to the porch and inhaled a deep breath of the fresh Montana air. In two days, her parents and Mr. Smith would be on their way back to New York. She would miss

Mother and Father, especially since she and Mother had come to an understanding. At the same time, however, Emilie would be relieved when her life returned to normal.

And she could return to grieving over Thad.

Edging down the steps, Emilie took in the bright blue sky. Except for a distant "moo" in the background from a calf, all was peaceful. Fall had arrived, and soon the leaves on the trees would change and winter would be upon her. Emilie would have to take a considerable hiatus from driving the automobile. She recalled when she worried about not being able to travel to Missoula to see Thad, whom she believed lived there.

Now she knew that the man she loved lived right next door, and no travel to Missoula would be necessary.

Not that it did her any good when he no longer returned her love.

Would her heart forever remain broken?

Fighting discouragement, Emilie continued down the path, stopping occasionally to inhale the last remaining scent of her garden blooms. She kicked at a partially-dried mud puddle with the toe of her expensive boot, not caring whether it soiled her footwear.

Emilie knew just the remedy to her downcast mood. She would go for a ride in her automobile. It had been far too long since she sat behind the wheel of her prized possession. Too long since she had tasted the freedom of the wide-open road.

With Mother, Father, and Mr. Smith all preoccupied away from the house, no one would ever know her biggest secret.

Nearly running toward the barn, Emilie took one last look about her just to be sure her family was still away. She figured she had a least an hour before they returned.

An hour was just enough time to put her dismal thoughts of Thad behind her and revel in some much-missed independence.

Cranking the engine, Emilie climbed into the sleek smooth seat and placed her hand on the steering wheel. She cared not that her hair wasn't fastened beneath a hat. Time was limited and Emilie aimed to take advantage of her freedom, as short as it may be.

Her foot on the pedal, she drove down the lane, passing the house, then curving along the fence line between the Wheeler and Evanson properties. If she could have, Emilie would have closed her eyes to enjoy the air of liberty rushing through her.

It rained yesterday and puddles still dotted the landscape, some deeper than others. Emilie expertly maneuvered the Model T, carefully avoiding the deepest of puddles. However, there was one puddle not far ahead she knew she could not avoid. She would have to see about having Jep or one of her other hired hands fill it in with dirt and soon.

A thought occurred to her then. Emilie had always been one to take the safe route. What if, just this once, she drove swiftly through the mud puddle and splashed the water all about? Instead of exercising caution, what if this one time, Emilie saw just how fast the Model T could go through water?

Her focus narrowed to one thing, and one thing only, and her tunnel vision failed to see the totality of her surroundings.

As Emilie stepped on the gas pedal of the Model T and approached the puddle, a huge grin lit her face.

If only Thad were here to attempt this adventure with her.

The wheels squealed and an enormous splash arose around both sides of the Model T. Dots of mud spattered on her hands and arms. Emilie made a note to leave enough time for a bath before her parents' return.

Just when Emilie thought all was going well during her mini-adventure, she heard a noise. A yelling man, perhaps?

Hard to tell over the putter of the engine.

But why would a man, or anyone for that matter, be out and about, especially since she had seen no one?

"ALMIRA!"

The sound of her given name caused Emilie to ponder pushing on the brake. Had she hit a cow? No, the cows all appeared safely behind the fence. Had she imagined the noise?

"ALMIRA!"

There it was again. Emilie stopped the automobile, then gazed from left to right.

That's when she saw him.

Emilie gulped. The discovery of Mr. Smith standing on the roadside covered in mud had certainly done something to her day.

It brightened it.

But it for certain had not brightened Mr. Smith's day. The arrogant man stood palms to his sides and a frown of disgust lighting his face.

Emilie offered a prayer seeking the Lord's forgiveness, then cautiously took a step from the Model T and began her walk toward Mr. Smith. "I'm dreadfully sorry, Mr. Smith."

Well, maybe not dreadfully.

Mr. Smith said nothing; he only scowled at her. His revenge would be to tell Mother and Father that Emilie had driven the Model T.

They would likely never forgive her.

Emilie took a full gander at Mr. Smith's appearance. His overpriced once-white suit was spattered with polka-dots of mud and his fedora slumped in a puddle, squished and soggy. His newly polished leather shoes were now waterlogged and no longer shiny. Mr. Smith's face sported mud droplets as he sneered.

Something did strike Emilie odd then in that moment as she stared at her nemesis.

No longer stiff, oiled, and perky, his mustache was now droopy and wilted.

Unable to hide her amusement, Emilie broke out in spontaneous laughter, her body shaking and her eyes tearing with regalement. She placed a hand over mouth, but it did little to muffle the unladylike snickers that arose from her toes to her throat.

Emilie nearly choked doing her best to cease the giggles at Mr. Smith's expense. She raised a hand to her forehead. "Oh, dear," she gasped. "Oh, dear, indeed."

And Vera and Mother, in their return from town in the buggy, approached just in time to witness it all.

NOT ONCE in all of her life had Emilie seen Mother's eyes protrude the way they did at that moment.

Not once in all of her life had Emilie ever witnessed Mother rendered speechless.

Mother gaped first at Emilie, then at Mr. Smith. Vera covered her mouth with her hand and closed her eyes.

The precious woman was likely praying, and for good reason.

"Your...your daughter, Mrs. Crawford, is an unseemly and undignified woman," Mr. Smith seethed.

Emilie caught Mother's eye. What would she say regarding Emilie's recklessness?

Mother said nothing for a moment, then stiffened her narrow shoulders. "Do not refer to my daughter that way, Donald."

"But...but..."

"No buts about it. You have been nothing but an insolent cad toward my daughter since you arrived."

If Mother's eyes had bulged upon discovering Emilie, the automobile, and Mr. Smith's predicament, Emilie's eyes bulged all the more.

Had Mother just rebuked Mr. Smith?

"Mrs. Crawford, do take that back."

"I will not. Vera, would you please take me to the house? I fear I must momentarily recline from all of this excitement. Almira, perhaps you and I can meet and speak this evening after supper."

"Yes, Mother."

"Very well then." Mother took another deep breath and stared straight ahead, as Vera beckoned the horses to continue down the lane.

Emilie stole a hasty peek at Mr. Smith, as she climbed back into the automobile. His crusty expression left her no question as to his feelings about the predicament in which he had found himself. His thin lips were twisted into a glower and his nostrils flared. She inwardly giggled, as she thought of how he reminded her of a bull in a bull fight she had once seen.

Really. He is already perturbed, so what would be the harm in...

Emilie turned the wheel to navigate the motorcar into the opposite direction. Yes, she would be repenting of this action long into the night. But some things were worth it, right?

Backing slowly into the large puddle, she allowed the plan within her mind to take form. With a heavy foot, she pressed on the gas pedal. The automobile gave a lurch before sputtering the mud from the puddle up in all directions. Most notably on Mr. Smith. "ALMIRA!" he bellowed.

Mud freckles spattered onto her shirtwaist.

But Emilie cared not.

Feeling rather brave, she craned her neck to see that Mr. Smith was now fully covered in mud from head to toe, with the exception of two beady eyes tossing her an irate glare.

Serves you right, Mr. Donald W. Smith, III, for not being where you were supposed to be —fishing with Father!

As swiftly as she could, Emilie motored on her way back to the barn.

And Mr. Smith?

He stomped all the way back to the house, his no-longer shiny shoes splashing up more mud onto the backs of his pant-legs. And his mud-entrenched self camouflaging his appearance.

And Mother? Emilie thought she caught a glimpse of a smirk on her face as she rode with Vera back to the house.

AFTER SUPPER, Emilie joined Mother in the parlor for their conversation. Mr. Smith retired early, and the looks Father repeatedly gave Emilie boasted intense concern. "Your mother will be discussing this incident with you," he chastened her just after hearing of the episode.

True to Father's promise, Mother had an opinion about the events of the afternoon.

"Mother, thank you for defending me against Mr. Smith earlier today."

Would Mother's defense be short-lived? Did she regret it?

"Now, Almira. Do understand one thing. You were quite improper spraying mud all over Mr. Smith. In the social circles in New York, you would be deemed a rabble-rouser. Gossip about you would spread throughout the city and polite society would keep their distance from you. You could even be shunned in some social circles. The motoring of the vehicle alone would be cause for talk."

Emilie slid down a bit in her parlor chair. Mother's lecture, while not unexpected, did cause Emilie to regret the occurrence. "Mother, for a second, I honestly did not see Mr. Smith on the road."

"Is that true, Almira?"

"Indeed, Mother."

"And the automobile?"

"I'm rather taken with it, Mother. The independence it provides is like none other. Morris motors me occasionally, but at other times..."

"Am I to understand that you motor quite frequently?"

"Yes, Mother."

"What am I to do with you, Almira? Such a spirited young woman. You'll be thirty in a couple of years. Ought you not to revel in such foolish escapades?"

"If only you could partake in frequent automobile rides, you would understand."

"Nonsense. Now you sound like your father."

Emilie folded her hands in her lap.

"Nonetheless..." Mother paused with a sniffle and an inhalation, as if attempting to catch her breath.

"Mother, are you quite all right?"

Mother said nothing, but sniffed again.

"Mother?"

The next thing Emilie knew, Mother was laughing. And not just a calm and reserved laugh, but an all-out expression of amusement. "Oh, Almira. Really!"

"Begging your pardon?"

Mother appeared to be gasping for air and tears ran down her cheeks. Emilie had never once seen her in such a condition. Should she ask Jep to fetch the doctor?

"You...you...Mr. Smith..." Mother continued to laugh a glorious laugh that sounded like music to Emilie's ears. Before she could stop herself, Emilie was giggling too.

Mother reached across the sofa and clasped Emilie's hands. "Oh, Almira. The look on Mr. Smith's face. All disrupted and upset. I shan't ever forget it."

Emilie recalled Mr. Smith's appearance as well. "And his polka-dot white suit and then his mustache..."

"Oh, yes. His mustache. Wilted like a dead flower," guffawed Mother. She gave a snort with her laugh, then covered her mouth in embarrassment. But it was short-lived. "And then, and then, Almira, you doused him with mud all over again. The poor, dear man."

Poor, dear man indeed!

After a few moments, Mother attempted to contain herself. "Well, for goodness. What would polite society think of me behaving in such an uncivilized manner? A sobering thought, indeed." She did her best to put on a serious presence.

But Mother didn't succeed.

Nor did Emilie.

And on that day, Emilie formed a bond with her mother that changed their entire relationship.

It was the only thing she would fondly accredit to Mr. Smith.

CHAPTER THIRTY-EIGHT

Thad parked his automobile in front of the orphanage. The children must be inside for studies, he reasoned, for he saw that no one was outside of the institution. He imagined them hard at work with their writing and arithmetic, quieted from their usual rambunctious selves. Thad reached into the backseat for the bat and ball. The children loved it when he played a game of baseball with them.

The orphanage and its occupants had stolen Thad's heart ever since he heard Mrs. Hagen speak of it during a church service a few years back. God stirred something mighty within him to help the foundlings who so desperately needed male mentors to care about them.

Had it not been for his grandparents, Thad, as an orphan, might have resided in a place such as this. The children were fortunate to have Mrs. Hagen and her dedicated staff to care for them. He prayed daily that her dream for all of the children to find permanent homes would someday come to fruition.

In honor of the grandparents who raised him when Thad was orphaned, he visited a few days each month to play ball with the children and to make a financial donation.

Thad sauntered up the steps to the front door. One of the children, little Ephraim, once told Thad there were fifteen steps. "And I should know, Mr. Evanson. I falled down several of them one day goin' to recess."

Thad thanked the Lord profusely Ephraim hadn't ended up with more than a few scratches from his fall. A smile lit his face. Not that he would ever let on as such, but Ephraim was his favorite. The boisterous six-year-old youngster had stolen his heart from the moment he met him. Perhaps there was something in the boy that reminded Thad of himself at that age. So full of energy and always seeking the next activity; yet, contemplative and thoughtful. Someday, if Thad ever married, he would adopt Ephraim and be the loving father the boy never had.

Marriage.

Thad's mind wandered to Emilie. He had hoped to marry her one day. Disappointment and regret rippled through him.

But to marry Emilie had simply not been in God's will.

Yet, he couldn't imagine her finding happiness with Mr. Smith.

Brushing aside the continual thoughts of Emilie and all he had lost because of a silly argument, Thad opened the door and wandered inside. Mrs. Hagen sat at her desk to the left of the foyer.

"Mr. Evanson, what a pleasure to see you." The kind woman in her fifties waved at him. "The children will be so happy you've arrived. Ephraim speaks of nothing else after you leave each visit."

"Well, he'll be pleased to know that I brought the bat and ball once again."

"After the noonday meal, I'm sure you could persuade the children to join you in a game."

"Thank you, Mrs. Hagen. I think I enjoy it as much as they do."

She smiled. "A grown-up child is what you are, Mr. Evanson. I declare that is why the children are so taken with you. Right now they are listening to a story. Would you care to peek in on them?"

Thad nodded and followed Mrs. Hagen to the library. He stood at a distance in the doorway where neither the children nor the reader of the story could see him.

And that's when he noticed.

Emilie sat in the rocking chair, reading to the children with little Adelia on her lap.

Thad knew she volunteered her time at the orphanage from what Sheriff Keats had told him. It didn't surprise him from what he knew of Emilie's gentle nature. Someone drawn to the less fortunate, as Emilie was, would surely seek to volunteer her time with orphaned children.

A lump in his throat formed. Taken aback by her beauty, Thad stared. It was likely unfair that she didn't know he was there, and for that he ought to feel guilty.

He listened as Emilie made voices for the characters that caused even the eldest of children to giggle. Her voice stirred feelings within him.

Feelings of a longing so deep it hurt.

Feelings that would never die.

Even if Emilie had a suitor, one who planned to marry her and whisk her away from her Montana ranch to New York City, Thad would forever love her.

And forever regret the day he lost her.

Thad pushed the thoughts aside. Right now, he would partake in her beauty from afar.

A few minutes later, he took a step forward into her line of vision. When Emilie finished reading, she closed the book. The children begged for another story, and Emilie tittered, that charming lilt in her voice. She looked up from the book, and her eyes connected with his. The surprise in those sparkly amber eyes was unmistakable.

The children saw Thad and dashed toward him, their enthusiasm apparent. But Thad neither heard nor saw them. His attention remained focused on Emilie.

"Thad?" she asked as she approached him.

"Hello, Emilie."

He could see the questioning expression in her eyes. "I come to play ball with the children a few days a month."

"I never knew." She paused. "I read to them each month as well."

"I didn't see your automobile outside."

"I usually park in the back."

"Can we play ball, Mr. Evanson?" Ephraim asked.

"Soon," Thad answered, not taking his eyes from Emilie's face. He wanted to tell her he missed her. That he was glad to see her. That he loved her. That he was sorry. But the words wouldn't come.

"Mrs. Wheeler, Mr. Evanson," Mrs. Hagen interrupted, as she approached them. "We should be thrilled if you would both stay and partake in the noonday meal with us. What do you say?"

With effort, Thad averted his eyes to Mrs. Hagen. "That would be fine, ma'am."

"Oh, good, Mrs. Hagen gushed. "And you, Mrs. Wheeler?"

"I don't think I could impose."

"Oh, you're not imposing. It would be an honor. Afterwards, you can stay and watch the children join in a ballgame with Mr. Evanson. I daresay it is quite thrilling. Oh, dear me. Do the two of you know each other? Mr. Evanson, this is Mrs. Wheeler. Mrs. Wheeler, this is Mr. Evanson."

"Yes, I'm acquainted with Mr. Evanson," said Emilie.

Thad tried to discern if that was a good thing from her point of view. Likely not since they had parted ways. "We're neighbors," he said.

"Oh, what a marvelous state of affairs. Now then, Mrs. Wheeler, what do you say? Shall I have Annette prepare a place setting for you?"

"I'm not sure..."

Thad knew the hesitation was because of him. If only their circumstances had been different. If only he could tell her how he felt. If only she wasn't betrothed to another. Before he could stop the words from exiting his mouth, he said, "Please stay, Emilie."

Emilie bit her bottom lip, like she always did when she was considering something. He remembered all those times together when he'd witnessed that silly little quirk. Thad missed those days.

"I will stay."

He wanted to embrace her. Plant a kiss on those full lips. Tell her it was downright ridiculous that some half-witted argument had ended their courtship. But Thad restrained himself. While Emilie would be able to stay for the meal, and hopefully the ballgame, she wouldn't ever be in his life the same way again.

Not when she was now engaged to another.

Not when she would be leaving for New York City soon.

Thad had missed his one chance with her.

CHAPTER THIRTY-NINE

With nearly twenty children, five staff members, and Emilie and Thad, the long narrow wooden table was filled to capacity. Excitement and loud chitchat commenced until Mrs. Hagen blew a whistle. Immediately, the chatter ceased and all eyes focused on the director of the orphanage.

"Children, we have two very special guests with us today. Mrs. Wheeler and Mr. Evanson. Please show them the utmost of respect during their extended time with us today. Mr. Evanson will be organizing a ballgame after our meal. Please be sure to finish your assigned tasks before leaving the dining area. Mr. Evanson, would you kindly lead us in prayer?"

Everyone around the table reached for the hand of the person next to them. Thad met Emilie's eye. She nodded, and he clasped her hand loosely in his. Her heart flip-flopped in her chest.

It had been so long since her hand had been enveloped in Thad's strong calloused hand. Emilie's heart yearned for those days when the love between them blossomed.

Couldn't they reconcile their quarrel? Or had she missed her only chance with him?

Pushing such thoughts aside, Emilie watched as Thad, to her left, bowed his head. The children and staff followed his lead. "Dear Heavenly Father, thank You for the food we are about to receive. Bless the hands that prepared it and let it nourish our bodies. We ask also, Father, that You would keep all of the children safe during the ballgame. In Jesus's Name, Amen."

A lively round of "amens" ensued, followed by the clanging of dishes as the meal items were passed around the table.

Emilie pushed the green beans around on her plate. Mrs. Hagen suggested she and Thad sit side-by-side. Had the woman suspected there was more to their relationship than merely neighbors? Not that Emilie minded sitting next to Thad and listening to his hearty laugh whenever a child said something humorous.

Not at all.

She did feel a bit self-conscious, however. Perhaps she should have left before lunch. Emilie had come to spend time with the children and read them a story. Not to stay the entire afternoon. But to tell Mrs. Hagen she had other things to do with her day would have been an out-an-out lie. With Mother, Father, and Mr. Smith gone, Emilie's days weren't nearly as full. She loved visiting the orphanage, but she didn't love the uncomfortable feelings and emotions that arose whenever in Thad's presence.

"I heard you reading to the children," Thad said, interrupting her thoughts.

"They delight in hearing the stories. That one happened to be my favorite as a child."

"The children are fond of you."

"And of you. It appears some are eating far faster than their stomachs can digest the food, just to play a ballgame."

Thad's mouth curved upward in the quirky grin she had grown so accustomed to in their times together. "Ballgames are important, Emilie. Perhaps you would like to join us and be the first batter."

Emilie's eyes widened. "Surely not. I have not an ounce of athleticism."

He chuckled then, a pleasing and husky laugh meant all for her. Emilie reveled in it for a moment. Could they salvage what had gone wrong between them?

"Best you eat your meal, Mrs. Wheeler, before you go hungry and have no energy to join in a ballgame, much less stand on the sidelines."

The temptation to playfully slug Thad in the arm was almost too much, but Emilie refrained. "I think I shall survive just fine, but thank you kindly, Mr. Evanson, for caring about my welfare."

"I do care about you, Emilie." Thad's words this time were soft, almost to the point of being inaudible.

Had she heard him correctly? He had been so understanding and sympathetic when she told of losing the baby. He'd held her in his arms and offered reassurance.

Dare Emilie tell him she cared for him too?

"Are you ready to play ball yet, Mr. Evanson?" Ephraim asked, slipping out of his chair and sidling up next to Thad.

"I am just about finished, Ephraim."

"Good, 'cause you and me gots to win this one."

Thad chuckled and wrapped his arm around the small boy. "Winning isn't the most important thing, Ephraim, but I guarantee we will have fun."

"What's gar-en-tee?"

"It means something I am sure of."

Ephraim cocked his head to one side. "Can I be on your team?"

"Reckon that would be fine."

"Good, 'cause we are always on the same team. Say, can I hit the ball first?"

"Why don't we let someone else hit the ball first today, Ephraim? It's gentlemanly to let others go first."

Ephraim pondered the suggestion for a minute. "Sure. Okay." He reached his thin arms around Thad's neck and gave him a hug. "I wish you were my pa, Mr. Evanson. Then we could play us a game of ball any ol' time we like."

Emilie saw a wistful look in Thad's eyes. Did he wish he was Ephraim's father? She recalled Thad telling her how he almost married once. He would be a loving father.

Regret filled her heart and her mind.

"Mrs. Wheeler?"

Emilie's thoughts were interrupted by Adelia, who, sitting on Emilie's right-hand side, began tapping on her arm.

"Yes, Adelia?"

"Are you gonna come watch the ballgame?"

"I am. It sounds like it's going to be a lot of fun."

"I'm not so good at ballgames. Mr. Evanson, well, he helps me, 'cause I'm just a little girl."

Emilie smiled at Adelia. Just as she noticed Thad had taken to Ephraim more than any of the other children, so it was the same for her with Adelia. From the first time Emilie met the little girl with a limp, she had taken to the four-year-old.

If Emilie ever had the opportunity to be a mother, she would adore a daughter just like Adelia.

Marriage.

The thought flitted through her mind. The possibility of a life with Thad had seemed so imminent just a few short months ago.

Now all of that hope was gone.

The realization struck a chord of pain in her heart.

A HALF-HOUR later, the children lined up for team-picking. Thad chose two of the eldest boys as captains of their teams. As if knowing from past games that Thad and Ephraim were one unit, one of the boys picked both of them for his first pick. On it went until all of the children were chosen. Adelia, who stood on the sidelines ran to Thad as soon as the team-picking was over. "I am always on Mr. Evanson's team," she said, her blue eyes bright.

Mrs. Hagen set two chairs side by side. "Here's a chair for you, dear." She folded her rotund self into one of the chairs. "Most of the other staff enjoys standing on the sidelines. Me, I like the comfort of a chair to watch the big game."

"Thank you, Mrs. Hagen. I must say I'm looking forward to watching, as I've never seen a game like this before."

"But aren't you from New York City, dear?"

"I am. However, Mother would never take kindly to me attending a ballgame."

Miss Coverly, a tall, thin, spinster-type woman who taught the older children their lessons, stepped forward and announced, "Let the game begin!" Everyone clapped and cheered.

Mrs. Hagen motioned to a young, apprehensive woman standing near the steps. "Jessie, would you care to join us?"

Jessie avoided Mrs. Hagen's eye and instead stared at her tattered shoes. "No thank you," she said, her voice barely audible, before going back inside.

"Would you like for me to go after her?" Miss Coverly asked.

"Thank you, but we'll leave her be," Mrs. Hagen answered. To Emilie, she said, "that was Jessie Breithaupt. She recently arrived here, and we know little about her. The poor dear works for room and board, but she barely speaks a word."

EMILIE HAD no idea the rules of the game. From what she could tell, one person on one team hit the ball and the other team did their best to keep the ball-hitter from stepping on the "bases" that had been strategically placed in the yard in a diamond formation.

"I think Mr. Evanson fancies you," clucked Mrs. Hagen.

"Begging your pardon?"

"I've seen the way he looks at you."

"I know of no such thing," said Emilie, hoping that wasn't a lie. She could only surmise what Thad's feelings were for her as of late.

"Surely, dear, you see it too." Mrs. Hagen appeared hopeful. "Such a handsome couple the two of you would make, and with you being neighbors and all. How convenient."

Convenient indeed. If only they hadn't been enemies first.

CHAPTER FORTY

Emilie followed the trail of stepping stones through the gate into the family cemetery. She clutched a bouquet of flowers in her hand and a painful wistfulness in her heart. She first rested some blooms on Newt's grave before journeying to her baby's grave marker. Taking a seat, she allowed the tears to flow freely as she gathered her thoughts.

As Emilie always did when she visited, she read the engraved words: *Beloved Baby Wheeler, gone before I ever had a chance to know you.* "You were so cherished," she whispered.

The birds chirped around her with nary a care in the world. The aroma of hay combined with flowers floated on the breeze.

Emilie swallowed hard. "I still don't know why the Lord took you home before I had a chance to meet you. I will never know the answer to that question. But since coming to know Him, He has given me a peace I can't quite explain. The hurt of losing you will never go away, but Jesus has given me the grace to carry on without you. Even though some days it might feel impossible."

Would the emotions always be fresh?

A bumblebee landed on one of the blooms, diligently undertaking its task at hand. Emilie watched him for a few minutes, marveling at the intricate creation.

Her son would never see bumblebees or collect bugs or scare a younger sister with worms. A sob rose in her throat. "I hope someday to have other children. I've even contemplated adoption from the orphanage." Emilie paused. "There's this little girl there named Adelia. You would have liked her. She is just the most precious child and has a limp from an accident." She sighed. "But even if I adopt Adelia or have other children, I'll never forget you, my firstborn. I'll never forget what may have been. I grew to love you from the moment I knew I carried you and one thing I do know is I will see you again someday." The newfound realization lent a sense of peace.

A temperate breeze swept through the enclosed cemetery and the trees swayed, their branches shielding the graves from the sun. Emilie smoothed her hand along the grave marker's flat surface. "I read from the Psalms this morning. Psalm 55:12 says, '*Cast thy burden upon the* LORD, *and he shall sustain thee.*' I have cast my burden of losing you and missing you on the Lord. I know He will...He will sustain me, for He promises such."

Lord, please sustain me. It was the prayer of her heart every time she thought of her son.

Emilie sat for several silent minutes, reflecting on the verse. The Lord would sustain her. His love was unfailing, and He would help her with the loss of her child.

THAD OPENED the envelope and read the letter from someone he had not heard from in three years.

Dearest Thad,

I hope this finds you doing well. Aunt Jane has decided she wishes to visit Montana, as she is enthralled by the uncivilized West. I suggested Hollow Creek. Would you kindly retrieve us from the train depot in Missoula on September 20? We plan to stay for five days and will need a return ride to Missoula for our departure.

Please let me know by telegram at your earliest convenience.

I await your response.

Catherine

Thad read and re-read the letter several more times before folding and placing it back in the envelope.

He scratched his head. Why was Catherine contacting him after all this time? Surely Aunt Jane would be more "enthralled" with somewhere like Idaho or Wyoming.

Besides, Thad had no desire to reunite with Catherine.

But a man is always a gentleman. Grandma's voice echoed through his mind.

Best to let Catherine know as soon as possible that Thad would retrieve her and Aunt Jane from Missoula. He was sure, to Catherine's dismay, that she and her aunt would have to board at the humble Hollow Creek Hotel.

Thad sauntered into the post office to send his telegram. September 20 was less than two weeks away. What did the Lord have in mind for Thad and Catherine?

It couldn't be to rekindle their courtship, could it? Thad's mind was consumed only with thoughts of Emilie. He hadn't thought of Catherine in years.

CATHERINE WAS exactly as Thad remembered her. Hoity-toity, presumptuous, and pretty.

"Hello, Thad. You remember my Aunt Jane?" Thad had only met Catherine's aunt a few times, but he couldn't forget the aristocratic air of the crochety older woman.

"Hello, ma'am." Thad tipped his hat. "A pleasure to re-meet you," he said in as jovial tone as possible.

Aunt Jane snorted. Clearly she was not amused. "Yes," she harrumphed, then ambled away to look at a nearby shop, leaving Thad and Catherine alone.

Catherine patted his arm. "You must think me quite forward. I wasn't sure if I should come for a visit," she said, pooching out her lower lip in an exaggerated pout. "I couldn't be sure, after all, if you had married another."

Thad's thoughts went immediately to Emilie. He had been close to proposing to her before their disagreement. If he had, would Emilie have said "yes?"

"Thad?"

Catherine's high-pitched voice brought him back to the present. "I'm glad I haven't been replaced," she said, a glint in her eyes.

Thad avoided her statement.

"We should get on the road to Hollow Creek." He led Catherine and Aunt Jane to the automobile.

The drive to Hollow Creek gave Thad plenty of time in between Catherine's drivel to contemplate the real reason she had paid him a visit.

THE FOLLOWING day, Thad retrieved Catherine and Aunt Jane from the Hollow Creek Hotel to attend church. From their sour expressions, he figured neither was amused at staying at the unpretentious hotel.

No greeting, just a huff from Aunt Jane. "No indoor plumbing. Who stays at a place like that?"

"I'm sorry, Aunt Jane, truly I am." Catherine pouted. "I wish I could have warned you."

Aunt Jane stiffened her narrow shoulders, which severely contrasted her ample hips, making her appear as though an exaggerated pear. "Well, I never expected to stay somewhere so unsophisticated."

"Begging your pardon, Aunt Jane, but didn't you wish to visit somewhere uncivilized?" Thad asked.

"Well, I never!" Aunt Jane stomped toward the automobile and waited for Thad to open the door for her.

Catherine inched next to Thad and whispered. "Oh, Thad. You mustn't speak to Aunt Jane that way. You'll offend her."

"Sorry," he muttered. *But to my way of thinking, Aunt Jane is offended by nearly everything.*

"Are we going to services or not?" Aunt Jane demanded. "For if we are not, then I shall go back inside that hideous abode and recline for the remainder of the day."

Thad remembered Aunt Jane from when he courted Catherine. The woman, whom Catherine deemed an admirable person, remained exhausting and onerous. In the years since Catherine's mother passed, Catherine had grown particularly fond of her paternal aunt. But Thad had never seen the "charm" of the older woman.

"We could walk to the church since it's such a short distance," Thad offered.

Aunt Jane touched a hand to her thin gray-streaked mousy-brown hair. "I do declare. I want to arrive in style at the services. Not walk. My aching bones simply cannot tolerate such a lengthy stroll."

Thad's eyes traveled the seventy-five feet to where the steepled church stood. By the time he fired up the automobile, loaded everyone, and drove there, they could have walked there twice. Even with Aunt Jane's slow pace.

For as obstinate as the woman was, Thad was surprised she allowed him to call her "Aunt Jane," rather than Miss Strom.

He assisted Aunt Jane and Catherine into the motorcar, gave the automobile a good crank, then climbed in for the meager distance to church.

Services, as usual, were full. Thad, for the second time, decided to attend Grace Church for a chance to see Emilie. He scanned the area outside of the church and spied her not far from where he stood with his guests. Thad took a deep breath. He missed her. Missed talking to her; missed sharing about their day; and missed holding her in his arms.

Somehow, someway, he had to mend the ridiculous rift that had started between them and had only grown bigger with each passing day.

If only she wasn't promised to another.

At least Emilie had spoken to him at the orphanage. That was a start. But would she forgive him? "Thaddeus!" snapped Aunt Jane, her hands on her wide hips. Thad's attention jerked at the voice of the obnoxious woman. Why was it that she presumed his full name to be Thaddeus? *It's Thad. Just Thad*, he wanted to retort, but held his tongue.

"Aren't you going to introduce us?" sneered Aunt Jane, her nostrils flared, lips pursed, and her one pointy eyebrow quirked.

"Uh..." To not be in Aunt Jane's good graces was nothing new, but the troublesome woman did make even the toughest of men concede to her demanding requests.

Aunt Jane remained scrutinizing Thad, awaiting his answer. Her hazel eyes never blinked.

She reminded Thad of a bull about ready to charge its target. Thad did his best not to chuckle. "Yes, Aunt Jane. I will introduce you."

"It's about time you came to your senses and ceased dilly-dallying. What a lack of manners you have, young man."

Thad bit his tongue at Aunt Jane's chastisement. The alternative was not advisable. Especially with onlookers. "Yes, ma'am."

"Now proceed henceforth."

Instantly, Aunt Jane put on a different demeanor. Her overly-large mouth that usually spouted orders curved into a fake smile, as she and Catherine stepped up beside the reverend.

"May I present to you Jane Strom and her niece, Catherine Strom," Thad mumbled.

Reverend Arkley greeted them. "So nice of you to pay a visit to Hollow Creek. How long will you be staying?"

Thad noticed that Emilie, Vera, and Morris were immediately behind Aunt Jane.

"We'll be regrettably staying for only a couple more days on this visit," touted Catherine.

"Yes, regrettably." Sarcasm lined the two words uttered from Aunt Jane's thin lips.

"It is a pleasure to meet you, Reverend. I'm Thad's betrothed."

Reverend Arkley arched an eyebrow and regarded Thad, who gave a slight shake of his head. "Thad is an upright man. You could do no better."

Thad wanted to pull the reverend aside and tell him that Catherine wasn't his betrothed. Not anymore, and hadn't been for three years. But Catherine continued to gush all the more. Aunt Jane stood, her wide forehead creased and her pointy nose tilted upward, not speaking so much as a syllable.

After many attempts, Thad finally caught Emilie's eye. A question lined her pretty face. Had she heard Catherine's remark? What must she think?

From the pain in her eyes, Thad knew the answer. She had heard. He shook his head ever so slightly. Would Emilie understand that Catherine had exaggerated what she'd said? Instead of maintaining eye contact, Emilie averted her gaze.

"Emilie," Thad called. He started toward her, taking large strides. He needed to speak with her. If she heard what Catherine said, things would be even worse between them.

But Catherine grabbed his arm and pulled him back. "Thad, where are you going?"

"Yes, Thaddeus, where are you going?" snarled Aunt Jane.

And Emilie hadn't even turned her head at the sound of his voice when Thad had called her name.

Would they ever make amends?

Before Thad could give his dilemma more thought, Floyd trotted up beside him, thumbs hooked into his suspenders. The ranch hand sized up Aunt Jane with an approving eye. "Well, howdy there, little lady. I don't believe you and me's had the priv-o-lidge to meet. May I be given the blissful pleasure of escortin' ya into the church?" Before Aunt Jane could respond, Floyd continued. "Yer likely wonderin' where I learned all them fancy words: blissful, escortin', well I done learned them at the saloon. Ya see, this man there was talkin' 'bout..." Floyd gulped and avoided Thad's eye. "Meanin' I don't spend time no more in the saloon or nothin', it's just somethin' I reckon I heard a long time ago. So what do ya say? Can I do some blissful escortin'?"

Aunt Jane snapped her long neck back and took in an eyeful of Floyd. It took all of Thad's self-control not to start chortling at the woman's obvious displeasure.

"The audacity and the gall! Whom, pray tell, are you speaking to?"

"Why, you, of course. Ain't no one else here as purdy as you." Floyd winked, his wrinkled face becoming all the more furrowed.

Aunt Jane's face turned red. But not with the pleasing blush Thad had seen on some women when they were complimented by a man's words. No, Aunt Jane's appearance was the opposite—more of the ruddy look that highlighted the oversized brown mole on her left cheek. "How dare you speak to me in such a condescending manner," she shrieked, her lips curling into a permanent scowl.

Thad looked around to see if anyone had heard the exchange. No one seemed to be paying Aunt Jane and Floyd much mind. For that, Thad was grateful. He stroked his chin and did his best not to laugh at the duo's outlandish behavior.

Floyd took a step toward Aunt Jane. "Not meanin' no disrespect, ma'am. It's just that I ain't never seen you here a'fore, and..."

"That will be enough." Aunt Jane waved her arm to dismiss Floyd. "What makes you have the inkling that a cultured woman of my respectability would want anything to do with the likes of you?"

Instead of becoming offended, Floyd merely grinned. "I best be gettin' into the church. Mebe you and me can meet up after the sermon."

"I think not."

Floyd chuckled and sauntered off into the church.

"What a hideous man, and what is that foul odor?" Aunt Jane pinched her long, pointed nose.

Thad almost felt sorry for Floyd.

Almost.

CHAPTER FORTY-ONE

At her unrelenting insistence, Thad promised Catherine and Aunt Jane he would show them his home on Monday. "In the newspaper article I read, it stated that your cattle operation has grown extensively." Catherine rested a hand on his arm and leaned toward him.

Thad nodded, but said nothing, and drove the two to the Evanson Ranch. He recalled speaking with the reporter from his hometown in Illinois about his humble beginnings. He had not anticipated Catherine reading the article. When they went their separate ways, Thad never expected to see her again.

They passed first by Emilie's home. He saw her outside amongst the trees that had lost most of their leaves and his breath caught. She was as lovely as the day he had first met her.

"Ooh," squealed Catherine, her shrill voice causing Thad to cringe. "Is that your home?"

"No, that's the Wheeler Ranch."

"Such a shame, for I would surely like to live in such a house."

Of course Catherine would want to live in such a house. It was impressive, even by city standards and the view of the mountains was unmatched.

"Are you sure it's not your house?" she pouted, her long face appearing even longer.

"Quite sure." What had he ever seen in Catherine?

A few minutes later they arrived in the front of Thad's home. Shabby in comparison to Emilie's mansion, for sure. It needed new paint and the porch could stand some repairs.

Curious that his quest for everything to be perfect in his life hadn't extended to his home.

"Why are we stopping here?" snapped Aunt Jane, her voice hasty and clipped. "I am most certainly not in the mood for social calls to people I do not know."

Catherine held a hand to her chest. "Nothing is wrong with the automobile is there? Father says sometimes automobiles can be unreliable."

"There's nothing wrong with the automobile," Thad said, realizing his voice almost sounded like a hiss. He stopped the motorcar. "This is my home."

"Begging your pardon?"

"This is my home, Catherine. Would you like me to give you a tour of the grounds? We recently built a new barn to replace the prior one."

"I declare it's an absolute necessity that you rebuild the house," retorted Aunt Jane. "I cannot in good conscience allow my only niece to live in such an abode. And really, who cares about a pathetic barn?"

A pathetic barn? It's impressive if I do say so myself.

Thad squinted at Aunt Jane in the backseat. Why would Catherine wish to live there? Unless...

"I will handle this, Aunt Jane. It won't be easy, but I will handle it."

"Handle what, Catherine?"

"Thad, please do not take offense, but I am not the least bit interested in seeing the new barn. Maybe we should take Aunt Jane back to the hotel and perhaps you and I could go for a drive."

"Yes, of that I would be most agreeable," said Aunt Jane. "This venture has been utterly boring. All I have seen are cows and more cows. Please, do take me back to the hotel so I may recline on the hard straw bed."

Thad didn't miss the sarcasm in Aunt Jane's voice. Was there no pleasing the woman? No wonder she never married.

"Poor Aunt Jane. She really cannot handle much fanfare these days," said Catherine after they had returned her aunt to the hotel. "Seeing your home caused her so much disturbance. She was expecting so much more. Truth be told, so was I."

Two miles later, Thad pulled to the side of the road to a peaceful clearing by the river. "Aren't the mountains a sight to behold today?" he asked, opening the door for Catherine.

"Indeed," she answered, but didn't bother to look in the direction of the mountains.

So opposite of his Emilie, who loved God's creation, especially the mountains and her flowers.

His Emilie? Thad shook his head. She was his Emilie no longer.

More like Mr. Smith's Emilie.

Thad led Catherine to a picturesque location near the river. "Catherine, the weather is set to change anytime. The nights have grown colder, and there's talk of snow any day now."

In response to Thad's words, Catherine pulled her wrap tightly around her shoulders. "Aunt Jane and I so hoped we could make our visit and return to Illinois before winter begins. I'm told it arrives quite early in Montana."

"Sometimes it does."

Catherine faced him, her face tilted upward, and she fluttered her lashes in a way that likely had an effect on male admirers.

It once had an effect on Thad. But no longer and not for some time. He'd become older, wiser, and more discerning. "What is the real reason you came to Hollow Creek?"

"I told you in my letter. Because Aunt Jane wished to visit somewhere uncivilized. She spends so much time reading books these days and has heard so much about the Wild West." Catherine paused. "I think she half thought she would see a wagon train or a shootout while we were here." She placed a hand on his arm. "Thad, I have missed you so."

Thad searched her eyes, attempting to determine if she told the truth. When she decided to break their engagement, there had been no remorse for three years. Why now?

"Do you not believe that I miss you?"

"I don't know what to believe, Catherine."

"I still love you, Thad." She sighed. "But I might as well confess the truth. We came here for a visit, not so much for Aunt Jane, although she did make mention of visiting the uncivilized West." She paused. "Truth of the matter is that we came for me."

"For you?"

"Yes. I hoped I would be able to assuage the guilt within me for breaking your heart those years ago. I see now what an error I have made."

Broke my heart? "Catherine..."

She fluttered her eyelashes at him again. "Please, Thad, allow me to finish. You see, when I read that article in the newspaper, I knew I had made a grievous error. So, I talked Aunt Jane into accompanying me for a visit. I knew once you and I spoke, we would be able to reconcile. "

"I'm not..."

Catherine held a finger to his lips. "Thad, I know some things will be an adjustment for both of us, to be sure. With the Evanson Cattle Company as successful it is, you are fortunate to be able to turn the everyday burdens of the ranch over to your foreman."

"Turn it over to my foreman?"

Pete was more than capable, but Thad loved running the ranch.

"Yes, and as such, you could return to Illinois with me, and we wouldn't even have to worry that your home is less than desirable."

"I'm not returning to Illinois. Montana is my home."

"You would still own your home here, such as it is. We could return by train often during pleasant weather. The rest of the time, you could manage your ranch from Illinois. Father has already promised an office for your use at a modest price."

"Catherine, I am not leaving Montana."

Catherine's shoulders slumped and she sniffed. "I was worried you might say as much." Reaching into her reticule, she retrieved a handkerchief and dabbed her eyes. "I know that with true love, one must compromise at times. Such is the case for me this time. What if we reside in Montana during the summer months and during the remainder of the year we take up residence in Illinois? That *was* your home, Thad."

"*Was* my home, Catherine, while my grandparents were alive."

"And then you sold their meager farm and moved here. What would they say if they knew you sold their farm?"

Her attempt to place guilt on him irritated Thad. "I had already discussed it with Grandpa long before he and Grandma passed on. He knew it was my dream to own a cattle ranch, and he supported that plan."

Catherine waved him off. "Anyhow, I believe my idea about residing in both places during different times of the year makes sense."

"You are assuming we marry, then."

"Absolutely. Remember when we courted how we talked of our dreams?"

How you talked of your dreams.

Thad shook his head. "What made you change your mind about me? Was it the newspaper article?"

"However do you mean?"

"When you saw I was making something of myself, was that when you changed your mind. Did you envision I might someday be a wealthy man?"

"You are a wealthy man now, are you not?" Catherine's voice elevated in pitch.

"Indeed. The Lord has blessed me in a mighty way. With His help and hard work, I grew the ranch to what it is now."

"Then all is well."

Just as he'd thought. "It was my wealth that encouraged you to contact me?" It was more of a statement than a question, for Thad already knew the answer.

Catherine's face paled. "Thad, don't make me admit that."

"I know how important money is to you."

"I only want what's best for us. That's why I tried so hard to convince you to work for Father at his business. We could have a home now far beyond even that extraordinary home on the way to your house."

"As you recall, I didn't want to work for your father."

Catherine reached up and took his face in her hands. Unease riveted through him. Before he could take a step back from her, Thad heard the sound of an automobile. He glanced up in time to see Emilie pass by. His eyes connected with hers for a brief moment as she drove by.

What must she think? Even from this distance, there was no mistaking the anguished look in her eyes. *Emilie, it's not what you think!* He longed to run after her and tell her the truth. About everything.

Thad stepped away from Catherine.

"You must be reasonable, Thad Evanson. This would work for all of us."

"Begging your pardon, Catherine?"

"I do declare, you've not heard a word I've said. Perhaps if you spent less time just staring at that passing automobile and turned your attention to me instead, I wouldn't have to repeat myself." She huffed. "I said that I do believe this arrangement will work best for all of us."

"All of us?"

"Yes. Me, you, Father."

"Your father should have found someone else to work for him by now."

"Oh, he has found another employee to take your place. You really disappointed Father, you know."

Thad sighed. When Catherine broke their engagement, he had taken it hard. He felt as though he hadn't measured up to Catherine's expectations. He couldn't stay in Illinois and work for her father merely because that's what she wanted. Thad would never have been content. When he had told her as much, she had broken the engagement and decided they could no longer marry.

Catherine had refused to follow him to Montana.

Just as Thad refused to remain with her in Illinois.

But if Emilie wanted him to, Thad would have moved to Missoula before he knew she resided here in Hollow Creek.

"Thad, if we marry, it will benefit everyone. Father's business..."

"What about your father's business?"

"It isn't doing as well as it once was." Her hand trembled as she wiped away a tear. "It leaves me quite despondent to give it thought."

Thad shook his head. Why had he not noticed before her inclination toward theatrics? "I am sorry to hear that, Catherine, but I'm not sure how our marrying will benefit him."

"Perhaps as an employee and also financially you could assist him until the business gets a foothold again."

"That's what this is about?"

"Thad, please do not be angry with me. I do care for you."

"I'm sorry, Catherine. I can't marry you."

"Whyever not?"

"I don't love you."

"Love matters only so much. If only Aunt Jane hadn't been so persnickety and demanding about marrying only for love as they do in the dime novels, then she wouldn't be a spinster to this day."

"Love matters to me, Catherine."

"What of Father?"

"I'm sure he has other means to assist his business in gaining a foothold again. Are you destitute?"

"Destitute?" Catherine jerked her head back and laughed. "Heavens no. We are far from destitute. But we have had to sell one of our homes."

"Then all will be well."

Catherine did nothing to hide her sullen face. "Do you love another, Thad? Have I been replaced?"

"As a matter of fact, yes, Catherine. I do love another. Very much so."

"There's no changing your mind?"

"No.

"I declare then. I can't believe you could be so obtuse. Do return me to the hotel. Tomorrow, I must insist you drive Aunt Jane and me to Missoula where we may catch the next train."

Thad nodded and followed Catherine to the automobile.

Now if only he could fix what was broken between he and the woman he truly loved.

CHAPTER FORTY-TWO

While in town, Morris retrieved some correspondence from the post office for Emilie. She hoped it might be good news.

My Dearest Almira,

I hope this finds you doing well. After we attended church in your little village, I decided to begin searching for such a church here. As you know, in New York City, there are dozens of options. The driver took me to a location outside the city where I found a humble church with a reverend much like the one at Grace Church. The message was excellent, and I daresay conviction filled my heart. Your father was a bit skeptical at first at the thought of attending services, but soon became amenable to my suggestion. (Of course, I also became amenable to him owning an automobile for us to journey back and forth to the church).

As such, he and I have frequented our new church five Sundays in a row now. I must admit I had absolutely no idea of the magnitude of what Jesus did for us. Thank you for insisting we attend services when we visited you.

How is the young man to whom you have given your heart? Almira, dear, I know you to be a bit stubborn, so I want to encourage you to settle whatever differences you have with this man. Pleased am I that he is wealthy in his own right. The reverend told us to pray in burdensome times. It brought to mind the burden you obviously carry regarding the two of you.

Dear daughter, I wish only for the best for you in all things. While I am utterly disturbed that you choose to stay in Montana, which is such an uncivilized place, I also understand it is where you feel you belong. Should you desire to visit your father and me in New York City—and we hope you do—we would welcome you with open arms. I promise we will not insist you stay.

On a lighter note, remember Donald, the one whom your father thought would make a good match for you? Suffice it to say, the man is a disreputable scoundrel, and I am thankful you did not marry him. He was found embezzling from his father's company. Can you believe such a thing?

As I am learning, God watches over us and was certainly watching over you regarding Donald.

Do write and let me know how you fare.

With Much Love,
Mother

Emilie folded Mother's letter and placed it on the bureau in her room. She was thankful Mother started attending church regularly and had softened to the idea of Emilie continuing to reside in Montana. Mother had come a long way since her visit to Hollow Creek. Obviously, the Lord was working in more lives than just Emilie's.

The house suddenly felt hot and muggy. Perhaps Emilie should take advantage of the unseasonably warm day and go for what could be her last drive in the Model T before winter set in.

Minutes later, she climbed into the automobile and motored down the road. She welcomed the breeze on her face to combat the perspiration dampening her forehead. For some reason, her body started to ache and the headache she had amassed late yesterday lingered. At times, dizziness overtook her. She ought not to be driving, she knew, but needed time to escape and think. The weather had turned colder in recent weeks, and she knew these last few days of freedom in the automobile were numbered.

On the open road, Emilie could set free her thoughts, and today, she had many. She hadn't stopped thinking about church services yesterday. She had been taken aback the moment she heard the woman in front of her say Thad was her beau. Had he been courting someone all along and hadn't told Emilie? Sadly, it would not surprise her. He had lied about other things. Or had this woman replaced Emilie when he broke off their courtship?

Emilie attempted not to stare at the petite dark-haired woman with perfectly-pinned curls, who inspected her from head-to-toe, as if judging every aspect of her appearance. Emilie felt self-conscious and wished she had worn a different ensemble.

The woman had put on airs for some time, as she stood speaking with the reverend in her high-pitched voice.

Beside Thad's betrothed stood an older and taller woman. A homely woman, at best, Emilie thought, then chastised herself. *Lord, please forgive me for my uncharitable thoughts.*

For the briefest of moments, she caught Thad's eye. What had he been thinking? Did he miss the times they shared? Emilie certainly did. She thought she saw an inkling of hope at the orphanage that things between them could be restored. But now...

Emilie prayed during the entire church service that the Lord would direct her thoughts and mind to the sermon at hand, rather than on Thad and his fiancé.

After the service, Emilie, Vera, and Morris were walking to the automobile when she had heard Thad beckoning her. However, instead of responding, Emilie quickened her step.

The entire misunderstanding between her and Thad had grown far out of proportion. She continually prayed for guidance and even considered speaking again with Vera about it.

And now, Thad's heart belonged to someone else.

Perhaps because of that, she need no longer worry about repairing the rift between them.

The thought bothered Emilie almost more than she could bear.

The road ahead curved slightly as she approached a perfect setting near the river. She slowed the motorcar and noticed another Model T was parked by the side of the road. "Is that Thad's?" she inquired aloud, knowing the answer to her own question.

Emilie drew closer to the other automobile. She saw Thad and his betrothed near the river. She held his face in her hands. Had they been about to kiss? Or had they already kissed?

Emilie's heart broke all over again.

Surely there was some way they could reconcile. Emilie needed to summon the courage to apologize for her chicanery. She needed the opportunity to tell Thad she loved him. Wanted to be in his life again.

But it was obvious he didn't feel the same.

Thad so fleetingly glanced her way when she drove by that Emilie thought she imagined it. She returned her eyes to road, not wanting to comprehend the courtship between the man she loved and someone else.

Emilie hadn't felt well all weekend. Her stomach roiled as though the food she ate earlier might make a reappearance.

Who knew a broken heart could be so painful?

CHAPTER FORTY-THREE

Due to the conversation Thad shared with Catherine the day before, the trip to Missoula contained minimal dialogue. Once in a while, Aunt Jane would offer a negative comment or complaint. Thad did not even attempt to do more than grunt at her continual pessimistic rambling. He had too much on his mind to deal with her dramatic behavior.

Emilie motored by at about the time Catherine held his face in her hands. An uncomfortable gesture in and of itself, not to mention the added awkward addition of Emilie viewing the act of affection. What had she thought? Did she really believe Thad was Catherine's beau? All indications at church pointed to that exact assumption.

How he wished he didn't have to make the lengthy trip to Missoula. Instead, Thad wished he could visit Emilie and set things to right. He would tell her Catherine wasn't his betrothed and hadn't been for over three years and then he would ask her if she would reconsider her engagement to Mr. Smith. Thad would take Emilie in his arms and declare his love for her and offer apologies for his part in ending their relationship.

But it was not to be so. Instead, Thad would spend the next few hours motoring to Missoula and seeing to it that Catherine and Aunt Jane boarded the train safely. Then, because Pete mentioned it would likely snow tomorrow, Thad would climb back into his automobile and travel back to Hollow Creek post haste.

Thad stole a glance at Catherine. She glowered in her seat, arms folded and face set in vexation because of his comments to her.

Good riddance! Thad hadn't asked Catherine to come to Hollow Creek, and he no longer had any feelings for her. Hadn't for years. Never did he want to be harsh or insensitive, but he was thankful for the chance to set things to right with Catherine.

Now if he could do the same with Emilie.

Thad sighed. He rounded a bend in the road and slowed as a mule deer crossed. After Catherine and Aunt Jane recovered from their dramatic show of consternation, Thad was again alone with his thoughts.

After delivering them to the depot, Thad visited a place he thought he would never again step foot inside.

Miss Julia Mathilda's Fine Dresses.

If a man was going to have a chance at winning back the heart of the woman he loved, that man best come prepared with a special gift.

Even if his third time venturing into the boutique was an act of courage in itself.

The Lord hath not given me a spirit of fear.

Before even entering the dress shop, Thad poked only his head through the door. His eyes scanned the interior just to be sure the establishment wasn't full of women ready to pounce on a poor, unsuspecting man such as himself.

Relieved the boutique appeared empty and none of his female enemies lurked in the corners, Thad took one slow step inside, followed by another.

Yea, though I walk through the valley of the shadow of death, I will fear no evil: for thou art with me.

Thad recognized Henrietta behind the counter. When she saw him, her mouth fell open and her eyes bulged. "Please excuse me. Begging your pardon," she said and toddled off toward the back room where Thad heard her distressed call, "Miss Mathilda!"

Within moments, Miss Julia Mathilda made her entrance into the front of the store. Thankful he was the lone customer at the moment, he glanced at his pocket watch and determined to make his purchase and leave the boutique in less than ten minutes.

"Hello, sir. Do you need to purchase a hat today?" The right corner of Miss Mathilda's mouth quirked upward a bit.

"No, Miss Mathilda. Today, I am here to purchase that brooch set you showed me on my last visit."

If he could have captured Miss Mathilda's shocked facial expression permanently on a tintype, Thad would have done so. Her already-round eyes protruded and stared back at him. It brought back a memory to Thad of the time when he was just a young'un and accidentally gripped the frog he had found a bit too hard. The frog's eyes nearly bulged out of its head.

Miss Mathilda's jaw dropped and she took a hold of the counter. When she recovered, she took a deep breath and spoke. "Very well, sir. I will retrieve it for you now." She opened the display case and removed the cameo brooch and matching earring set.

Thad opened his wallet and placed the necessary funds on the counter. "Would you mind wrapping it for me?"

"Not at all. So you have finally righted your senses and have decided to purchase this exquisite gift for your wife of ten years?"

Should he correct Miss Mathilda in her assumption? Or just go along with her theory? He chose the latter. Never again did he wish to experience Miss Mathilda's profound disappointment in him. And unless he returned to purchase Emilie another present, he didn't plan to visit Miss Julia Mathilda's Fine Dresses ever again.

"I'll return forthwith," Miss Mathilda said, and made a hasty retreat to the back room. Minutes later, she wrapped the brooch and earrings in a padded velvet box and handed it to Thad. "May your lovely wife enjoy her delayed anniversary gift."

"Thank you, ma'am."

As Thad strolled down the boardwalk and back to his automobile, he offered a prayer, his hundredth since his estrangement from Emilie.

Lord, I pray Emilie will give me ten seconds of her time. Ten years with her would be more than I could ever ask for. I pray I have the opportunity to prove my love for her and that You would help me be worthy of her.

CARRYING TWO fine Evanson Cattle Company steaks and Emilie's brooch and earrings, Thad plodded up the stairs to Emilie's porch. He took a deep breath and prayed again. Would God's plan for Thad's future include Emilie? What if she didn't believe what he had to say? What if she didn't want anything to do with him? What if…

While Thad waited for a response to his knock, he turned and gazed out over the open fields. It had rained for half of his return trip from Missoula last night, making the journey more adventuresome than Thad would have liked. Today, rain mixed with snow appeared likely.

"Thad?" Vera's drawn face and pensive expression caused him concern.

"Hello, Vera. Is Emilie home?"

Tears formed in Vera's eyes, and she stepped aside. "Please do come in, Thad."

"Is everything all right? Is Emilie all right?"

"She's very ill, Thad. Doc says it's influenza. She may…she may not make it."

No. Not his Emilie. Not the woman he loved.

Why had he spent so much precious time being angry with her?

Regret choked him.

If she died...

"I'm afraid it is true. Do come in."

Thad followed Vera into the entryway of Emilie's home, and he noticed Doc coming down the stairs. "Hello, Thad."

"Doc."

"How is Emilie doing?" Vera asked.

"I'm afraid not well. Her temperature has escalated. I'm going to go check on a few other patients. I'll be back in a couple of hours. In the meantime, keep a cool cloth on her forehead as often as you can. I've left some cinnamon on her bureau. Mix it with milk and try to get her to take some. It will assist with the fever. Right now, she's alternating between chills and sweats." Doc placed his hat on his head.

"Can I see her?" asked Thad.

"I would recommend against that. This is a dangerous illness. Three folks in town have already lost their lives to it. We don't need it to become an epidemic because of stubbornness. Please. Go home and get some rest so you don't get it as well."

"But it's important that I..."

"Thad," urged Morris, "You should listen to Doc. Vera, Hattie, and I will take turns with Emilie and keep watch over her. We haven't even allowed any of the outside help to enter the home for fear they will get the influenza and share it with their families. Vera and I both had the it years ago as children and Hattie was exposed when her sister had it."

"Doc, Vera, Morris, I'm thankful for your suggestions, but I'm going to Emilie. I love her and I'm not going to lose her." He handed Morris the parcel with the brooch and earrings and the steaks. "Is she upstairs?"

"A word of warning," said Doc. "If you go to see her, you will be quarantined to the house until the fever has passed."

"I'll stay here as long as it takes to get her well." Thad eyed the stairs around the corner. "May I go to her now?"

Morris shook his balding head. "Can't say as I blame you, son. I know if it was my Vera, I'd be wanting to be there with her."

"It's settled then. Please lead the way to her, Vera."

Vera nodded and led Thad to the stairway. "Her room is the first on the right at the top of the stairs."

Thad passed Vera and took the stairs two at a time. He cared not if he got the influenza. He only had one thing on his mind.

And that was taking care of Emilie.

CHAPTER FORTY-FOUR

Emilie never experienced such weakness and achiness in all her life. There wasn't a part of her body that didn't throb. At times, she shivered so much she thought she might shake plumb off her bed. At other times, it seemed Morris had stoked the fire in her room a bit too much, making the heat overwhelming.

Lord, I beseech thee to please heal me.

The influenza had come on so suddenly, with no warning. She had turned around shortly after seeing Thad and his betrothed and returned home. Within minutes of entering the house, Emilie stumbled, then awoke in her bed.

Somehow, Vera, Morris, and Hattie delivered her to her room. Doc arrived at some point, although Emilie didn't remember much of his visit.

Attempting to find a comfortable position, she moaned as the achy pain shot through her arms and up through her neck. Her legs were rendered useless.

Her body shook violently. Soon, someone would be in to check on her again, and when they did, Emilie hoped she would have the energy to ask for the blankets to be placed up to her chin.

Had Morris recently added wood to the fire?

She had no concept of time. She was certain her friends checked on her often, but with dozing in and out of semi-consciousness, she couldn't remember when the last time had been.

"Emilie?"

She opened her eyes to see Thad…was it Thad? Or was she hallucinating? Someone stood in the open doorway. She closed her eyes again. Surely she was dreaming. Thad would never visit her after their misunderstanding, and certainly not while she languished with influenza.

Was that a hand she felt on top of hers? Emilie forced her eyes open. She saw someone peering over her. It looked like Thad. Could it be?

"Thad?" her voice in her ears came out as a ragged whisper. It hurt to speak.

"It's me, Emilie." He leaned over and kissed her on the forehead. "I'm here to take care of you."

Why had he come? How had he heard of her illness? She attempted to process all of the questions in her mind, but her head throbbed with an intense pounding.

"Don't try to talk, Em."

It was Thad. For he was the only one who ever called her that.

Unless Emilie was dreaming.

Which she hoped she wasn't.

Thad's hand gently squeezed hers. Emilie had so many questions to ask him, but she struggled to remember them.

"Doc said you have the influenza. Nasty stuff. Apparently several in town have it." Thad let go of her hand and she heard him stand and walk somewhere in the room.

Or at least it sounded like he stood and walked somewhere. With her ears so clouded, Emilie couldn't be sure.

Thad returned after a few moments and placed a new cloth on her head, replacing the warmed one. The cold wet cloth caused her to shiver. "Are you cold?"

"Yes," she heard herself whisper.

Thad pulled the quilt to her chin. "Lord, I pray You would heal Emilie."

He was praying for her.

Emilie closed her eyes and relished in his words to the Lord. "*When thou passest through the waters, I will be with thee; and through the rivers, they shall not overflow thee: when thou walkest through the fire, thou shalt not be burned; neither shall the flame kindle upon thee.*"

He was quoting Scripture. The words comforted her heart.

She struggled to recall the day when Thad had introduced her to the Lord. Not her perception of the Lord, but the Lord as He really was. Then Pastor Shay at the Missoula church had reiterated things from the Bible about Jesus.

"Doc says you need to have some cinnamon mixed with milk. It'll bring down the fever."

Emilie attempted to shake her head. She'd already had some of the obnoxious concoction and didn't desire any more. Besides, to swallow with a parched throat was far too painful. If she struggled to swallow water, how would she ever succeed in swallowing the cinnamon milk?

Especially since she had always detested cinnamon. Except, of course, when mixed with apple in pie à la mode.

Her mind reverted to all those times eating the dessert with Thad at the restaurant in Missoula. Good memories.

Would she ever have the chance, or the ability to tell Thad she loved him? That she was sorry? She couldn't speak much, but if she could write...

That, too, was out of the question with the pain and weakness in her hands and arms.

"I know you aren't fond of cinnamon, but this will make you feel better."

He placed a hand at base of her neck. A second later, he tipped a cup toward her mouth. She took a tiny sip and did her best to swallow.

"Good. That's good, Emilie." He rested her head down on the pillow.

"How is our patient?" Was that Vera's voice?

"She took a small sip of the cinnamon milk. I'm not sure how much we'll get her to take. She's not overly fond of cinnamon," Thad said.

"That is true, and she's a stubborn one. Between the two of us, we should be able to get her to take enough to help with that fever."

"Vera, how long has she been like this?"

"She said she started feeling poorly the day before last. Yesterday, when she arrived home from a drive, she collapsed on the floor. Praising God, I am, that Morris, Hattie, and I were able to bring her to her room. My first thought was to put her in the parlor. But here at least, she is in her own bed."

"Vera?" Emilie's voice rasped.

"Yes, Emilie?"

"Is...is Thad...is Thad here?" Emilie had to be sure Thad was here and not just a figment of her imagination.

"Yes, my dear one, Thad is here."

Even a sigh of relief was too much effort, but Emilie was thankful. So very thankful Thad was here. She closed her eyes. Fatigue overtook her.

"Thank you for caring for her, Vera."

"Emilie is very dear to us."

"To me, too."

"She has missed you, Thad."

Emilie dozed in and out during Thad and Vera's conversation. When she awoke again, Thad was holding her right hand and speaking to her. How much of what he said had she missed?

"Anyhow, Em, I'm right sorry for all the lying about who I was and where I lived. I hope you can forgive me."

Emilie hoped he could forgive *her*. She wished she could force her scratchy and dry throat to articulate the words seeking that forgiveness.

"I love you, Emilie."

Had Thad just said he loved her?

If she'd had the strength, Emilie would have smiled at the words. Hoping she indeed heard correctly, she knew two things to be true.

One: that she loved Thad also.

And two: that she would recover. She must.

For she needed to tell Thad of her feelings for him as well.

CHAPTER FORTY-FIVE

Emilie's gaunt face and near unresponsiveness troubled Thad. He hoped Doc would be back soon. At least between he and Vera, they had been able to get Emilie to drink some of the cinnamon milk and a minimal amount of water.

Most of all, Thad prayed.

Prayed for Emilie's healing.

Prayed for another chance with her.

Vera appeared in the doorway. "Thad, why don't you have a bite to eat. Cook has prepared the steaks you brought."

He didn't want to leave Emilie's side.

Vera seemed to sense his apprehension. "I will be with her. Besides, I must change her clothing again."

"All right." Thad reluctantly got up from his place on the chair beside Emilie's bed. The aroma of steak and potatoes waffled through the doorway and his stomach growled, reminding him he hadn't eaten in some time. "I need to get word to my help that I'll be here for a while anyhow."

"At least until Doc says the quarantine is over."

Weariness overtook him from the long and stressful drive back from Missoula in the inclement weather, and now with Emilie's illness. A decent meal would do wonders in helping eliminate his exhaustion.

Morris and Hattie had already eaten so Thad sat alone at the table. Photographs lined one of the shelves in the dining room, combined with trinkets. Thad finished eating, then stood to peruse the shelves. He recognized the photographs of Emilie's parents, two of Emilie as a young girl, one of her and Newton Wheeler at their wedding, and one of just Mr. Wheeler.

From Thad's calculations, it had been about a year and a half since her husband had passed. Was there any room in Emilie's life for him? And what of Mr. Smith?

First, she had to first recover from her illness.

Hattie appeared in the hallway. "Is there anything I can retrieve for you, Mr. Evanson?"

Thad shook his head. "I'm fine, Hattie, thank you." He paused. "Wait, there is one thing. I know the help cannot come into the house because of the quarantine. How do you get their attention if you need something?"

"There's a bell on the porch, sir, that I can ring. If the wind isn't blowing too hard, Jep or one of the other men will hear it. Did you need something?"

"I need to let my hired help know I'll be here for a while with the quarantine."

"I can take care of that for you, Mr. Evanson." Hattie rushed to the door, opened it, and tugged on the rope holding the bell. "Hopefully, one of them will hear it."

Light snow whirled around outside, promising a chilly evening. From his location, he could see his own home in the distance through the fluttering snow. When Thad had stood at his window, he could see Emilie's house—and this window—perfectly. How many times had he done so? Even before he knew her?

A rap at the door interrupted Thad's thoughts. Hattie rushed to open it, but kept her distance from the visitor. "Hello, Jep."

"Hattie, is everything all right?"

Thad watched the exchange between the two young people. They appeared to be quite fond of each other. Even courting perhaps? Thad grinned wistfully as he recalled when he and Emilie briefly courted while meeting in Missoula.

All that seemed so long ago now.

With Emilie fighting for her life, would they get another chance?

"Mr. Evanson has a message to give you."

Jep nodded his strawberry-blond head. "Hattie, reckon I sure do miss you."

"I miss you too, Jep."

"How's Mrs. Wheeler?"

"There's no change. Keep praying."

"I am. Of that you can be sure. Reckon all of us are praying mighty hard for her."

The gratitude that so many would pray for Emilie overwhelmed Thad. "Jep, I have an errand I need attended to."

"Sure thing, Mr. Evanson."

He stepped onto the porch, keeping his distance from Jep. The cold air hit him even harder after having spent so much time in the overly-warm house. "I need to get word to my help that I could be here for several days, depending on when Doc lifts the quarantine. Could you ride over and let Pete and Floyd know?"

"Will do, sir."

"If possible, I'd like to speak to Pete."

"I'll let him know."

When Pete arrived at Emilie's house a half hour later, Thad informed him of some items to tend to on the ranch. But he also had an even more important request. "Pete, one thing..."

"Sure, Thad, what is it?"

"Could you ask Anne to get a prayer circle going for Emilie?"

"I'd be honored, and my Anne is just the woman to accomplish that task."

"I knew she would be. Thank you."

Pete plopped his hat on his head and turned to walk down the steps of the porch. "I'll be praying for Emilie and you too, Thad."

"Much obliged for that, thank you."

The more prayers Thad could collect for Emilie, the better.

"Oh, and Pete?"

"Yes?"

"I've been such a fool. I've let something as absurd as an argument come between Emilie and me. What if…"

"You were foolish. You both were. But there's grace and forgiveness for that. Right now, you and Emilie's staff and Doc take good care of her and do your best to speed her healing. Everything else is up to the Lord."

Thad knew Pete was right. Still, he wished he could go back in time and change things. He had learned an important lesson. As Pete mounted his horse and rode toward Thad's ranch, Thad kneeled beside the chair on the porch and gave his heavy burdens to the Lord.

Doc arrived an hour later. Emilie's prognosis hadn't improved. "I want you to keep a cold cloth on her head at all times. Warm packs will assist with easing the pain from the aches she is experiencing, as will this aspirin." Doc handed Vera a tin of aspirin. "Continue trying to feed her chicken noodle soup and keep her hydrated. This, along with a lot of prayer and rest, is what she needs right now."

"How are the other folks in town faring?" Vera asked.

"I'm sorry to say that we lost another one this morning. This influenza is deadly."

Another resident had passed? Thad offered a prayer for that person's family. Likely dehydration played a role in their succumbing to the virus. "Emilie's having a difficult time swallowing."

"Her throat is raw and red and her glands swollen, so that stands to reason. Keep doing what you're doing. You and

Vera take turns and make sure both of you get some sleep. It won't do, Thad, to have you come down with it too. You'll do Emilie no good if that happens."

"Yes, Doc."

"Good. Now, I will be back tomorrow morning. If anything changes, please have Jep or Digby fetch me. I will make a few more rounds tonight, then I'll be home for the remainder of the evening unless I'm out on a call."

Vera took the night shift and Thad slept in one of the spare rooms on the first floor. He fell asleep with a prayer for Emilie on his lips.

EMILIE AWOKE to the wind howling and some sort of decadent smell in the air. Was that pancakes? She inhaled again, then attempted to sit up in her bed, to no avail.

She was far too weak.

Emilie opened her eyes and saw Thad slouched in the chair on the right, eyes closed and long legs extended in front of him. He snored low rhythmical puffs of breath. A smile lit her lips.

She loved that man.

While her arms and legs remained fatigued and achy, Emilie could honestly say she felt better.

Much improved, indeed.

And gracious, but that smell! What she wouldn't give for some of Cook's pancakes draped with maple syrup right about now. Her stomach growled. Emilie eyed the water pitcher. If she leaned just right and far enough, she could reach the pitcher and perhaps pour herself a glass of water. While she couldn't do anything at the moment about her rumbling stomach, she could do something about her parched throat.

However, try as she might, she could not render enough strength to even prop herself up on one elbow, let alone roll over and lift a water pitcher.

Fatigue from even the attempt left her exhausted.

Emilie settled back and closed her eyes. She could certainly sleep for hours. *Thank You, Jesus, that I feel much better.* How long had she been debilitated with the influenza? What had happened in that time? When had Thad arrived? Were he, Vera, Morris, and Hattie avoiding the illness?

"Emilie?"

Her eyes fluttered open and she saw Thad standing over her. A crease on his cheek indicated where he had pressed it against the side of the chair while sleeping.

"I'm sorry, Thad. Did I wake you?" Her voice sounded raspy and hoarse to her plugged ears.

He leaned over and placed a kiss to her forehead. "No, not at all. I must have fallen asleep right after I came back from eating breakfast. Vera sat with you last night, and I've only been here for a couple of hours." He paused, his voice full of thick emotion. "Are you feeling better, Em?"

"I am."

Thad studied her and his eyebrows furrowed. "We were so worried about you. I was so worried about you."

Emilie watched as he closed his eyes and whispered a prayer of gratitude. Were those the tears in his intense blue eyes?

"I feel a lot better, Thad. But I'm so hungry and thirsty too."

The corners of his mouth quirked up into a crooked grin. "That's good to hear, Em. Mighty good to hear. I can do something about that." He poured a glass of water from the pitcher. Then, with all the tenderness Emilie expected, he assisted her to a propped-up position on her pillows. "Careful now," he said while tipping the cup to her lips.

Emilie desired to drink the entire cup of water and then some. But she knew better, so instead, she took slow sips, willing her body to fight the weakness while she drank.

"Better?" Thad asked, placing the pitcher back on the side bureau.

"Much better. Thank you. Is that pancakes I smell?"

"It is. Your cook whipped up a batch of some of the best pancakes I've ever tasted. I'll see what I can do about rounding you up something to eat. I'll be right back."

Emilie reclined on her bed again, noting that her legs, hips, and back had become stiff from reposing in one position for too long. She closed her eyes and tried to imagine the taste of Cook's fluffy golden-brown pancakes and the rich and thick syrup. Maybe a slice or two of bacon would accompany the pancakes.

Within moments, Vera, Morris, and Hattie joined Thad in Emilie's room. Hugging, praising, and plentiful conversation ensued.

Vera leaned over and placed a hand to Emilie's forehead. "I thought her fever might have broken last night. Jep went to fetch Doc. I can think of no words I would rather hear today than that our Emilie is on the mend."

"Amen to that," Morris said.

Hattie's brow furrowed. "We were ever so worried about you, Mrs. Wheeler. You gave us quite the fright."

"Are you all feeling well?" Emilie asked.

"We are fine. Morris and I both had the influenza as children. Hattie and Thad seem to be doing well."

"Thank you all for taking such good care of me."

"We would have it no other way. It's what folks do for people they love." Morris shot a glance at Thad, and Emilie wondered at Thad's expression. Did he love her? But what about the woman by the river?

"I would dearly love to have some of those pancakes, Vera."

Vera shook her head. "I'm sorry, Emilie, but there will be no pancakes for you just yet. I imagine Doc will say only broth for today. Then tomorrow, Cook will whip up for you all the pancakes you can eat."

Emilie prayed Thad would forgive her for their disagreement and that it wasn't too late to reconcile with him. She hoped he hadn't promised to spend his future with someone else.

Then she thanked the Lord for healing.

For friends who cared.

For Thad.

Thank You, Lord. I am blessed.

CHAPTER FORTY-SIX

"Thad, did I hear you say...I was so incoherent...did I hear you say that you...that you love me?"

He reached for her hand and kissed her fingers. "You heard correctly, Emilie. I love you."

"But what about your betrothed?"

"My betrothed?"

"Yes. When I was at church, a woman indicated you were her beau."

Thad appeared thoughtful. "Ah, you must mean Catherine."

"Catherine?" Had that been the woman's name? Why did that day at church seem so very long ago? Hazy thoughts filled Emilie's memory.

"Catherine and I courted when I lived in Illinois. She took it upon herself to travel to Hollow Creek with her Aunt Jane in an attempt to see if I would care to rekindle our courtship."

"Did you agree to do so?"

"No. I'm not sure I ever really loved Catherine. She is a shallow woman and wanted me to work for her father after we married. My dream has always been to own my own ranch in Montana. Catherine, on the other hand, had no desire to relocate to Montana. We reached an impasse and went our separate ways."

Emilie wished she could prop herself up more comfortably in her bed, but she was still so weak. "Yet, she sensed there was some hope in reuniting with you."

"Yes. She at first told me her reason for traveling to Hollow Creek was because Aunt Jane wished to visit the uncivilized West." Thad shook his head. "One thing about Catherine is that she has never been much good at lying."

"I thought for sure you had replaced me after our...our disagreement and broken courtship."

"About that, Emilie..." Thad squeezed her hand. "I sent Catherine and Aunt Jane on their way. I had no intention of reuniting with Catherine and when she explained about wanting to marry, her ideas were absurd to say the least. Upon further questioning, she admitted she was prepared to marry me for my wealth, as she and her father had fallen on some hard times."

"But when I drove by on that day, it appeared the two of you—" Emilie knew her face blazed with red at such an intimate inquiry.

"She did place her hands on my face. Catherine was doing her best to convince me to give our courtship another chance. I was having none of it." Thad leaned forward until he was mere inches from Emilie's face. He stared into her eyes. "The woman I intend to marry is someone else."

Emilie's heart thrummed in her chest. In her weakened state, could she handle what Thad was about to say—if he said what she hoped he would?

Thad leaned toward her and his eyes searched hers. "Emilie, I'm sorry for the way I acted. I was such a hypocrite. Here I was, so angry about you lying about who you really were, and I had done the exact same thing. I was prideful and stubborn. I know we both had our reasons, but the lying wasn't right."

"I'm sorry too, Thad. I never meant to hurt you."

"Nor did I mean to hurt you. When I found out that my neighbor was the woman I had fallen in love with, I was shocked."

"As was I. Here I was, in love with a man who had allowed his cows to run amuck all over my property."

"That will never happen again, Emilie. That's a promise. I should have seen to it that the fence was fixed long ago. I am ashamed to say there were some bad feelings between your late husband and me. Reckon we never quite got along. But that was no excuse not to make sure my cattle didn't trespass onto your land. Will you forgive me for that?"

"Yes. And will you forgive me for my role in our misunderstanding?"

"I will, Emilie."

Thad reached into his pocket and pulled out a box. "I purchased this for you at Miss Julia Mathilda's."

Emilie opened the box to reveal the brooch and earrings. "They're exquisite, thank you."

"Am I too late in asking for your hand in marriage, seeing as you are betrothed to that New York City fellow?"

"New York City fellow? Oh, you must mean Mr. Smith." Emilie giggled at Thad's expression of confusion. "You couldn't offer me all the flower gardens in the world to marry Donald W. Smith, III."

"He mentioned he intended to marry you."

"Mr. Smith may have felt that way at one time, but after hearing my views on women's suffrage and getting splattered with mud, he quickly changed his mind."

"Splattered with mud?"

Emilie shook her head. "I really had no idea he was there when I went splashing through that mud puddle in the automobile." She proceeded to share with Thad the entire story of the demise of Mr. Smith's suit and mustache.

Thad chuckled. "Reckon I don't have to worry about competition from that fellow."

"Not at all." A thought occurred to Emilie. "And to think that I thought Floyd was Mr. Evanson."

"And to think that I thought Mrs. Wheeler was an old crotchety woman." He winked at her. "She is quite the opposite. Young, smart, and beautiful." Thad paused. "There is one question I do have."

"Yes?"

"What about Newton? It wasn't that long ago when he passed. Is there room in your heart for me?"

"Yes, Thad. There is room in my heart for you. Plentiful room and then some."

He leaned over and kissed her on the forehead. "What do you say we start over? Emilie Crawford Wheeler, will you court me?"

"I will, Thad Alexander Evanson."

"And, Emilie Crawford Wheeler?"

"Yes."

"Do you fully understand that my intention to court you is because I aim to make you my wife?"

"And do you, Thad Alexander Evanson, realize that my intention to agree to enter into courtship with you is because I aim to accept your marriage proposal?"

"Yes, I do."

Thad kissed her again, this time softly on the lips.

First the Lord's healing.

Then reconciliation with the man she loved.

Could Emilie be more blessed?

WHEN THAD entered the dining area a few minutes later, he was greeted by a round of applause by Vera, Morris, and Hattie.

Thad chuckled at the ovation. It could only mean they'd witnessed his and Emilie's reconciliation.

"Oops," admitted Hattie. "I might have eavesdropped. A little."

When Thad gave her a questioning look, she continued. "I overheard you professing your undying love to Emilie, and I may have swooned a bit before sharing the news with Vera and Morris."

"And now we're all swooning," declared Vera.

Morris shook his head. "You ladies might be swooning, but I, on the other hand, am not."

"But you are in celebration of Emilie and Thad's declaration of their feelings for each other, are you not?" Vera asked.

"Reckon I am." agreed Morris.

Vera placed a hand to her heart. "Ah, to be young and in love."

Morris sidled up next to his wife. "And what of being old and in love?"

"That's the absolute best," said Vera, planting a kiss on Morris's cheek.

EPILOGUE

One year later

Morris opened the door of the automobile and Mother stepped out. Father stretched as he exited the Model T, and Morris unloaded the luggage.

"Oh, darling!" squealed Mother, as she sashayed up the porch stairs.

Emilie gave Mother a hug. "I'm so glad you and Father are here for a visit."

"We truly wouldn't miss it. Although we were here for the wedding in June, we couldn't wait another full year to see you."

"I just hope we will have ample time to visit before the snow decides to fall," grumbled Father, hoisting one of Mother's four bags on to the porch, lending a hand to Morris, who was struggling with the other three.

Morris chuckled. "We've had a pleasant early fall season so far. I'll take your bags to your room for you."

"Now, do tell, Almira, where are the children?" Mother shielded her eyes and perused the fields.

"They are over there throwing the ball with Thad."

"Throwing the ball? My granddaughter?"

"Now, Mother. You will be elated to know that Adelia also adores dolls, toy dishes, and sewing with Vera."

"Still, I'm not sure my granddaughter...?"

Father rolled his eyes. "Now, Cecelia, remember we promised not to be too opinionated on this trip."

"Oh," said Mother. "We did promise that, didn't we?"

Emilie giggled at Mother's pout. "Now, now, Mother. Do have a seat. You too, Father. Hattie will bring us some lemonade presently. The children will be finished shortly and you will have the chance to meet them. I do know you both will enjoy spoiling them."

"Oh, yes," said Mother. "Your father and I brought all sorts of presents for them."

"They are both thrilled to meet their grandparents."

"Well, as they should be," said Mother, feigning shock. "What is there not to like?"

Father cleared his throat and boasted his usual ornery expression. "We are likeable for the most part."

Mother and Father took a seat on the chairs on the porch. Hattie appeared and offered everyone a refreshing glass of lemonade. "I do declare the trip was positively exhausting. You know I never sleep well on the train, nor at any of the stops."

"That's because you are too busy snoring," chortled Father.

"Well, I never! I don't snore." Mother cast a crusty look at her husband. "Your father didn't sleep well either. But we are looking forward to that delightfully comfortable bed Hattie always makes up for us when we visit."

"We are glad to have you here. Besides the lack of the sleep, was your trip uneventful?"

"It was," said Father. "By the way, Almira, I couldn't wait to tell you your mother finally agreed to allow me to purchase an automobile."

"Father, that is marvelous news!" Emilie didn't let on about Mother's previous correspondence indicating that very fact.

"One might think so, but there is one problem."

"Oh?" Emilie did hope her father had picked a good-quality automobile.

"Yes. Your mother here likes to drive it far too often."

"Oh pish-posh, Ernest. Your father makes it sound as though I monopolize the motorcar. He couldn't be more incorrect. You see, sometimes the chauffer drives us to important charity events and such."

"But tell Almira what happens when we decide to take a leisure drive," prompted Father. Mother's usually pasty white skin took on a bright red hue. "It is only fair, Cecelia," added Father.

"Do tell, Mother."

"Well, you see, whenever your father and I are going for a leisure drive, I have Pierre, you remember him, don't you?"

Emilie nodded. She recalled the stuffy butler quite well.

"Pierre picks a number between one and ten. Then your father and I try to guess the number. We only get one guess each, mind you. Whoever is closest to the number Pierre picked gets to drive the motorcar."

"I'm sure you can speculate who wins most of the time," said Father, with a shake of his near-bald head.

"You don't even have to guess, Almira. I will just tell you. It's me!" Mother clapped her hands together with such glee that Emilie wondered if she'd ever been so thrilled in all her life.

"Congratulations, Mother."

"Well," harumphed Father, folding his arms across his chest. But he gave Mother an appreciative glance and a wink. "I am rather proud of how well she drives."

"Yes, and I haven't hit anyone yet. Not another motorcar, not a person, and not even a small creature running across the road."

"Well," said Father. "There was that snake that was slithering across the road on our way to our picnic."

"He doesn't count."

While Mother and Father continued to playfully tease each other with laughs and winks in between their silly words, the children and Thad approached the house.

Emilie had never felt so much love in her heart. The man she adored and the two children they had recently adopted filled her life with so much love. Her parents, whom she had developed a closer relationship with, were staying for the next week. And then there was the surprise she and Thad were about to announce...

Emilie couldn't be more blessed.

Greetings abounded. "Mother and Father, I present to you your grandchildren, seven-year-old Ephraim and five-year-old Adelia."

Mother rushed forward and enfolded the two children in her embrace. "I am so very happy to meet you both." She plopped kisses on their foreheads, then hugged them again. "I've waited a long time for grandchildren. Look, Ernest, aren't they just perfect?"

Adelia climbed onto Father's lap. "Is it true that you are my grandfodder?"

"Uh, yes, yes, Adelia, it is true." He patted her on the arm.

Father had never been the affectionate type. But with his and Mother's newfound love for the Lord, so many things were beginning to slowly change.

"I have a gift for each of you. Oh, Morris!" Mother yelled inside the door. "Could you please bring me the paisley-colored luggage?"

Adelia hopped from Father's lap and she and Ephraim awaited Mother's surprise.

Moments later, Morris delivered the luggage to Mother. She opened the bag and pulled out two expertly-wrapped presents. "There are more gifts where these came from," she whispered, as she handed them to each child.

Adelia opened hers first. "Thank you, Grandmudder." She hugged the baby doll to her chest.

Ephraim hurriedly opened his next. "Thank you!" He exclaimed and drove the Model T die cast car around on the porch, all the while making car sounds.

"Don't tell them, but I have some candy from that candy store you always loved as a child," Mother whispered to Emilie.

"You spoil them, Cecelia," Father rebuked.

But Emilie could see beyond Father's pretend gruffness that Father delighted in this just as much as Mother did.

"Mother and Father, Thad and I have some other exciting news for you."

"More exciting news? Dear me. I am not sure my heart can take it." Mother placed a hand to her heart.

Emilie and Thad exchanged a knowing glance. Then he took her hand in his and nodded at her to share the news.

News that she had barely been able to contain since her parents' arrival. "I have had such a difficult time keeping this news under my bonnet, as the saying goes."

"Do go on," prompted Father, never known for his extreme patience.

"Thad and I are going to be adding to our family."

"Oh, that is wonderful! I love that you will be adopting more." Mother beamed and hugged each of the children again.

"We will likely adopt more children, Mother, but I was talking about another way we are adding to our family."

"Oh!" Recognition dawned on Mother's face and this time she gently hugged Emilie. "Are you saying what I think you are saying?"

"Really, dear, do try to be more vague," teased Father.

"Yes, Mother, we are going to have a baby."

Celebration ensued and Emilie wondered for a minute if her parents might jump up and down in their excitement. And much to Mother's and Father's enjoyment, the children shared all the many names they had decided the baby should be named.

Emilie's eyes misted. God had blessed her with two children and soon a third. She took her gaze toward Heaven. And someday, she would be reunited with her firstborn son.

Thad motioned for Emilie to walk around the corner of the house with him. She put her arm through his and together they strolled down the steps and to the side of the house away from the commotion. Thad wrapped his arm around Emilie's waist and planted a kiss on her cheek. "I love you, Emilie Evanson," he said.

"And I love you, Thad Evanson," she answered.

He lifted her off her feet and swung her around in his arms, then placed her back on her feet again and planted a lengthy and passionate kiss on her waiting lips.

"But goodness, where did Almira go?"

Emilie and Thad shared a laugh at Mother's exaggerated concern, then shared another kiss, followed by another.

And in her heart, Emilie cherished the treasures of celebrating new life, second chances, and true love.

AUTHOR'S NOTE

One of the most interesting things about writing historical romance is research. For *Love in Disguise*, I wanted to give readers a sense of time and place from an era so long ago. As is always the case, there are fictional liberties taken by authors for a variety of reasons. Street names, the Bellerose Hotel and Restaurant, and the Missoula Garden Park were figments of my imagination, as was Miss Julia Mathilda's Fine Dresses. Although, I am sure there were clothing stores just like hers. Be on the lookout for more of Miss Mathilda. Something tells me she might have a guest appearance in another book.

Aviator Eugene Ely was a real person. As I mentioned in the story, he did arrive in Missoula and presented quite a show for his spectators. It would appear from newspaper accounts that those spectators arrived by streetcar or train. For the sake of the story, Thad, Emilie, Vera, and Morris arrived by Cadillac.

Sadly, Mr. Ely died two days shy of his twenty-fifth birthday in Macon, Georgia, during a performance when his plane crashed.

Researching old cars was a definite highlight of my research. Because Emilie and Thad had passengers, I gave them both touring cars, although I think if given the choice without author interference, they may have chosen the two-seater runabouts. My dad, who is an antique car enthusiast, took my siblings and me to many car shows in our youth. I'm still fascinated by the vehicles of yesteryear.

ACKNOWLEDGMENTS

To my husband. You are my love of a lifetime, and I couldn't pursue this dream without you. Thank you for your patience while I dove headlong into the early 1900s (and sometimes forgot to come back to the current century!)

To my daughters, for all of your encouragement and support. I appreciate you taking the time to read through my chapters, offer input and suggestions, and help me make my novels the best they can be.

To my beta readers, who diligently searched for plot holes and inconsistencies. Your suggestions were invaluable.

To Zoe Ann Stoltz, Reference Historian at the Montana Historical Society Research Center, for your assistance regarding information on Eugene Ely's arrival to Missoula.

To my readers. May God bless and guide you as you grow in your walk with Him.

And, most importantly, thank you to my Lord and Savior, Jesus Christ. It is my deepest desire to glorify You with my writing and help bring others to a knowledge of Your saving grace.

Let the words of my mouth and the meditation of my heart be acceptable in your sight, O Lord, my rock and my redeemer. ~ Psalm 19:14

About the Author

Penny Zeller is known for her heartfelt stories of faith and her passion to impact lives for Christ through fiction. While she has had a love for writing since childhood, she began her adult writing career penning articles for national and regional publications on a wide variety of topics. Today Penny is a multi-published author of several inspirational books. She is also a homeschool mom and a fitness instructor.

When Penny is not dreaming up new characters, she enjoys spending time with her husband and two daughters while camping, hiking, canoeing, reading, running, cycling, gardening, and playing volleyball.

She is represented by Tamela Hancock Murray of the Steve Laube Agency and loves to hear from her readers at her website, www.pennyzeller.com, and her blog, *random thoughts from a day in the life of a wife, mom, and author,* at www.pennyzeller.wordpress.com.

Made in the USA
Monee, IL
22 February 2022

91529023R00215